"Nan Rossiter is at the peak of her storytelling abilities with *Under a Summer Sky*, which is told with the kind of compassion, grace, and wisdom that is nearly unrivaled in contemporary fiction."　　　　　　　　　　　　　　　　　　　　—Examiner.com

"Real and touching. . . . *Firefly Summer* makes a charming, ideal summer read."　　　　　　　　　　　　　　　　—*The Recorder*

"This captivating and emotional novel tells a heartwarming story about love lost and found, family secrets, and a lot of truth. The author's true grit and honesty is a real eye-opener, and readers will enjoy the different time frames of flashbacks and future casts between the siblings and how they have grown. When tragedy strikes, we're not quite sure what happens in between; it takes more than several factors to digest everything. But, the four very different sisters are now well past their fifties, and it's amazing that their memories remain, as if the good ole days in Cape Cod just happened yesterday. This is the perfect book club pick."
　　　　　　　　　　—*RT Book Reviews*, four stars, on *Firefly Summer*

"Rossiter examines the effects of war, loss, and secrets in this coming-of-age book-within-a-book. There cannot be triumph without failure, or happiness without tragedy. Steadily paced and with a protagonist one can only root for, this is a great read for summer at the pool or beach. Fans of Elin Hildebrand and Nancy Thayer will enjoy this Nantucket tale."
　　　　　　　　　　　　　　　　—*Booklist* on *Nantucket*

"There are moments of pure gold in a story that will touch readers' hearts. With wonderful characters and a charming idyllic setting, *Nantucket* does pack an emotional wallop along the lines of a good Kristan Higgins book."　　　　—*RT Book Reviews*

"Rossiter returns to the characters from her novel *Nantucket* in this coming-of-age story. Sally Ryan, the proud owner of Nantucket coffee shop Cuppa Joe, is publishing a book about her life story. As readers learn, Sally had a very unremarkable childhood, living with her widowed father in Medford, Massachusetts. Her life forever changes when she meets Drew McIntyre, gets pregnant, and marries him at a young age. Fearful of Drew and encumbered by Catholic guilt (she believes her miscarriage resulted from one of her misdeeds), Sally believes that the marriage can't be dissolved. She travels to Nantucket, finds a place to stay, and begins working at a local coffee shop. After meeting Coop, a Vietnam vet, Sally enjoys their close friendship, which evolves into an on-again, off-again romance they try to keep secret. While the story of Sally's life is a page-turner, it's the manner in which she is finally able to reconcile her faith with her relationship with Coop that will resonate."   —*Publishers Weekly*

Praise for Nan Rossiter

"Sinking into a Nan Rossiter book is like coming home."
—Robyn Carr, *New York Times* bestselling
author on *Promises of the Heart*

"A multileveled, beautifully written story that will glow in readers' hearts long after the last page is turned."
—Kristan Higgins, *New York Times* bestselling
author on *Promises of the Heart*

"Full of family, friends, and faith, Rossiter's novel depicts a couple and a community who may sometimes struggle but ultimately find the positives in life. Readers who enjoy Lisa Wingate and Melody Carlson will enjoy the depiction of a southern beach hamlet where love and family thrive."
—*Booklist* on *Promises of the Heart*

"With a winning cast of characters and a compelling plot, Nan Rossiter's *Promises of the Heart* is a story that will warm your heart, lift your spirits, and renew your faith in humanity and the hope of happy endings."
—Marie Bostwick, *New York Times* and
USA Today bestselling author

"Another trademark Nan Rossiter story, crafted with the tools that sustain us: heart, hope, and family! A touching novel that explores the meaning of faith and family as one couple's search to complete their home merges with one child's need of a life-saving second chance. Once again, Nan Rossiter weaves together a multilayered tale of the endurance of love and a reminder that the things we most wish for can come true, if we're open to receiving them in unexpected ways. These characters stayed with me long after the last page was turned!"
—Hannah McKinnon, author of *The View from Here*
on *Promises of the Heart*

"A gripping story of three sisters, of love lost and found, and a family's journey from grief to triumph. A sure winner."

—Debbie Macomber, #1 *New York Times* bestselling author on *More Than You Know*

"Eloquent and surprising. . . . I love this story of faith, love, and the lasting bonds of family."

—Ann Leary on *The Gin & Chowder Club*

"Nostalgic and tender . . . summons the passion of first love, the pain of first loss, and the unbreakable bonds of family that help us survive both."

—Marie Bostwick, *New York Times* bestselling author on *The Gin & Chowder Club*

"An intimate portrayal of a family in crisis, with good character development and a bucolic setting."

—*Publishers Weekly* on *Words Get in the Way*

"The setting, with its sea breeze and quaint charm, is immediately inviting, adding to the overall sense of familiarity that the author so beautifully evokes. . . . To read this book is to feel like you've come home." —*Hartford Books Examiner* on *Summer Dance*

"Rossiter accurately captures the nature of life's fleeting passage and offers a meditation on the need to capture and hold onto every precious moment."—*Connecticut Muse* on *Under a Summer Sky*

"I am never disappointed with Nan Rossiter's wonderful tales and her ability to include the love of animals. The delicious recipes included are just a plus in *Under a Summer Sky*. It's refreshing to read a story of this caliber and be left with contentment and faith in the lasting bonds of family." —*Fresh Fiction*

A GOOD MEASURE

ALSO BY NAN ROSSITER

Promises to Keep

Promises of the Heart

Summer Dance

Firefly Summer

Nantucket

Under a Summer Sky

More Than You Know

Words Get in the Way

The Gin & Chowder Club

The Seattle Public Library
Columbia Branch
Visit us on the Web: www.spl.org

Checked Out Items 6/20/2022 13:54
XXXXXXXXX0645

Item Title	Due Date
0010105550932	7/11/2022
A good measure : a novel	
0010102146544	7/5/2022
News of the world	

# of Items: 2

Renewals: 206-386-4190
TeleCirc: 206-386-9015 / 24 hours a day
Online: myaccount.spl.org

Pay your fines/fees online at pay.spl.org

A GOOD MEASURE

A Novel

❧

NAN ROSSITER

HARPER

NEW YORK · LONDON · TORONTO · SYDNEY

HARPER

P.S.™ is a trademark of HarperCollins Publishers.

A GOOD MEASURE. Copyright © 2022 by Nan Rossiter. All rights reserved. Printed in the United States of America. No part of this book may be used or reproduced in any manner whatsoever without written permission except in the case of brief quotations embodied in critical articles and reviews. For information, address HarperCollins Publishers, 195 Broadway, New York, NY 10007.

HarperCollins books may be purchased for educational, business, or sales promotional use. For information, please email the Special Markets Department at SPsales@harpercollins.com.

FIRST EDITION

Designed by Jamie Lynn Kerner

Library of Congress Cataloging-in-Publication Data has been applied for.

ISBN 978-0-06-307624-2

22 23 24 25 26 LSC 10 9 8 7 6 5 4 3 2 1

For the good Lord above, who has blessed
me so richly!
May I always boast in You and Your gift of salvation
through grace by faith!

Give, and it will be given to you.
A good measure, pressed down,
shaken together and running over,
will be poured into your lap.
For all the measure you use, it will
be measured to you.

—LUKE 6:38 (NIV)

A GOOD MEASURE

1

⁓

LIGHT BLUE FLAMES LICKED THE DENTED BOTTOM OF THE OLD COPPER TEAKET-
tle, making it rock like an unsteady sailor. A moment later, the soft
whistle emanating from its spout escalated into an urgent scream.
To some, the sound—like the cry of a hungry baby—might be un-
nerving, but to Libby Tennyson it was welcome. She hurried into
the kitchen, carrying the small denim overalls she'd been mending and clicked off the burner. The ancient kettle squeaked and
sputtered indignantly, and then—like a baby that has just latched
on—settled contentedly. Libby poured steaming water into the
pot and dunked a single bag several times before putting the top
on to let it steep. The delicate Wedgewood china—miraculously
unchipped—two-cup pot and vintage kettle had both been handed
down to her from her grandmother, and Libby had never been able
to make a "pot of comfort" without thinking of the indomitable
force of nature that Gram had been.

Elisabeth McCormack Jansen, or "Bet," as she'd been called
by her husband—and after whom Libby had been named—was a
new wife and expectant mother when the Great Sadness—as she
called it—struck the nation, and one of the many lessons the young
woman learned during those lean years was that two—even *three*—
cups of tea, strong enough to provide a measure of comfort, could

be made from a single bag. Bet Jansen's thrift was legendary. Her family loved to recount her resourcefulness—from canning and pickling every kind of fruit and vegetable (including watermelon rind!) to being able to "make do" with whatever she had on hand, even concocting a delectable, hearty version of Stone Soup (minus the stone) with the last of the root vegetables in her cellar. She also had the eccentric habit of mixing breakfast cereals, and whenever her grandchildren declined to give her favorite combination— Corn Flakes and Honey Grahams—a try, she'd tease: *You don't know what you're missing!* She washed and reused aluminum foil, served boiled hot dogs on toasted white bread, smothered with spicy mustard and sweet homemade pickle relish, had the mildly obsessive habit (before OCD was a diagnosis) of wrapping her bread in two plastic bags to keep it fresh, and she religiously touted the health benefits of prune juice, insisting that one small glass kept her "regular" while dutifully squeezing a small daily glass of fresh OJ for her husband. To say that Henrik Jansen was not a fan of the thick brown substance of which his wife sang praises would be an understatement. In fact, whenever she offered him some, he made a silly scrunched-up face that made his grandchildren fall apart in giggles . . . and made Gram roll her eyes. Gram had been a tiny wisp of a woman with a heart the size of Tennessee, and although her spitfire spirit and stalwart faith had the power to move mountains, she maintained her frugal ways all her life, even after her cup once again overflowed with blessings. And her youngest granddaughter— and namesake—was cut from the same cloth.

Libby set her hen-shaped egg timer for seven minutes—just like her grandmother had—and waited for her tea to steep. It was true—she and Gram had a great many things in common—so many, in fact, that her grandfather had teasingly called her Mini-Bet. Not only had they shared the same name, but Libby had also inherited her grandmother's cornflower blue eyes and kind smile, her silky brunette-turned-prematurely-silver hair, and her never-idle hands; and both women, try as they might to have daughters, had only given birth to sons—Bet, five strapping boys, the youngest of whom was Libby's dad, Dutch; and Libby, six of her own—and now, Libby mused wistfully, they had one more thing in common—the aching sadness of becoming widows at much too young an age.

Libby watched the sun slip out from behind the slate-gray clouds and make its first appearance of the day before sinking below the dark horizon. It had been raining since dawn. The weatherman said there was even a chance of snow!—a rare occurrence in eastern Tennessee, especially in late April, but at that moment, the fiery orb was sending coral streaks across the sliver of cobalt sky, and casting an ethereal golden light on the ancient oak tree that stood like a sentinel in the middle of their windswept fields. The Tennyson Tree, the boys called it—the tree under which Cale—and now Jack—were buried.

Melancholy hour, Libby thought—the time of day that had once kept her so busy making dinner, helping her boys with homework, and prodding them to finish their chores that she hadn't had time to notice the setting sun. But now, as it streamed through the windows, washing the walls with a golden light, all she could hear was the tumbling teasing voices of her sons echoing through the rooms, along with her husband's stern commands. A lifetime of memories. Sweet memories.

It had been eight months since Jack died and Libby still couldn't believe he was gone. She kept expecting him to come through the door and pull her into a playful hug. Tall, handsome, and strong as a bear, Jack's six-foot-four frame and larger-than-life personality had filled a room, but after a valiant—albeit brief—battle with cancer, he'd become a shadow of the man she'd married. And then, on a sun-kissed summer day—the kind of day that should have found him out baling hay or harvesting corn—he'd succumbed to the dreadful disease, and his fighting spirit had slipped away, a whisper on the wind. Four months after that, Dutch died, too. Her two anchors in life taken from her, and it had been more than she could bear.

She turned from the window, poured a cup of tea, and held it in her hands, letting the heat seep into her aching joints. "Oh, Jack," she whispered, feeling tears sting her eyes, but when she heard the knob of the mudroom door turn, she quickly brushed them away.

"Grandma?" a small voice called.

"In here," Libby called back.

"Oh, no! Hold on . . ." the flustered voice called, and then, "Dang it, Gran! Is it okay if Goodness and Mercy come in? Because they're *in*!"

"It's okay, hon," Libby assured her granddaughter as the two tiger cats—one orange, one gray—scampered across the worn linoleum. She smiled, remembering how Chase—who had an affinity for rescuing and befriending orphaned animals—found two kittens behind the shed when he was around seven years old, and it had been at around the same time he'd been tasked with memorizing the Twenty-Third Psalm, so when the kittens imprinted on him and started following him everywhere he went, he christened them with their biblical names.

"Sorry," Ellie said as she kicked her barn boots onto the mat. "Cats are so sneaky—they just slink around, spying on you. I think they were waiting in the shadows for me to open the door."

"Probably," Libby said, chuckling as she watched the cats curl up together on the soft fleecy dog bed near the woodstove. "Are you and Dad done milking?"

"Almost. Uncle Eli and Uncle Grayson are helping him. He said I could come in for a minute. Boy, it's really gettin' to be mud season out there!"

Libby nodded, remembering all too well the mud and manure her six sons and husband tromped through when they were feeding and milking their five hundred cows. The washing, hanging, ironing, and folding of laundry (not to mention the pairing of socks!) had been endless. She certainly didn't miss it . . . or did she? Now, the thankless chore fell to her sons' wives. Matt, Eli, and Grayson continued to run the farm, but they'd all married country girls who'd known the mud they were getting into.

"Would you like a cup of tea?" she asked, eyeing her grand-daughter.

"Earl Gray?" the little girl asked hopefully, shaking off the chill and holding her hands out to the woodstove.

"Is there any other kind for a day like today?"

Ellie swept her blond hair out of her cornflower blue eyes—a combination of genetic traits that ran as strong as thistle in the stubborn Tennyson line. "Lemon, too, please."

Libby poured a second cup, squeezed in a slice of lemon, picked up the overalls, and brought both to the table. "These are little Jack's."

Ellie eyed the knees. "Were you able to patch 'em?"

"Does a cow give milk?"

The little girl smiled. "How come you always do that, Grandma?"

"Do what?"

"Answer a question with a question."

"How come you ask so many questions?"

"You just did it again!" Ellie exclaimed. She held her hands over the cup and breathed in the fragrant citrusy steam. "Grampa used to do it, too," she added, smiling. "I miss him . . . and Dutch."

"Me too," Libby said, "and I think it comes from having so many children asking so many questions all the time."

Ellie blew softly on the surface of her tea. "Why *did* you have so many kids?"

"So we could put them to work, of course," her grandmother teased, as if the answer should be obvious. "As you well know, there are plenty of chores around here."

"True," the little girl agreed. From the moment she'd been able to walk, Ellie had accompanied her dad to her grandparents' farm to "help" with all those chores—from feeding the chickens to leaning her cheek against the warm belly of a big bovine and skillfully tug on its smooth teats, squirting fresh milk into a bucket *or* into the open mouth of one of the many barn cats that patrolled the premises. Ellie had been—as her dad loved to tease—*born an old farmhand.* Now she eyed her grandmother. "Gran, did you ever want a girl?"

Libby nodded. "Oh, yes. I have so many recipes and kitchen secrets to pass along . . ."

"Good thing you have me," the spunky ten-year-old chirped.

"Good thing!" Libby agreed.

"Mom says I broke the all-boy streak."

"You did indeed . . . *and* now we have Maddie on our team, too."

Ellie nodded, thinking about her younger brother and all her cousins. Out of ten Tennyson grandchildren, only two were girls— Ellie and her newest cousin, Madison . . . and although there were two more buns in the oven—as her mom, Jodi, liked to say, the gender reveal confetti for both expectees had been blue. "Maybe Uncle Gage and Uncle Chase will have girls."

"Maybe," Libby replied, trying to tuck away her worry by taking a sip of tea. Gage, her second oldest, at thirty-seven, had recently gotten engaged, and he and his fiancée, Maeve Lindstrom, were planning to get married on the farm in June, but Libby didn't know what the future held for her youngest son. At twenty-eight, Chase's life was unfolding in ways she hadn't expected—or maybe she'd just been in denial, and with a mother's heart, she worried— despite Gage's reassurance—that Chase might never experience the wonder of being a dad.

"What's wrong, Grandma?" Ellie asked softly.

Libby looked up, instantly pulled back to the present, and mustered a smile. "Nothing, hon," she lied, and then eyed her granddaughter's cup. "Would you like some more tea?"

"Maybe a spot," Ellie replied, mimicking her favorite British

TV character, Hyacinth Bucket. "Just to warm it up," she added with a grin.

Libby brought the teapot over and warmed up both of their cups.

"We have to remember to watch *The Great British Baking Show* and *Keeping Up Appearances* this Saturday," Ellie said, thinking ahead to her weekly sleepover night, a routine that had begun shortly after her grandfather died.

"Don't we always?"

"We didn't last week."

"Why is that?" Libby asked, frowning.

"Because we played cribbage and lost track of time."

"Oh, right," Libby said, nodding.

Just then, the mudroom doorknob turned again, and a second later, Libby's third-oldest son, Matt, peered in, his cheeks ruddy from working outside. "You ready, kiddo?"

"Hello to you, too," Libby said.

"Hi, Mom," he said, smiling. "I'd come in, but I don't think it would make you happy," he said, gesturing to his muddy boots.

"That's quite all right," Libby said, nodding as Ellie wrapped her arms around her.

"See you tomorrow, Gran. The sun's supposed to come out."

"Do you think we'll recognize it?" Libby teased, squeezing her.

"I'm told it's a big fiery ball," Ellie said, laughing.

"Well, we'll just have to keep an eye out for it then."

"Love you."

"Love you, too. Don't forget your brother's overalls."

"Oh, right!" Ellie said, picking them up. "Thanks . . . and thanks for the tea."

"You're welcome."

Through the kitchen window, Libby watched her son and granddaughter walk to his truck and then glanced at the kitchen clock—it was still early enough. She could easily make it down to the Coffee Bean. She didn't have to stay long—just long enough to say hello to her two oldest friends and the other ladies from town who'd lost their husbands in recent years. She bit her lip, considering, then looked down at her clothes. She'd have to change . . . *and* it was getting dark—she didn't like to drive in the dark . . . not to mention she still had more mending . . . *and* she wanted to get up early and have the coffee ready when the boys got there in the morning. *Maybe next time*, she thought. She poured the last of the tea into her cup, put another log in the old Vermont Castings woodstove, and walked back to her sewing chair with Goodness and Mercy trotting after her.

2

PAYTON CHILDS UNLOCKED THE DOOR OF HER SHOP AND TURNED ON THE LIGHTS. It felt as if she'd just turned *off* the lights and locked the door, but here she was, back again, less than six hours later. *Day in, day out, lock, unlock. Where did the time go?* She glanced at the clock and yawned at the early hour. She'd kept the shop open late the night before—as she did every Thursday—for a small gathering of her mostly widowed friends (*mostly* because Callie Jasmine was divorced, but claimed it was *like* being widowed). The group—who affectionately called themselves the Guild—had been started by Payton and her friend, Ames Finley, after their husbands—Lonny, a tractor and small engine repairman; and Frank, a dairy farmer—died of heart attacks within six months of each other. The two women had consoled, confided, and found comfort in each other's company, and then they'd invited other friends whose husbands had died, and their circle had grown. Over the last several months, they'd also made it their mission to convince Libby Tennyson to join them, but their slender, silver-haired childhood friend always had an excuse. They weren't giving up, though. The three women had been friends since childhood—they'd gone to kindergarten together, and they'd had children who'd gone to kindergarten together, and Lonny and Jack had been best friends so their lives were deeply intertwined and rich with shared milestones and memories. Payton and Ames knew it would be good for Libby to get out of the house and join them. The Guild was a support group of sorts—in the beginning, they'd always gathered at Payton's house, but after she opened the shop, they moved the meetings there—it was more centrally located, and it saved Payton from having to keep her house tidy all the time. The Wine-Drinking Widows—as Cashen called them—had been getting together for nearly two years, though, so Payton thought she should be used to the once-a-week late night. It was unlike her to feel so tired, but then again, maybe she shouldn't have had that third glass of wine . . . or maybe sixty-five was finally catching up with her . . . *or* maybe it was time to call her doctor and make an appointment—it had been a while since she'd had her thyroid checked and her numbers fluctuated more than a politician in an election year!

"Cash, you comin' in?" she called, peering into the darkness, but when her twenty-eight-year-old son didn't respond, she realized he still had his earbuds in. She walked over and rapped loudly on the window of their old Chevy pickup, and when he looked up, his glasses reflected the screen of his iPhone.

"Be right in!" he called. "I just wanna finish this game."

Payton sighed, and let the shop door slam, putting an exclamation mark on her disapproval. "Those damn games!" she grumbled. "*And* those damn earbuds!" She didn't mind that Cash listened to music—she and Lon had raised him on their favorite music from the fifties and sixties so he'd grown to love it, too, but when he put his earbuds in, he disappeared into a world of his own. That was one of the reasons she'd bought the shop—besides needing something to do with her own time—she needed something for Cash to do. When he was little, her son had been diagnosed with Asperger's, a term associated with autism; and although he was on the high end of the spectrum, and smart as a whip, especially when it came to math and music, his bright mind was consumed by video games, and Payton felt as if she was constantly battling with him to find something more productive to do. Playing games and blocking out the world didn't help his social skills—which had always lagged behind those of other children his age, and as he'd approached adulthood, she worried what the future held for him, especially when she wasn't around anymore. Cashen needed to have his own income and his own purpose in life. For years, she'd been praying—with a mother's heart—for an answer . . . and for the assurance that he'd be okay when she was gone. Then, one afternoon, when she'd run into town to pick up a zipper to mend his jacket, she'd found the fabric store vacant . . . *and* the building for sale. She'd peered through the window, walked around back to the small courtyard framed with raised flower beds, and had an epiphany.

"What happened to the Calico Cat?" she'd asked Ames that evening when they'd been sitting on her front porch, having a glass of wine.

Ames sipped her chardonnay. "Callie moved it up to the Tractor Supply Plaza. She says it's a better location."

Payton frowned, wondering how she hadn't heard this news since Callie was in their group, and she wondered if maybe her epiphany wasn't such a great idea after all—if a fabric store didn't do well downtown, how would a coffee shop do?

She shouldn't have worried, though. Unable to shake the feeling that it was meant to be, she'd contacted a real estate agent, and with some of Lonny's life insurance, she purchased the little brick storefront for a song and put Cash to work. After consulting a contractor to make sure the wall dividing the store into two rooms wasn't weight-bearing—or hiding any wiring or plumbing, she handed her son a pair of Lon's old mechanic's goggles and a sledgehammer and said, "Have at it!" Cash had grinned gleefully as he lifted the heavy hammer and began swinging away, crushing the plaster and transforming the two rooms into a bright, airy space with a hidden fireplace at one end. After clearing the debris, they pulled up the sun-faded linoleum and discovered there was wide-board oak flooring underneath. Within a week, she hired Ron Carlson, a friend of Lonny's and semiretired handyman, to sand and refinish the floor. Ron also installed wainscoting along the bottom half of the newly Sheetrocked walls; and then, after she and Cash sanded, primed, and painted the walls slate blue and the wainscoting and trim around the windows linen white, she asked Ron to come back and install commercial-grade kitchen appliances, including two refrigerators, a dishwasher, three coffee machines, two cappuccino makers, and a long glass case for baked goods. Finally, she bought a retro-style cash register, set it on her new slate-gray granite countertop, and on the wall behind it, painted the inspirational quote:

BE STRONG
BE BRAVE
BE FEARLESS
DRINK COFFEE!

Payton's vision had been seeded by prayer, and she'd loved every minute they'd spent bringing it to life; and Cashen, for his part, had seemed to embrace his mom's dream and make it his own, too. Together, they filled dumpsters, sanded, painted, and found all the physical labor and planning cathartic. They worked from dawn to dusk, and then sat on milk crates in the middle of the debris and devoured pizza or Chinese food. Finally, exhausted, they headed home, collapsed into their respective beds, and didn't hear a sound till morning. It was a wonderful memory they both cherished.

As construction progressed, they pored over equipment and furniture catalogs—Cashen insisting on putting two cozy chairs and a couch and table in front of the fireplace—and Payton choosing small country farm tables and chairs for the rest of the space, along with sets of colorful ceramic Fiestaware plates and old-fashioned white diner mugs. The final touch had been hanging the beautiful sign Dan McGee had painted with a steaming mug of coffee and two coffee beans on it, encircled by the shop's name: The Coffee Bean—a name that was ten times better than her original idea, *Rocky Bottom Coffee*—which Ames said sounded like the coffee would be full of grounds!

On the day of the grand opening, Payton enlisted Ames's help, not only for moral support, but also to help keep an eye on her three new employees—Cashen, and his two best friends, Rylee and Jessie, who were also on the spectrum. Despite a few minor hiccups and a few mugs of spilled coffee, the day had been a huge success, and now, three years later, the Bean—as it was affectionately known in town—was a bustling (and mandatory) stop for all the local farmers, picking up supplies, moms who'd dropped their kids off at school, and bleary-eyed college students recovering from a late night of studying . . . *or* partying, and their busiest time of day was between six and ten.

Payton yawned as she dropped premeasured filter packs into coffee machines and hit their *start* buttons. This was Cashen's job, but he was still in the truck, and it was getting late. She looked through the boxes on the shelf, trying to decide on a flavor of the day. Finally, she settled on Smoky Mountain Coffee's Organic Fogbuster—a rich dark roast that could perk up the sleepiest brain—dropped in the packet and pushed the *start* button, but just as she did, the back door banged open and Cashen came in and immediately saw all the green lights. "I said I'd be right in," he said, frowning.

"I know you did, but it couldn't wait. You always say, 'Coffee doesn't brew itself,' and besides, I had a hankering for a nice hot cup of Fogbuster."

"You made *Fogbuster*?!" he asked, his voice rising. "We just had that on Monday."

"Well, we're having it again," she said, holding out the whiteboard marker. "Are *you* writing it in, or am I?"

Cashen pushed her hand away. "YOU write it in! I was planning to make Black Bear today—we haven't had it since March third."

Payton blinked. *How the heck did he remember the date of the last time they'd had the sweet berry-chocolate-flavored coffee?* She frowned, suddenly wondering if he remembered every flavor they'd served over the last month? *The last year?!* She knew he had a good memory—he could listen to a song someone played on the piano and replay it perfectly *without music*, but she'd had no idea he kept a mental inventory of the flavors they brewed every day. "I'm sorry, Cash," she said, trying to diffuse his frustration, "but you should've come in."

"I said I'd be right in," he growled, his boyish face aflame.

Payton was all too familiar with her son's temper—*and* mood swings, but she was also well-versed at calming him down. "How 'bout I get a cup of Fogbuster to clear the cobwebs from my brain, and we use the rest for iced coffee?" she suggested. "It's supposed to be nice today and people might like to have iced coffee for a change, especially with the weekend almost here."

Cash's frown faded as he considered the idea, and then nodded.

"All right, when it's finished brewing, transfer the Fogbuster to pitchers and put it in the fridge," she said, handing him the marker, "and write Black Bear in as the flavor of the day."

"Okay," he said, "but, in the future, remember I have it all planned."

"Got it," she said, kissing his cheek and turning to fill a mug with steaming black coffee. "I will absolutely *try* to remember."

3

AMES FINLEY DROPPED A HANDFUL OF SPINACH INTO HER NEW SMOOTHIE MAKER, checked the recipe again, added one apple, sliced and cored, a banana, a half a cup of blueberries, two dollops of yogurt, several frozen chunks of mango, peach, and pineapple, and a cup of unsweetened cranberry juice. "This is gonna make a lot," she murmured, checking the recipe one more time. "Okay, here goes." She put the top on—or, as it turned out, the bottom, flipped it over, and set it in the base. It immediately began to buzz and whir and in no time at all the chunks of fruits were transformed into a thick swirling purple liquid. Ames eyed it skeptically, took a tentative sip, and licked her lips. "Wow, that's really good—you'd never know it has spinach in it!" She slurped down half of it. "Now," she said triumphantly, "the next time Payton asks me if I tried it, I can say yes!"

She knew her friend had her best interests in mind when she gave her the smoothie maker for her sixty-third birthday—which was now nearly two years ago, but then, when she'd proceeded to ask her at least once a week if she'd tried it, Ames had grown weary of hearing the question. Even Cash—who she loved with all her heart—had taken up the cause, repeatedly asking her: Mrs. Finley, did you try your new smoothie maker yet? and she was about ready to bop him!

"That's what I get for telling her I wanted to start taking better care of myself," she mused, recalling how, after Frank died, she'd taken a long hard look at the way they'd been living and blamed herself for not insisting he take better care of himself. The doctor had repeatedly told her husband he needed to lose weight, drink less beer, eat fewer doughnuts . . . and less bacon . . . and steak, and try to force down an occasional vegetable—and make it something green, not just corn on the cob slathered in butter and salt. If he didn't, the doctor warned, he wouldn't live to see his sixty-fifth birthday, and although Ames had tried to get Frank to listen, he always waved her off like a pesky fly, and every time she put a spear of broccoli on his plate, he slipped it to their black Lab, Ned, who'd eat just about anything!

And then it happened. The memory of that morning was etched in her mind like the brand on an old steer. She'd made lunch at 11:30—just as she always did, but when Frank—who was famous for saying: *You can call me anything, but* don't *call me late to dinner*—hadn't appeared, she'd gone to investigate . . . and found him in the field behind the barn, slumped over the steering wheel of his still-running tractor. She'd called—and then shouted, but he hadn't responded—hadn't even stirred, and with an anxious heart, she'd shaken his knee, but the movement had only made his hand fall to his side. "Frank!" she'd cried. "Wake up!" She'd turned off the tractor, and even though he was twice her weight, she'd managed to pull him down without bumping his head and begun frantically pumping his chest and breathing into his lungs. But it was too late.

In the months that followed, she'd been stunned—shocked, really—unable to wrap her mind around the idea that her husband would never track mud through their kitchen again. Frank Finley was gone from this earth. He'd never sit in the threadbare recliner that was molded in the shape of his short stout body; he'd never snore the night away in the bed they'd shared for forty years. He was gone from the drudgery of daily life around their run-down farm, and it left her . . . well, numb . . . and empty. Their now twenty-eight-year-old daughter, Quinn—who'd always locked horns with him—tried to console her, but, from a distance, her daughter's words had little effect. Until one Sunday afternoon, Quinn said, "Mom, I know you miss him, but think about it—now you can do whatever *you* want. You can live your life on *your* terms without him telling you what to do . . . without having to do everything *his* way.

"You can go hiking with Ned. You can join the church choir. You can even play softball again—I still remember Mrs. Childs talking about how you two used to play on the same team, but how Dad always made a face when you said you had a game and wouldn't be home for supper. You couldn't even come visit me . . . but now you can travel anywhere in the world. Every time you talked about going on a cruise or on a bus tour, Dad put the kibosh on it, but now you can do all those things. Think about it, Mom . . . for the first time in your life, you are *free*."

Ames had listened to her daughter's words, and they'd washed over her like a gentle wave, soothing her weary body. At the same time, it seemed as if a heavy curtain was being pulled away from a long-shrouded window, and the golden light streaming in was full of promise. "I hadn't thought about it like that," she'd answered quietly. "I'm so used to him being here . . . so used to our life together."

"Forty years is a long time," Quinn had said. "It's a big change. Why don't you think about coming for a visit? We can drive along the coast or hike in the mountains—we can even go to Yosemite— you always said the national parks are on your bucket list."

"Maybe," Ames had replied uncertainly.

"Promise me you'll think about it," Quinn had urged, and Ames *had* promised.

"I love you, Mom. Everything's gonna be okay."

"Love you, too, sweetheart," she'd replied, and when she'd hung up, she'd looked out at the setting sun, her daughter's words

echoing in her mind: *Mom, for the first time in your life, you are free.*
"Free," she'd whispered. What an odd feeling!

She poured the last of the purple liquid into her glass and took
another sip. So much had changed since that day. For starters,
she'd realized she had no interest in running the farm by herself
and she'd sold the land and barns to a young farmer who talked
about building a house on the land and restoring the farm to its
original glory—something Frank had never had the energy or
gumption to do. Ames had known Quinn had no interest in moving back to Tennessee, so what was the point of keeping it? The
only thing she had kept was the little ranch-style house in which
she and Frank had lived and ten acres of the rich dark earth next to
the house, which she'd turned into a community garden.

Finley Farm had been an instant hit with the organically
minded young families who lived in town—the ones who wanted
to buy local, live off the land, and eat what they grew—all con-
cepts they seemed to think they'd come up with on their own.
They were a friendly bunch, though, and Ames loved stopping by
to check on them. She usually found them hard at work, weeding
and cultivating—it was like having a garden, but not having to
care for it (not that she minded weeding), but these youngsters
and their rosy-cheeked kids showed up at all times of day and did
the work, leaving Ames to prune and dig in her flower and herb
gardens—a chore she'd once loved, but for which she'd eventually had no time.

She also latched on to some of Quinn's suggestions. She
took Ned on long walks or on hikes in the nearby mountains.
The fresh air, blue sky, and lovely colors soothed her spirit like
a gentle balm, and they both lost ten pounds! And although she
hadn't joined the choir (yet!), she had let it be known that she
was interested in playing softball again, and when word got out
that Amesy O'Connor Finley—who'd been star catcher in high
school—was interested in playing again, an argument ensued
between the teams. Finally, her former team, Benny's Bomber-

ettes—a rowdy, beer-drinking group of old-timers that included
Payton—insisted that *they*—with two injured players—had the
greatest need, and Ames happily donned her old number—17—
and trotted into left field (because her knees were too stiff to play
catcher). That first season had ended with the Bomberettes coming back from a 4–1 deficit—thanks to a grand slam by Payton—to
defeat their archrival, Jimmy's Ace Hardware Nuts & Bolts, and
take home the league trophy.

Ames set her glass in the sink, filled it with sudsy water, and
gazed out the window, thinking about the conversation she'd had
with Quinn the evening before. They'd been talking about the coffee shop and she'd mentioned how she and Payton hadn't yet been
able to convince Libby—who lived just down the road—to come on
Thursday night, and Quinn had stopped her. "Wait, I thought the
Guild was for widows . . ."

"It is . . ." Ames said, frowning and trying to remember if
she'd ever told her daughter about Libby's husband. "I told you . . .
um . . . *didn't* I tell you about Jack?"

"Um, *no* . . ." Quinn had replied.

"He had cancer—inoperable. Didn't last six months."

"Oh, no!"

"Libby's already been through so much," Ames continued,
"losing Cale, and then, four months after Jack, her dad died."

"Wait, Dutch died, too?!" Quinn had sounded stunned.

Ames knew her daughter had loved Chase's grandfather and
had always thought of him as a sweetheart who loved teasing the
kids. And although she'd only been nine when Cale was killed
in a farming accident, she'd been just as shocked and dismayed
as everyone else, shedding tears of her own when she saw tears
streaming down her best friend's face at his big brother's funeral.

Ames nodded. "I'm sorry, I thought I told you this . . ." She
paused. "I didn't tell you about the funerals? And seeing Chase?
He gave such a lovely eulogy at Jack's funeral . . ." She paused. "My
memory must be going, hon. I'm really sorry."

"It's okay, Mom, but if I'd known, I would've sent Chase a card. I might've even come home for the funerals."

"Well, now I really wish I'd told you. It would've been nice to have you come home, even if it was for a sad reason. I know you're busy with the restaurant, but I miss you."

"I miss you, too, Mom . . . *and* don't forget, you promised you'd come visit me."

"I know," Ames replied. "And one of these days I'm going to surprise you."

"That's what you keep saying."

"I just don't know what I'd do with Ned."

"You can leave him with Mrs. Childs—I'm sure he'd be fine."

"Mm-hmm," she said, sounding unconvinced. "Anyway, we've been trying to get Libby to come on Thursday nights," she continued, remembering the beginning of their conversation.

"She will . . . when she's ready," Quinn assured her. "It takes time." She paused. "Do you happen to know what Chase-me is up to now?" she asked using her old nickname for him. "Or where he's living?"

"Payton said he and a friend from college have their own travel agency in DC, but they're moving—or they've moved—to Savannah—near Gage."

"Okay," Quinn said. "Maybe I'll see if he's on Facebook yet—I used to check, but he never was. If he is, I'll send him a message, but if he isn't, maybe you can get his address from Mrs. Tennyson, so I can send a note."

"Okay," Ames said. "I'm sure he'd love to hear from you. He really *did* give a nice eulogy for Jack . . . *and* he's as handsome as ever."

Quinn smiled, remembering her friend. "He's definitely a looker."

Ames nodded but didn't say anything more, and after they'd hung up, she wondered why Quinn and Chase had lost touch— they'd been inseparable when they were growing up. They'd even gone to their prom together. Ames always thought they made a cute couple, and she'd secretly hoped they'd end up together, but then Frank had dashed her hopes by telling her about a conversation he'd overheard them having on the front porch. Frank was constantly eavesdropping, and that was one thing Ames didn't miss about him: he was a nosy busybody . . . *and* a gossip. But she now knew—thanks to the eulogy Chase had given—that her husband had been right.

She washed and rinsed the smoothie maker and set it in the dish drain, and for the millionth time, prayed, with a mother's heart, that some handsome fellow—who loved hiking and kids and dogs—would come along and sweep her sweet daughter off her feet. More than anything in the world, she wanted Quinn to be loved by a man who would put her first in his life. It was something she never had.

4

CHASE TENNYSON LEANED BACK IN HIS CHAIR AND SLOWLY SWIPED HIS FINGER through the condensation on his glass before downing the last of his iced tea. He licked his lips, savoring the fresh lemon, but wished it was something stronger . . . and it would be, if it wasn't for Liam.

"The least you can do is wait till after five," Liam had teased when he'd come home early the day before and found Chase sipping a vodka tonic.

"It's five o'clock somewhere," Chase quipped. "And it's *not* an everyday occurrence," he added defensively. "Besides, we're living on the beach now . . . we should enjoy it."

"Mm-hmm," Liam replied, squeezing his shoulder.

Chase shook his head. "I can't help it—the tick-tock's moving too damn slow. I keep thinking about the sun sinking, like it did when we were in Mykonos." He smiled at the memory of the trip they'd taken to Greece the previous year. "Hey, Alexa," he called to the speaker on the counter, "play 'Day Drinking' by Little Big Town." And as the playful party song filled the kitchen, he eyed Liam. "You want one, don't you?"

Liam glanced at the clock. "What the hey," he replied with a grin.

Chase laughed, knowing it didn't take much to convince him. He also knew, deep down, that his partner was right to call him out on his lack of self-discipline—he was absolutely capable of overdoing things. Liam called it his "devil-may-care" attitude and said he "tended to push the envelope." Both were valid observations, but Chase always countered by saying he was just *embracing life . . . seizing the day*. And besides, he hadn't always been this way. Growing up in the shadow of five older brothers, Chase had known, early on, that he was different. His mom said he had a gentle way about him. She called him her old soul and told his dad he had his own song to sing. She said he'd been born with a tender heart and an extra dose of compassion. On report cards, his teachers noted his affinity for befriending and fiercely defending his less popular—and often bullied—classmates. They called him the little boy with the big heart, and when he graduated from elementary school, he was given the much-revered "Good Citizen Award" because he always helped—without being asked—his friend Cashen Childs, a classmate with autism who struggled with the rigors of school. On the farm, Chase also took under his wing any animal—mammal or fowl—that was being neglected by its mother or in the case of Happy—the little freemartin calf that was almost turned into veal by his father—by becoming her advocate, savior, and best friend.

But as he'd grown taller, Chase had known there was something else. With piercing blue eyes, a shy gentle smile, and long dark lashes that were the envy of every woman he ever met, he was constantly drawing the attention of girls in school, and although he dated a couple of times, it never felt quite right . . . and then, as his world grew wider—*and wilder*, Chase grew wiser. He discovered how unkind and unjust the world could be, and out of necessity, he became keenly aware of everything happening around him. He learned to be cautious and to keep things to himself. At the same time, under the watchful eye of his protective and mischievous older brothers, his wry, fun-loving, devil-may-care attitude had blossomed . . . and it was accompanied by

"So I've heard," Liam replied, "but I still haven't had a chance to try it."

"Did you look for it? They're supposed to be carrying it."

"I did look, but sorry, mate. No joy."

"Well, we'll just have to take a trip to the farm—it's the creamiest coffee ice cream you'll ever taste and it has chunks of the most decadent chocolate brownies. Man, oh, man—it's to die for! Besides, we haven't seen my mom since Christmas, so we're long overdue."

While he had the freezer door open, Chase filled his glass with ice. "You want a cocktail . . . or the whole rooster?" he asked, looking up with an impish grin.

Liam glanced at the clock. "I think I'll just have a glass of wine."

"Suit yourself," Chase said as he poured a generous amount of Tito's into his glass and splashed tonic over it. He squeezed a lime into the still-fizzing bubbles and then reached for a corkscrew. "Red or white?"

Liam looked up from his laptop. "Red," he said, continuing to scroll. "Sheesh! I have at least three hundred emails."

"You're a popular guy," Chase teased as he opened one of the boxes stacked in the corner, looking for a wineglass. "We really need to start unpacking."

"Mm-hmm," Liam murmured distractedly. "I bet ninety percent are business related."

Chase finally found a glass, poured the wine, and set it on the table. "And you thought we wouldn't do well, but here we are, two years later, buying a house on the beach."

Liam looked up. "You're right, but I should've known, with you at the helm, we'd have nothing but success."

Chase grinned and took a sip. "Not just me—you have the business sense."

"Business sense will get you nowhere without someone who's a genius at marketing," Liam countered, taking a sip of his wine.

"Do I hear a trace of sarcasm in your voice?" Chase quipped, eyeing him.

"Me?! Noo . . ."

"Ha! Well, it *was* a good idea." Chase leaned back in his chair, slowly swiped his finger down the side of his glass, and thought about the business outline he'd been working on that afternoon to promote their new office in downtown Savannah. He felt the relaxing sensation of the alcohol and as he watched Liam tap away on his keyboard, his mind drifted to the first time they'd met . . . and how they'd come up with the idea for their business.

The syllabus for Advance and Advantage—affectionately known to the business majors as Entrepreneurship 101—stated that the goal of the required course was to: *Find a unique need and fill it.* The bulk of the work (after coming up with that unique need) involved outlining a marketing strategy: from advertising that included a website and social media pages, and pinpointing an audience to financing and projecting annual income and expenses. At the end of the semester, students—who had the option of working in teams—were expected to present their business at a symposium attended by professionals . . . *and* potential investors.

On the first day of class, Chase had sat in the last row of the small lecture hall, recovering from a presemester blowout and waiting for Dodgy Doug—the old codger who'd taught the class since the beginning of time—to waddle in, but when a tall, slender boy with sun-bleached chestnut-brown hair sat in front of him, Chase couldn't help but notice. At the end of class, he'd slung his backpack over his shoulder, and the boy had stood, too, and turned to look back. "Ole Doug is a piece of work," he remarked, shouldering a leather satchel.

"He is," Chase agreed.

The boy extended his hand. "Liam Evans."

"Chase Tennyson," Chase said.

They'd chatted as they stepped out into the late summer afternoon and continued to talk about the amount of work the class entailed. Finally, Chase, on a whim—and suspecting they might have more in common than the pursuit of a business degree—suggested they work together. "Divide and conquer," he'd said with a grin, and Liam, to his surprise, had agreed.

That night, over a six-pack—because Chase said beer-storming *always* produced better results than "plain ole brainstorming," they'd come up with an idea for a travel agency that would specialize in finding safe, friendly, and welcoming destinations for the LGBTQ community. They worked long and hard on their project, growing ever closer as they did, and ultimately their hard work paid off—Pride Travel was a huge hit at the end-of-the-year symposium, and their professor, seeing its potential, introduced them to one of the professionals in attendance who had deep pockets. The young woman had given them her card and said to absolutely call.

That was nearly five years ago now! Chase sipped his drink and felt his stomach rumble. He looked over at Liam. "What did we say we were having for dinner tonight?"

Liam looked up. "I thought we were getting pizza from that place Gage and Maeve recommended. Huca something . . ."

"Oh, yeah," Chase said, his face brightening. He opened his laptop and began searching for the website of the restaurant his brother and soon-to-be sister-in-law had recommended. "Huc-A-Poo's Bites & Booze," he said, finding it. "My kind of place." He sipped his drink as he perused the menu and read the pizza options out loud. "Here's one," he said. "The Omnivore . . . *The garbage can of pizzas served with a bunch of meats and veggies.*"

"Perfect!" Liam said, taking a sip of his wine and looking out at the rain. "Do they deliver? Because I really don't feel like going back out."

Chase consulted the website again. "They do," he confirmed. "Is a large enough?"

"Sure," Liam replied, turning his attention back to his emails.

Chase tapped the number into his phone, ordered, gave them

the address of their beach cottage, and hung up, looking dismayed. "Forty-five minutes! I don't know if I'll last that long."

"You'll be fine."

Chase got up to freshen his drink and then clicked on his Facebook page and noticed a new "friend" request. He had never been a big fan of social media and only had a few "friends." The catalyst for joining had been the need to promote Pride Travel, and it was only later that he'd made a personal page.

He clicked on the request and the name that popped up brought back a rush of memories. "Quinn Fin," he murmured, smiling wistfully. "Hmm . . . I don't know."

Liam looked up quizzically.

"An old classmate sent me a friend request."

"How come you don't know if you can accept?"

Chase took a sip of his drink. "Something that happened . . . but if I could've ever fallen for a girl, it would've been Quinn Finley."

Liam watched curiously as Chase scrolled down his friend's page.

"Pretty as ever, though. Blond hair, blue-sky eyes, tan, athletic . . . and the kindest person you'll ever meet." He looked at Quinn's information. "My mom said she moved to San Francisco after college . . . I wonder if she lives near your parents." He continued to scroll, looking at her pictures, and then stopped and laughed. "Oh, wow! You have to see this picture!" He turned his laptop so Liam could see a photo Quinn had posted several years earlier. It was of two ten-year-old towheaded kids with their arms thrown over each other's shoulders, holding blue ribbons and grinning from ear to ear; behind them were two big brown-and-white cows with eyes the color of melted chocolate. The caption read: TBT! BFFs with our bovines and blue ribbons. #crossmyheart

"Wow! Is that *you*?!"

Chase nodded.

"What were the ribbons for?"

"4-H—it's a youth agriculture program we were in when we were kids—they say it's to help develop leadership skills, but we just had fun raising and showing our cows at the fair." He smiled. "Now, look at this one . . ." He clicked on a second picture and Liam studied it with a slow smile. It was of a high-school-age Chase wearing a dark gray suit with his arm around the girl—now grown up and wearing a long dark blue dress. The caption read: My sweet prom date! #crossmyheart

"I didn't know you went to your prom."

"Yep," Chase confirmed. "Damn," he said wistfully. "I haven't seen Quinn in years."

"What's with the hashtag?"

"Just something we used to say to each other."

As he said this, a notification of a new message popped up and when he clicked the icon, the drop-down bar showed it was a message from Quinn. Liam nodded. "Looks like she wants to reconnect." He looked up. "Does she know?"

Chase nodded. "She knows—she was the first—and only—person I . . ." But before he could finish, the doorbell rang, and he pushed back his chair. "That was quick!"

5

WHEN LIBBY WALKED ALONG THE MOSS-COVERED STONE WALL THAT FRAMED their farm, she always imagined an old farmer working in the hot sun, carefully choosing each stone before setting it in place. Stone walls took planning, and this wall—which had stood the test of time—was a testament to the farmer's skill and care. She also wondered, as she walked, what worries he might have had and what prayers he had prayed. If he'd had children, he would've had plenty to pray about. She considered the stones, too, each one spotted with pale green curls of lichen—and realized that many of them had probably never been touched again. She also loved to listen to the chipmunks scolding her as they scampered through leaves and scooted into crevices, only to peek back out and watch her pass. She watched the chickadees and warblers, too, light on the uppermost wall and sing breezy summer songs or warn the others of her presence. In one direction, the wall ran the entire length of the road. In the other, it rolled up and down the hills of their six-hundred-acre farm, occasionally interrupted by white wooden gates that could be swung wide so the herd could move from one pasture to another.

In front of the wall, at the end of the driveway, was where Jack had planted their mailbox. For years, Bill Wright, the mailman, had tried to get Jack to move the box to the beginning of the road—which had no outlet—so he wouldn't have to drive the extra mile every day just to deliver a bill or two and the monthly *American Dairymen*, but Jack had never obliged. Even Bob Garret, who delivered the *Knoxville Daily Sun*, took up the cause for a while, saying Jack . . . or Libby . . . or one of the boys drove, rode, or walked past the box at least twice a day, but Jack wouldn't budge. *He paid his damn taxes and the least the damn government could do was deliver his damn mail to his damn box . . . and the same went for his damn newspaper!*

But now Jack was gone, and when Bill mentioned it to Libby, she had Matt moving it the very next morning.

"How come Grandpa never moved the mailbox?" Ellie asked as they planted blue blotch, true blue, and deep orange pansies around the new cedar post.

"Why do you think?" Libby asked as she pulled cube-shaped clumps of pansies from their plastic trays and handed them to her granddaughter.

"Because Tennysons are as stubborn as the day is long," Ellie said, using the phrase her mom used when she talked about the Tennyson side of the family.

"Precisely," Libby said. "Let's just hope *you* missed out on that trait."

"Dad says I did *not*," Ellie said as she brushed dirt from her hands. She stood to admire their work. "I *love* orange and blue together."

"That's because they're opposites and they complement each other, like red and green or purple and yellow."

"I know, but of all the colors, orange and blue look the best together."

"That explains why you didn't pick the purple and yellow pansies."

"Yup." She looked at the old mailbox her dad had put on the new post. "I think you should get a new mailbox, Gran."

Libby eyed the dented green box. "You're probably right. Maybe I'll ask your dad . . ."

As she said this, a pickup truck came around the corner, and Libby turned, recognized her childhood friend and neighbor, Payton Childs, and waved.

"Good afternoon, you two!" Payton called cheerfully. "Your pansies look so pretty. Just the sight of them lifts my spirits."

"Thank you," Libby replied, wiping her brow with her arm. "It's definitely nice to see the sun again."

"It is indeed. And how are you, Miss Ellie?" Payton asked. "You look as if you've grown a foot since the last time I saw you."

"I'm fine, thank you," Ellie said, grinning, "and I probably look that way because my pants are too short." She looked down at her ankles—which drew her grandmother's attention, too.

"My heavens, El, those pants *are* too short!"

"I know. Dad always asks me if I'm expecting a flood."

"Remind me when we get back to the house and we'll see if we can find some longer pants—after six boys, I have closets full of 'em . . . in all lengths."

Ellie looked alarmed. "That's okay, Gran. I don't want to wear boys' pants—I'd rather wear high waters!"

Libby frowned. "Well, that's silly—they're perfectly good pants. Uncle Gage says farm kids don't care what they wear."

"Well, he'd be wrong about me," Ellie declared. She turned back to Payton and quickly changed the subject. "Where's Cash today, Mrs. Childs?"

"Oh, he's still at the shop. He stays late on Fridays to clean the floors. Then we get pizza for supper."

Ellie nodded. "That sounds fun."

"*And* . . . how are *you* doin'?" Payton asked, locking eyes with Libby.

"I'm fine," Libby assured her. "I've got El to keep me company . . . *when* she's not too busy."

"Well, you know, we ladies are still gettin' together every Thursday night and you're more than welcome to join us. It'd be good to get out of that big house and away from all those memories."

"I know . . . and one of these days, I might just take you up on it."

Payton smiled. "I'm gonna hold you to that," she said, and then she eyed Ellie. "Remember, Miss Ellie, you heard it, too—you're my witness!"

The little girl grinned. "I'll remember."

Payton swept her hand through her short, salt-and-pepper hair and pulled on her baseball cap. "Well, I'm off to pick up Ames—we have our first softball practice tonight."

Libby frowned. "I hope the fields aren't too wet."

"You and me both!" Payton said, waving. "You take care!"

After she'd gone, Ellie eyed her grandmother. "How come you don't go on Thursday nights, Gran?"

Libby leaned down to pick up the empty flower trays. "Oh, I guess I'm just happier being home, cozied up with a good book and a cup of tea."

"You can do that any night. I think you should go. Mrs. Childs and Mrs. Finley are always so nice—they make me laugh. You need to laugh more. You know what the Bible says—a cheerful heart is good medicine, but a crushed spirit dries up the bones . . . *and* a day without laughter is a wasted day!"

Libby eyed her granddaughter. "The Bible doesn't say that!"

"It says the first part."

Libby smiled. "How'd you get to be so wise?"

"Being 'round you . . . *and* reading a lot," Ellie replied. "Did you hear about the big shark they found off the coast of Nova Scotia last year?"

"I don't know if I did . . ."

"You'd remember because it was over seventeen feet long and it weighed more than thirty-five hundred pounds!"

"Wow!" Libby exclaimed. "That is big!"

"They estimated she's over fifty years old! *And . . .* guess what they named her."

"I don't know," Libby answered, wishing she had half the enthusiasm for learning as her ten-year-old granddaughter did.

"Nukumi—it's named after a legendary wise old grandmother figure of the Native American Mi'kmaq people," Ellie replied, putting her arm around her grandmother's slender waist. "Just like you."

"Ha! *Old* maybe, but I don't know about legendary . . . and *you,* my dear, are much wiser than I am," Libby said, pulling her close as they walked along the road.

"It must run in *your* side of the family," Ellie said. "The Tennyson side is stubborn, and the Jansen side is wise."

"Well, I think you got an extra dose from the Jansen side."

"We can only hope," Ellie said, using a phrase she'd often heard her grandmother say.

"True!" Libby replied. "So, what kind of tea are we having today?"

"Hmm . . ." Ellie put her finger to her chin. "How 'bout peppermint?"

"Peppermint it is."

6

AMES LIFTED THE SHARK-FIN-SHAPED LID OFF THE TREAT CANISTER—AN ACTION that always triggered the menacing theme from *Jaws* . . . and always made Ned's ears perk up. "Okay, mister," she said, eyeing him. "On your bed." The big black Lab hurried over to his fleece-covered bed and Ames knelt in front of him, gazing into his sweet brown eyes. "You can come next time, when it isn't so wet out. You don't need to lie on the cold grass. You'll be much cozier right here on your bed . . . or on *mine*," she added, knowing that, as soon as she left, he'd trot down the hall, hop on her bed, and sprawl across it like a king. She gave him the treat and kissed his furrowed brow. "I'll be back . . . *and* maybe I'll even bring you some pizza crust." Hearing two of his favorite words, Ned thumped his tail, and Ames chuckled. "See you in a bit," she said, grabbing her softball glove and hurrying out through the open garage.

"I can't believe we have practice already," she said, climbing into Payton's truck.

"It's a sure sign of spring!" her friend said cheerily, but as she put the truck in gear, she looked over and saw Ned gazing out the window. "I thought we were bringing him."

"Nah, it's too wet. He's better off at home."

"Sorry, Ned," Payton called. She loved the old Lab almost as much as his "mom" did. Maybe more. "He could stay in the dugout, you know . . ."

Ames shook her head. "He's fine. The sooner we go, the sooner he'll be asleep, dreaming happy dog dreams."

"Mm-hmm," Payton replied, sounding unconvinced.

"Did you finish the book club book yet?" Ames asked, tying her cleats as they drove.

Besides being founding members of the Guild and playing softball together, Payton and Ames were in the same book club, but, unlike the weekly Thursday meeting of the Guild and the twice-weekly practice or game of the softball team, the book club only met once a month, and they didn't meet in the summer. This month they'd been plodding through the last book before their summer break—Virginia Woolf's *To the Lighthouse*—and Ames, despite all the rave reviews she'd found on Amazon, thought it was "a snoozer."

"I *have*," Payton said, "but I'll definitely be bringing a large sippy cup full of wine to the meeting. Let me know if you want one."

"I definitely do," Ames said, chuckling. "I haven't finished it . . . and I honestly don't know if I'll be able to. I can't get through a single page without falling asleep . . . and that's *without* wine. I don't know why Ellen picks such tired old books. I think we should read a page-turner once in a while."

"Why don't you suggest one?" Payton asked, looking over.

"Maybe I will," Ames said, gazing out the window. "I'll have to think of one before we start up again in September."

"It would probably help if you didn't read other people's reviews on Amazon and let them cloud your opinion."

Ames chuckled, knowing it was true. "I have to do my research—I'm always skeptical of the books she picks and I want to know what I'm getting into."

"Well, how about reading the positive reviews, too?"

"I *do*," Ames said, knowing full well she was more likely to click on the one-star reviews first.

"Are you still up for pizza?"

"If you are, but I probably should've driven so you wouldn't have to take me home."

"I don't mind—you're just down the road."

"Cash might mind."

"No, he won't. He'll have his nose in his phone and he won't even notice."

"Okay," Ames said, and then, even though she'd been planning to wait for Payton to ask her, she blurted, "I tried the smoothie maker!"

"No way!" Payton exclaimed, feigning shock.

"Way," she replied, laughing.

"And?"

"And it was great."

"What did you make?"

"A recipe called Rise and Shine."

"Was it good?"

"It was. It had spinach, apple, and lots of frozen fruit, *and* I felt healthy all day."

"Good," Payton said, nodding. "I'm glad you finally tried it."

"Me, too."

They passed the abandoned textile mills and pulled up behind the ramshackle wooden bleachers that had been leaving splinters in the hind ends of townsfolk for generations. "I thought they were gonna replace the bleachers this year," Payton grumbled.

"It got moved to fall," Ames said—she always knew what was happening in town—"but I wouldn't hold your breath." As they climbed out, the wind whipped around the truck like a mini-tornado and pulled their caps off their heads. "Sheesh!" Ames said, grabbing hers before it could scuttle across the parking lot. She tightened the plastic closure, pulled it back on, and stopped at the fence to watch their teammates warm up. "Ready?" Payton asked, slapping a softball into her glove.

"I guess so," Ames said with a chuckle.

Payton trotted out past the pitcher's mound—one of the many things she loved about her old friend was her unflappable spirit. It was true, she had worried about her after Frank died. For a while it had seemed as if Ames might never smile again, but then Quinn— good ole Quinn, as Payton often called her—had reminded her mom that life with Frank had been anything but easy and said that Ames could now enjoy life on her own terms. Her daughter's words had hit home, too, because that same afternoon Ames had shown up at Payton's front door with a bottle of chardonnay, and as they'd watched the stars come out, she'd told her everything Quinn had said.

Ames threw the ball and then swung her arm around, stretching it. "A little stiff."

"It's been a long winter," Payton replied, tossing the ball back.

They threw it back and forth, each lost in the memory of their younger days—when the wind didn't feel so cold and their bodies didn't ache so much. Finally, feeling warmed up, Ames called, "Want to pitch a few?"

Payton nodded, took her place at the mound, scraped her toe through the dirt, wound up, and fired it straight over the plate, leaving Ames's hand stinging inside her mitt. "You still got it, ole girl!" she teased.

"That's what you always say," Payton said, laughing.

Practice lasted for an hour and a half, and afterward the team gathered around the dugout and Jen McAllister dragged a cooler out from behind the bleacher. "Who wants a cold one?"

"Meee!" a chorus replied.

"Wish we could, ladies," Payton said, checking her phone, "but we have a dinner date with Cash."

"Booo!" Several women jeered affectionately as Ames and Payton headed to the truck.

They pulled away, waving, and Ames turned up the heat in the truck and held her hands in front of the vent. "My hands are frozen!"

"Mine aren't," Payton said, unzipping her sweatshirt.

"Is your thermostat still broken?" Ames teased.

"Goin' on ten years now," Payton said, shaking her head. "I don't think it'll ever be normal."

Ames knew how much Payton's core temperature fluctuated. She was constantly zipping, unzipping, covering, uncovering, pulling on, pulling off—it was an endless cycle. "Did you ever make a doctor's appointment? I thought you were gonna get your thyroid checked."

"I am, but I've been busy . . . *and* I keep forgetting, and when I *do* remember, it's after hours."

"You should write yourself a note."

"I should—what a novel idea!"

Ames laughed. "Want me to order ahead?"

"Sure."

"What are we getting?" she asked, pulling her phone out of her pocket.

"The usual—medium pepperoni for Cash and a large for us—whatever you want."

"Half mushroom, half bacon . . . or Hawaiian?"

"Oooh, Hawaiian—we haven't had that in a while."

Ames ordered the pizzas and when they stopped at the shop to pick up Cash, she started to climb out. "Hafta spend a penny."

"You can't wait till we get to the restaurant?"

"Nope," she said. "You have hot flashes and I have an overactive bladder—we've reached that wonderful stage of life when we have old lady problems."

"That's because we *are* old ladies!" Payton said.

Ames laughed and saw Cash coming out. "Hello, there, young man," she called. "Hold the door for me, would you?"

"Hello, Mrs. Finley," Cash replied, barely looking up from his phone as he held the door.

"Eye contact, kiddo," she admonished gently, and Cash looked up and smiled.

"I'll be right out." Ames went inside, used the ladies' room, and as she passed back through the kitchen, she stopped and jotted two words on a sticky note and stuck it to Payton's favorite mug. Then she closed the shop door and hurried out to the truck.

7

CARRYING TWO HOT LATTES AND TWO OF GOOSE FEATHERS CAFÉ'S SIGNATURE sandwiches, Chase stepped onto sun-dappled Barnard Street, but as he pulled his sunglasses down from their perch on top of his head and tried to read a text from Liam at the same time, he almost tripped on the legs of a man dozing in one of the café's outdoor chairs. "Whoa!" he exclaimed, sidestepping. "Sorry 'bout that!"

"No worries," the man replied, pulling his legs in. "We jus' sittin' here a spell," he said, his dark eyes blinking in the sunlight.

Hearing him use the word *we*, Chase looked down and realized there was a little white dog under his chair. "Hey, pupper," he said, juggling his food so he could hold out his hand for a sniff. In response, the skinny little pit bull stood up and wiggled her whole hind end. "What a cutie," Chase said, propping his sunglasses back on his head. "What's her name?"

"Marmalade," the man replied, "cuz she's so sweet." Upon hearing her name, the little dog wiggled closer, her bony rib cage outlined under her short white fur.

"Nice!" Chase said. He knelt down to give Marmalade a proper hello, and as he stroked her ears, he noticed she was tethered to the man's chair with an old, frayed rope, and behind her on the ground was a piece of cardboard with the words ARMY VET WILL WORK

FOR FOOD! scrawled across it. He frowned, but when he stood, he hid his concern and reached out to shake hands. "Chase Tennyson. How do you do, sir?"

The man stood politely, and Chase—who was over six feet tall himself—realized the man was four inches taller, and his hand was the size of a bear's paw. "Matthias Abraham," he replied. "How do you do, my friend?"

"I'm well, thank you," Chase replied. "I have a brother named Matt, but it's short for Matthew."

The man smiled. "My mama named me after the thirteenth apostle."

"The one who replaced Judas," Chase said with a knowing smile.

Matthias nodded. "You know your Bible."

"Skipping Sunday school was not an option in our house."

"In ours, neither," Matthias said, chuckling. He started to sit back down, but just as he did, a café employee peered out.

"I'm sorry, sir, but these tables are for customers."

Matthias nodded, and started to stand, but Chase stopped him. "Would it be all right if I joined you?"

"I thought you were in a hurry."

"I thought I was, too, but . . ." he said, tapping his phone, "my friend just bailed on me."

Matthias gestured to a second chair. "You're welcome to join us."

The employee rolled her eyes and disappeared, and Chase emptied the contents of his bag on the table. "Have you had lunch? Because now the other sandwich is gonna go to waste."

Matthias bit his lip—he *hadn't* had lunch. "Thanks, son, but I can't take your food."

Chase frowned. "At least take this coffee then—it's just gonna get cold." As he said this, he pictured Liam working at their new office just a few blocks away, waiting for him to return with lunch and some much-needed caffeine.

"All right," Matthias said with a slow smile. "It'd be a sin to let a cup of coffee go to waste."

"It would." Chase agreed, smiling at the small victory. He took the cap off his cup and nodded to Matthias's hat. "Which branch of the service were you in?"

"Army," the man replied, taking a sip of the frothy coffee.

"Vietnam?"

Matthias nodded. "Medic."

"That must've been a tough tour, especially as medic—I can't even . . ."

"I try not to think about it."

Chase unwrapped his sandwich. "You sure you don't want the other one?" he asked again, gesturing. "It'll get soggy and then I'll just have to throw it away."

Matthias felt his stomach rumble. "Well, I wouldn't want it to go to waste. Would it be all right if I give a couple morsels to my pal?"

"Of course," Chase said, taking a bite.

Matthias unwrapped the sandwich, lifted a corner of the rye bread, and eyed the contents.

"It's Havarti, cucumber, tomato, and avocado topped with sprouts," Chase said, licking a dollop of pesto mayo off his finger.

"Interesting," Matthias replied, breaking off a hunk. He held it out to Marmalade—who took it politely. "What do you think, Marm?" he asked as she wiggled around him. He broke off another piece and while Chase watched, the old man—who was as thin as a rail—made sure she had something in her belly before he did, and the reality of it all made the food in his mouth taste like cardboard.

"Here, Marm," Chase said softly, holding out the last bite of his first half, and the soulful look in her eyes immediately stole his heart. He looked up. "Are you from Savannah, Mr. Abraham?"

"Please call me Matthias . . . and yes, all my life."

"Family?"

"I did have family . . . I mean, I *do* have family—I have four children, but they are with their mother in Atlanta, and the oldest three are on their own."

Chase nodded and sipped his latte.

"I used to drink a bit and it got me into a heap o' trouble. Before the war I didn't touch the stuff—my mama said it was the devil's drink, and I steered clear o' it, but when I got back, things were different, and it helped me shut out my memories—memories o' the devil hi'self."

"It *is* the devil's drink," Chase acknowledged. "But it can be a hell of a lot of fun, too."

"It can be . . ." Matthias looked up, his eyes shadowed, ". . . until it isn't."

Chase pressed his lips together. It was a truth he knew too well.

"Tha's why I'm in the situation I'm in, and I feel worse for my Marmy-girl." When he said her nickname, the little dog lifted her head off her paws and gazed at him adoringly. He sighed. "But tha's where we at and I guess it could be worse. At least we live someplace warm." He finally took a bite of the sandwich and licked his lips. "Hey, this is pretty good."

Chase smiled and nodded.

"Do you live in Savannah?"

Chase swallowed, then said, "Tybee Island. We just moved here from DC."

"DC," Matthias mused thoughtfully. "I always wanted to go there," he added wistfully. "Two monuments I'd like to see—the Vietnam War Memorial—to find the names of the fellas I knew . . . and to stop by and see ole Abe."

"You should go," Chase said. "The monuments are amazing."

Matthias sighed. "Maybe someday—it's on my bucket list."

Chase watched a shadow of regret cross the man's face, and then Matthias looked up and mustered a smile. "What brings you to Savannah?"

"My partner and I just moved our business here. We've been wanting to get out of DC and we visited Savannah last summer to see what it was like—one of my brothers lives here, and we fell in love with it."

"Nice," Matthias said. "How many brothers do you have?"

"Four." Chase pressed his lips together before continuing. "I had five, but my oldest brother died when I was nine."

"Oh, man, I'm sorry to hear that."

"Thanks—it was a long time ago. My brother Gage has lived here for ten years—he's the second oldest. I think it'll be nice to be near him. My other brothers live in Tennessee near our mom."

Matthias smiled. "It's good to be 'round family. There ain't nobody like 'em."

"Do you see your kids?"

"Sometimes. I wish I saw 'em more." He gave Marmalade the last of his sandwich and then crumpled up the paper. "I can't thank you enough for the sandwich and coffee, young man," he said, standing, "and for taking the time to chat with an old man. It means a lot."

"You're welcome, Matthias," Chase said, realizing he was planning to leave, and standing, too. "Maybe we can do it again sometime."

"That'd be nice. We'd like that, wouldn't we, Marmy-girl?" He looked down and she wiggled her whole hind end.

Matthias picked up the tattered rope, discreetly tucked his cardboard sign under his arm, gently squeezed Chase's shoulder, and ambled away. Chase watched them go, and after they turned the corner, he cleaned up his own trash, glanced at his watch, and hurried back inside to get another coffee and sandwich for Liam.

8

A_MES_ WOKE WITH A SHIVER, BUT WHEN SHE TRIED TO PULL UP HER QUILT, IT wouldn't budge, and when she tried to roll to her side, she felt a heavy lump pressed against her legs. "Oh, Ned," she groaned, giving him a gentle shove. "You're taking up the whole bed again!" The big Lab thumped his tail and rolled onto his back for a belly rub. "Oh, no you don't, you big lug," she admonished, rolling him in the other direction and freeing the covers. She scooted into the warm spot he'd left behind, pulled the quilt up to her chin, and closed her eyes, but it was pointless—she was wide awake.

She opened one eye, peered at the clock, realized Payton and Cash were already up, showered, and brewing coffee at the Bean, and felt guilty for lying there. She definitely shouldn't have stayed up so late, finishing that damn Virginia Woolf book. With a sigh, she pushed off the covers, swung her legs over the side of the bed, and tried to find her slippers, but when her big toe bumped into a soggy tennis ball, she decided to turn on the light. "Good thing I didn't stand up," she mumbled. "I probably would've twisted my ankle!" She blinked at the brightness of the lamp, located her slippers, slipped her feet into them, and shuffled down the hall. When she returned, Ned was sprawled across the bed, all four legs up in the air, snoring like a freight train. "You're worse than your father was," she said, recalling her husband's loud snoring.

"Ready for breakfast?" she asked, and in one continuously fluid movement, Ned flipped, stood, and leapt from the bed. Ames chuckled. "I guess you are." She followed him down the hall, let him out through the garage, and while he took care of business, filled his bowl with kibble. A moment later, he pushed open the door with his nose and bolted to his food. As she measured coffee, Ames listened to him happily crunching and slurping, and when the sound of her coffeemaker joined in, sputtering and dripping, she smiled, thinking, *There's something comforting about a morning routine and morning sounds . . . and the older I get, the more comforting they become. Thank goodness for Ned. I don't know what I'd do without him!*

When the coffeemaker finished dripping, she filled her mug with coffee, added a little cream, and settled into her favorite chair in the living room. She cradled the mug, letting the warmth seep into her hands . . . *and* her soul, and watched the sky brighten. Not wanting to break the lovely peacefulness, she just sat there, sipping her coffee, and as she did every morning, gave thanks for her warm and safe—albeit small and cluttered—home. A moment later, Ned trotted in, still licking his lips, hopped up on the couch adjacent to her chair, and curled into a ball. She reached over and stroked his head and thought about the conversation she'd had with Quinn the night before. *I miss you, Mom. You should come for a visit before softball really gets going. If you don't, the whole summer'll go by again. I looked up flights and they're not that bad. You can get a round-trip from Knoxville to San Fran for cheap. I'll send you the link . . .*

Ames sighed. The thought of leaving Ned made her heart ache. She missed her daughter, but in the six years she'd had Ned, she'd never left him for more than four hours. She couldn't imagine leaving him for a week . . . *or more!* She pictured him wandering around the house, looking for her—or worse, in a lonely, cold kennel—where he would be expected to relieve himself on a concrete slab—oh, the indignity!—and she was certain her sweet, faithful Lab would be lost without her . . . *and* the comfort of their routines. Not to mention she'd worry about him the whole time and what fun would that be? "I don't know how you'd manage without me," she whispered, stroking his soft ears. Ned sighed contentedly and Ames shook her head—she'd just have to tell Quinn she couldn't come—not while she still had Ned.

She opened her devotional, saw the reading for that day was from the book of Esther, and opened her bible to find it. "Where are you, Esther?" she sang softly, leafing through the pages trying to recall if she'd ever had to find the elusive book before. The only thing she knew about the obscure book was that it was in the Old Testament. Finally, she found it—right where it had always been, between Nehemiah and Job.

"There you are, ole girl," she said, chuckling. She began to read, but when she finished the assigned verses, she was still intrigued and decided to continue. A half hour later, she'd finished the entire story of the queen who risked everything to save her people, and when she looked up, she realized the sun was streaming through the windows. "My goodness!" she said. "I guess I got carried away." She scratched Ned's ears. "We need to get going, don't we?" She picked up her empty coffee mug, put it on the counter, and went down the hall to change. When she returned, Ned was waiting in the kitchen with his leash in his mouth—something he'd been doing since he was a puppy. "You're such a good boy," she said, "but we don't need that today." She took it from him, tied it around her waist, and then held the door out into the garage open, and he bounded down the two steps, through the open garage door, and out into the sunshine. "I think spring might finally really be here," she said, catching up to him.

They headed down the quiet country road and as they passed the sign for Finley Farm, Ames spied an old Subaru with a NO FARMS NO FOOD sticker on its bumper and turned in to say hello to Sarah Whitman, one of Quinn's old classmates. Ned raced ahead to greet the young woman who was just pulling her gardening tools from her trunk. "Morning, Sarah," she called.

"Morning, Mrs. Finley," Sarah called as she knelt down to greet Ned.

"You're getting an early start."

"I am. I thought I'd take advantage of this beautiful day. I'm itching to dig in the dirt so I thought I might put in some asparagus and beets and see if they take."

"Ever the optimist," Ames teased.

Sarah's green eyes glinted in the sunlight. "It's a tough job, but someone has to do it."

Ames nodded. "Where's your helper?"

"He's in school this year!" She shook her head. "I can't believe he's old enough. That's another reason I'm here—it's so much easier to get things done."

"I know what you mean. Before you know it, though, he'll be all grown up, so enjoy every minute."

"I'm trying."

"Well, have fun digging in the dirt. You've inspired me—I have several packets of sunflower seeds to get in the ground."

"I'm glad I inspired you," Sarah replied. "Have a nice walk."

As Ames waved goodbye to her daughter's old friend she felt an unexpected twinge of mom-envy. Even though Quinn owned her own restaurant and seemed happy, she'd never been in a serious relationship, and Sarah—who was a year younger—was already married *and* a mom—precisely the things Ames dreamed for her daughter. She looked heavenward and whispered, "You know my heart, Lord. Please bring someone special into Quinn's life, too." Then she followed Ned back out to the road.

They neared the fields where they'd kept their cows and her thoughts drifted back to the last years of Frank's life. Toward the end, he'd decided to give up the dairy business and just plant corn and hay to sell, but when he started selling their cows, too, it had broken her heart. She'd begged him to keep her two favorites, but he refused, and she'd watched tearfully from the kitchen as her beloved Belle and Lucy trudged up the ramp into a stranger's trailer.

Now, as she walked through the tufts of tall buttercups, she saw John—the young farmer she'd sold their land to—unloading hay from his pickup into the round metal trough they'd always used. Almost immediately, a parade of Ayrshire and Jersey cows plodded toward him. "Life goes on," she murmured. "Who would have thought we'd have cows in these fields again?" she said to Ned when he wandered over to watch. She waved to John and then headed back up the road, but as they neared the house, she stopped to pick some wildflowers, and when she caught up to Ned, she found him pushing the door between the garage and the house open with his nose. "You're so smart!" she said as she followed him inside and lifted the lid off the treat jar.

9

JUGGLING A TRAY OF EGG SALAD SANDWICHES, HOMEMADE CHOCOLATE CHIP cookies, and a pitcher of lemonade, Libby pushed open the screen door. "Lunch!"

Matt and Gage looked up. "Be right there, Mom," Matt called back.

Libby set the tray on the picnic table and watched her sons prying a rotten board from the barn. "It's going to be more work than you thought."

Gage wiped his brow. "Even if we weren't having the wedding here, it needs to be done. It should've been done a long time ago."

"Well, we've had a few things going on around here, as you well know."

"I know," he said, "and I haven't been much help."

"It's not that bad," Matt said in his usual glass half-full style. "We put a new roof on it five years ago, and the frame is rock-solid. It just needs a few boards here and there, and some fresh paint.

Just then, Gage's yellow Lab, Gus, raced around the corner of the barn dragging a long stick, but when he smelled the sandwiches, he stopped in his tracks, lifted his nose, and trotted over to the table.

"Oh, man, what the heck did you get into?" Gage asked, eyeing the brownish-black goo that was smeared into his thick fur.

Matt chuckled. "Looks like he found something really good—and gooey—to roll in!"

"Dang, Gus! What the heck?" Gage said again, and when the big Lab wiggled closer, he put up his hand. "Oh, no you don't!"

Libby laughed. "What is it with dogs and manure?"

Gage shook his head. "I don't know." He eyed Gus again. "But you can go lie over there," he said, pointing to a spot near the barn. "You just got yourself uninvited."

Gus sniffed the air around the table hopefully, but Gage pointed again, and with his tail and ears hanging, Gus walked over and dutifully lay down in the shade.

"I think he'd make a good search and rescue dog—he has such a strong nose," Libby said.

Matt took a sip of his lemonade. "He could also be one of those drug detection dogs."

"Now what fun would that be," Gage asked, "when you can run free all day, explore, roll in smelly stuff . . . and mooch food off people?"

"Do you take him to work with you?" Libby asked.

"Most days," Gage said, her question reminding him of the new house they'd just started working on in Savannah. "In fact, before he came around the barn just now, I would've said he's calmed down and spends a lot of his time lazing on the grass . . . but he would've just proved me wrong."

"What are you working on?" Matt asked, pouring a glass of lemonade for each of them.

"We're restoring an old Georgian-style home that belonged to a Southern family with roots that go back generations—slave owners for sure . . . *and* it's rumored to be haunted. After the last family member died, the bank was named executor and they broke the land up into lots and sold them without any trouble, but they couldn't even give away the house—it's been on the market forever. They were just about to tear it down when an unsuspecting couple from New York City showed up and bought it for a song. They had no idea it was haunted, but after spending one night, they moved to a hotel and brought in an old Creole woman who specializes in voodoo to get rid of the evil spirits."

"That's crazy," Matt said, shaking his head.

Gage nodded. "It *is* crazy, and that's why I have the rest of this week off—Ben said he didn't need his employees around when evil spirits were being exorcised. I don't know if I believe any of that stuff, but Ben does. He says he's been in old homes that definitely didn't feel right—gave him a chill and some really bad vibes."

Libby took a sip of her lemonade. "You two remember the old Hollister house on Witness Road?"

Matt nodded. "How could we forget? The name of that road is creepy enough."

"We used to go fishing over there and then dare each other to go up on his porch and knock on the door," Gage added.

Libby nodded. "Well, back when Dad and I were dating, Mr. Hollister was still alive. We never saw him in town because he was pretty self-sufficient—tended his own garden, hunted in the hills, and fished under the bridge near his house—that was the only time we ever saw him, when he was fishing. Other than that, he kept to himself. One summer night, though, something happened at that house. People heard shouts and screaming—like someone was being murdered, but the next morning, he was sitting in his rocking chair on the front porch and everyone figured he was fine. But he stayed in that chair for days . . . *and* nights, his chair slowly rocking back and forth. Finally, the sheriff decided he better check on him and sure enough, he was dead as a doornail . . . but that chair was still rocking back and forth."

"Oh, man, that's creepy," Gage said, raising his eyebrows. "Is his house still there?"

"It is," Matt said. "It's all overgrown and the roof is falling in."

"Did they ever figure out what happened?"

Libby shook her head. "For some reason, even though the circumstances were suspicious, he didn't have any family and the state didn't do an autopsy. But even if he'd just had a heart attack, why would the chair rock? The air around him was as still as a dead possum . . . and it smelled like one, too." She shook her head. "Your father loved to drive home that way after a date—even though it took longer—and he always slowed down because he knew it gave me the heebie-jeebies. We'd be just about to pass the road when he'd slow down and say, 'Ooh, let's go this way—I know how much you love it!'"

"Didn't he work for Mr. Hollister when he was a boy?" Gage asked.

Libby nodded. "He did some yard work for him, but when his father—your grandfather—who was a minister, found out, he forbade him from ever going there again. It was very odd. I think he still went sometimes if Mr. Hollister needed a hand.

"Anyway, afterward, everyone thought the house was haunted."

"Well, I know we kids did," Matt said, laughing. "I *never* went up on that porch, but Chase—he would. We'd dare him and he'd hop right over the fence, stand on the porch, and recite 'Jabberwocky' or a few verses from 'The Raven.' That boy had no fear."

"That's because he had five big brothers he was trying to impress, *and* who he knew would protect him," Libby said.

"True," Gage said, taking a bite of his sandwich. "Anyway, the house we're working on now must've been beautiful in its heyday, but it needs a lot of work now. The restoration will take the better part of a year."

"What about your artwork?" Libby asked. "I thought, after your art show, you were going to devote more time to it?"

"I'm trying to," Gage said. "If I'm not too tired, I draw at night . . . but with the wedding coming there's so much to do. I am working on the cover of our wedding invitation."

"I didn't know that," Libby said in surprise. "Is it a drawing?"

"It's a watercolor . . . of sunflowers because they're Maeve's favorite."

Libby smiled. "How *is* Maeve?"

"She's fine. Busy with all the planning. She wanted to come this weekend, but one of the girls at work is out on maternity. We'd also have to find someone to take care of the chickens, and she didn't want to ask Macey again—she's busy, too. Harper has soccer twice a week and sea camp after school, and with Ben working so much, she's juggling both their schedules. Everyone's busy," he said. "You know how it is, Mom."

"I *do* know," Libby replied. "At least, I *used* to know. I'm not as busy as I once was. Back when you were little, I didn't know which end was up!"

"Well, now you can relax—you deserve it," Matt said, taking another half sandwich.

Libby sighed. "I know, but sometimes I wish I was busier. I always looked forward to this stage of life, when it would be just Dad and me . . . I never expected to be alone."

Matt squeezed her hand. "We know you didn't, Mom, but Grayson, Eli, and I are always here, and you know you're welcome to come over to our houses anytime—for supper or just to say hi. Plus, you have Ellie—she loves spending time with you, especially Saturday night sleepovers."

"I know," Libby said. "I don't know what I'd do without her. She's such good company and she's always teaching me new things. Just the other day she was telling me about some predatory cat someone spotted down in Texas. I forget the name of it . . ."

"Was it a jaguarundi?"

"Yes! She said it's a medium-size cat—slender and muscular

with a big bushy tail, and it's so rarely spotted that some people think it's a myth. Where does she learn this stuff?"

Matt chuckled. "She reads all the time—everything she can get her hands on, but she seems to especially like magazines and books about animals. *Nat Geo* is her favorite."

"She's a fountain of knowledge."

Gage smiled. "I bet she and Ben and Macey's daughter, Harper, would hit it off. Harper reads all the time, too, and she loves marine life, especially sea turtles. She and Maeve have their own book club. The last books they read were the *My Side of the Mountain* trilogy."

"I read those," Matt said.

"I think we all did."

"I wonder if Ellie has read them," Matt mused thoughtfully. "She loves anything about birds."

"I think they're in the bookcase," Libby said. "You can take 'em home."

"Or you and she could read them together, like Maeve and Harper," Gage suggested.

"We could," Libby agreed.

"By the way, Mom," Matt said, "I heard Mrs. Finley and Mrs. Childs have been trying to get you to go to the coffee shop on Thursday nights. Have you gone yet?"

Libby pressed her lips together. "Where'd you hear that?"

"From a little bird," Matt teased.

Her boys eyed her, waiting for her answer, and she shook her head. "I haven't gone because the weather's been crummy, and I don't like to drive in the dark."

"I'd be happy to drive you there . . . and pick you up," Matt said. "In fact, today is Thursday—you should go tonight."

"I'm not going when Gage is here."

"I'm gonna be here all weekend, Mom, and I can drive you into town for a little while, if you like."

Libby shook her head. "I don't think so. Maybe when the weather gets better."

"Mom, it's beautiful."

She shook her head again and pushed the plate toward him. "Have another sandwich."

Gage took another half of a sandwich and then realized Gus had stealthily edged closer so that he was now lying at his feet. "Hey, you're supposed to be over there," he scolded, but Gus just thumped his tail, and Gage relented, giving him a corner of the sandwich. "Right after lunch, you're gettin' the hose!"

10

"Are you sure you'll be okay?" Payton asked.

"We'll be fine, Ma," Cash said, sounding exasperated. "It's not even busy."

She pulled on her jacket and watched Rylee sweep the floor as Jessie wiped down tables. "Okay, no funny stuff. We close in an hour, and I'll probably be back before then. The Guild is coming tonight, so we'll be having an early supper."

Cash closed the register and made a note on a piece of paper because he liked to keep a running total of the exact amount in the drawer. "I know. I know. Can I get Chinese and eat here? Then you won't have to take me home."

"Sure," Payton said, knowing her son enjoyed hanging out at the shop on Thursdays, and usually came up with an excuse to stay. "That might be a good idea."

Cash grinned. "Of course it's a good idea—those are the only kind I have."

"Mm-hmm," Payton teased, raising her eyebrows. She kissed his cheek. "Call me if you have any problems."

Cash groaned. "We won't have any problems, Mom. You worry too much."

"You're right," she said, making a funny face at him. She

walked toward the door. "I'm going out for a bit, you two. If I'm not back before you leave, have a good night."

"You, too, Mrs. Childs," Rylee said, looking up from sweeping a small pile of dirt into a dustpan.

Jessie looked up, too, her eyes smiling, and hurried over to give her a hug. "Have a good appointment, Mrs. Childs. Don't worry about a thing. Cash is a good boss."

Payton laughed, knowing how much Jessie loved her son. "I know he is. Okay. If I'm not back, I'll see you tomorrow."

"Take your time, Mrs. Childs," Rylee called. "We got this!"

Payton smiled—she knew she shouldn't worry. Cash had run the shop by himself before and he was probably more responsible when she wasn't there. On top of that, Rylee and Jessie had been working for her since the shop opened and they knew how to do their jobs.

She walked to her truck, climbed in, and as she shifted into reverse, her thoughts shifted to her appointment. She hated going to the doctor. If it wasn't for the sticky note Ames had left on her coffee mug, she would've purposely kept forgetting to call, but the note had left her no excuse. Julie, Dr. Hamlin's receptionist, had searched his schedule for an opening that was "later in the day"— and squeezed her in on the following Thursday, so here she was. Julie also sent an order for bloodwork to the lab, and Payton had fasted and gone the next morning. Now, she parked the truck in front of the office and climbed out, but as she walked across the parking lot, her heart started to pound, and she tried to remember if she'd taken her blood pressure medicine the night before.

The waiting room was empty, and before she even had a chance to sit down, Jackie, Dr. Hamlin's assistant, peered around the doorway. "How're you, Payton?"

"Able to sit up and take nourishment," she replied, mustering a smile. "The usual aches and pains, but I *am* getting older, you know."

Jackie chuckled. "Aren't we all?"

They went into the first exam room they came to, and Jackie motioned to the scale.

"Must I?" Payton asked, grimacing.

"I'm afraid so," Jackie replied.

Payton stepped on gingerly, hoping her light step would somehow register less weight, but as Jackie slid the gauge up and up, Payton shook her head. "Sheesh! Can you take a couple off for clothes and shoes?"

"I can," Jackie agreed. She opened the patient portal on her laptop, reviewed Payton's medications, updated her chart, and then reached for the blood pressure cuff. Payton rolled up her sleeve and tried to relax. She closed her eyes, felt the cuff squeezing her arm, and tried to picture a sunny beach with gentle waves lapping the shore. "One sixty-two over ninety-eight," Jackie announced, breaking the tranquility of the scene. "A little high."

"I guess so," Paton muttered.

"It might just be white coat syndrome—is it usually high when you come in?"

"I don't remember, but it must be since I take medicine for it."

Jackie nodded. "Do you ever take your blood pressure at home?"

Payton shook her head. "I don't have a monitor."

"You should get one. They're not expensive, and then you can check yourself when you feel relaxed." She opened a cabinet and pulled out a monitor. "This is a good one—you can probably find it online."

Payton studied the simple device and nodded, making a mental note. "Could you write the name down?" she asked. "I probably won't remember."

"Absolutely." Jackie jotted the brand and model on a slip of paper and handed it to her. Then she closed the portal on her computer and smiled. "You're his last patient so he'll be right in."

Payton nodded. "Thanks, Jackie."

Payton leaned back in the chair and pulled her phone out of her pocket to see if anyone—namely Cash—had tried to reach her, but there were no messages. She tapped her Facebook app and scrolled through her newsfeed. She only had a handful of "friends" so it usually didn't take long for her to see what everyone was up to, but when she came to a post by Quinn, she stopped. Ames's daughter had shared a beautiful photo of a pelican standing on one leg, and behind it the sun was setting—the scene reminded Payton that Ames hadn't mentioned visiting her daughter lately. She'd have to remember to ask her.

There was a tap on the door and Dr. Hamlin peered in. "Well, well, well, look who it is," he teased cheerfully. "Long time, no see, young lady."

"I know," Payton said, sliding her phone into her pocket. "Don't take it personally."

"I never do," he said, sitting on a stool and clasping his hands together. "How've you been?"

"I've been well, thank you. How've you been?" she asked politely, changing the subject.

"Same ole, same ole. Busy, but that's okay." He eyed her. "How's my buddy, Cash?"

Payton smiled. "He's fine. Closing the shop tonight."

"Good. You need to let him do things on his own. He's perfectly capable."

"I know he is, but I still worry."

Dr. Hamlin nodded. "I know it's not easy, Payton, but it would be good for him to become more independent. Maybe even let him get a place of his own someday."

"Oh, I don't know about that. He can't even remember to put his clothes in the laundry!"

"If he was given the chance, he might surprise you. Besides, you—and I—aren't going to be around forever."

"I know. That's why I'm here." She searched his eyes. Nason

Hamlin had been her doctor for all of her adult life—and even though she avoided visiting him—she considered him to be a trusted friend.

"So what's going on? I know you wouldn't come see me if you weren't worried about something."

She chuckled. "This is true, and it's probably nothing, but I just don't seem to have the energy I used to . . . and I *really* think my memory is going," she added. "Just the other night at my book club meeting I couldn't even remember the name of the main character!"

He smiled. "Well, it's normal for people our age to slow down and become forgetful, but reading is good exercise for our brains, so keep it up . . . even if you forget some things." He turned to the laptop on the table. "Did you go get your bloodwork?"

"I did—last week."

He scrolled down the screen, tapping and searching. "Looks like your blood pressure is a little high," he said. "Have you been taking your medicine?"

"When I remember."

He eyed her. "It's important to remember. Why don't you put it near your toothbrush and take it at night, right after you brush your teeth?"

"Okay, I'll try that."

He eyed her again. "And if that doesn't work, maybe you should consider getting a pill tray."

"Oh, no! Pill trays are for old people!"

He raised his eyebrows as if she was stating the obvious, and then turned back to scrolling. "Here it is." He studied the screen for a minute and frowned. "Well, your thyroid numbers are definitely low, so that would explain your lack of energy."

"Would it also explain my weight gain?"

"It could," he said, reaching for his stethoscope. He listened to her heart, felt the glands in her neck, and then gently pressed the hollow below her Adam's apple, but when he hesitated a few extra seconds and continued to probe the area, she looked up and realized he was frowning.

"Uh-oh, what's the matter?" she asked.

He shook his head. "It's probably nothing, but just to be sure, I'd like you to get an ultrasound—there's a little bump there and it's best to get it checked out."

Payton gently touched the spot he'd been probing, and sure enough, there was a tiny bump that she'd never noticed before. "Should I be worried?"

"Nope, I don't want you to worry," he said. "You already do enough of that," he teased, trying to lighten the mood that had just settled over the room. "I'm also going to lower the dose of your thyroid medicine, and then we'll check it again in six weeks. I'll send the script to the pharmacy and the script for the ultrasound to the hospital. You just have to make the appointment."

Payton nodded, feeling stunned. "It's always something."

"It's a good thing you came in," he said, searching her face, "and I mean it about *not* worrying, Payton. It's *just* an ultrasound. And don't go looking it up on the internet, either."

Payton nodded, but after she thanked him and walked numbly through the office and out into the parking lot, she immediately pulled out her phone.

11

CHASE RINSED THE LAST PLATE AND SET IT IN THE DISH DRAINER. "WHY DON'T
we go tomorrow? We can surprise my mom. Gage is at the farm for
the weekend because he and my brothers are working on the barn,
getting it ready for Gage and Maeve's wedding. It'll be fun . . . *and*
you'll finally get to try Rocky Top . . . you know, that coffee ice
cream with the brownie chunks I keep raving about."

"You don't have to convince me," Liam said, drying the plate
and putting it in the cupboard. "But don't you think it's kind of
crazy to drive all the way to Tennessee to see Gage when he lives
here?"

"We won't just see him. We'll see my mom and brothers, too.
It'll be fun, and the weather is supposed to be nice."

"I'm always on board for a weekend away, especially now that
we're finally getting settled."

"Perfect! I just need to do some laundry tonight. Do you have
any?" Chase dried his hands on a dish towel and pulled open the
doors to the laundry room.

"I do," Liam said, opening one of the last unpacked moving
boxes and lifting out a jug of detergent.

Chase turned on the washer, poured in some detergent, and
sorted through the basket, dropping their light-colored clothes

in first. "I ran into Matthias and Marmalade today," he said when Liam returned with an armful of clothes. "You know, the veteran I told you about a week or so ago?"

"The one you gave my sandwich to?"

"Yes, that one," Chase said, laughing. "And, in my defense, I did buy another sandwich for you."

"An hour later . . ."

"Well, I think he was a little hungrier than you."

"Mm-hmm. Anyway, how is he?"

"I don't know—he seemed sad. I offered to buy him a cup of coffee, but he said he was all set. I think he had a half-pint of something stronger in his pocket."

Liam nodded. "I keep meaning to tell you I saw something on Savannah's Facebook page about a food kitchen that's looking for volunteers, and I know you've been talking about helping out, like you did in DC, so I sent the link to you."

"Okay, thanks," Chase said.

"And on the topic of Facebook, did you ever connect with your friend from home—you know, the girl you went to the prom with?"

Chase raised his eyebrows, suddenly realizing he'd never responded to Quinn. "No, I forgot. The pizza came, we had a couple of drinks . . . and then *you* distracted me," he added with a grin.

Liam handed him the fabric softener, pulled a few more items out of the box, including the old towels they used when they washed their cars, and then he broke the box down and added it to the pile of cardboard near the door. "Maybe we can stop at recycling tomorrow and get rid of all these boxes."

"Any idea where recycling *is*?" Chase asked, closing the laundry room doors.

"No, but they probably have a website."

Chase sat down in front of his laptop and typed *Tybee Island recycling* into the search box, but even before he finished, the local recycling center popped up, and he studied the map. "Looks like it's on our way, but they don't open till eight."

"Did you want to leave earlier than that?"

"I guess not. I'm gonna be up for a while, waiting for the laundry," Chase said. "There's another load after this one."

"Do you want me to wait up?"

"Nah, I got it—I'm not that tired."

"Okay, well, I might read for a bit."

"Which means you're going to fall asleep," Chase teased.

"Maybe," Liam replied with a grin. "I did get up early this morning to go running."

"Um, did you go alone?" Chase teased, raising his eyebrows, since he'd accompanied Liam on the six-mile run around the island.

"Um, no. Someone went with me . . ."—he feigned puzzlement—"but I can't remember who."

Chase rolled his eyes and shook his head at the same time. "Go read."

"Okay," Liam said, laughing, and then he hesitated, and Chase looked up. "Maybe while we're at the farm, we should tell your mom we're engaged."

"Ha! Maybe!" Chase said, making a funny face. "That ought to be interesting."

"I thought she was okay with it . . . with *us*."

"She is okay with it—at least she says she is, but sometimes I wonder how she feels, deep down. She always tells me the only thing she wants for me—for *us*—is to be happy *and* healthy. She doesn't want me to be alone—to never have someone in my life, but I think she'd prefer that someone was a girl. She definitely doesn't want me to miss out on being a dad."

Liam leaned against the counter. "Well, we're gonna be dads. We both want kids."

"I know, but we're obviously not gonna have them in the conventional way. Gage said she mentioned it to him last summer. She told him she thinks it's confusing and unfair for kids to have two dads and not a traditional family. She thinks they'll get teased."

"What did Gage say?"

"He told her we would make awesome parents. He said the only thing that matters to kids is being loved, and that there are plenty of heterosexual couples who should *not* be parents. He thinks she's coming around. He also asked me if we were thinking of adopting."

"And what did you say?"

"I said I wasn't sure—that we hadn't really talked about it."

Liam put his hands in his pockets. "I'm open to adopting. There are so many kids that need homes. I'd love to help a little kid like Harper—she's such a pistol!"

"She is," Chase agreed, picturing Ben and Macey's adopted eleven-year-old daughter. "They really lucked out when they got her."

"And look at Mason—Maeve put him up for adoption when he was a baby, and what an amazing person he is . . . so, yeah, adoption is definitely an option, but I wouldn't rule out finding a surrogate mom, either—that would be cool."

"It would be," Chase agreed. "We'll have to see what happens, but you're right—we *do* need to tell my mom, so maybe this weekend . . . and your parents sometime soon, too. We've been engaged since Christmas Eve and we've hardly told anyone."

Liam nodded. "I want to tell my parents in person, too, although I doubt they would ever come to my wedding . . . *if* we even have one."

Chase nodded solemnly—he knew Liam's parents had been less than understanding when their only son had opened up to them about being gay. "Well, I'm happy to come along. You know me, any excuse for a trip to California."

"We'll have to figure out that one. Meanwhile, I'm gonna go pack, and then read, but if I fall asleep, consider this good night."

Chase stood up and pulled Liam into a kiss. "Good night. Love you."

"Love you, too."

Chase searched his eyes. "Your parents will come around."

"Maybe," Liam said with a sad half smile.

They lingered for a moment and then Liam reached for the book he was reading, *Journey of Souls*. "Don't stay up too late."

"I won't," Chase replied as he went back to the laundry room and switched out clothes. With one load in the washer and one in the dryer, he freshened his drink, reached for his laptop, clicked on his Facebook page, found Quinn, and scrolled through her pictures. "Yep, pretty as ever," he whispered, smiling, "but looking a little older, my friend. I can't believe we're twenty-eight—how can that be?" He tried to figure out if she'd ever met someone special, but he only saw pictures of friends, a calico tiger cat named Clementine, and the majestic California coastline, so if she had met someone, she hadn't posted any pictures of him. She *had*, however, done a lot of hiking. Several photos were location-tagged *Yosemite*, and in one in particular, she was gripping the infamous cables with one hand while letting go with the other to give a triumphant thumbs-up as she reached the summit of Half Dome. "You go, girl!" he whispered, smiling.

He continued to scroll and discovered she owned her own restaurant, aptly named Quince Café, and then he came across a picture he hadn't noticed before. It was of the two of them after their prom. They'd changed their clothes—he was wearing jeans and a Zac Brown T-shirt, and she was wearing cutoff shorts and her favorite old hooded sweatshirt. He had his arm draped around her shoulders and they were holding red Solo cups and standing near a bonfire. The image was smoky and golden, but the half smile on his face reminded him of the aching sadness he'd felt that night, and the memory suddenly washed over him like a wave. The keg, the foamy beer, the fire reaching higher than the trees after they'd thrown on a pile of old wooden pallets . . . the music and laughter as she'd drawn him away from their friends. It had been the first time for both of them and when she'd pulled him down into the tall grass in the field behind the barn, he'd prayed with all his heart that he'd find the answer he wanted—the answer that evaded him . . . but afterward, he'd known. For sure.

She hadn't known, though, and he hadn't told her. Not then. Not that night.

He read the caption she'd written under the picture: First time! #crossmyheart. "Damn, Quinn," he whispered. "I trusted you . . . you promised." He bit his lip as he hovered his cursor over the *accept* button. "I still love you, though . . . and it's all water under the bridge now."

He clicked the tab and then read her message:

> Hi Chase, I just heard about your dad and
> Dutch . . . and I'm so sorry.

12

WHEN PAYTON CAME THROUGH THE DOOR OF THE SHOP, CASH LOOKED UP FROM his phone and, with a frown, pulled out one of his earbuds. "Did you pick up Chinese?"

"Oh, no, I completely forgot," she said, shaking her head in dismay. "I—I" she stammered, unable to form a coherent sentence, and then it suddenly dawned on her that she shouldn't even try to explain because she didn't want him to worry. "I'll order it right now. They never take long—it'll be quick, and I'll head right over to pick it up."

"They deliver, you know."

"Do you want them to deliver?" she asked distractedly. "Because I can go—it's just around the corner."

"Whatever's easier, Mom. I can walk over and get it, too." He noticed her hands trembling as she looked for the number and frowned. "What's the matter? Are you okay?"

"Oh, yes! I'm fine. Just a little distracted."

"How was your appointment?"

"It was fine. No worries," she assured him.

"Good."

"So, sesame chicken?"

"Mm-hmm. Dumplings and an egg roll, too, please."

Payton called in the order. "Do you mind walking over to pick it up?" she whispered with her hand over the phone.

Cash looked up. "Nope, I don't mind."

Payton nodded and uncovered the mic. "No, we'll pick it up."

She hung up and riffled through her bag. "Here's a twenty," she said, holding it out. "They said it would be ready in ten minutes so you should probably head over soon."

Cash took the money and dropped it on the counter next to him. "I will . . . I just want to finish this game."

Payton sighed and started to reply, but then bit her tongue. She glanced at the clock—the ladies would start arriving soon, and although Rylee and Jessie had made the shop shine before they left, she still needed to do a few things to get ready. She quickly pushed three tables together to make one long one and then pulled open the "Guild Cabinet"—as Cash called it—to get out a tablecloth, wineglasses, small plates, and a corkscrew. She started to measure decaf into a regular-size coffeemaker for anyone who wanted coffee instead of wine and then looked up and realized Cash was still sitting at the counter. "It's been ten minutes, Cash."

"I'm *going*," he said, sounding annoyed and pushing back his stool so it clattered to the floor. He picked it up roughly and headed for the door, but he didn't get far.

"Don't forget the money!" she called, and he stormed back. "And make sure you wait for your cha . . ." But before she could finish, he'd stuffed his earbuds in his ears and walked out, letting the door slam behind him.

Payton clenched her jaw. *How is he ever going to manage on his own when he can't even remember to do simple things? What in the world will happen to him if, God forbid, something happens to me?* She clicked on the coffeemaker and then leaned against the counter and felt tears fill her eyes.

"Yoo-hoo! Anybody here?" a cheerful voice called, and she quickly brushed her tears away.

"In here," she called back.

Ames bustled in and set a plate on the counter. "I made lemon poppyseed muffins—from scratch this time, so I have no idea how they'll be." She chuckled, but when she turned and saw the tears glistening in Payton's eyes, her smile faded. "Oh, no! What's wrong?"

Payton shook her head, and Ames searched her friend's face. "Tell me," she said softly. "Is it Cash?" She looked around. "Where *is* Cash?"

"He went to pick up Chinese food so he'll be right back . . . unless he gets lost."

"He won't get lost," Ames assured her. "What's wrong then? What happened?"

Payton took a deep breath. "I had my appointment . . ."

"Oh, right. I forgot. How'd it go? Did you ask him if there's anything he can do to fix your temperature gauge?"

"No, but I had bloodwork last week and my thyroid numbers are off again—which would explain why I'm so tired . . ." Ames waited for her to continue, but Payton just leaned against the counter and shook her head.

"What else did . . . ?" she asked.

"He found a tiny lump on my thyroid and he wants me to have an ultrasound."

"Oh," Ames said. "What does he think it is? Did he say?"

Payton shook her head. "He called it a nodule and told me not to worry . . . and *not* to look it up."

"But you did, anyway."

Payton nodded. "Thyroid cancer is caused by excessive exposure to radiation, and the only radiation I've had are x-rays at the dentist's office. It seems like they want to do x-rays every time you go, and although they cover your chest with that protective cover, they don't always use the throat cover." She shook her head, tears welling up in her eyes. "Honestly, how much can your teeth move in one year?!"

Ames pulled her into a hug. "How come you don't listen?"

she asked. "Don't you know the internet makes everything sound worse than it is?"

"I needed to know. I worry about Cash . . ." Just then, the back door swung open, and Payton pulled away and eyed her friend. "Don't say anything," she whispered.

"I won't," Ames assured her. "Cross my heart."

Payton cleared her throat and wiped her eyes. "Did you have enough money?"

"Yes," Chase answered brusquely, pulling a clump of crumpled bills out of his pocket and plopping them on the counter. He started to pull the small white cardboard boxes out of the bag and then slipped a set of chopsticks out of their red paper sleeve.

"Hello, there, young man," Ames said.

Chase looked over and then quickly looked away. "Hello, Mrs. Finley. I didn't know you were here."

"I'm here," she said, smiling, "*and* I brought your favorite treat."

Chase looked up again. "Chocolate cupcakes?" he asked hopefully.

"Lemon poppyseed."

"Those are my *second* favorite." He turned back to his supper and Ames turned to Payton and shrugged. Payton just rolled her eyes, but then she took the plate and set it next to the wineglasses.

"I also brought *your* favorite," she said, producing a bottle of chardonnay. "It was so nice out today, I decided it was time to switch back to white."

Payton smiled. "It *is* time to switch—I've had enough of winter *and* cabernet."

"You don't have to have any, though, if you don't feel like it."

"Oh, I feel like it!" Payton said, shaking her head and reaching for the corkscrew.

Ames nodded and squeezed her hand. "I'm sure everything will be okay."

Payton searched her friend's eyes. "Thank you. We'll get through it, won't we?"

"We will, together," Ames assured her, holding out two wine-glasses. "We always do."

Payton filled the glasses and put the bottle on the table. "To dear old friends," she said quietly.

"Absolutely!" Ames replied, clinking her glass, and as she leaned forward and softly kissed her friend's ruddy cheek, the front door opened, jingling the chime as a parade of ladies came in, chatting and carrying plates of food and bottles of wine.

"We're here!" they called, laughing.

"GRAN, COME QUICK!" ELLIE CALLED, PEERING AROUND THE MUDROOM DOOR.

"What is it?" Libby asked, hurrying in from the next room. "Is everything okay?"

"Everything's fine. You have to come listen," Ellie said, pulling her out into the yard.

They stood in the dusky light, and the sound of peepers filled the air. "I love peepers," Libby said softly. "It's like a spring symphony."

"Not the peepers, Gran," Ellie whispered urgently. "Listen!"

They stood still, but the only other sound Libby could hear was the rhythmic clank and whoosh of the milking machines as Matt and Gage ushered their plodding bovines into their stanchions and filled their troughs with hay. "I don't hear anything," she whispered.

"Shhh," Ellie said, squeezing her hand, and Libby nodded, straining to listen. And then an odd sound—a short buzzy *meeeep*—filled the evening air. A moment later, they heard a second *meeeep* from another part of the field, and Ellie grinned. "Hear them? It's the woodcocks!" Her voice filled with awe. "They came back."

Libby smiled and they stood listening . . . until Gus bounded out of the barn and the whistle of wings signaled that the funny little birds were flying away. "Oh, Gus!" Ellie cried in dismay. "You scared them."

"They'll be back," Libby said, putting her arm around her granddaughter, "but thank you for telling me. I love that sound."

"Me, too," Ellie agreed.

"Are you coming in for a cup of tea tonight or are you still helping in the barn?"

"I'm coming in," the little girl said, walking with her grandmother.

"What kind of tea shall we have?"

"I don't know," Ellie mused thoughtfully. "What do you feel like?"

"How about lemon-ginger?"

"With honey?"

"Is there any other way?"

Ellie held the door open. "Did you know *woodcock* means little chicken of the woods?"

"I did not, but it makes sense."

"They have other funny names, too, like timberdoodle, bogsucker, Labrador twister, and mudsnipe."

"Ha!"

"Have you ever seen their mating dance?"

"I haven't," Libby said, filling the kettle with fresh water.

"Oh, you have to see it—it's so funny!" Ellie said, slipping her phone from her pocket to find the video she'd seen of a woodcock and its babies bobbing back and forth, and up and down in a dance that was reminiscent of Michael Jackson.

Libby held the phone and laughed. "My goodness! Even the chicks know how to do it."

"Yeah," Ellie agreed. "They come out of their shells knowing how!" She reached for the box of tea and dropped a single bag into the teapot. "Also, their ears are between their eyes and at the base of their bill. They evolved in such a way that their brains are actually upside down!"

"How odd."

"Mm-hmm. And you know how most birds mate for life and both help with parenting? Well, that's definitely not the case with timberdoodles. The male gets as many females prego as he wants and he doesn't lift a feather to help raise the babies."

"Prego?" Libby asked, raising her eyebrows.

"*You* know, Gran," Ellie said, sounding exasperated because she had to explain. She opened the cabinet and reached for the honey. "*Pregnant*," she said, "but actually, in the case of birds, he doesn't get her pregnant the same way as with mammals. With birds, males fertilize the eggs—which I *know* happens in mammals, but with birds the baby doesn't grow inside the female. It grows inside the egg, outside the female . . . in the nest . . . under the mom . . . because the dad doesn't help one bit."

"Got it," Libby said, turning off the burner and pouring the hot water into the teapot. "He doesn't set a very good example."

"No, he doesn't, but there are humans that don't set good examples, either. Anyway, the mom makes her nest in a little hollow in the ground with some leaves and then she lays one egg a day, until she has exactly four. After the fourth egg—and not before, because she wants them all to hatch at the same time, she sits on the nest for nineteen to twenty-two days. When the babies hatch, they're able to leave the nest in a few hours, and if they're in any danger . . . or if their mom sounds the alarm, they instinctively know to freeze. By four weeks, they're already almost full-grown!"

"Wow! That *is* quick!"

"Yes," Ellie said, nodding, "but sadly, in the wild, their life span is less than two years—one point eight to be exact. However, if they don't die, they can live to be as old as seven."

"My goodness! That's a long time."

Ellie stirred in her honey. "But the *worst* parents are the brown-headed cowbirds. They don't even build nests. They just lay eggs in other birds' nests and leave them there. They never do a thing—they don't even hang around to see them hatch, and then the other birds end up taking care of them. I've read that, back in the day, cowbirds used to migrate with herds of cows—that's how they got their name—and that's why they didn't hang around to raise their young. They were always on the move."

"Well, that would explain such irresponsible behavior," Libby said, taking a sip of her tea.

"Mm-hmm," Ellie agreed. "The oldest cowbird lived to be almost seventeen years old!"

"My goodness! That's a very old bird!"

Ellie nodded. "One time, I saw a picture of a cardinal that was half male and half female—it was half red and half tan." She pulled out her phone. "I'll show you a picture."

Libby frowned. "That sounds like a chicken we once had. Chase named her . . . *or him* . . . Scramble. Grandpa thought its egg must've been double-fertilized, and wanted to get rid of it, but Uncle Chase rescued her and she—*or he*—followed him everywhere."

Ellie nodded as she continued to search for a picture of the rare cardinal. "Uncle Chase is so cool."

"He is," Libby agreed. "One of a kind, and animals know it—they just love him. They know a sweet understanding soul when they find one. Your dad called him an animal whisperer."

"I hope to be a bird whisperer someday," Ellie said, still searching her phone. "Here it is," she announced, holding her phone for Libby to see.

Libby studied the picture. "The Lord works in mysterious ways, doesn't he?"

Ellie nodded. "He does. Mom says he likes to stretch our minds . . . *and* she says he has a sense of humor—that's why he gave us little Jack, who climbs on everything and just about gives her a heart attack!"

"He's at that age."

They sat quietly, each lost in their own thoughts, and then there was a sudden loud commotion on the porch. "Sounds like Gus has the zoomies!" Ellie said, getting up quickly. She peered out the screen door into the misty evening air and saw Gus racing up and down the porch, and then she saw the reason why. "Uncle Chase is here!"

She pushed open the door and Chase and Liam came into the kitchen, laughing with Gus still wiggling around their legs, tail wagging.

"Hi, Uncle Chase," she cried, jumping into his arms.

"Hey, kiddo," he said, giving her a big hug. "How are you?"

"I'm fine! Gran and I were just talking about you."

"You were?!" he said, looking over her shoulder at his mom.

"Yep," Ellie confirmed, and then she slipped from his arms and hugged Liam, too. "Hi, Uncle Liam!"

Liam knelt down to hug her, and Chase laughed and eyed Liam. "*Uncle* Liam?"

"Well, he is, isn't he?" Ellie said, grinning.

Chase looked at his mom and smiled. "Well, maybe," he said, and then he pulled her into a hug. "Hi, Ma," he said softly.

"Hi, Chase," she said, holding him before letting go to hug Liam, too. "What a nice surprise! We haven't seen you two kids since Christmas!"

"I know! That's why we're here."

14

"DID YOU SEE THE PHOTO QUINN POSTED THIS MORNING?" AMES ASKED, PULL-ing her phone out of her pocket. "Her little Clementine must have the sweetest personality!"

"That reminds me," Payton began.

"*What* reminds you?" Ames asked, looking up from her phone.

They'd picked up a pizza after their softball game, and instead of eating in as they usually did, they'd brought it home and they were now sitting on Payton's front porch, watching the sun set. Payton took a sip of the "roadie" she'd grabbed from the team's cooler and scratched Ned's ears. "I saw a picture on Quinn's page the other day of a pelican and . . ."

"Oh! I saw that, too," Ames said. "Wasn't it gorgeous?"

"It was . . . *and* it reminded me that *you* are supposed to visit Quinn."

"Oh, that. I don't know if I'm going to. I think I'm gonna have to wait till after Ned is gone."

"After Ned is *gone*?! He's only six years old and he will probably live to be at least twelve, maybe older! You're going to wait six more years to visit your daughter?! You can't do that. Life is too short, and by then, you'll tell me—if I'm still alive—that you're too old!"

"Well, she could come visit me, too, you know—she hasn't

been here since Frank's funeral . . . and I'm sure you will still be alive. You're too stubborn to leave this earth."

Payton chuckled, knowing she was right—she could be stubborn when she had to be, but maybe that was a good thing because the ultrasound she'd had that morning—thanks to a last-minute cancellation when she'd called to make the appointment, had resulted in the worrisome news that she'd have to go back for a biopsy, and she was suddenly—and stubbornly—resolved to face whatever was happening inside her body head-on.

"Quinn's busy running a restaurant. Trust me, that's a tough business to leave unattended, and besides, you're retired, and I'm sure she wants to show you around—where she lives and her restaurant. You've never even seen an ocean. In fact, I don't think you've ever been out of Tennessee!"

"That's not true," Ames countered. "I've been to Kentucky *and* North Carolina."

"Oh, boy!" Payton teased, rolling her eyes.

"You haven't seen an ocean, either."

"I have—I went to Myrtle Beach when I was little."

"Oh, boy!" Ames replied. "That was so long ago it barely qualifies."

"It qualifies!"

Ames took a sip of beer and licked her lips. They normally drank wine on Friday nights, but the weather was so nice—such a change from the week before—that cold beer tasted good. "Anyway, I just don't know what I'd do with Ned . . . or who would bring in my mail and water my plants."

"Ned can stay here, and Cash and I can look after the house."

Ames shook her head. "I appreciate the offer, but I don't think so. Ned and I have our routine, and he's so used to it—we get up, he goes out and has breakfast, I make coffee. We sit together while I do my morning reading, and then we go for a walk. Every day is the same and animals like routines. If I left him, he'd be lost, and I'd be worried about him."

Payton rolled her eyes. "*You* like your routine. *You* are the home-body. I'm sure Ned would be fine with a little excitement in his life, wouldn't you, pal?" she murmured, rubbing her socks into his fur. Ned thumped his tail lazily.

"I'll take care of Ned, Mrs. Finley," Cash interrupted, peering through the screen door. He came out and sat on the porch next to the big black Lab and Ned laid his head on Cash's lap.

Payton smiled. "See? He'd be fine."

Cash nodded. "Ned loves me. I'll even stay at your house."

Payton—who was about to take a sip of her beer—stopped, her smile fading. "You can take care of him here, Cash. This is practically his second home."

"He might like it better at his house, Ma."

Ames looked over at Payton with raised eyebrows. "Hmmm. *I'm* supposed to get over *my* worries and let go, but someone else we know isn't ready to do the same."

"There's a big difference between leaving a dog in the care of a friend and letting a young person—who doesn't always demonstrate that he's responsible—live on his own."

"Is there?" Ames teased.

"I'm responsible," Cash countered. "I'm twenty-eight, Mom, and I take perfectly good care of the shop when you're not there. I count the register every night and I set it up in the morning. I make coffee, wait on customers. I'm sure I can feed and walk Ned, and I can bring in the mail and water the plants, too. *You* never let me try, Mom—that's why you don't think I'm responsible. Besides, if you'd let me get a dog, you'd see that I know how to take care of one."

Payton swallowed. Everything he said was true, but at the same time, she still wasn't ready to let go. "You do plenty of things that *aren't* responsible, Cash . . . the worst of which is playing video games nonstop. Just last night, when you were supposed to be picking up Chinese food, you just sat there and lost track of time, and then you forgot the money and slammed the door—how is that responsible?"

Cash gently lifted Ned's head off his lap and stood up. "You need to give me a chance," he said, sounding frustrated, and then he went inside.

Ames cleared her throat. "He's right, you know. Besides, my house is just a little two-bedroom ranch—how much trouble can he get into?"

Payton clenched her jaw. "I have a lot going on at the moment," she whispered. "I don't need anything else to worry about."

"I know you do," Ames replied quietly, "and I don't mean to upset you. When do you have to go back?"

"Thursday."

"They couldn't get you in sooner?"

"They said I was lucky to get in then—they had a cancellation."

"Are you okay?" Ames asked gently.

"I'm fine. I just want to know what's going on. Not knowing is worse."

Ames nodded. "Callie Jasmine had thyroid cancer. She said they told her if you're gonna get cancer, thyroid is the one to get."

"You told her?!" Payton asked.

Ames looked up, surprised by the tone of her friend's voice. "No, no, of course not," she sputtered, making a mental note to call Callie as soon as she got home. "She was talking about it a while back, and she said she had her thyroid removed and it was no big deal. She actually said it's pretty common."

Payton took a sip of her beer and seemed to relax. "It's still scary to have the word *cancer* used when it concerns your own health." She looked over. "It gives you pause, you know? It makes you think about what's really important."

Ames nodded and reached over to squeeze her hand. "Well, you are very important to me, my dear, and I'll be praying it turns out to be nothing, but if it turns out to be *something*, I'll pray even harder for a positive outcome . . . because I don't know what I'd do without you."

Payton searched her friend's face. "I feel the same way about you, my dear, and I also feel that life is too short, and that's why you should visit Quinn."

Ames shook her head and smiled. "I'll tell you what . . . if you let Cash take care of Ned at my house, I'll visit Quinn."

Payton rolled her eyes. "Ha! You got me."

"I do," Ames replied, chuckling.

"Well, all I can say right now is I'll think about it."

"Okay, well, Ned and I are heading home. Let's go, ole pal." She nudged him with her foot and the big Lab pulled himself up, wagging his tail. He gave Payton a kiss, and then he lumbered down the steps.

"Good night, my dear," Ames said, standing.

Payton stood up, too, and gave her friend a hug and a kiss on the cheek. "Make sure you call Callie and tell her not to say anything," she teased.

"I did *not* tell Callie," Ames said as she walked toward her car.

"Mm-hmm," Payton answered, sounding skeptical.

15

"So?" Chase asked, watching Liam's face. "What do you think?"

Liam licked the ice cream in his chocolate-dipped waffle cone. "Pretty good."

"Pretty good?!"

"Just kidding," he said, laughing as he tried to free a chunk of chocolate brownie with his tongue. "It's *amazing.*"

"Right?! I told you . . ."

"You *did* tell me," Liam confirmed. "I was a fool to doubt you."

"You were," Chase agreed, licking his own ice cream and sitting on the porch steps next to him. "We make the cones at the shop, too. Did you watch when we were there?"

"I did," Liam confirmed. "It's cool how they use an actual waffle maker and then wrap them around a mold."

"Yep, it doesn't get any fresher."

"How long has your family had the shop?"

"A couple of years," Chase replied, trying to remember. "It opened a little over a year before my dad died, because it was early summer and he died the following August. It was always a dream of his and I'm glad he was able to see it happen. For as long as I can remember, my mom made ice cream for family picnics and they always talked about having a little stand at the farm, but then they decided it was too far off the beaten path and there would be too much traffic on the road, so they bought a lot in town. Instantly, Tennessee Tennyson's Dairy Bar became legendary. My sisters-in-law run it. We also employ a bunch of kids, some special needs kids, too."

"Is it open year-round?"

"It is. It's not as busy in the winter, but we still sell cheese, yogurt, milk, and eggnog."

"Mmm. I love the eggnog."

"Everyone does. We can hardly keep it in stock at Christmas-time." He looked up and saw Gage coming across the driveway with Gus trotting beside him.

"You gonna teach Liam how to milk a cow?" Gage asked, shaking out the paintbrush he'd just cleaned.

"That's a good idea!" Chase replied. "Right after we finish these." He held his cone away from Gus's eager nose . . . and tongue, but when the big dog licked the air hopefully, he laughed. "I don't think you should have brownies, mister. Your dad's gonna have to make a Plain Ole Vanilla pup cup for you."

"He's already had at least ten pup cups since we got here."

"I'll save you the bottom of my cone," Chase promised, "even though it's the best part." And Gus, as if he understood, sat down right in front of him to wait.

"Are the cows headed in?" Chase asked.

"Like clockwork," Gage said, gesturing over his shoulder.

Chase looked past him, saw a long line of cows plodding toward the barn, and smiled wistfully—he loved being home. There was something so safe and comforting about life on the farm, and no matter where he was in the world, he could look at his watch and know exactly which chores were underway. If it was four A.M., the lights were on inside the barn and the steam was rolling off the round bellies of the hungry bovines as they ate breakfast and were relieved of their milk; in the evening, it happened all over again; and, in between, there were plenty of other chores being tended to—from mucking stalls to stacking hay. The cows counted on and loved their routine.

Chase licked his ice cream one last time and then, as promised, held the last bite—which still had a puddle of melted ice cream in it—out for Gus, who gobbled it down with the same enthusiasm as Cooper—the internet sensation who devoured an entire cone at the drive-through in one uncivilized gulp. "Hey, leave my fingers!" Chase said, laughing. "Hasn't your dad taught you any manners?" he asked, scratching the dog's noble nose.

"I've tried," Gage said apologetically, "but he forgets."

Chase looked over at Liam. "So, you ready to milk some cows?"

"Sure," Liam replied, petting Gus's big head and giving the last of his cone, too, but when he wiped his hands on his napkin, he suddenly started to sneeze, and then his eyes instantly began to water.

Chase watched him curiously. "Are you allergic to dogs?"

Liam wiped his eyes with his thumbs and shook his head, but then he started to sneeze again. "Geez. I don't know," he said. "I've never reacted like this before."

"Maybe it's all the hay," Gage suggested.

"Maybe," Liam said. "I'll just wash my hands and face and see if it helps."

"Okay," Chase said, and then he eyed Liam's clothes—jeans, a button-down oxford shirt, and new buck shoes. "It might be a good idea to change. Do you have other shoes with you?" he asked. "If not, I'm sure we can find some boots that'll fit . . . and I probably have a T-shirt you can wear."

Liam stood up and nodded, still wiping his eyes.

Chase shook his head and turned to his brother. "We'll be right out."

Ten minutes later, Liam—wearing a faded Tennessee State Fair T-shirt and an old pair of Muck boots—followed Chase over to the barn, but as they crossed the driveway, they heard a cacophony of mooing and shouting. "Uh-oh!" Chase said, raising his eyebrows. "Sounds like the ladies are upset."

A moment later, they saw Gage and Matt trying to usher the entire herd outside, and when Gage saw them through the doorway, he called, "Lily ended up in Josie's stall, so we hafta try again."

Chase nodded and hurried into the fray, but Liam stepped back to stay out of the way. He leaned against the wall and watched Chase fall easily into the job of smacking the rumps of the cows to get them moving. "Let's go, ladies," he prodded. "Don't worry, you're still gonna get supper and your tanks will be emptied. I know it's Lily's fault, but you'll hafta talk to her about it later."

The cows mooed loudly, complaining and resisting and still determinedly trying to get to their designated stanchions, but finally they all plodded outside again, and when they were allowed to turn around, they managed to lumber in the correct order, and the previous chaos dissipated into happy contentment as they munched their suppers and felt teat cups suctioning to their swollen udders.

Chase motioned to Liam to follow him to the last stall, but instead of attaching a milking machine, he set a low wooden stool next to the cow and put a bucket under her. "Give it a go," he said, grinning, and Liam rolled his eyes, sat down, and began tugging, but he had little success. Finally, laughing, Chase knelt beside him, leaned his forehead on the warm belly of the cow. "Like this," he said, expertly massaging and pulling down on the teats, and releasing forceful squirts of milk into the pail.

Liam put his hands on the teats and tried to mimic the movement Chase had just used, but he couldn't seem to master it until Chase closed his hands around his and moved them up and down. A moment later, a small gray barn cat appeared, and Chase aimed the teat in her direction and gently squirted the creamy milk into her mouth.

Finally, Chase hooked the teat cup to the cow instead and they stood up and watched the cat clean up all the milk that had spilled. "Not bad for a beginner," Chase teased.

"I'm only a beginner when it comes to milking cows," Liam said, grinning, and then he looked around to see where Matt and Gage were before he pulled Chase into a corner and softly kissed him. "Somethin' about the way you milk a cow turns me on," he whispered.

Chase grinned, his blue eyes sparkling with mischief, but when he saw Gage walking toward the door, he quickly pulled away, and innocently scratched the ears of the cow they'd been milking. He cleared his throat, and over the clanking of the milking machine, began to explain the social hierarchy in a herd of cows. "Some are bossy, and some are calm, and some are timid, but they all know their place, and it was just displayed by their reluctance to cooperate."

Liam smiled. "So, they're like a bunch of old ladies."

"Exactly," Chase said, laughing.

They watched Gage walk out of the barn, and Chase started to pull Liam back into the corner, but then Ellie appeared with Gus at her heels.

"Everyone's here," she announced, "and supper's ready."

"Hello to you, too," Chase teased.

"Sorry," she said. "Hello!"

"We'll be right there."

"Okay." Ellie eyed them and then spied the milk pail. "Did you show Uncle Liam how to milk?"

"I tried to," Chase said, grinning, "but he's a slow learner."

Ellie laughed. "Well, he'll get it . . . *if* he stays long enough." She reached for Liam's hand and pulled him toward the door. "You don't have to help—you're the guest."

"Guest? I thought I was family," Liam joked, allowing himself to be pulled toward the house.

"You're gonna be family . . . when you marry Uncle Chase," she said matter-of-factly, and Liam eyed Chase with raised eyebrows.

The sky was on fire when Matt closed the barn doors and caught up to Gage and Chase, who were already walking toward the house. "So, when are you gonna tell Mom?"

"Tell her what?"

"You know what."

Chase frowned. "Not sure what you mean."

"I have a very perceptive ten-year-old, you know—she sees all and knows all."

"Ha!" Chase said. "Well, I don't know what she *thinks* she sees . . . *or* knows . . ."

Matt put his arm around his little brother's shoulder. "She says you and Liam are getting married."

Chase laughed. "I don't know where she got that idea."

"Are you?!" Gage asked. "Because that would be awesome! We love Liam."

"Yeah?" Chase asked, laughing.

"Absolutely! He fits right in with the fam."

Matt nodded. "Ellie loves him . . . and she's a pretty good judge of character."

"Well, thanks," Chase said with a smile. "We've been talking about it. We want to start a family, but I wasn't sure how Mom would take it . . . and Liam is worried about his parents."

"How come?" Gage asked. "They're not on board? I thought they lived in California."

They stopped walking before climbing the porch steps and Chase looked over his brothers' shoulders at the apricot sky. "Living in California doesn't automatically make you open-minded and accepting."

"I know," Gage said. "I was teasing." He smiled at him. "You should tell Mom. She'll be fine . . . especially if you tell her while we're all here."

"You think? Because Liam and I were just gonna tell her by ourselves tomorrow before we head back."

Gage looked at Matt. "What do you think?"

Matt shrugged. "I think it's up to Chase and Liam." And then he eyed his youngest brother. "I hope you know how happy we are for you, brutha. Congrats, man!" he said, shaking his hand and pulling him into a hug.

"Yeah, congrats!" Gage said. "I can't wait to tell Maeve. She will be thrilled. In fact"—he clapped Chase's shoulder—"we should have a double wedding."

"Ha!" Chase said, remembering how much his father had initially struggled with the news that his youngest son was gay. "Dad would roll over in his grave if we got married in his barn."

"No, he wouldn't—you're his son and he loved you with all his heart."

"Thanks," Chase said, his eyes glistening. "You have no idea how much that means to me. How much it means to both of us. I'll talk to Liam about it."

"Good!" Gage said, smiling. "Now, let's go eat—I'm starving!"

16

LIBBY SWITCHED OFF HER BEDSIDE LAMP AND SANK INTO JACK'S PILLOW. FOR ALL forty-three years of their marriage, she'd slept on the left side of the bed and he'd slept on the right, but the first night after he died, she'd slipped into the curve of the mattress where his body had been, hugged his pillow, and wept. The sheets hadn't smelled of death and darkness and sorrow. They'd been fragrant with the gentle honey soap with which she'd washed him, and they'd smelled of the boy with whom she'd fallen in love—a mixture of musk, sweet hay, and sunshine.

The next morning, however, her daughter-in-law, Jodi—who'd come over to help—had stripped the sheets before Libby could stop her, and it had broken her heart all over again. In hindsight, it had been just as well because she might never have washed those sheets again! Now, though, when she washed them, she always put a drop of Jack's favorite aftershave on the corner of his pillowcase. For as long as she could remember—from the time he was seventeen, driving her home past the haunted house on Witness Road to all the roast beef dinners at the firehouse and Bean Hole bean suppers they'd attended at the church as a family—Jack had worn the same aftershave, and the scent made her feel as if he was by her side.

After that, Libby had never gone back to her side of the bed. Instead, she slept on his side, gazing at the stars through his window and breathing in the lovely scent of his pillowcase. Tonight, she lay still, listening to Gage wash up, and Chase and Liam talking. Finally, the house grew quiet. She waited expectantly for Chase to break the silence with his usual tribute to the old TV show *The Waltons*, and a moment later, it came: "Night, Gage. Night, Liam. Night, Mama!" She heard Liam chuckle as he replied in kind, and then she answered, too. Finally, it was Gage's turn: "Night, Liam. Night, Mama. Night, John-boy!" he called back.

Chase laughed, and Libby smiled. *It's so nice to have my boys home, sleeping in their old rooms.* Even though Ellie slept over every Saturday, there was something comforting about the boys being home. She treasured hearing their voices, the sound bringing back a rush of memories of the bustling life they'd once shared. The chaos of weekday mornings—all hands on deck to help with chores before wolfing down breakfast, grabbing lunch bags, and racing for the bus; or on Sundays, utter chaos ensuing as she ironed shirts and pressed slacks of all lengths, getting everyone dressed in their Sunday best, tying ties, locating bibles, and making sure everyone had something in their offering envelope. Those were the days of family picnics, watching NASCAR races on TV, or sitting in the cool shade outside, and later on, after everyone was tucked in, leaning against Jack's soft shirt while they sat on the porch and he recited the only poem he knew—"The Village Blacksmith."

She looked out the window at the stars and felt a tear trickle down her cheek and plop onto the pillow. "Oh, Jack," she whispered, "I miss you so much," and then she began to murmur the last three stanzas of the famous Wadsworth poem, amazed at how tragically prophetic it was . . . except it was *she*, and not the mighty blacksmith, who'd been left to toil through her days . . .

> . . . *He needs must think of her once more,*
> *How in the grave she lies;*

And with his hard, rough hand he wipes
A tear out of his eyes.

Toiling,—rejoicing,—sorrowing,
Onward through life he goes;
Each morning sees some task begin,
Each evening sees it close;
Something attempted, something done,
Has earned a night's repose.

Thanks, thanks to thee, my worthy friend,
For the lesson thou hast taught!
Thus at the flaming forge of life
Our fortunes must be wrought;
Thus on its sounding anvil shaped
Each burning deed and thought.

If she could only have one of those lovely days back . . . if only she'd known, at the time, how precious their life was!

Weary as Libby was—she'd definitely *earned a night's repose*—the relief of sleep still eluded her, and her mind drifted to her childhood friends, Payton and Ames. Through all their lives, they'd been there for one another—from their school days to their wedding days, and from their child-rearing years to the loss of their parents—and in her case, her oldest son. But through it all, they'd stood resolutely by one another's sides. Payton was right—she did need to get out of "this big old house full of memories"—it would be good for her! Payton and Ames had both lost their husbands so they knew how hard it was, as did all the women who gathered at the Coffee Bean on Thursday nights. Somehow, they'd all persevered and learned to smile again—a feat that often felt impossible to Libby. She even wondered, sometimes, if she would ever feel true joy again.

She gazed into the darkness, remembering how Payton had

draped her arm around Ames's shoulder at Frank's funeral and pulled her close. She knew her two oldest friends had always been each other's best friend—they'd played on the same basketball and softball teams, and they'd shared what seemed to be an almost impenetrable bond, but they'd also always made sure to include her—Friday night movies, Saturday night sleepovers, or just meeting for milkshakes and cheeseburgers—she was one of them! It wasn't until Payton and Ames had switched from drinking milkshakes to drinking beer and wine that they'd begun to drift apart . . . and then, after she'd started dating Jack, the separation grew wider, but now, here they were, nearly fifty years later, all widows, and their friendship seemed to be coming full circle. How crazy this journey called life—with all its twists and turns—was! Libby rolled to her side and pulled Jack's pillowcase close and breathed in the lovely scent that still made her heart pound. "I'll go to the coffee shop, Jack," she whispered. "I know you'd want me to . . ."

17

PAYTON WRAPPED HER HANDS AROUND HER COFFEE MUG, PULLED A BLANKET over her shoulders, and sank into the Adirondack chair on her back porch to watch the sunrise. She treasured the peacefulness of Sunday mornings. When she'd first opened the Coffee Bean, they'd been open seven days a week, but her earnestness had lasted six months. She—and Cash—both needed a day off, and they'd picked Sunday. Cash called it *Lazyday*.

"Even God took Sunday off after creating the world," she had told Ames, "and the Bible says *we* are supposed to take it off too."

"You don't need to convince *me*. I'm all for you taking a day off—you deserve it."

"It's a rule people don't honor anymore."

"Chick-fil-A is closed on Sundays," Ames reminded her.

"That's the only place. I remember when we were little, nothing was open, except church. Every store in town was closed. If you were out of something, you were out of luck. People should go back to that—it would be good for their health . . . *and* their sanity! They'd spend more time with their families, more time doing relaxing things like fishing, reading books, and daydreaming. More time watching the clouds drift by. We need more cloud watching and less go-go-go!"

"Those were simpler times," Ames agreed.

Payton took a sip of her coffee now. "They were simpler times," she whispered, "and I wish we *could* go back to them." As she said this, a pair of female cardinals landed on the top of a nearby bush. Payton didn't stir, and held her breath as she watched them—they were so close, and then one began flying to the feeder and bringing seeds back to the other. The display of affection happened repeatedly, and she wondered if the cardinal that stayed on the bush was a baby . . . or maybe it was an older adult. *God certainly works in mysterious ways*, she thought, smiling.

Suddenly, the cardinals flew off and Payton's thoughts drifted to Ames and the offer—or rather the *challenge*—she'd made a couple of days earlier: *If you let Cash take care of Ned, I will visit Quinn.* She sipped her coffee. She really wanted Ames to visit Quinn, but she really *didn't* want Cash to stay alone at Ames's house. What if he left the oven on? Or the water running? Fire and flood were both real possibilities, and he was such a sound sleeper, she was sure he wouldn't wake up. In fact, she'd probably have to stay with him . . . which she would happily do, but then they'd have to leave early to open the shop and Ned wouldn't get his walk, and they couldn't leave him alone all day. She'd have to go back to let him out and make time for a walk, be there to feed him, and she had enough on her mind without having to worry about her friend's dog. At the same time, she still wanted Ames to visit Quinn, dang it! So maybe she should just close the shop for a week, but she was sure Ames would find out and be mad—madder than a hornet whose nest was disturbed. She chuckled at the thought. Silver-haired, kind-faced, mild-mannered Ames definitely had a temper when someone tried to pull the wool over her eyes.

Payton took another sip of her coffee as the debate continued in her head. Of course, Ames *did* live just up the road, and if Cash *did* have a problem, she could be there in a heartbeat. In his defense, he did take good care of the shop when she wasn't there, counting the drawer and waiting on customers—he could be re-

sponsible when he had to be. Besides, maybe taking care of Ned—
having to walk him, play with him, *and* pick up after him—would
cool his desire to have a dog, and that would be a huge positive because she was tired of hearing about it!

Suddenly, feeling nauseated, Payton pushed off the blanket—
she'd come to recognize the queasy sensation to be a signal that
her core body temperature was about to rise like a thermometer
with a match under it, and sure enough, a moment later, she was
perspiring. She sighed—*when will these damn hot flashes end?* She
closed her eyes and waited, thankful for the cool morning breeze,
and then reached up and touched her neck, hoping the tiny lump
had miraculously disappeared, but it was still there and her heart
sank, a renewed wave of worry washing over her. Jack had died
just six months after being diagnosed. Were her days numbered,
too? And what *would* happen to Cash? She could hear Dr. Hamlin's
words echoing in her head: *I know it's not easy, Payton, but it would
be good for him to become more independent. Maybe even get a place
of his own. If he was given the chance, he might surprise you. Besides,
you—and I—aren't going to be around forever. . . .*

Feeling chilled again, she pulled the blanket up, leaned back,
and was surprised when a Carolina wren landed on the railing. It
seemed unaware of her presence and promptly started singing its
heart out, welcoming the new day. In spite of herself, she smiled,
the unabashed cheerfulness of the little bird lifting her spirits,
but a moment later, footfalls inside the house made the little bird
fly away, and with it, her brief respite from gloom.

"Mornin'," Cash said, peering through the screen door.

"Mornin'," she replied.

"Can I make pancakes?"

Payton bit her lip to keep from groaning, the image of a messy
kitchen filling her mind. "Why don't you just have cereal, Cash?
There's a new box of Lucky Charms in the pantry."

"Because I woke up feeling like pancakes."

Payton shook her head—she just wanted to sit on the porch, enjoy her coffee, and not have to clean up a messy kitchen.

"You don't have to help. I can do it myself," he said, as if reading her mind.

"Go ahead," she relented, knowing that once her son had an idea in his head, there was no changing it.

She heard him shuffle across the linoleum and, determined not to let him upset her peace, took another sip of her coffee, but as she listened to cabinets and drawers opening, mixing bowls clinking, the griddle clicking on the hot stovetop—she began to feel guilty. She loved her son dearly, so why was she so impatient with him? Why did she always feel annoyed by him? And why was she always so quick to find fault? He was just trying to live his life the best he could and make his way in the world, and his success was constantly being hampered by a grouchy old woman who wouldn't let him do anything. Who wouldn't even let him try! What was wrong with her? How had they gotten to this point? After twenty-eight years of prodding and expecting him to rise to her expectations, but acting as if she was disappointed—for no real reason . . . except that she was weary . . . *and* resentful of what sometimes felt like a lifetime sentence of caring for him.

When they'd worked on refurbishing the shop together, they'd had so much fun—it had been *their* project and even though it had initially been her dream, he'd made it his, too. They'd worked side by side, planning, talking, and busting their butts until they were exhausted; and then eating takeout food together and laughing! Now, she wished, with all her heart, they could go back to that sweet time of enjoying each other's company, instead of always being crabby. She closed her eyes—she was tired of even thinking about it, and she just started to doze off when his voice broke the silence. "Pancakes are ready!"

"That was quick," she murmured. She pulled herself up, folded the blanket, picked up her coffee mug, and opened the door, fully expecting to find the kitchen looking like an F4 tornado had blown through, but instead, it was spotless. The dishes he'd used, except for the bowl of batter, were washed and in the dish drainer, the counters sparkled, and the table was set with placemats, napkins, silverware, glasses of orange juice, butter, maple syrup, and a small centerpiece made up of pansies.

"Happy Mother's Day!" he said with his sweet shy smile.

"Oh, my goodness! I forgot it was Mother's Day!" she said, shaking her head and giving him a hug. "Thank you, hon."

"You're welcome," Cash pulled away to flip three golden blueberry pancakes from the hot griddle, and then artistically framed them with two links of sausage. "Here you go," he said, setting the plate on her placemat.

"Where are yours?" she asked, as she refilled her coffee mug.

"Right here," he said, spooning more batter onto the griddle.

"Do you want one of these?" she asked.

"Nope, you go ahead. Mine will be ready in a minute."

"Should I wait?" she asked.

"Nope. Eat 'em while they're hot."

She sat down, buttered and drizzled syrup over her pancakes, and took a bite. "Mmm," she said. "These are *ah-may-zing*, and what a nice presentation, too!"

"I learned from the best," he said, grinning and sitting across from her. "Oh!" he said, standing back up so abruptly he almost knocked over his chair. He hurried over to the sink, reached behind the flour and sugar canisters, and came back with a white envelope.

"Is this an original *Cashmark*?" she asked, smiling and using the name he wrote on the back of the cards he'd been drawing for her since he was little.

"It is," he confirmed, grinning.

She slipped the homemade card from the envelope and studied it. It was a drawing of a coffee mug with the words: BEST MOM

IN THE WORLD on it. She pressed her lips together, opened it, and through the blur of tears, read the words he'd carefully printed:

> *Thank you for all you do for me and for loving me no matter what! I LOVE YOU!*
> *Love, Your Son, Cashen*

"Oh, Cash," she said, looking up, her eyes glistening.

He furrowed his brow. "You're not supposed to cry, Mom," and because her tears worried him, he gestured to her plate. "You should eat. They're gonna get cold."

She nodded, wiped her eyes, set the card in front of her, took another bite, and tried to keep from crying, but when he looked up, he noticed a tear trickling down her cheek. "What's the matter, Mom?" he asked. "Why are you crying?"

"I'm just happy, Cash," she lied, her heart aching with the very real possibility that he would be on his own sooner than she ever expected. "I'm happy to have such a good son, and I'm crying because I love you, and you make me very proud."

Cash beamed. "You make *me* very proud, too, Mom."

She searched his boyish bespeckled face. "Thank you, Cash. That means more than you know."

18

⚮

"Happy Mother's Day!" Chase said, kissing Libby's cheek and holding out the bouquet of wildflowers he'd picked after helping his brothers with chores.

She looked up from the scrambled eggs she was stirring in her old cast iron pan. "Thank you, hon," she said. "These are beautiful!" She put down her fork and reached into the cabinet for a vase. "Are your brothers coming in? Because these eggs are almost ready."

"Yep, they said they'd be right in." He poured a mug of coffee and opened a different cabinet in search of some aspirin.

"Do you have a headache?" she asked, frowning.

"I do," he said, chuckling. "My own fault," he added, recalling the liter-size bottle of Jack Daniels he and Liam and his brothers had passed around the bonfire the night before.

"How late were you up?" Libby asked, shifting her attention to the bacon.

"*Too* late," he replied, swallowing some Tylenol with his coffee. He looked over at the sputtering pan. "Why don't you let me do that?" he said. "You shouldn't be making breakfast. We should be cooking for you."

Libby laughed. "It's okay," she said, but she relinquished her fork. "Do you want an apron?"

"Do I want an apron?" he teased, rolling his eyes. "What do you think?"

"Well, I know how particular you are about your clothes."

"I'm wearing jeans and a T-shirt, Mom."

Libby eyed her handsome son, put her hand on his tan cheek, and gazed into his summer-sky-blue eyes. "I'm so glad you and Liam came for a visit. It was such a nice Mother's Day surprise."

"You're welcome," he said, reaching up to place his hand on hers. "I wish I could take credit for knowing it was Mother's Day, but quite honestly, I forgot. I just wanted to come home because we hadn't seen you since Christmas and it's been too long. I miss you . . . and the fam."

"We miss you, too. I'm glad everyone could come over last night—it was just like old times."

"It was," Chase said, smiling. "We had quite the bonfire."

"I know! It was so bright the firelight was dancing on my bed-room walls."

"Is Liam up?"

"I haven't seen him."

"I'm not surprised. He's not used to partying with the Tenny-son boys."

"Do you think you should check on him?"

"I will, but there's something I wanted to talk to you about first—while we have a minute."

Libby frowned and searched his face. "Is everything okay?"

"Yeah, everything's fine," he said. "In fact, everything is great." He pressed his lips together and leaned against the counter. "We were gonna tell you together, but last night, I started to think it might be better if I talked to you alone . . . and Liam said it was fine."

Libby's heart started to pound—*What was this about? What news did he have to share?* "What is it?" she asked.

Chase took a deep breath and slowly let it out. "I hope you'll be happy, Mom," he began tentatively, "because Liam and I want to have a family . . . and we plan to get married. We're engaged—we actually got engaged when we were here for Christmas—do you remember when we went for a walk after church on Christmas Eve?"

Libby nodded slowly, her heart still pounding. She knew how serious her son was about Liam, and she'd known all along that news like this would likely come, but now that it was here, she was still surprised. She loved Chase with all her heart, and she loved Liam, too, but deep down, she struggled sometimes. She couldn't tell him this, though—his gentle heart was much too precious to her, and she knew he would remember this moment for the rest of his life. Suddenly, she heard a clear but quiet voice in her head: *Just love him! Love him with all your heart—that's all that matters!* She blinked in surprise. "Oh, Chase," she said softly. "I've always prayed you'd find the right person to love—and that that person would love you back just as much." She pulled him into a hug. "I'm so happy for you."

"Thanks, Mom," Chase said, beaming. "That means more than you know."

Just then, Liam shuffled into the kitchen, wearing sweatpants and a T-shirt and rubbing his temple, and Chase looked over his mom's head, and gave him a thumbs-up.

Liam smiled. "Happy Mother's Day, Mrs. Tennyson," he said.

Libby pulled back. "Thank you, Liam . . . but I think you need to start calling me *Mom*, like all my boys."

He laughed. "I can do that," he said, giving her a hug.

Chase turned his attention back to the bacon and began lifting the long strips to a waiting plate. He'd just transferred the last piece when the screen door squeaked and Ellie clumped in with Gus at her heels. She kicked her barn boots onto the mudroom floor. "Uncle Gage says he has a long ride home and needs to get going soon," she called out, relaying the message that had been assigned to her.

"We have a long ride, too," Chase said, eyeing Liam.

"You're leaving, too?" Ellie asked, a shadow falling over her rosy cheeks.

"Afraid so, kiddo."

"Dang!" she muttered, and then she moved closer and whispered, "Did you tell her?"

Chase leaned down, and whispered back, "Yes!"

"Good," she said, giggling and reaching for a piece of bacon.

"They're hot," he warned.

"Not for me!" she said, taking a bite. "I love bacon!" She grinned at Liam, turned, and almost tripped on Gus, who was sitting behind her. "You want a piece, too, don't you, boy?" she asked, breaking off the end as he thumped his tail.

There was a commotion on the porch and then Matt pushed open the screen door, laughing as he walked in, followed by Gage, Grayson, and Eli, all of whom had—from years of habit—stopped to take off their boots. "Happy Mother's Day, Mom!" they called, giving her hugs.

Libby laughed. "Thank you! I couldn't feel more loved than I do right now!"

Ellie gave her a hug, too. "Happy Mother's Day, Gran! All this love is your reward for having all these kids!"

"It is indeed," Libby said, smiling.

〰️

19

"THANK YOU FOR THE BEAUTIFUL ROSES, HON!" AMES SAID, SWITCHING HER phone to speaker and setting it on the counter so she could continue chopping nuts for her banana bread.

"You're welcome, Mom," Quinn said, and then she paused. "What in the world is that noise?"

Ames laughed. "I'm chopping walnuts. Is it too loud?"

"A little."

"Okay, I'll mash bananas instead."

"Mom, why don't you just sit for a minute and talk? I can't stay on long because I have to get back to work."

"Okay. Do you want to call me back so we can FaceTime—like we did the other night—and I'll answer on my new iPad?"

Quinn laughed. "Okay, I'll call you back."

Ames quickly washed her hands, grabbed her iPad, and sat out on the porch with Ned. A moment later, her daughter's beautiful face was right in front of her! "Happy Mother's Day!"

"Thank you, honey! It's so good to *see* you! This newfangled technology is so amazing. It's almost like being together."

"Almost," Quinn said, laughing. "Except actually being together and being able to give you a hug would be much better."

"So, when are you coming home?" Ames teased.

"Ha! Very funny. That's another reason I'm calling—for Mother's Day, I'm also giving you a plane ticket so you can come visit *me*."

"Oh, hon, it's not the money. I can afford a plane ticket."

"I still want to treat. You know it's not easy for me to get away, and since you're retired—you could easily come visit for a week."

Ames nodded. "I know, and I actually have some news about that."

"Yeah?" Quinn said, tucking her wispy blond hair behind her ear, just like she'd done since she was a little girl. "What is it?"

"Well, you know how I said I didn't want to leave Ned?"

"Um, no . . . I don't remember you saying that, but if *that's* the reason you won't come, that's crazy—Ned will be fine! Can't you leave him with Mrs. Childs?"

"Well, that's what I was going to tell you. Payton never seems to want to let Cash do anything on his own . . ."

"Oh, how *is* Cash?" Quinn interrupted, fondly remembering her old classmate. She and Chase had both looked out for Cash when they were kids. He'd struggled socially in school and become easily upset, but he'd also been a genius at math and a talented artist. Chase had been first to take him under his wing—always standing up for him, especially if he was being picked on, but there were times when Chase hadn't been around and then, Quinn had stepped in and gotten Cash to "just breathe" until he calmed down.

"He's fine—all grown up, just like you, but he's aching for independence and Payton just won't let go. The other day, though, she and I were talking about me visiting you and when I said I was reluctant to leave Ned, Cash piped up and offered to house-sit and take care of him. It was no surprise," she continued, "that Payton pooh-poohed the idea, but then I told her I would leave Ned and visit you, if *she* would let Cash stay with him . . . and you're not gonna believe it, but she called me a little while ago and said she's going to let him!"

"So you're coming for a visit?!"

"If you still want me to . . ."

"Of course I want you to!" Quinn practically shouted, a smile lighting her face. "What changed Mrs. Childs's mind?"

"She didn't say, although she did say Cash had made her a very nice Mother's Day breakfast, and she seemed more cheerful than she's been lately."

Quinn nodded. "So when do you want to come?"

"Well, that's the other thing. It's a little up in the air because Payton might need to have surgery—she won't know for another week. I also wasn't sure of your schedule."

"Whenever you can come will work for me," Quinn assured her, but then she frowned. "Why does she need surgery?"

Ames sighed. "I'm sworn to secrecy."

"Ma, I'm in California. Who'm I gonna tell?"

"I don't know. You're on social media so you keep in touch with people."

"I won't tell anyone, but if you don't want to say anything, that's fine, too."

"She doesn't want Cash to worry—that's why it's a secret, but her doctor found a tiny lump on her thyroid and she had an ultrasound, but it was inconclusive, so she has to have a biopsy. If it turns out to be cancer, she'll have to have it removed."

Quinn nodded. "That's not as big a deal as it seems. I have a couple friends who had their thyroids removed, and they said their recovery wasn't that bad. They also said if you're gonna get cancer, thyroid is the one to get."

"I heard the same thing from Callie Jasmine—she had it, but Payton's still worried. It's easy for us to say *don't worry*, but when the word *cancer* is used regarding your own health, it's scary."

"Of course," Quinn agreed. "Are you waiting till she finds out or . . ."

"Payton thinks I should go soon, so if she needs me—or Cash—I'll be back."

"Okay!" Quinn said happily. "This is awesome—I mean, you coming, of course!" As she said this, her little tiger cat hopped up on her lap, peered into the camera, and meowed. "You're gonna get to meet your grandma, Clem!" Quinn said, and the cat swished her tail and meowed again.

Ames laughed. "She's so sweet—I can't wait to meet her." Then she leaned down, turned her iPad, and nudged Ned. "Say hello to Quinn and Clementine, Ned."

The big dog sniffed the screen, his wet nose filling the camera and Quinn laughed. "Hey, Neddy!" she said. "I miss seeing you, ole pal!" Ned thumped his tail. "I'm so glad you have him to keep you company, Mom."

"He *is* good company," Ames agreed, "but he hogs the bed more than your father *ever* did!"

"Wait! You let him on the bed?!"

"Yep," Ames said, nodding. "There're no rules around here anymore! He lies on your old bed, too, because the sun shines across it every morning."

"Love it!" Quinn said. "Well, do you want me to find a ticket for you, or do you want to look?"

"I think it would be better if you find it—you're much better at that sort of thing, and you know your schedule, so whatever works for you."

"Okay. I'll look tonight as soon as I get home and I'll text you." She smiled. "I'm so glad you're coming, Mom. We're gonna have so much fun."

"I'm glad I'm coming, too. It will be so good to see you—in person! And give you a hug."

"All right. Well, I better run. It doesn't take much for chaos to ensue at the restaurant, especially today. Enjoy the rest of your day . . . and your banana bread. Maybe you can bring some out when you come," she added hopefully.

"With chocolate chips or just walnuts?"

"With chocolate chips, of course!" Quinn said, remembering her mom's luscious recipe.

"Okay," Ames said, laughing. "I'll wait to hear from you on timing and tickets."

"Sounds good! Love you, Mom!"

"Love you, too, hon!"

Quinn waved and Ames waved back and then her daughter's face disappeared. Ames sighed and looked out across the field. It had been wonderful to see her, and she was excited about seeing her in person, but she still worried. "Ah, worry," she whispered, "why do you torment me? Dear Lord, help me have faith so I don't worry so much." Then she nudged Ned with her foot. "Shall we go have a banana?" she asked, and he perked right up and headed for the door, tail wagging. "I guess I'm gonna have to make a list of all the things you like to eat . . . *and* I'll have to write down our routine so Cash knows what to do."

〰️

20

"I thought the feeders were on this shelf," Libby said, straightening up. "But now I'm not sure where they are."

"Did you look in the pantry?" Ellie asked as she scooped sugar into a measuring cup.

"Why would I put them in the pantry?" Libby asked, sounding exasperated.

Ellie shrugged. "It's a fourth of a cup of sugar to one cup of water, right?"

"Yes, I think so," Libby answered. "I haven't put them out in several years, so they could be anywhere."

"They must be in a safe spot," Ellie teased, knowing how her grandmother was famous for putting things in safe spots, and then not being able to find them. "Want me to look?"

Libby sighed. "You'd probably have better luck than me."

Ellie handed her the spoon, disappeared into the pantry, and began scanning the long wooden shelves lined with homemade jams and pickles.

"We may as well make a cup of tea while we're at it," Libby mused.

"Okay!" Ellie called back as she rummaged around in some boxes.

"What kind would you like?"

"Hmm . . ." Ellie murmured thoughtfully as she continued to look.

"Can't hear you, hon."

"How 'bout Constant Comment?" Ellie called back.

"Good choice," Libby said, reaching for the little basket of assorted teas she kept on a shelf above the stove and taking out a slim red package of the tea with "the curious blend of orange peel, cinnamon, and other aromatic spices." Constant Comment had been one of her grandmother's favorites. She filled the kettle with fresh water, lit the back burner, set the kettle on it, and dropped the tea bag into her pot, draping the tag over the side.

"Can we open this, too?" Ellie asked, holding up a jar.

"Where was that?!" Libby asked in surprise. "I searched high and low for marmalade when Uncle Gage was here."

"It was right in front," Ellie replied, grinning.

Libby shook her head in dismay. "We can open it. Shall we have it on toast or pound cake?"

"Oooh! Pound cake!"

Libby laughed and set two plates on the counter. "Milk, honey, or lemon in your tea?"

"A little milk, please." Ellie brushed her bangs out of her eyes. Most of the time, she loved the way her bangs fell across her face, except when she was looking for something. She stood up, pushed her hand back through her hair, held it there, and noticed a cardboard box in the corner with the word *Hummer* scrawled across it. Triumphantly, she dragged it out and pulled open the flaps. "Found 'em!" she announced, lifting out two hummingbird feeders.

"Where?" Libby said, appearing in the doorway.

"Right there," Ellie said, gesturing to the corner. "They couldn't've been in a cabinet because they were in a box."

Just then, the kettle started to whistle and Libby, still shaking her head, hurried back to the stove. She clicked off the burner, gave the pot of simmering sugar water a stir, and clicked that burner off, too. Then she poured the steaming water into the teapot, put the top on to let it steep, and set the timer for seven minutes.

"Constant Comment always reminds me of Christmas," Ellie said, lifting the top to dunk the bag a few times, and breathing in the steam. "Mmm!"

Libby smiled. "That's what my grandmother used to say." She opened the marmalade, cut two thick slices of buttery pound cake, set them on the plates, and smoothed the sweet orange jam laden with curls of orange rind across the surface. "Here you go."

Ellie set the plates on the table and scooted into her seat to wait. Finally, the egg timer went off and Libby brought the teapot over and poured the dark citrus tea into their cups. Ellie poured a little milk into hers and stirred it with a silver spoon. "Did you know a hummingbird's heart weighs a fraction of an ounce and beats eight hundred times a minute?"

"Eight hundred times!" Libby exclaimed, sitting across from her. "How can that be? I'd think it would wear itself out."

"And the heart of a blue whale weighs four hundred pounds and can beat as little as ten times a minute when it's diving . . . *and* it can be heard two miles away!"

Libby chuckled. "How do you know this?"

"We've been studying the heart in science." She blew softly on the surface of her tea. "A resting hummingbird also breathes two hundred fifty times per minute, and its wings beat an average of fifty times a *second*!"

Libby shook her head. "God has certainly made some amazing creatures."

Ellie nodded. "Hummingbirds also migrate for hundreds of miles, *and* they travel alone. They return to the same feeders and gardens every year, so if you haven't put your feeders out the last couple of years, they probably missed them."

Libby took a sip of her tea. "How long do they live? Maybe they will come back this year."

"Seven or eight years, but there was one hummingbird in Colorado that lived to be twelve!"

"How do they know that?"

"They caught it and put a band on its leg."

"Do they mate for life?"

Ellie shook her head. "The male hummingbird goes to great lengths to attract a female, zipping around like a fighter pilot, but then he doesn't do anything to help raise their babies. He's a deadbeat dad just like the woodcock. The mother does everything. She lays two tiny eggs—smaller than jellybeans!" She took a bite of her cake. "You make the best pound cake, Gran . . . *and* the best marmalade. It's so much better than those little plastic containers they have at the diner."

Libby said, "Once you've had homemade jam, nothing else compares."

Ellie licked her lips, savoring the sweetness. "Can I help you make jam this summer? You said you have a lot of kitchen secrets to share."

"Absolutely. I need all the help I can get."

Ellie smiled. "How old were you when you met Grandpa?"

Libby took a deep breath and slowly let it out. "I was fifteen and he was seventeen."

Ellie sipped her tea, trying to imagine her grandparents so young. "Do you have a picture?"

"Somewhere. Probably tucked away in a safe spot," she said, chuckling.

Ellie laughed, too. "How did you meet?"

"He was doing some yard work for *my* grandparents—he had his own business. He'd just moved to town with his family because his father, your great-grandfather, was the new minister at the Baptist church."

"Did he ask you on a date?"

"He did," Libby said, nodding, "but my parents said I couldn't date anyone until I was sixteen, so he had to wait, but that didn't stop him from coming around." She laughed. "He was tall and handsome and had the bluest eyes I'd ever seen."

"I remember his eyes," Ellie said. "They were the color of the summer sky."

"They were. And all the boys inherited them. I have brown eyes and I *had* dark hair," Libby said, reaching up to touch her now-silver hair, "but Grandpa's genes were stronger..."

"You mean more stubborn," Ellie interrupted with a grin.

"Yes," Libby agreed, chuckling, "and now, all the grandkids have blond hair and blue eyes, too. You included," she added, smiling and wrapping her hands around her cup. "I miss him so much," she said, her eyes growing misty.

"I miss him, too," Ellie said softly, biting her lip uncertainly as a sad silence fell over the kitchen, the only sound coming from the old Seth Thomas wedding clock in the next room. "Gran, where did Grandpa ask you to marry him?"

"Oh, my goodness! That's a long time ago," Libby said, mustering a smile, "but I remember as if it was yesterday. We were at the fair, standing on a grassy knoll behind the tractor pull and your grandfather was acting as nervous as a long-tailed cat in a room full of rocking chairs. I didn't know what was wrong with him! It was a beautiful night, though, typical fair weather. The lights of the Ferris wheel and the carousel were spinning and swirling, people were laughing and squealing, and we could hear the bells and whistles of all the games, and your grandfather—who was usually as brown as a bean by late summer—was as pale as a ghost. I honestly thought he'd eaten a bad potato ... and then, out of the blue, he turned to me, knelt down on one knee, and blurted out, 'Elisabeth McCormack Jansen, will you marry me?' No frilly words—just a straight-up question. I was so surprised I started to cry—which really worried him, but then I managed to stammer *yes*, and, a moment later, like spreading wildfire, the announcer calling out the results of the tractor pull declared: 'Well, well, well! Jack Tennyson finally got up the courage to ask Libby Jansen to marry him! It's about darn time!' And everyone around us started cheering, which made all the color—and then some—return to your grandfather's face."

Ellie listened intently. "Wow, Grandma, I never heard that story before!"

"We had some good times, your grandfather and I." She paused, thinking back and mused, "He always seemed so serious, but he was an old softie. We had some tough times, too, but we got through them. One day at a time, Libby, he used to say to me. One day at a time."

"And that's how you're getting through now," Ellie said gently.

Libby nodded. "It is," she agreed, "and your company is helping more than you know."

"You should go to the coffee shop tonight, Gran."

"I should," she said, squeezing her granddaughter's hand. "We'll see."

21

⁂

"THE TECHNICIAN TOLD ME TO TIP MY HEAD ALL THE WAY BACK AND TO LIE STILL. Then he numbed the area, but it still hurt because he had a very hard time getting the needle into the damn thing . . . and then he had to do it two more times!"

Ames nodded sympathetically. "Did he say when you'll get the results?"

"Maybe tomorrow, but probably next week since it's already Thursday."

Ames looked around the shop. "Where's Cash? I brought chocolate cupcakes."

"You did? Darn! He wanted to go home—said he didn't want to hang around with a bunch of old ladies." She rolled her eyes. "One thing that will never change is his mood swings."

Ames chuckled. "Well, we're all guilty of that, ole girl." She took a sip of her wine. "Are you gonna let him learn to drive?"

"I don't know," Payton said with a sigh. "Let's see how he does taking care of Ned."

Ames reassured her, "I'm sure he'll be fine—Ned loves Cash. If he can't have me, Cash is the next best thing." She looked at the clock—it was after six. "Where the heck is everyone?"

"Sue Metcalf and Holly Meissner both said they were running late because they worked at the Thrift Mart all day, but Kathy Hyland said she'd be on time, and Callie and Heather said they'd be early so I'm not sure where they are. I'm not sure about Lynda or Lynn, either, but they didn't say they *weren't* coming." She picked up her glass and walked over to the couch. "I need to sit."

Ames picked up her glass and sat next to her. "If you're tired, you know, we don't have to get together."

"I know, but it keeps my mind off things." Payton took a sip of wine and tried to relax. "What time is your flight on Saturday?"

"Early," Ames replied, reaching for a cheese and cracker. "I think it's at 6:15, so I should be there by 4:15."

"I don't think you have to get there two hours early anymore."

"Well, since I've never flown, I'm gonna get there early."

"That's right! I forgot you've never flown."

"Have *you* ever flown?"

"Not commercially, but Lonny and I went to an air show once, and they were giving rides in a little red-and-black Waco, and we went up." She smiled wistfully. "He loved planes."

"Do you miss him?" Ames asked.

Payton half nodded. "I do, but sometimes I think life is easier now. I don't know." She looked over at her friend and reached for her hand. "I have you and that fills my heart in a different way . . . a nice way."

"I know what you mean," Ames said, searching Payton's eyes and giving her hand a gentle squeeze. "I don't seem to miss Frank as much. My life is definitely less stressful now." She chuckled. "Who would've thunk it?"

"Do you need a ride to the airport?"

"No, no. I'll drive myself—you have to be here to open."

"If you plan to be at the airport at 4:15, I can easily drive you *and* be back in time to open. In fact, we can leave Cash with Ned and he can take him for a walk once it's light out. It would be so much easier for you than trying to figure out parking and where you're going."

"Are you sure?"

"Absolutely," Payton replied.

"Okay. I also need Cash to come over so I can go over every-thing with him."

"We can come over after softball practice tomorrow."

"Perfect."

Just then, the shop door swung open, bells chiming. "We're here!" Sue and Holly called, bustling in with plates of food. "Pour us some wine!" Sue said, laughing. "What a day we've had! I think I went through twenty bags of clothes at the Thrift Mart! Oh, and I found this cute plate someone dropped off with a black Lab on it," she said, holding it out to Ames. "Doesn't it look like Ned?"

"It does look like Ned!" Ames said, giving her a hug. "Thank you!"

A few minutes later all the other ladies arrived, and soon, everyone was chatting cheerfully over glasses of wine or mugs of decaf. "We've raised enough money at the Thrift Mart this year to give out twenty $1,000 scholarships," Sue announced. "That is a record!"

"Wow!" Payton exclaimed. "Everyone must've spent the last year cleaning out their closets!"

"They must've," Sue said. "We had a lot of nice things, and people were looking for ways to save money, so we had a lot of new business."

"That's great," Ames said, holding up her glass. "A toast to the Thrift Mart and all the ladies who work so hard to help our young-sters pay for college."

"Hear! Hear!" everyone said, holding up their glasses.

They resumed chatting, uncovering plates of bruschetta, lemon bars, brownies, and even a lovely charcuterie that Sue had made on a board someone had donated to the Thrift Mart, un-used and still in the box, and then the chime on the door jingled and they all looked up.

"Libby!" they cried in delight.

Libby smiled and closed the door. "It was such a nice night . . . and it's even still light out . . . and since I had to run to the store, I thought I'd stop by and see what you all were up to."

"We're so glad you did," Ames said, giving her a hug.

"Yes, we are," Payton agreed, hugging her, too. "Come in and sit. We have all kinds of food," she said, gesturing to the table while Sue pulled an empty chair up next to her. "What would you like to drink? We have wine, coffee, tea . . ." She looked over at Callie, who always drank tea. "Is the water still hot?"

Callie nodded. "I have a pot of Tazo Passion steeping right here," she said, pointing to a ceramic cobalt blue teapot, "and there's more than enough."

Payton turned back to Libby. "How does passion tea sound?"

Libby laughed. "I've never had passion tea, but I'd love to try it." She looked around the cozy shop—she had been inside the store when it was the Calico Cat, but she hadn't stopped in after it became the Coffee Bean. "This is really cute," she said, sitting down between Callie and Sue—who made her feel right at home. "It must be odd for you, Callie, to be in here now that it's a coffee shop."

"Actually, I'm used to it," Callie said. "Payton changed it so much. If you remember, there used to be a wall right here," she added, motioning to the center of the room.

"I *do* remember," Libby said, "but I don't remember the fireplace . . ."

"That's because it was behind a fake wall," Sue explained. "Payton and Cash found it, quite by accident."

Libby nodded. "Well, it's beautiful. I'll have to bring Ellie in sometime for tea—she will love it."

"How is Ellie . . . and all your handsome boys?" Sue asked. "I haven't seen them in a coon's age."

"They're fine," Libby replied, smiling as Ames sat down next to them. "Gage is getting married this summer—he and his fiancée are having the ceremony in the big barn, which we haven't used for milking in years, but they've been restoring it, getting it ready—replacing boards and painting."

Sue nodded. "Barn weddings are all the rage right now."

"I know," Libby said. "It's funny how things come into style. Back when we got married, if you had your wedding in a barn, people thought you couldn't afford a nice venue, but nowadays, old farms charge a small fortune to host a wedding."

"That's so true," Callie said, shaking her head as she poured tea into their cups. "People buy old farms and turn them into gold mines. I had my wedding reception at the firehouse. I should've known it wasn't going to work out back then," she mused regretfully.

Callie held out a saucer of lemon slices as Libby reached for her tea. She took one, squeezed it in, and then took a sip of the rich red tea, savoring the unusual flavor. "Mmm, this is good—it tastes so . . . tropical."

Callie nodded. "It's made with hibiscus, rose hips, orange peel, and lemongrass—it's my favorite. It's really good iced, too."

"I'll have to get some."

"I was just talking to Quinn the other day," Ames said, taking a sip of wine. "She asked how Chase was doing."

"Oh, he's fine. He's actually getting—" Libby began, but then stopped midsentence. "He was just visiting last weekend. It was so nice to see him."

"That Chase is one handsome boy," Callie said, smiling. "I remember how close he and Quinn were when they were younger—they made such a cute couple. I always thought they'd end up together, but I guess not. Does he have a girlfriend?"

Libby shook her head. "Nope, no girls . . ." she answered, her throat tightening. She turned to Ames. "How *is* Quinn?"

"Oh, she's fine," Ames said, smiling gently at her old friend, knowing she'd changed the subject on purpose, and knowing

Callie must not have attended Jack's funeral—the funeral at which Chase had given such a heartfelt eulogy for his father, and in doing so, revealing truths about himself.

"I'm actually flying out to see her on Saturday."

"You are?" Libby said in surprise. "How exciting! Are you going for a week?"

"I am."

"Who's taking care of Ned?" Callie asked.

"Cash is staying with him at the house."

"Wait!" Sue whispered, eyeing her. "Payton is letting Cash house-sit?"

"She is," Ames confirmed, laughing because they all knew how protective their friend was of her son, especially since he was usually at the shop with them on Thursday nights and they had all witnessed many of their mother-son interactions. "We made a deal. At first I was reluctant to leave Ned, so Cash volunteered to watch him. But Payton was hesitant about that, so I said I'd go visit Quinn if Cash could take care of Ned. And we both agreed!"

"Good!" Sue said. "She needs to let him spread his wings . . . and you definitely need to visit Quinn."

Ames nodded. "I know. I'm really looking forward to it." She looked at Libby and smiled. "We have to let the Lord stretch our faith sometimes, otherwise we miss out."

"This is true," Libby agreed, smiling knowingly at her old friend.

As the evening grew late, the women thanked Payton for another fun night and headed out. Finally, only Ames, Payton, and Libby—who, no matter where she happened to go, always stayed to help clean up—were left.

"I'm so glad you came," Payton said as she picked up empty glasses.

Libby nodded. "I'm sorry it's taken me so long—I've wanted to come, but I think I felt like I would be acknowledging that I really am a widow." Her eyes suddenly filled with tears. "I try to be strong for the boys and Ellie, but I'm really not . . ." As she said this, her tears spilled down her cheeks. "I miss him so much and I still can't believe he's gone."

"Oh, Libby," Payton said, putting her arm around her. "We know what a shock it is . . . and how hard it is—that's why we've wanted you to come."

Ames nodded. "We are always here for you—anytime you need to talk or a shoulder to cry on. You don't have to pretend to be strong."

Libby wiped her eyes and chuckled. "Look at me—you guys have turned me into a puddle!"

"It's good to be a puddle sometimes," Payton said, laughing. "We're not supposed to keep it all in. Isn't that what Chase used to tell Cash when they were little? 'It's not good to keep it in, buddy—it's not healthy'—I can remember hearing him tell Cash that on several occasions when he was upset. God bless that son of yours—he was wise beyond his years."

Ames nodded in agreement. "He certainly was . . . and still is."

Libby wiped her eyes. "Thanks, you two. Just being here makes me feel better."

"Well, we do go back a few years, don't we? There's a lot to be said for old friends."

"There is indeed," Payton said, pulling them both into a hug.

22

CHASE GRABBED HIS JACKET, SWITCHED OFF THE LIGHT, AND STEPPED OUT ONTO the sidewalk behind Liam. "Got yer everythin'?"

Liam patted his pockets. "Yep. Phone, sunglasses, wallet. Got *yer* everythin'?" he asked with a laugh, knowing how often Chase didn't remember his *everythin'*.

Chase felt his back pockets for his phone and wallet, and then the front of his shirt where his sunglasses usually hung. "Dang! I don't have my sunglasses."

"Uh, they're on top of your head."

Chase reached up, felt them, and laughed. "Yep, they are! Do you have the keys?"

"I thought you had 'em."

Chase felt his front pockets now. "Nope. Must be on my desk." He went back inside, located his keys, hurried out, and as he locked the door, Liam stepped back to admire the new sign they'd hung that morning.

"Looks good!"

Chase stuffed his hands into the pockets of his faded Levi's and eyed the elegant wooden sign. "It does. I'm glad we went with PRIDE TRAVEL and not RAINBOW TRAVEL—it definitely sounds better."

"I'm glad we went with clear stain and not paint. The new logo looks awesome."

Chase glanced at his phone. "We better get moving."

They walked through City Market and down toward the river, weaving their way through shoppers and tourists. "It's such a nice night," Liam commented. "I meant to ask you—did you make reservations?"

Chase shook his head. "Maeve did."

"I hope so because it'll be hopping on a Friday night."

"I'm sure she did," Chase said as they reached the restaurant. Rocks on the River, known for its fresh Georgian seafood and contemporary southern fare was in the Bohemian Hotel. Its upstairs bar, Rocks on the Roof, not only had an intoxicating selection of craft cocktails, but it also had an intoxicating view of the Savannah River, and that's where they found Gage and Maeve already imbibing.

"Hey!" Chase said as they came up behind them.

"Hey, yerself!" Gage said, standing to shake his brother's hand and pulling him into a hug. When he released him, he turned to Liam and did the same. "How's it goin', bro? I can call you that now, right?"

Liam laughed. "Absolutely."

Maeve stood up, too, and Chase eyed his beautiful ginger-haired sister-in-law. "Hey to you, too," he said softly.

Maeve smiled. "So . . . I hear congratulations are in order!" she said, hugging him.

"They are indeed," Chase replied, grinning impishly as Liam hugged her, too.

"Well, dinner is on us tonight," Gage said.

"No way," Chase countered. "You don't have to."

"We want to. Besides, you treated last time."

"When *was* last time?" Chase asked, laughing. "I was trying to remember, because Liam made the comment that we live in the same town now, but we had to drive all the way to Tennessee to see you last weekend."

"I think last time was in March—we went to the Cotton Exchange."

"Oh, right," Chase said. "That was a fun night." He sat down next to Liam and eyed their drinks. "What are you drinking?"

Maeve glanced down at the menu. "Hmm . . . it's called Practice What You Peach—Tito's, peach liqueur, spiced vanilla syrup, fresh lemon, and sparkling wine. It *is* yummy. Want to try it?" she asked, holding out her glass.

Chase took a sip and licked his lips. "Mmm . . . love me some Tito's!"

Liam took a sip, too, and nodded. "That *is* good!"

They looked at the menu and Chase—knowing how much Liam liked mango, eyed him over the top of his menu. "Looks like they've even got your number."

Liam nodded. "Yup, It's the Mango for Me."

They placed their orders and, within moments, the waiter, who introduced himself as Alex, brought their drinks. Gage lifted his glass. "May God bless you with a lifetime of happiness and enduring love. Congratulations!"

"To you as well!" Chase said, grinning, as they clinked their glasses.

Maeve smiled and took a sip of her drink. "I might have to get another one of these, it's so good."

"Whoa," Gage teased. "You're gonna have *two* drinks?!" He winked at Chase and Liam. They both knew Maeve wasn't a big drinker, and none of them had ever even seen her slightly tipsy.

"Maybe," she said, laughing, and then she looked at Gage. "Did you tell them about our new chickens?"

"No, I forgot," Gage said. "You can tell them."

"Okay," she said, chuckling. Maeve looked at Chase and Liam. "We got two baby chicks back in February," she began, "and they're just getting old enough to start laying eggs."

"Did you name them?" Liam asked. He loved the names the Tennyson family came up with for all their animals, but Mother Clucker—the name of one of Gage and Maeve's other hens—was, by far, his favorite.

"We did," Maeve said. "One is Foghorn, and the other is Egg Nog."

Liam laughed and nodded approvingly.

"Nice," Chase said, sipping his drink.

"So, anyway," Maeve continued. "Foghorn has been laying eggs for about . . ."—she looked at Gage questioningly—". . . two weeks?"

He nodded. "Yeah, at least two weeks."

Maeve went on, "But Egg Nog, nothing, and she almost seemed like she was getting depressed, because every time Foghorn lays an egg, she starts clucking and strutting around like she's found the cure to cancer, and all the other hens go see each other's eggs—hers included and cluck their approval.

"Well, poor Egg Nog—she just sits on her nest with everyone else, but nothing happens, so I think she was beginning to feel really left out. But this morning, lo and behold, she laid her first egg *and* . . . oh, my goodness! She started clucking at the top of her lungs, telling everyone within two miles about her great accomplishment, and then all the other hens went to check out her egg and started clucking, too—it was almost as if they were congratulating her. It was too funny."

Chase listened to Maeve telling the story, and at the same time, watched Gage listening, too, and he could tell, by the adoring look on his brother's face, how much he loved Maeve, and his heart swelled with happiness for them. Sweet Maeve, who'd never had chickens before, had embraced every part of his brother's life, and every one of his interests. And even though he and Liam shared a love that was just as deep and caring *and* enduring, he knew there were people in the world who didn't understand and wouldn't accept them. Who wouldn't even try, and it made his heart ache.

Maeve smiled and looked at Gage again. "I think she was still strutting around tonight when we left, right?"

"She was," Gage confirmed.

Chase shook his head. "Hens are too funny. They are so proud of themselves when they lay an egg, especially the first time." He looked over at Liam. "When I was little, we had a chicken that was half rooster and half hen."

"I remember that chicken!" Gage said. "You named him . . . or her Scramble."

Chase nodded. "I read about this phenomenon. Animals or birds that are half male and half female are called gynandromorphs, and they're not as rare as you think."

"What causes it?" Maeve asked.

"Our dad always said the egg must've been fertilized twice, but in biology class we learned that they think it happens when the cells of a female egg develop with two nuclei—each with a different chromosome. Then, when the egg is fertilized with two male chromosomes the egg ends up having both male and female chromosomes.

"Anyway, our dad wanted to get rid of Scramble, but he . . . or she," he said, repeating Gage's wording, "followed me everywhere and my mom wouldn't let him."

"Nature—and God's creation—is so interesting. He has quite an imagination when he makes everyone—and everything—so different."

"It makes the world more colorful and interesting," Liam said.

"It definitely does," Chase said, grinning.

Just then Alex came back over. "Y'all ready to order?"

"I am," Chase said. "I looked before we came."

"I did, too," Liam said, laughing.

Gage eyed Maeve. "Ready?"

"I am . . . *if* I can go last."

Gage gestured to Chase. "Have at it."

Chase looked up at the waiter. "I know you're known for your seafood, but I'm gonna have the Southern Steak Frites, medium, and . . ."—he motioned to his glass—"a refill."

"You got it," Alex said, without writing anything down. He turned to Liam. "You, sir?"

"I'll have the same," Liam said, "but my drink was the mango."

Alex nodded and turned to Gage. "And for you, sir?"

"Well, Alex, since you're not taking notes, I'm gonna make it easy for you and have the same as them"—he indicated Chase and Liam—"except my drink was peach, and I'd like my steak rare."

Alex nodded and turned to Maeve—who was still poring over her menu. She looked up with a smile and raised her eyebrows. "And . . . I will have the . . ." She looked down again. "I think I'm gonna have the crab cakes . . . or maybe the seafood ravioli?" She looked at Alex—who had spiky blond hair, a clear tan complexion, and couldn't have been older than seventeen. "Which do you recommend?"

Alex smiled. "The crab cakes. Definitely."

"Sold!" she said. "And my drink was peach, too."

"You got it," he said, gathering their menus. "I'll be right back with your drinks."

Chase and Liam watched him walk away, and then eyed each other. "He's so gay," Chase said, laughing.

"Oh, yeah!" Liam agreed.

Maeve eyed them with a puzzled look on her face. "How do you know?" she asked. "I would've never guessed."

Liam shrugged and looked at Chase. "We always know."

Chase nodded and smiled. "We do," he confirmed. "We always do . . . and I'm sure he knows about us, too."

Just then, Alex came back with their drinks.

"Right?" Chase said, eyeing him.

Alex laughed. "Yep."

"Unbelievable," Maeve said, laughing. "You're like twins with a secret language."

Chase smiled. "It's called gaydar, but *you* people can't talk that way about *us*. Only *we* can talk that way about us."

Maeve laughed and took a sip of her drink. "Hmm, I think this one's a little stronger."

"Probably," Liam said, laughing. "Thanks to Alex."

She rolled her eyes. "Anyway, I . . ." She looked at Gage. "*We* wanted to ask you guys if you could put together a honeymoon package for us."

"Absolutely!" Chase said. "Where do you want to go?"

"Well, that's the thing," she said. "Gage wants to go to the Grand Canyon, but I would sort of like to go somewhere . . . well, more exotic."

"The Grand Canyon is exotic," Gage said, sounding wounded.

Chase and Liam both laughed, and Chase shook his head. "You can go to the Grand Canyon anytime. You need to go somewhere romantic for your honeymoon."

"Like Greece, right?" Maeve suggested hopefully.

"Exactly!" Chase said. "We went to Mykonos a couple of years ago and it was *ah-may-zing*!" He eyed Liam for confirmation. "Wasn't it?"

"It was. I would definitely recommend Mykonos. We can tell you all the cool places to go, the restaurants. You will love it."

Gage eyed them. "The question is: Will *I* love it?"

"Of course! You're there with the woman you love. How could you *not* love it?"

"I don't know," Gage said. "I kind of had my heart set on watching the woman I love ride a burro down a dusty trail into the most iconic canyon on the face of the earth."

Chase laughed. "You can do that on your first anniversary."

Gage shook his head, feigning defeat, and then sipped his drink.

"Oh, don't look so disappointed. You'll get to see your best girl in a skimpy bikini."

"This is true," Gage said, looking over at Maeve, whose eyes looked a little glassy. "Hmm," he teased. "I think we better get some food in you or I'll be carrying you home."

"What?! I'm fine," she said. Then she looked at Chase and Liam. "There is something else we wanted to talk about."

"What's that?" Chase asked, sipping his own drink and feeling a little tipsy himself.

"We'd really love it"—she glanced up at Gage and he nodded approvingly—"if you guys would get married with us."

"Ha! You've had too much to drink, little sister, and it's gone right to your head," Chase teased.

"No, we mean it. We think it would be fun." She looked to Gage for support. "Tell them."

Gage nodded. "We do mean it. You can invite whomever you like." He looked at Liam. "Your family—parents, grandparents, siblings, friends, whoever . . ."

Liam pressed his lips together and frowned. "My grandparents are gone . . . and although my sister might come, I honestly don't know if my parents would; they might not even come if we got married in their backyard. We haven't told them yet, so I'm not sure what they'll say." He looked at Chase. "We're figuring out when we're gonna tell them."

Gage said, "Well, we'd still love having a double wedding at the farm and a big family celebration after."

Chase smiled. "That is really kind . . . *and* generous of you." He looked at Liam. "We'll have to figure all this out and let you know."

"Okay," Gage said, "but please know that it would really make it special for us."

"Okay," Chase said. He eyed Maeve. "You sure about sharing your big day?"

"Absolutely! We love you guys and we're so happy for you."

Chase chuckled. "We're happy for you, too, but I think we need to cut you off till your dinner gets here," he teased, and, as if on cue, Alex appeared, carrying all four dinner plates.

23

AMES SQUEEZED HER EYES CLOSED AS THE 757 BEGAN ITS DESCENT INTO SAN Francisco International Airport, but the lady next to her—who'd been her guiding angel the whole trip—looked over and said, "You should watch—it's beautiful! You can see the ocean."

Ames opened her eyes. "You mean we're going to survive this landing?"

"Absolutely. I fly all the time. We'll be fine."

Reluctantly, Ames peeked out the window and there it was, the endless blue ocean. "My goodness!" she whispered. "It goes on for*ev*er!"

"It does. You're lucky it's such a clear day. I don't know how many times I've landed here in a blanket of fog."

Ames shook her head. "I don't know how pilots fly in fog and clouds. I would panic if I couldn't see what was in front of me."

"Oh, they learn to trust their instruments—I'm sure it becomes second nature."

"It must take an extraordinary amount of faith," Ames said. She watched the tiny cars traveling on the highway, and the roofs and pools growing bigger, and she was amazed by the bustling nature of humanity—everyone going somewhere!

Finally, the ground came up very fast and they bumped into a landing, the air screaming as the flaps went up, and then, just like that, they were there. "See? Piece of cake," the lady said, smiling.

Ames nodded. "I can't thank you enough for being a voice of calm reassurance and comfort."

The lady smiled as she stood up and reached into the overhead compartment for her carry-on. "You're welcome. I hope you have a lovely visit with your daughter."

"Thank you." Ames leaned down to pull her small personal bag from under the seat in front of her, but when she looked up again, the woman was gone. She sighed, retrieved her own carry-on, and walked up the aisle. "Thank you so much for getting us here safely," she said, smiling at the handsome young pilot standing near the exit.

"You're welcome," he replied.

Then she paused and searched his face. "You really don't look old enough to be piloting a big plane like this."

He laughed. "Well, now that we're safely here, I can tell you that this was my first official flight with actual passengers on board."

"Good Lord!" Ames exclaimed. "I'm glad you didn't tell us before!" She shook her head. "Well, bless you, young man, and may you have a long, safe career." She paused, frowning. "Isn't there a term pilots use for clear skies?"

"I think you must mean CAVU—it stands for ceiling and visibility unlimited."

"Well, I hope you always have CAVU skies," she said, releasing the handle of her carry-on to give him a hug.

"Thank you, ma'am," he replied, his blue eyes sparkling.

Ames looked behind her, realized she was holding up the line, squeezed his hand, and continued up the ramp, towing her luggage.

Uncertain of her whereabouts, she texted Quinn to let her know she'd arrived and then followed a young couple she recognized from the plane toward the exit where she saw her daughter waiting.

"Mom!" Quinn cried, wrapping her arms around her. "I can't believe you're here!"

"I can't believe it, either!" Ames hugged her daughter for a full minute before pulling back to hold her face in her hands. "You look wonderful!"

"You do, too, Ma," Quinn said softly. "I'm so glad you're here."

"I'm so glad, too," Ames replied.

"How was your flight?"

"It was fine. We had the cutest young pilot—he said it was his first time flying a plane with actual passengers."

"Wow!" Quinn said in surprise and then frowned. "I'm really glad it went well then."

Ames saw her daughter's concern and laughed. "Everyone has to have a first time at everything, right?"

"I guess," Quinn said, "but with flying, a little experience is always nice."

"True, but you can only get experience by doing it. Anyway, he did a good job and I wished him well and gave him a hug."

"Of course you did," Quinn said affectionately.

As they made their way to Quinn's car, she said, "I took the weekend off . . . well, for the most part. I *do* have to go in for a little while tomorrow, but I thought we could drop off your stuff, meet Clem, have a quick bite—because you're probably starving, and maybe drive down to Monterey for dinner, although there are some nice places nearby too. How does that sound?"

"I am a little hungry—all they gave us on the plane was a bag of pretzels, but where I'd really like to go for dinner is the Quince Café!"

Quinn laughed. "Okay, I'll have to see if I can get us in!"

FIFTEEN MINUTES LATER, QUINN PUSHED OPEN THE DOOR OF HER SUNNY APART-ment, and Clementine hurried over to greet them, swishing between their legs and telling them all about her morning. "What a sweetheart," Ames said, kneeling down to give her daughter's tiger cat a proper hello.

Quinn smiled. "She *is* a sweetheart, and very vocal. When I get home from work . . . or from anywhere, she meows up a storm, telling me everything." Quinn scooped her into her arms. "*You* are a mush, aren't you?"

Clem pressed her nose against Quinn's, making her laugh. "Would you like some coffee?"

"I'd love some! I didn't have any this morning because I didn't want to have to use the bathroom," she said, "so I haven't had my caffeine fix yet."

"Oh, wow! If I don't have my caffeine by nine o'clock, I get a headache, but I also know all about not wanting to find a bathroom. When my friends and I climbed Half Dome, we weaned ourselves off caffeine for a week beforehand so we wouldn't need coffee and then we didn't drink anything that morning because we didn't know where we'd be able to *go* when we were hiking. We did end up drinking a lot of water on the way up, but we never needed to go because our bodies kept using all that hydration! Afterward, though, we found out there were some facilities along the way."

Ames shook her head. "I still can't believe you hiked Half Dome!"

Quinn nodded as she heated water to make coffee in her Chemex. "It took sixteen hours and a lot of water breaks . . . *and* a lot of encouraging each other. And then, when we finally reached the cables and looked up at the steep rock face . . . well, it's more than a little intimidating. There are people coming down while you're going up, and everyone goes at their own pace—some very slowly while others are in a hurry—but you can't go all that way, and *not* reach the summit, so we put on our gloves and held on to those cables with death grips."

"Well, I'm glad you made it up—*and down*—in one piece."

"Me, too, because coming down is a completely different

adventure. We were only on the summit for about a half an hour when we started to see lightning in the distance, and then everyone wanted to go down at the same time, but you can only go so fast when there are people in front of you. It was more than a little nerve-racking," Quinn said, remembering the experience with a mixture of pride, elation, and relief. Even though it had been one of the most challenging and stressful things she'd ever done, she was glad she'd done it. "By the time we got all the way down, our knees were aching."

"I bet," Ames said, shaking her head and watching her daughter pour hot water over the coffee filter.

"I picked up some chocolate croissants, too," Quinn said, motioning to a paper bag on the counter. "I'm gonna nuke 'em so the chocolate melts."

"I love chocolate croissants," Ames said, welcoming Clementine onto her lap.

"I know you do."

Quinn sat across from her, and Ames took a sip of her coffee. "It's so good to see you, sweetheart," she said, smiling.

"It's so good to see you, too, Mom," Quinn said, reaching over to squeeze her hand. "Now, try one of these croissants—I got them at the bakery down the street and they are the best!"

Ames nodded and then raised her eyebrows. "That reminds me! I brought a loaf of banana bread with walnuts and chocolate chips for you."

Quinn's face lit up. "You remembered!"

"Of course, I remembered," Ames said, taking a bite of her croissant. "I'm your mom."

24

"GRAM, I'M HERE!" ELLIE CALLED, DROPPING HER BACKPACK ON THE MUDROOM floor, but just as she did, Goodness and Mercy scooted between her legs and chased each other into the kitchen. "G and M are in!"

"That's okay," Libby called, coming into the kitchen with an armful of books. "Those two are always sneaking in." She set the books on the table. "Have you ever read these, El?" she asked, spreading them out. "Your dad and your uncle Gage read them when they were your age, and your dad thought you might like them."

Ellie looked at the covers. "Hmm . . . *My Side of the Mountain*," she murmured thoughtfully. "I don't think I have . . ." She picked each one up and read the back. "Is it a series?"

"It is. The author, Jean Craighead George, loved to write about nature and animals."

Ellie frowned. "Did she write the *Julie of the Wolves* trilogy? Because if she did, I read all of those and *loved* them."

"She might've . . . I'm not sure. These are the only books I have by her."

"*Julie of the Wolves* is about an Eskimo girl who lives in the wild with wolves—they helped her survive—she even learned to speak their language!"

Libby nodded. "That must've been pretty amazing."

"It was. Did you know that wolves mate for life?"

"I did not."

"They will also die for their mate or another close family member."

"I had no idea they were so devoted."

Ellie nodded and studied the backs of the books. "Thanks, Gram. I'll definitely read these." She stacked them in a pile. "Maybe I'll even start tonight."

"After Hyacinth?"

"Of course," Ellie said, grinning. "*And* cribbage."

The kettle on the stovetop began to sing and Libby's face brightened. "I have a new kind of tea for you to try."

"What kind is it?"

"It's called passion tea. I had it the other night at the Coffee Bean."

"Wait! You went to the Coffee Bean with the ladies?!"

"I did," Libby said, pouring hot water over one of the tea bags Callie had given her.

"How was it?"

"It was nice. A lot of fun actually."

"Are you gonna go again?"

"Maybe," Libby said, setting the timer for seven minutes.

"What did you talk about?"

"Oh, you know . . . girl stuff," Libby replied.

Ellie laughed. "Did you drink wine? I hear they all drink wine in that group."

"What do you think?" Libby asked, raising her eyebrows.

"I think you had tea, because I have never seen you drink wine."

"Correct. And that's why I have this new tea for you to try," she said, turning off the timer. She poured the tea into two cups. "Lemon?"

"Yes, please."

Libby squeezed a sliver of lemon into both cups and carried them to the table. "Have you been to the Coffee Bean?"

Ellie nodded. "Mom gets coffee there sometimes, but I've never eaten there."

"Well, we will have to go sometime."

"Maybe we could go after church tomorrow," Ellie suggested hopefully.

"Oh, hon, I don't think they're open on Sunday."

"Oh, right. I forgot," Ellie said, a shadow of disappointment crossing her face.

"But we'll go soon—we'll have a girls' lunch."

Ellie blew softly on the surface of her tea and then, out of the corner of her eye, saw something small streak past the window. "I think I just saw a hummer!" she exclaimed, getting up to look. Libby joined her at the window and they watched in the fading sunlight as two male rubythroats hovered near the feeder and then zoomed away. A moment later, a female landed and had just begun to take a long sip when one of the males returned and began flying up and down like a big pendulum. "What in the world is he doing?!" Ellie whispered.

"He's showing off, trying to impress her."

Just then, the second male dove into its path midswing, and they raced off together. "They're both trying to get her attention!"

Finally, the female zoomed away, too, and Libby sat back down. "Your tea is getting cold."

Ellie joined her and took a tentative sip. "Wow, this is good!"

"I know," Libby said smiling at her granddaughter's enthusiasm for the new flavor.

Ellie's face suddenly lit up with a smile. "You'll never guess what kind of bird I saw this morning."

"What kind?"

"A whip-poor-will! I was walking along that little piney path behind our house, and she was just sitting in the leaves under a juniper tree. I wouldn't've even noticed her, except that, when she saw me, she got up and started dragging one of her wings along the ground, pretending to be injured, and then I saw she had two eggs."

"Lucky you! I can't remember the last time I saw a whip-poor-will."

Ellie nodded. "They lay their eggs on the ground, just like a woodcock—which I think is kind of silly. It's a wonder they're not extinct! Anyone could come along and accidentally step on the eggs . . . or purposely eat them."

"Well, that's how God made them," Libby said, "and somehow they manage, just like all his creatures."

"Including *us*," Ellie said, smiling. "God made us all different, too, and we manage somehow and do the best we can."

"So true," Libby said, her granddaughter's words plucking her heartstrings and making her think of Chase, who always strived to do his best, no matter what he faced—from taking under his wing every living thing that needed help to probably one of the hardest things, telling his father he was gay. That had not been an easy conversation, but Chase had countered Jack's biblical argument with his own interpretations of the Bible, and he'd gently, but firmly convinced his father that being gay wasn't a choice. Now, he was getting married, and she wondered what Jack would think if he were alive. She knew her husband had loved their youngest son with all his heart, but with all that love came worry, and neither she nor he would ever want Chase to be hurt or ridiculed. Life was hard enough . . . and that was the hardest part . . .

"I love listening to the whip-poor-wills when I'm lying in bed at night," Ellie said, interrupting her thoughts. "It's such a cheerful summer sound."

"It is," Libby agreed.

"Did you know that whip-poor-wills purposely time the laying of their eggs so they hatch ten days before a full moon so that, when they do hatch, the moon will give them enough light to forage for bugs all night long so they can feed their babies?"

Libby shook her head. "That's incredible. How do they know?"

"God must tell 'em," Ellie said matter-of-factly.

"He must indeed," Libby replied.

Just then, they heard a clump on the porch, and a moment later, Matt pushed open the door. "You two all set for the night?"

"We are," Libby replied. "We're having grilled cheese and tomato soup for supper, watching our favorite show, playing a game or two, reading, and going to bed."

"Sounds like a good plan," Matt said, smiling. "Do I get a hug?" he asked, eyeing his daughter.

"Yup," Ellie said, running over and jumping into his arms.

"Be good."

"I'm always good!"

He laughed. "Okay, see you tomorrow."

"Not if I see you first!" she said, grinning as he set her back down.

"Thanks, Mom," Matt said.

"Oh, hon, you don't need to thank me. It's my pleasure to have such good company every Saturday night." She looked over at Ellie. "I don't know what I'd do without her . . . without all of you keeping me going."

He half smiled, knowing how much his mom missed his dad . . . *and* her own dad. "Okay, well, Eli, Grayson, and I will be back in the morning." He eyed Ellie. "Be ready for church."

"I will," she promised.

"Love you both," he said. "G'night!"

"Love you, too," Libby replied, and then added, "Maybe next Saturday, you can leave Jack here, too, and you and your lovely wife can go on a date."

"A date?" Matt said, laughing as the screen door closed behind him. "What's that?"

Libby smiled as she watched him walk to his truck. "A date is something you need to make time for," she murmured, "because all too soon, the time is gone." As she said this, she felt Ellie's hand slip into hers.

"I'll be your date anytime, Gran," she said softly.

Libby looked down. "Thank goodness I have you, hon!" she said, giving her granddaughter a hug.

"You have all of us, Gran."

"I know I do—I'm truly blessed."

25

PAYTON HUNG UP THE PHONE AND LEANED AGAINST THE COUNTER, JULIE'S WORDS
echoing in her head: *He wants you to come in, Payton. Can you be here
at 3:30 this afternoon?* She'd answered that she could, but before she
could ask why, Dr. Hamlin's receptionist had hung up.

But Payton wasn't born yesterday. She knew that when test results showed there was nothing wrong—nothing to worry about,
you simply got a message: *Everything looks fine. We'll see you in a year.*
Even after all the mammograms she'd had in her life, she'd always just gotten a form letter stating that everything was normal
and to remember to schedule one for the following year, but when
you got a call and were asked to come in, well, she'd seen enough
movies to know that wasn't a good sign. For some reason, doctors
always want you to come in so they can give you bad news in person. Why was that? Why couldn't they just tell you over the phone?
Did they not want you to be alone when they told you your life was
threatened? Were they afraid you might jump out a window or have
a nervous breakdown? Didn't they know that *just by asking you to
come in*, you'd know that an ominous cloud was forming over your
world? Didn't they think you knew that being summoned to the
doctor's office was akin to being escorted to the gallows?

"Dang it," she whispered, tears springing to her eyes. She

looked down and realized Ned—who'd been coming to the shop with them all week—was gazing at her with worried eyes. "Oh, Ned," she said, kneeling down and burying her face in his fur, "can you believe this is happening?" Ned wagged his tail consolably and she pulled back and looked into his sweet brown eyes. "We'll get through it," she said resolutely, trying to ease her own worry as much as his. "We just have to put it in God's hands and keep the faith." Ned thumped his tail in agreement and then, satisfied that she was going to be okay, moseyed back to his bed.

"Ma, we need you out here," Cash called, poking his head into the kitchen.

Payton hurried out to the front of the shop and realized there was a line snaking out the front door. "What the heck?" she said. "Did someone put a sign out that says Free Coffee?"

Cash shook his head. "I don't know what happened. Rylee came in and said there's a bus parked up the street." Payton nodded and started to help Jessie fill orders while Cash continued to man the register, but despite the long wait, the steady stream of customers seemed unhurried, and kept themselves occupied by chatting and browsing the Tennessee-themed T-shirts and coffee mugs Payton also sold in the shop. Finally, after a full half hour of serving customers, the last two—attractive well-dressed women in their early seventies, set their purchases on the counter and ordered two medium hot lattes with whole milk and chocolate shavings. "Where are you from?" Payton asked as she cranked the little metal chocolate shaver over the foamy surface of their lattes.

"We'ah from Massachusetts—Nantucket," the first woman answered in a decidedly Boston accent, "and we'ah taking a bus tour of the East Coast. We've been to DC, Williamsburg, and tonight we're gonna stay in Pigeon Hole. On the way home, we're going to Gettysburg."

"It's Pigeon *Forge*," the second woman—whose face reminded Payton of Ames—corrected, nudging her. "We're going to Dollywood tomorrow," she added cheerily, "but this afternoon, we're goin' to the Tennessee Tennyson's Dairy Bar." She smiled. "I can't wait to try their ice cream. My grandkids vacationed down here last year, and my nineteen-year-old grandson is still talking about the Tennyson family's famous ice cream."

The first woman eyed her. "You should explain that Jon is on the autism spectrum and when he latches onto something, he never forgets it."

The woman nodded. "Yes, my grandson has Asperger's and my son's family has never taken a real vacation before because money has been tight, but last year they did, and it was very special for Jon—he *loves* ice cream and he considers himself to be a connoisseur."

Payton smiled and handed them their coffees. "Very nice!"

"Jon's getting his own apartment soon, too," the woman continued, "*and* his driver's license. His parents want him to be more independent."

Payton nodded, listening in wonder to the direction the simple conversation with strangers was taking. "Well, Tennyson's ice cream is the creamiest on earth, so I'm sure you'll like it."

The woman nodded. "I'm sure we will, too." She leaned forward and whispered, "I'm just a plain ole vanilla girl, so nothin' fancy for me."

The first woman chuckled. "You are anything but plain ole vanilla, dear," she said with a mischievous come-hither smile.

"Oh, you!" the silver-haired woman replied, laughing and affectionately nudging her.

Payton frowned uncertainly as a light flashed on and off in her preoccupied brain. *Were these two women flirting? Were they a couple? They seemed so comfortable . . . and almost intimate with each other, and they obviously enjoyed one another's company, but what exactly was their relationship?* "Well, Tennyson's *vanilla* is the best there is. I'm sure you'll love it."

"Thank you," the second woman said. "I'm sure we will." Then she looked at her friend. "Did you get the shirt you wanted?"

"Yes, I got two—one for me and one for you."

"You didn't have to do that."

"I wanted to." She looked at Payton and smiled. "Thank you."

As they walked away, their hands touched and they discreetly clasped pinkies before going outside with their coffees.

Payton watched them, smiling wistfully. "Hmm . . . maybe such a life is possible," she murmured, and then her eyes widened. "I wonder if Tennyson's Dairy Bar knows there's a tour bus headed their way!" She called Libby to warn her and then she looked up at the clock and realized it was after three! "I have an appointment," she called as she pulled off her apron. "Will you guys be okay?"

Cash looked up from the register. "I didn't know you had an appointment today."

"I forgot," Payton lied. "They called a little while ago to remind me."

"Okay," he said. "We'll be fine."

Payton nodded. Cash had been oddly helpful all week, *and* he seemed to be managing just fine on his own at Ames's house. He hadn't burned it down *or* flooded it, and he was even outside early every morning with Ned, both of them ready to be picked up. Maybe Ames was right—maybe he just needed the chance to prove himself. She grabbed her bag, and headed for the door, and as she walked through the now-empty patio behind the shop, she straightened a few chairs and grabbed a stray napkin that had blown to the ground, and it was then that she noticed—for the first time—how neatly manicured the gardens were. Clusters of black-eyed Susan, bee balm, and echinacea were all starting to come up, and everything around them was neatly weeded and cultivated. She knew Cash enjoyed gardening, but when had he found time to work out here? She always assumed that when he was sitting out here on his break, he was playing games on his phone, but obviously, he'd made time to tend the garden, too. "That kid," she murmured, half smiling. "It's getting so I never know what to expect."

Ten minutes later, Payton parked in front of the office and looked up at the building, knowing that when she came back out, her life would be different.

26

THE SLEEPY STREETS OF SAVANNAH WERE SHROUDED IN MIST WHEN CHASE KNELT on the sidewalk in front of Pride Travel to tie his running shoes. He stood up and swung his arms in circles, trying to loosen his shoulders, and then leaned over, keeping his long muscular legs straight, and held the back of his ankles, which made his hamstrings sing. He'd always been limber and athletic, but the last few years, he'd begun losing the easy flexibility he'd enjoyed as a youth. "I think I must've done something to my shoulder when we were working on the barn because it hasn't been the same since," he said, watching Liam stretch the arch of his foot on the curb.

"Well, we're not getting any younger," Liam replied. "Aches and pains come with the territory. They say getting old isn't for wimps."

"That's the truth," Chase agreed, "but we aren't even thirty yet."

"We will be before you know it."

Chase raised his eyebrows. "*And* we're gonna be old parents at the rate we're going."

As they trotted toward Forsyth Park, Chase set the pace. In the short time they'd lived on Tybee Island, Chase had fallen in love with the neighboring historic old city designed by James Oglethorpe. He loved the layout and the parks and the old houses, and he especially loved Savannah's mysterious and beguiling reputation as *the* most haunted city in the country . . . not to mention the undoubtedly spirit-filled Bonaventure Cemetery, which was the setting of the book he'd just read, *Midnight in the Garden of Good and Evil*. "Let's go to the cemetery!"

"Again?" Liam asked, shaking his head. "Now I know why you don't want to run on the beach—you just like running through that old creepy cemetery."

"I *do*," Chase admitted, laughing. "We've been running on Tybee Island since we moved here, and running on the beach makes my calves ache. Besides, it's fun to run in town, and since we have an office with an upstairs apartment now—*and* a shower, we can run before work." They turned onto East Anderson and continued along the quaint, quiet street, the only sounds coming from a delivery truck dropping off newspapers.

"Have you given any more thought to getting married at the farm?" Chase asked between breaths as they picked up the pace.

"I have, and I still don't know. I don't want to take away from Gage and Maeve's day, and I always thought we'd just have a small ceremony—you and me, and a couple of friends."

"I know what you mean—I guess I always imagined it that way, too," Chase said, shaking his head. "Even though my dad was accepting—or at least he *said* he was accepting, especially after *he* brought up the Bible and I countered with rules that are in the Bible that just don't make sense—like how it says planting two different crops together or wearing two different types of fabric are sins—I still think he might turn over in his grave if I got married on *his* farm." He paused. "On the other hand, I *do* love a big wedding, and I think it would be fun to have our families there."

Liam shook his head. "My sister might come, but I honestly don't think my parents will."

Chase wiped his cheek on his shoulder. "Do you still want to tell them in person?"

"I do," Liam said. "I just don't know when. We're so busy right now."

"Well, we'll just have to go—even if it's only for a weekend. We won't know until we ask."

Liam nodded. "I know."

They reached the entrance to the cemetery and Chase stopped. He pulled his arm in front of him, still trying to stretch his tight shoulder. "I heard Johnny Mercer is buried here. Let's see if we can find him."

The sun was still trying to burn off the morning mist, and the hazy light filtering through the Spanish moss gave the cemetery an ethereal golden glow. "Sheesh!" Liam said, looking around. "It's even spooky in the daytime."

"It is," Chase agreed, slowing to look at the names on the tombstones as they ran.

"Hey, there's a sign," Liam said, gesturing to a little arrow marker on the side of the road. They followed it, and moments later, they found themselves standing in front of the famous song-writer's gravesite. "What songs did he write?"

"He wrote the lyrics for a bunch of old classics . . . 'Moon River,' 'Days of Wine and Roses,' and 'One for My Baby' . . ." He pointed to a curved stone bench in front of the grave. "Some of the titles are written here."

"Oh, wow! I had no idea," Liam said, reading the titles. "He wrote 'Jeepers Creepers'!"

Chase nodded and stepped past the bench to look at the dates on the grave. "He was born in 1909 and died in 1976 . . . he was only sixty-six."

"Young," Liam said, standing beside him.

"Yeah, around the same age as my dad." He looked up. "Ready?"

Liam nodded and they continued through the misty cemetery, looking at the ancient tombstones and markers. "A lot of old spir-its in here." He noticed another sign, marking the way to another gravesite and slowed down. "Let's find Little Gracie Watson."

"Okay," Chase said, catching up. They followed the arrows until they were standing in front of a statue of a little girl. "Wow, she was only six! I wonder what happened to her."

Liam walked over to a sign that was posted nearby. "She died of pneumonia, and her spirit is one of the more active ones in the cemetery." He shook his head. "Do you believe this stuff?"

Chase laughed. "I don't know, but sometimes I feel as if the spirit of a loved one might be nearby . . . like my grandfather."

"I like that idea much better than a spirit haunting a house . . . *or* a cemetery."

"There's a house near our farm that everyone thinks is haunted. The old recluse who lived there died in his rocking chair and it was days before people realized he was dead."

"No way," Liam said, following him out through the entrance.

"Yeah, the story goes that his neighbors heard horrific sounds one night over at his place, but the next day he was sitting in his rocking chair so they all assumed he was fine, but three days later, he was still sitting there, rocking back and forth, and finally the sheriff went up on the porch to check on him and he was stone-cold dead."

"That's creepy," Liam said.

Chase agreed. "It *is* creepy. My brothers used to dare each other to go knock on the front door, but Gage would never go. Me, on the other hand—I'd stand on the porch and recite poetry."

"You're such a rebel."

"I know," Chase said, laughing.

They ran along in silence, each lost in his own thoughts, but when they turned into Forsyth Park, Chase noticed an older gentleman sitting on a bench with a little white dog next to him. "Hey! There're Matthias and Marmalade!" He slowed to a walk and stopped in front of them. "Hey there, Marmalade," he said, kneeling in front of her. The little dog stood up, sniffed his outstretched hand, and began wiggling her whole hind end.

"Well, look who it is, Marmy-girl," Matthias said, smiling.

"Our old friend, Chase." He pulled himself up, swaying a little, and extended his hand. "How are you, young man?"

"I'm fine, fine," Chase replied, shaking his hand. He gestured to Liam. "This is my partner, Liam."

Matthias turned to Liam. "Pleasure to meet you, Liam," he said, shaking his hand. "Any friend of Chase is a friend of ours, right, Marm?"

The little dog wiggled over to Liam as he leaned down to scratch her ears. "Hello, there, Marmalade," he said softly.

He stood up and listened while Chase and Matthias chatted. "You managing okay?" Chase asked, eyeing the paper bag on the bench, and what looked like a soggy sandwich in a newspaper next to it.

"Oh, sure, sure," Matthias answered, swaying slightly. "We doin' jus' fine, aren't we, Marm?"

Chase nodded, searching the old man's glassy eyes and finding it hard not to notice his trembling hands. Finally, feeling genuine concern, he threw caution to the wind and asked him outright, "Do you and Marm have enough to eat? Because you can come to our office—we have an apartment upstairs and a shower . . . or I can bring you some food . . . or a hot cup of coffee . . ."

"No, no, we're fine," Matthias assured, waving him off. "We doin' good, aren't we, girl?" he said, looking down, and Marmalade wagged her tail and sat down resolutely at his feet.

Chase frowned uncertainly, obviously not convinced. He wanted to help—he wanted Matthias to come back to the office with them so he could give him a plate of nourishing food and Marmalade food that was suitable for a dog . . . along with a big fresh bowl of water! He wanted to give Matthias the opportunity to take a hot shower if he wanted, and to sleep in a safe, clean place. But how do you help someone who doesn't want help? Who is too proud to accept help?

"Well, we best keep movin'," the old man said abruptly. "The officers don't like it if we stay in one place too long." He reached down to pick up his paper bag and he almost fell over.

"Are you sure you won't come with us?" Chase pressed.

"I'm sure," he said, and then he smiled. "Thank you, though. Your offer is very kind." He eyed Liam. "Nice to meet you, sir," he said, shakily reaching up to tip his cap. "C'mon, Marmy-girl," he said, untying the tattered rope from the end of the bench.

Chase and Liam both knelt down to pet Marmalade one more time, and in return, she leaned up and licked their cheeks. "Nice," Chase said, smiling. "Thank you for the kiss!"

"We'll see you soon," Matthias said, and then he turned and shuffled away with his little dog beside him.

Chase and Liam watched them go. "Dang! I wish he'd let us help him."

"Yeah," Liam agreed, rubbing his eyes and starting to walk back to the office. "We better get back—it's getting . . ." But before he could finish his sentence, he sneezed, and then he sneezed again. "What the heck?" he said between sneezes as his eyes started to water.

Chase caught up to him and looked over. "What the heck is right! I'm beginning to think we're never gonna be able to have a dog."

〜

27

It was Thursday before Ames and Quinn had a chance to drive down the Pacific Coast Highway to Monterey. "Oh, my goodness! It's beautiful!" Ames said as they hiked along the cliffs of Big Sur.

"I hope you wore your bathing suit," Quinn said, as they took a winding path to the beach, "because you can't go home without going for a swim in the Pacific."

"Payton said the same thing, and I *did* wear it," Ames said, "but I doubt I'll go in past my knees." They walked along the sandy beach, carrying their sandals and getting their feet wet. "I can't believe how quickly this week has flown by," Ames mused out loud.

"Well, we've been busy!" Quinn said. "We went to Yosemite, hiked up to the falls, had lunch at the Majestic."

"Yes, that was amazing!" Ames agreed. "I've seen pictures of the sequoias and the mountains, but pictures don't do them justice. It's sad to think some people live their whole lives and never get to see such grandeur in person. The next time I come out, I'm bringing Payton."

"That would be fun," Quinn said, smiling.

"I also love your café—it's so quaint and so . . . *you*!" Ames said, looking over. "I hope you know how proud I am of you, Quinn."

"Thanks, Mom," Quinn said, putting her arm around her.

"I'm proud of you, too, just for getting up the courage to leave Ned and come out here."

"I guess he's surviving—Cash sends me pictures all the time. He's been taking him to the coffee shop during the day, and Ned's been sleeping beside him at night. He doesn't seem to miss me as much as I thought he would."

"I'm sure he misses you. He'll run circles around you when you get home."

"Maybe," Ames said, laughing.

Quinn picked up a smooth stone and skipped it across the water.

"Your dad taught you to do that," Ames said.

"He did," Quinn agreed. "And he taught me how to fish, too—I remember."

"Do you miss him?"

Quinn took a deep breath and let it out slowly. "We should probably head back if we want to get some shopping in before dinner."

Ames frowned and searched her daughter's face. "I didn't mean to upset you, hon."

"You didn't upset me, Mom. I just don't think about Dad that much. I do miss the little things we did together, like skipping stones and fishing, but I don't miss the way he treated you." She pressed her lips together into a solemn line. "He was very dismissive and condescending, and he put pressure on you to stop doing the things you enjoyed, like softball and traveling. I think it was unfair . . . and unkind."

"Well, one good thing came out of our marriage," Ames said, gently placing her hand on her daughter's cheek, "and that was *you*! If I hadn't married your father, there would be no you, so it was meant to be."

Quinn laughed. "Well, the way he treated you for forty years—which is almost your whole life—is a high price to pay."

"There is no price too high for having you in my life."

"Thanks, Mom," Quinn said, wrapping her in a hug.

They walked back to the car, brushed off their feet, and headed into town for some shopping. Ames wanted to buy gifts for Payton and Cash, and in one of the first shops they came to she found a lovely silver necklace for Payton and a T-shirt for Cash that had the symbol for pi on it that looked like his favorite pepperoni pizza. Afterward, they found a quaint seafood restaurant and sat on the deck, overlooking the ocean. They dined on crunchy coconut shrimp, fire-roasted Baja salmon, and watching the sun set, and the whole time, Ames reveled in the company of the lovely young woman her daughter had become.

After seeming to dredge up unhappy memories by mentioning Frank, Ames tried to keep the conversation light, but finally, unable to suppress the mom-curious question any longer, she took a sip of her chilled sauvignon blanc and asked, "Soo . . . are there any new loves in your life that you've forgotten to mention?"

Quinn took a sip of wine, too, and grinned. "Wow, Mom, I'm impressed. You managed to hold off on asking that question a lot longer than I expected."

"I'm trying *not* to pry," Ames said, laughing.

"Well . . ." Quinn began, looking out at the ocean, "there's not really anyone worth mentioning, just a date now and then, but nothing serious." She looked back at her mom. "I guess I never really got over my high school crush."

Ames knew all too well who she meant. Quinn had been over the moon when Chase had asked her to their senior prom. They'd even gone out a few times, but then—before heading off to college—Chase had gently told Quinn he "just wanted to be friends" and even though he insisted it had nothing to do with her, she'd been crushed, literally. Ames eyed her. "You know Chase is gay?"

Quinn practically spit out her wine and laughed. "Why don't you just come right out and say it?" she teased.

"I'm sorry. Should I have said it another way?" Ames said,

sounding wounded. "I mean that has to be the reason he didn't fall in love with you."

"I'm sorry I laughed, Mom," Quinn said. "Your directness just caught me off guard, and yes, he told me that a long time ago. He said if he could've ever loved a girl, it would've been me, but that didn't make it any easier."

Ames nodded. "I thought he must've told you because somehow your dad knew. He was always eavesdropping, you know . . . and he was a talker, too. No secret was safe with him. He was the one who told me, and God knows who else he told."

Quinn frowned. "I didn't know Dad knew."

Ames nodded. "I know this won't help how you feel about your dad, but I've always suspected he was the one who told Jack."

"Oh," Quinn said softly, frowning. "Wow . . . I had no idea."

Ames took a bite of her salmon. "Do you ever hear from Chase?"

"I haven't heard from him in several years but, just recently—after you told me about his dad and Dutch, I discovered he'd finally joined Facebook and sent him a friend request."

"Did he respond?"

"It took about a week, but he finally accepted." Quinn took a sip of her wine. "I also messaged him that I was sorry to hear about his dad, but I haven't heard back."

"Maybe he's been busy," Ames offered. "Libby said he was visiting recently."

Quinn nodded. "From his pictures, it looks like he met someone. They've done a lot of traveling."

Ames sipped her wine and tried to remember if she'd told her daughter that Chase owned a travel agency. "I told you he owns—"

"Yes," Quinn said, smiling. "It's funny he and I both ended up owning our own businesses."

"It is funny," Ames agreed. "You two would've been a good match."

"Well, I guess God had other plans," Quinn said.

Ames searched her daughter's eyes. "I've been prayin', hon, and I'm sure he has someone good in mind for you. You just haven't met him yet. The Lord works in mysterious ways—you just have to keep the faith."

"I'm tryin', Mom," Quinn said, reaching for the dessert menu. "So . . . did you save room?"

"Of course!" Ames laughed. "I always save room for dessert!"

Payton pressed her lips together in a stubborn line. "Cash, I said I'd think about it."

He shook his head and rolled his eyes again. "Bye," he said, closing the door.

"Have a good night," Payton called. "Love you!"

"Mm-hmm," he grumbled.

Payton watched him walk up the driveway, call Ned, unlock the door, and go inside. She was accustomed to him not responding in kind when he was upset—it had been his modus operandi since he was little—his way of showing her he wasn't happy. She knew he loved her, and she knew he missed his father . . . and she knew he would be devastated if anything happened to her. He would regret the times he hadn't responded that he loved her, too. He'd feel guilty and might never forgive himself. She knew her sweet son—she knew what made him tick . . . and what triggered him, but she loved him with all her heart and she just wanted him to be safe and protected. From the day she first held Cash in her arms, she'd loved him with the fierceness and ferocity of a mother bear, and when he'd started school, and his classmates had started making fun of him for being different—for being socially awkward, for being a math nerd who never thought about his appearance—it had broken her heart. Many times, she'd picked him up from school and he'd had tears trickling down his sweet face, fogging up his glasses, and she'd wanted to protect him from those kids who were so thoughtless and unkind . . . and she still wanted to protect him. The only kids who had been kind to Cash, besides Rylee and Jessie, were Quinn and Chase. They'd always included him. Chase, especially, with his gentle ways and kind blue eyes, had always picked Cash first if he was the captain of the kickball team. It hadn't mattered to Chase if he missed out on picking the most athletic kid. What had mattered to him was the feelings of the boy who stood shyly to the side, expecting to be picked last. Chase had given Cash confidence and made him smile, and whenever Chase had come home for a visit after high school, Cash had just about knocked him over with a hug. "Hey, bro," Chase would say, laughing and hugging him back. "How're you doin'?"

"I'm fine, bro," Cash would reply, beaming and using the same moniker.

The memory of those moments, and Chase's genuine kindness toward Cash always brought tears to her eyes. Cash had other friends—Rylee and Jessie of course, but his bond with Chase elevated him. Being Chase's *bro* made him feel valued and proud, and more than anything, Payton wanted her son to have those feelings all on his own. Would getting his license and having his own car give him that same self-confidence and self-worth? He'd been taking such good care of Ned all week, walking and feeding him, keeping the house neat, bringing in the mail, watering the plants, weeding the garden, and being outside every morning when she came to pick him up. She was proud of him—he'd proven he could be responsible when given the opportunity . . . so why was she still holding him back?

She looked up at the house. It was getting dark, and he'd turned the lights on inside so she could see him tugging on a toy with Ned, and it made her smile—*I should probably let him get a dog, too*, she thought, but then she shook her head. *One thing at a time!*

She put the truck in gear and slowly pulled away. The ladies would be arriving at the shop any minute, and even though Ames wouldn't be there, Payton was looking forward to having a glass of wine and relaxing *and* having some adult company. It had been a long week—she'd been right about Dr. Hamlin wanting her to come in so he could tell her the biopsy had come back positive, and then he'd tried to sound upbeat: *If you're going to get cancer, thyroid cancer is a good one to get.* And even though she'd fully expected the bad news, she'd still been in a state of shock as she waited for Julie to schedule an appointment two days later with a surgeon. And now her surgery was scheduled. She just had to go get bloodwork . . . and ask Ames if she could drop her off and pick her up. She was sure her friend would, but she hadn't told her yet—she didn't want to upset her when she was on vacation, so she was waiting for her to get home.

Payton parked the truck behind the shop and hurried inside to get ready. She pulled out the tablecloths and was just about to get out the glasses and plates, when the chimes on the front door jingled. "Libby!" she said in surprise.

"Hi, Payton," Libby said cheerily. "I knew Ames wouldn't be here this week, so I thought I'd come over early and help you set up." She held up a plate. "I also made some deviled eggs. My hens are laying like crazy and I have too many eggs."

"Nice!" Payton said, giving her friend a hug and peeking under the foil at the eggs. "You make the best deviled eggs."

Libby laughed. "It's the curry . . . *and* a little mustard."

Payton nodded. "I knew it was something different, but I never knew what."

"What can I do to help?"

Payton looked around. "Want to help me put these tables together and then we'll spread out this tablecloth?"

"Sure," Libby said, setting the eggs on the counter.

"I'm so glad you came early. I was thinking about Chase earlier and how good he always was with Cash when they were growing up."

Libby nodded. "Oh, Chase loves Cash. He always talked about him when they were kids. He was amazed at how good he was at math—always figuring out hard problems in his head with such little effort. He thought he was funny, too, with the little jokes he told."

"Well, Cash thought Chase walked on water," Payton said. She looked up and searched Libby's face. "You have no idea how much it meant to me when he took Cash under his wing."

Libby smiled. "Chase was always that way. Even when he was little, he had a kind old soul. He loves to help people . . . and animals. That boy had more critters following him around . . ."

"He has a good heart, Libby." She looked up. "How is he doing?"

"He's fine. He was just visiting a couple of weeks ago—it was so good to see him."

Payton nodded. "Has he met anyone?"

"Hmm?" Libby said, looking up as if she hadn't heard the question.

"Has Chase met anyone?" Payton asked again.

Libby started to shake her head, but Payton searched her eyes. "You know, we've been friends our whole lives, Libby, and we've shared so many of our troubles and triumphs over the years. Nothing will ever change that."

"I know," Libby said, smiling. Then she bit her lip and nodded. "Chase has met someone. Actually, he's engaged."

"Wow!" Payton said. "Congratulations!"

"Thank you," Libby said. "I'm still getting used to it, though. Sometimes it's hard to understand how a boy is attracted to—and falls in love with—another boy, but I imagine they have a hard time understanding us, too, and yet they don't make a big deal about it. I'm so glad he's met someone, and we all love Liam."

Payton nodded. "It's funny you should say that because I've been thinking a lot about that, too . . . about how and why people fall in love. Sometimes people meet their soul mate right away and never have any doubts—those are the lucky ones! But oftentimes, I think too many times, people fall in love with the wrong person— someone who is already committed, or who doesn't love them back; and then there are those who think they're in love when they really aren't . . . or who settle for someone because they worry that they might never meet anyone else." She paused and smiled. "And then there're the people who marry someone to please others . . . or because it's socially acceptable . . . but those people aren't really being true to themselves . . . and I don't think they're ever truly happy."

Libby nodded. "More than anything else in the world, I want him to be happy."

"That's what all we moms want for our kids," Payton said.

"The prayer we pray most fervently is that our kids are happy and healthy and safe."

"So true." Libby said, taking her friend's hand. "I'm glad I came early."

"I am, too," Payton said, hugging her. "The only thing we can do for our kids, besides pray, is to simply love them for who they are. Nothing else matters."

Libby nodded.

"Okay, enough chitchat!" Payton said. "The ladies will be here any minute!"

And, as if on cue, the chimes on the front door jingled again.

〜

29

AMES TOOK A SIP OF HER WINE AND LEANED HER HEAD AGAINST THE WINDOW TO look out at the fields below—from thirty-five thousand feet the country looked like a colorful patchwork quilt, and the towering clouds—oh, my—was this God's view all the time?! She couldn't help but be amazed by the beauty, especially since she was looking at it through the eyes of someone who'd had a glass of wine! The pilot—who wasn't the cute young fellow who'd delivered her safely *to* California, but an old codger who looked like he was just hours away from retirement—announced that they were approaching Knoxville and would soon begin their descent, and Ames buckled her seat belt, feeling much more relaxed than she had on the way out. She was a pro at air travel now, and as she watched the ground grow closer, she wondered if Payton was waiting.

The wheels hit the ground with barely a bump and the reverse thrust thundered outside her window, but a moment later, they were pulling up to the gate. Ames switched off airplane mode on her phone, texted Payton that she'd arrived, pulled her carry-on from the storage area, and made her way out, nodding and thanking the pilot and flight attendants.

As she walked down the main corridor, towing her bag, her

phone hummed and she stopped to read the reply from Payton: We are all the way to the right when you come out of the terminal.

Ames stepped out into the bright Tennessee sunshine, looked to her right, and saw Cash standing near the truck on the sidewalk with Ned. "Oh, Ned!" she cried, and the big Lab stood up, wagging his whole hind end.

"There she is," Cash said. "There's your mom—I told you she was coming home."

Ames hurried toward them, and when she was close enough, Cash let go of Ned's leash and he bounded to her, almost knocking her over.

Ames knelt down, laughing as he slobbered her cheeks with kisses and wiggled his entire body. "Hey, ole pal," she whispered. "I missed you so much! Did you miss me?"

Ned wiggled his response as Cash reached down to pick up his leash again. "He missed you, but he was fine. We had no problems, right, boy?"

Ned wiggled around Cash and back to Ames, loving them both, and Ames stood and smiled at Cash. "Thank you for taking such good care of him, Cash, and thank you for sending all the pictures. It made it so much easier for me to be away, knowing he was in good hands."

Cash looked down. "No problem. We had fun. I'd be happy to do it anytime you want to visit Quinn."

Ames put her arm around him as they walked toward the truck. "Thank you. I will definitely take you up on that. Quinn says hello, by the way. She asked me how you're doing, and I told her what a big help you are at the coffee shop."

Cash nodded shyly. "Hello back. How is she?"

"She's fine," Ames said, stopping to pull out her phone and show him a picture she'd taken.

Cash studied the picture and smiled. "She's still pretty. The prettiest girl I ever knew."

Ames smiled and nodded. "She is. She's going to try to come for a visit this summer."

"Well, tell her she better come see me."

Just as they reached the truck, Payton climbed out. "You two having a private conversation over there?" she teased, giving her friend a hug.

Ames laughed. "No, I was just thanking Cash for taking good care of Ned."

Payton nodded as she lifted Ames's carry-on into the back of the truck. "We have to get moving. Security doesn't let you stay in this lane very long—they keep making people move. We had to go around three times and I don't want to be here when they come by again."

Cash started to climb into the narrow back seat of the truck with Ned, but Ames stopped him. "You want me to sit back there?"

He shook his head. "We're fine."

"If you insist," Ames said, climbing in. She looked over at Payton. "And how are you, ole girl?"

"I'm hangin' in there," Payton said, making a funny face at her friend that told her there was more to the story, and Ames nodded in understanding. "So! How was your trip?" Payton asked, changing the subject.

"It was really nice! We had such a good time, and it was wonderful to see Quinn."

"Did you get to eat at her restaurant?"

"Twice! The first night and the last night, we had dinner at a table overlooking the Golden Gate Bridge—what a view! She was so lucky to find that location—she said it was just a run-down little shack on a cliff when she bought it, but she had a vision, saw its potential and worked hard to make it happen."

"That's how you do it," Payton said.

"I have a vision," Cash said softly, looking out the window.

Payton looked in her rearview mirror at her son. "You *do*?"

"Mm-hmm."

"What is it?" Ames asked, turning around.

"I'd like to have my own pet-sitting service."

Payton looked over at Ames with raised eyebrows. "And who would help me in the shop?"

"You could hire someone else . . . *or* sell it and retire."

"Retire?" Payton exclaimed, almost driving off the road.

"Why not?" Cash said with a shrug. "You always talk about how tired you are. Mrs. Finley is the same age as you and she's retired. You could travel together."

Ames looked over at Payton and smiled. "He's right, you know. You *could* retire. If you sold the shop, you could have Cash invest the money and live off the dividends. You don't have a mortgage." She looked back at Cash. "And I would write a wonderful review for your pet-sitting business."

Payton frowned. "But I love the Coffee Bean. I've put so much into it—I did it for both of us, Cash, so you'd have a place to work." She looked in the mirror again.

"What if I don't want to work at a coffee shop all my life?" Cash said, looking directly into the mirror, searching her eyes.

Payton shook her head. This was so outside the box she didn't even want to continue the conversation. "We can talk about this another time," she said abruptly, hoping her son would forget about it. Cash looked out the window and didn't say anything more, and a tense silence filled the cab. Suddenly feeling very hot, Payton rolled down her window, and as soon as she did, Ned leaned over her shoulder and stuck his head out, his jowls and ears flapping.

Ames looked back and saw Cash gently stroking Ned's fur with a sad smile on his face. "I brought you all some presents," she said cheerily, trying to break the tense mood. She reached into her bag and pulled out a little clear bag of homemade dog treats in an assortment of shapes—hearts, bones, and fire hydrants. "They're peanut butter flavored," she said, giving one to Ned—who slobbered it down and immediately looked for more. She gave him another one and said, "That's it for now." She reached back into her bag and pulled out the T-shirt she'd found for Cash, which she'd wrapped in tissue paper.

He pulled off the paper, shook open the shirt, and laughed. "This is perfect! Thank you."

"What is it?" Payton asked, looking in the mirror, and he held it up to show her. "Cute," she said, nodding.

"Fits!" he said, pulling it on.

"Good!" Ames said. "I'm glad you like it, and I also have money for you."

"You don't have to pay me."

"What?! Yes, I do. You can't pet-sit for free."

Cash stroked Ned's ears, but didn't say anything, and Ames reached back into her bag and pulled out a small box with a bow on it. "And this is for you, but you'll have to wait till we get home."

Payton looked over, nodded, and smiled. "Missed you."

"Missed you, too," Ames said, squeezing her hand. "So what are you two having for dinner tonight?"

"Well, since we didn't have pizza on Friday, we thought we might have it tonight."

"May I join you?"

"Of course, silly," Payton said. "We were planning on it."

⸈⸉

30

"You're going to love it," Chase said as he walked the two young women toward the door. "Liam and I were in Rio de Janeiro a couple of years ago and the people were so welcoming and friendly. Plus, your hotel is right on the beach, and your room looks over the water. I wish we were going back!"

Liam, who was sitting at his desk, looked up. "Make sure you go to Rua Farme de Amoedo—that is *the* hot spot for the LGBTQ community. There are lots of chic boutiques and eateries." Chase nodded in agreement as Liam went on. "*And* bars! Make sure you go to the Explorer Bar—that was our favorite, right?" he said, looking to Chase for confirmation.

"Yep, there and the Clássico Beach Club–Urca–the view is to *die* for . . . and they have the best beef pastels."

Liam nodded in agreement. "You're gonna have such a good time!"

The women laughed. "We can't thank you enough. This is the best travel agency—we're going to tell all our friends about you."

"Awesome!" Chase said. "Thank you!"

"Yes," said the second woman, and then she looked at her partner. "We should post a review—that would help spread the word."

"Absolutely," said the first. "We will! We're so glad you moved to Savannah."

"We are, too," Chase replied. "We're growing very fond of low country charm and the pace of life." He opened the door for them. "Let us know how you like it."

They nodded. "We will."

"Have fun!" Liam called.

"Thanks!" they called back.

Chase closed the door. "They were nice. I love clients like that."

Liam nodded and looked up. "Sooo . . . I was looking at flights and they're not too bad right now."

Chase leaned back in his chair. "How soon are you thinking?"

"I was looking at next weekend."

Chase nodded. "If you want."

"You don't sound very enthusiastic."

"Well, you keep telling me they aren't going to embrace the news."

"You don't *have* to go."

"I'm going. Your parents seemed very nice when we went out to visit them back in college."

"That's because they thought you were my roommate."

"I *was* your roommate," Chase teased. "And I still am."

Liam rolled his eyes. "I hadn't told them yet, and after I did tell them, my father said he never wanted to talk about it again."

"Great," Chase said, raising his eyebrows.

"I know, but I have to give them a chance—they're my parents . . . and I love them."

Chase nodded. "I know you do, and that's why I'm going. We'll get through it together." He rubbed his stomach. "In the meantime, I'm hungry! What are we gonna have for lunch?"

Liam looked up from his laptop. "I want to book our flights first."

"Whenever you want to go, I'll be there, so book 'em, Dan-O."

Liam rolled his eyes. "Okay, it's an early flight."

"How early?" Chase said, looking up from the menu he was perusing on his laptop.

"Six."

"Ouch . . . but okay." He tapped his pen. "Nonstop?"

"One stop. Charlotte."

"Dang! I hate layovers. I thought you were a travel agent . . ."

Liam made a face at him. "We can do nonstop but it's gonna cost more."

Chase sighed, but managed to refrain from saying *whatever.* Liam hated the word and Chase didn't want him to think he was feeling put-upon. "So we're flying out early Saturday and back Monday?"

"Actually, I was looking at the Sunday night red-eye."

Chase tapped his pen again and nodded. Yep, he would definitely be useless on Monday.

"Is that okay?"

"Whatever you think," he said. "Meanwhile, *I* think we should get lunch from Goose Feathers—I've a hankerin' for that Havarti, cucumber, tomato, and avocado topped with sprouts deal they make. You want one?"

"What kind of bread did that come on?"

Chase scrolled to look. "Rye, but I bet you could get it on anything you want."

Liam clicked to the menu. "I think I'll just get the veggie panini."

"Hmm," Chase mused, looking at it. "That looks good, too, but I 'ma stickin' with The Telfair. You want a latte?"

"Sure, I can always use some caffeine."

Chase nodded, called in the order, and stood, tapping his back pocket for his wallet. "Okay, I'll be right back."

Liam looked up. "Hey . . ."

Chase looked back questioningly.

"No giving away my sandwich."

Chase laughed. "No promises there—if I see a hungry person, all bets are off."

He pushed open the door and stepped out into the steamy summer air. "Whatever happened to spring?" he mused, shaking his head. "It's downright hot out here." He walked along, looking into the windows of shops, and smiling at passersby. He'd just turned the corner onto Barnard Street and was about to cut through an alley when he heard someone call his name.

"What you doin' in our alley?"

He looked over and saw Matthias sitting in a doorway with Marmalade sitting on his foot.

"Hey," Chase replied, smiling. "I didn't know this was your alley."

"It's nice 'n cool back here, an' Mr. Policeman don't shoo us away."

Chase nodded. "How are you doing?"

"We fine. Jus' tryin' to keep cool in this heat. It sure got hot quick."

"It did," Chase agreed. He walked past a dumpster that smelled like rotting food and knelt in front of Marmalade. "How are you, little girl?" he asked as she wiggled around him, panting. He looked up at Matthias. "Do you guys have enough water?"

Matthias motioned to a plastic Cool-Whip container, half full of water. "Yep, filled that with the rain comin' down the spout last night." He grinned. "We can also get water from the public restrooms if need be."

Chase raised his eyebrows. "If you need water—or anything at all, Matthias—a shower, a place to sleep, something to eat, you can come to our office—Pride Travel—it's right around the corner . . . and it's air-conditioned, too, if you just want to get out of the heat."

Matthias chuckled. "If this ole body got used to air-conditionin', it might ne'er leave."

"That's fine," Chase assured him. "But I especially mean it about the water—you and Marm need to stay hydrated."

Matthias nodded. "No worries, young man. We used to this life o' ours." He looked down at his dog. "Aren't we, girl?"

Marmalade whipped her tail in agreement, and Chase shook his head. "Listen, I'm goin' to pick up some sandwiches and coffee. Do you want anything?"

"No, no," Matthias said, waving him off. "We all set."

Chase nodded. "All right, but I mean it about comin' to the office if you need anything."

"Thank you, kind sir. We will keep that in mind."

Chase eyed him skeptically. "Promise?"

"Promise," Matthias assured him.

"All right," he said. He extended his hand. "Take care of yourself . . . and your little pal."

"We will. You do the same," Matthias said. "The good Lord gave each of us a measure of faith, and he has blessed you, my friend, with an abundance—I can see it in your eyes."

Chase smiled at his friend's prophetic statement. "Thanks, Matthias," he said, and then he felt an odd wave of unease wash over him and his smile faded.

The old man nodded. "You're welcome."

Five minutes later, Chase was standing in line, waiting for the extra sandwich and coffee he'd ordered, and while he waited, he bought four bottles of water and a bag of homemade dog treats from a display on the counter. With his adjusted order filled, he hurried back to the alley, but when he got there, Matthias and Marmalade were gone. He frowned, trying to decide what to do with the food. Finally, he pulled a cardboard box out of the dumpster, packed everything in it, tucked the flaps under each other, and left the box in the doorway, hoping Matthias would find it.

❧

31

"CROWN ME, GRAN," ELLIE SAID, POINTING TO THE RED CHECKER SHE'D JUST jumped over two of Libby's black pieces—a move that had also landed her on the far side of the board.

"Hmm?" Libby said distractedly. "Oh, sorry, where'd you move?"

"I can't tell you," Ellie said, removing the two black pieces from play. "You have to pay attention."

Libby surveyed the board and realized that her little army was suddenly looking very depleted. "My goodness!" she exclaimed. "I guess I better start paying attention!"

Ellie stifled a giggle as she watched her grandmother study the board, realizing that every possible move was now a trap. "Which one ya gonna move, Gran? We haven't got all night, ya know," she teased, using the words her grandfather had always used when he was winning.

"Oh, dear," Libby said. "It doesn't look good, does it?"

Ellie laughed. "That's three in a row, Gran. Want to play again?"

Libby sighed and looked at the clock. "Isn't our show coming on?"

Ellie followed her grandmother's gaze and realized it was

almost seven o'clock and *The Great British Baking Show* would be starting. "Yes!" she exclaimed, picking up the board and sliding the checker pieces into the tattered cardboard box, the corners of which—after six boys—were barely being held together with yellow tape. She folded the board, laid it in, and carefully fit the top on.

"Tea?" Libby asked.

"Yes, please."

"What kind?"

Ellie put her finger to her chin. "How about chamomile?"

"Chamomile it is," Libby said, filling the kettle with fresh water.

"I'll go turn on the TV," Ellie said, disappearing into the living room.

Libby nodded, relieved to be relieved of the checker competition. She hadn't been able to focus because she'd been thinking about Payton, who'd quietly told the ladies at their last gathering that she was having surgery on Thursday, and unless someone wanted to host at their house . . . or unless Ames—who said she'd help Cash run the shop—wanted to keep it open, there wouldn't be a meeting. The group had agreed they wouldn't meet—because they couldn't meet without her! And then they'd immediately rallied around her, assuring her that all would be well, especially Callie—who'd had her thyroid out two years earlier and said it was easy-peasy, and they all assured Payton they would be keeping her in their prayers. Susan Metcalf—ever the organizer—had set up a meal train for anyone who wanted to make a dinner and deliver it to the house, and since everyone did, Payton and Cash could count on at least one full week of meals. Libby had signed up to make dinner on Saturday, and now, she was trying to decide between her favorite casserole—hot chicken salad—or a simple crustless quiche, the latter of which Payton might find easier to swallow.

Just then, the kettle started to whistle and she clicked off the burner, poured the steaming water over the tea bag, and set the timer for seven minutes.

"C'mon, Gran," Ellie called. "It's starting."

"Be right there," Libby called as she dunked the bag and thought about all the reassuring words the ladies had offered. She had wanted to say something positive, too, but the recent loss of her husband had kept her silent. Jack had died just six months after being diagnosed with cancer, and the news Payton shared had brought all the anxiety and grief she'd felt back to her. "I'll be praying hard," she whispered, hugging her friend as she left . . . and she'd been praying ever since.

The egg timer chimed, and she squeezed the teabag, poured two cups, put them on saucers, and carried them to the living room. "What did I miss?" she asked, setting them on the coffee table and sitting on the couch next to Ellie.

"Oh," Ellie said, moving closer. "Well . . . I think it's actually a repeat—it's the one where they're making pudding. Do you remember?"

"I'm not sure," Libby said, frowning. "Would you rather watch something else?"

"Oh, no, it's a good one. I don't mind watching it again."

Libby nodded and took a sip of her tea.

"Gran, did you know Sue Perkins is a lesbian?" Ellie asked, reaching for her tea.

"I did *not* know that," Libby managed to say after almost choking on her tea. "How do *you* know that?"

"I saw an interview on YouTube and she was talking about when she came out to her mom—it was pretty funny."

"Was it?" Libby said, setting her cup safely back on its saucer.

"Mm-hmm. She said she called her mom and said she was going to come over at four o'clock the next day, and her mom thought it was odd that she wanted to come over, and she kept asking her why she was coming over, and she said she told her mom they would discuss it the next day, but her mom continued to ask, and finally she said, 'Do you just want to tell me you're gay?' as if it wasn't a big deal."

Libby nodded, not knowing what to say.

"She's such a pip, isn't she?" Ellie said, laughing. "Her mom is just like you, Gran. I mean Uncle Chase is gay and it's not a big deal to you—he's your son and you just love him anyway. I mean, there's nothing you can do about it, right? That's how God made him, and you always say God doesn't make mistakes, right?"

"No, he doesn't make mistakes."

Ellie leaned against her to watch the show, and Libby's mind went back to the night Chase told her. It was the summer after his first year of college, and she'd gone into his room to say good night, and he'd stopped her and said there was something he wanted to tell her. She'd sat down on Grayson's bed across from him. She'd known a moment like this was coming—Frank Finley had overheard Chase talking to Quinn and, being the town gossip, he'd run right over to tell Jack the next morning. Neither she nor Jack had said anything to Chase—they hadn't known what *to* say. Looking back, now, she wished she'd reacted like Sue Perkins's mom had—as if it was no big deal, but she'd struggled a little more than that because she hadn't wanted Chase to ever be hurt . . . and then her son had asked the question she'd never forget: *Why did God make me this way?*

It was a question she'd often asked him herself afterward. Life was hard enough without having to worry about being teased, ridiculed, and not accepted. Sadly, there are still so many people in the world who aren't open and accepting, who don't care about a person's feelings . . . and who even physically target the lives of those who are different from them. Why couldn't people just live and let live? She never wanted her son to be hurt, physically or emotionally, but it had made her heart ache to think he would always have to carry this extra burden.

"I finished those books," Ellie said, pulling her back to the present.

"Which books?"

"That trilogy you gave me about Sam and Frightful—the peregrine falcon."

"Already?" Libby said in surprise.

"Yep. Now that school's out, I have plenty of time. Besides, they were really good. And you're not gonna believe this, but the other day, I saw a falcon flying over the trees behind our house. It was soaring up and diving down in the wind, barely moving its wings—it looked like it was having so much fun."

"I hope it wasn't looking for whip-poor-will babies."

"I don't think it was. It was up so high I don't think it was hunting. Plus, the whip-poor-will babies have already hatched and moved on."

"Already?!"

"Mm-hmm. I checked on them before school one morning, and when I got home that afternoon, there was no sign of them."

"That was quick!"

Ellie nodded. "Ten days." She sat on the edge of the couch and took a sip of her tea. "Did you know peregrine falcons can fly almost two hundred miles an hour when they're diving after prey?"

"No way!"

"Way," Ellie said.

"It's a wonder they don't crash!"

"They don't fly that fast all the way to the ground. They strike their prey in the air, and then either seize them with their talons or knock the wind out of 'em and finish 'em off on the ground."

"That's amazing," Libby said.

"Mmm," Ellie replied. "In the book, Sam has a weasel he named the Baron. You should read the books, too, Gran—you'd love 'em."

"I think I must've read them to at least one of the boys, but I really don't remember."

"I brought them back—they're in my bag."

Libby nodded, but she doubted she'd be able to get through

all three books as quickly as her granddaughter had—she could barely stay awake for the news.

"Oh, I forgot to tell you, Mom wants to go dress shopping for the wedding next week, and she wants to know if you'd like to go, too."

"Oh, I don't know," Libby said. "I haven't even thought about getting a new dress."

"You have to, Gran! You're the mother of the *grooms*."

"I guess you're right," Libby said, laughing. "It's been at least five years since we had a wedding, and I probably haven't bought a new dress since!"

"It's going to be so much fun," Ellie chirped. "I can't wait."

Libby nodded, suddenly realizing she was looking forward to it, too. "It's coming up soon."

"It is!" Ellie said, sitting up. "And we still have to make the candles for all the tables . . . *and* we have to make the strawberry shortcake."

"We have a lot to do," Libby said, smiling at the thought of being busy . . . and needed!

32

AMES PULLED INTO PAYTON'S DRIVEWAY AND WATCHED THE KITCHEN LIGHT blink out. A moment later, her friend emerged from the house and made her way down the walk. "Good morning," she said, climbing into Ames's car.

"Good morning," Ames replied, turning the radio station down a bit as she backed out.

"How are you?" Payton asked, holding her bag snugly against her.

"I'm fine," Ames said. "More importantly, how are *you*?"

"Able to sit up and take nourishment."

"I hope you didn't take any nourishment this morning," Ames said, eyeing her.

"If I did, could I get out of this?"

"You could, but you'd still have to make a new appointment." She looked over again. "You *didn't* eat or drink anything, did you?"

"Nooo, I *didn't* eat or drink anything," Payton replied, shaking her head.

"Good," Ames said, sounding relieved.

Neither of them spoke for several minutes, and the only cheeriness in the car came from the DJ promising the mist would burn off and it would be a gorgeous summer day in the low eighties. "Get your sunglasses out!" he said, and then George Strait's voice drifted through the darkness, singing "Amarillo by Morning." Payton looked out the window at the trees silhouetted in the darkness and listened, praying it wouldn't be the last time she heard one of her favorite songs.

"What's the matter?" Ames asked, looking over.

Payton shook her head, but didn't say anything, tears stinging her eyes as fear gripped her heart.

"Everything's gonna be okay," Ames said softly. "The surgeon said he's done this surgery thousands of times, he doesn't expect there to be any problems, and you'll be out by lunchtime."

"I know," Payton said, her voice choked with emotion. "It's just . . ."

"What?" Ames asked gently.

"If something *does* go wrong—say I have a bad reaction to the anesthesia or some other medicine—and God forbid, I don't wake up . . . what's going to happen to Cash?"

"Oh, my goodness! You are not gonna have a bad reaction . . ."

"How do you know? I've never even had anesthesia before."

"What?! You've never been knocked out before?"

Payton shook her head.

"What about when you had Cash?"

"All natural . . . *and* lots of pain. God was really trying to create that maternal bond!"

"Okay, what about when you had your colonoscopy?"

"Never had one."

"What?! You told me you did."

"I lied."

Ames rubbed her forehead. "Why would you lie about something like that?"

"So you'd stop bugging me."

"Well, *now*, not knowing how you're going to react to anesthesia is your punishment."

"I guess," Payton said glumly.

"Seriously, though," Ames said, "you are going to be fine. You are far too stubborn to die from a little anesthesia."

"But, if I do die . . . what will happen to Cash?"

"If something happens to you, I will look out for Cash."

"You promise?"

"Of course! He's like my second kid anyway."

"Well, thank you. I feel better."

"I'll let him get his license, though . . . *and* his own dog."

"Well, you'll be a better mom than me, so maybe he'd be better off."

"Could you stop with the self-pity? I'm just teasing."

"I know," Payton said with a sigh. "I've actually been thinking about letting him get his permit . . . if I survive this."

"I think it's a good idea," Ames said as she pulled into the hospital parking lot. "You want me to drop you off at the door?"

"No, no!" Payton said. "I can walk." And then she looked over. "Unless you weren't planning to come in."

"I'm coming in," Ames assured her as she pulled into a spot. "Is Rylee's mom picking Cash up so they can open the shop?"

"Yes, but you're gonna go over and check on them, right?"

"I am," Ames assured. "You need to stop worrying. The only thing you need to think about is relaxing and knowing that everything will be okay. God's got this!"

"Thanks, Amesy," Payton said, patting her hand. "I don't know what I'd do without you."

"I don't know what I'd do without you, either," Ames said.

They walked into the hospital and Payton checked in and dutifully held out her wrist so the nurse could attach her ID bracelet. Then they were directed to the fifth floor where nurses were already busy questioning, prepping, and taking the blood pressure of the other patients who were having surgery that day.

"You don't have to stay," Payton said, looking around. "I'll be fine."

"I'm staying till they take you," Ames said firmly.

Just then a young nurse approached. "Mrs. Childs?"

Payton nodded.

"C'mon back," she said cheerily.

Payton and Ames followed her to one of several small spaces separated by curtains and gave her a fabric hospital gown, paper slippers, and a paper cap. "You can leave your underpants on, but the rest goes in this bag," she directed, giving her a clear plastic bag. She reached up to close the curtain. "I'll be right back."

Payton rolled her eyes. "I hate hospitals."

Ames chuckled and shook her head. "I'll wait right outside."

"Okay," Payton said, unbuttoning her blouse.

Ames stepped outside the curtain. "Let me know when you're ready."

A moment later, Payton called, "I'm ready."

Ames stepped back in and eyed her friend's new outfit. "You look cute," she teased. "Especially with that hat—it looks like one of those old-fashioned shower caps."

"Thanks," Payton said. "I'm so glad I have you for moral support!"

"You're welcome," Ames said, grinning. "How 'bout I take your picture and post it on Facebook."

"Don't you dare!" Payton warned.

"Ha! You know I wouldn't."

The nurse returned with a soft heated blanket and had Payton snuggle under it on the propped-up bed. "Wow, I need a blanket warmer at home," she said.

The nurse laughed. "Don't we all?" And then she proceeded to ask Payton all the same questions she'd already answered, took her blood pressure again, noted it was a little on the high side (again), and jotted Ames's phone number on the chart so they could reach her.

A second nurse stood outside the curtain and announced they were ready to take her to surgery, and Payton mustered a smile and searched Ames's face. "Thank you for getting up early to bring me . . . *and* for staying."

"You're welcome, dear friend," Ames said, searching her eyes and reaching for her hand, which was ice cold. "Now, you just give all your worries to God," she said gently. "He's got this and he's got *you*!" She squeezed her hand, leaned down, and softly kissed her cheek.

Payton nodded. "Tell Cash I love him."

"I will," Ames assured her as the nurse started to wheel the bed away.

"I love *you*, too!" Payton said.

"I love you back," Ames said, smiling. She watched the nurse wheel the bed away, push the automatic door opener, and disappear down a hall, beyond which only patients and medical staff were permitted, and then Ames turned and walked toward the exit. When she got outside, the sun was just peeking over the horizon and the summer sky was streaked with coral and pink clouds, and through the mist she saw a brilliant double rainbow spanning the entire sky.

∽

33

LIBBY LEANED AGAINST THE FENCE IN THE WARM SUMMER SUNSHINE AND watched Matt try to get Buttercup, one of their young heifers, to bond with her new calf, but the new mom would have none of it. She mooed, stomped her hooves, and danced away from the strange little creature that had just emerged from her body, causing her so much pain.

"Why won't she let her nurse?" Ellie asked from her perch on top of the fence.

"It happens sometimes," Libby explained. "Buttercup's never been a mom before, so she doesn't know exactly what to do—sometimes cows have maternal sense and sometimes they don't. She might just be an ornery, high-maintenance cow—that happens sometimes, too."

Matt walked over. "I don't think she's gonna let him nurse. I put grain on his back to get her to clean him off, but as soon as the grain was gone, she wanted nothing to do with him."

"Do you want to try putting them in the same stall?"

Matt shook his head. "I'm afraid she'll hurt him with all her kicking. He's definitely hungry, though, poor guy."

Libby nodded. "Well, I can make a bottle and Ellie can give it to him."

"I thought of that," Matt said, "but I'm wondering if Rosie might let him nurse—she's always good with the new calves . . . and she's standing right over there, watching. She hears him bleating and she wants to help."

Libby followed her son's gaze. "I bet she would. She's such a gentle soul, and she always makes a good surrogate."

"I hate to take him away from Buttercup, though."

"Maybe she'll come around when she gets used to him . . . *and* when he isn't so eager."

"Maybe," Matt said. "I'll let her in, and see what happens." He unlatched the gate and the big chestnut-brown cow hurried over to the little bleating calf. Rosie immediately started to nuzzle and comfort him, and it didn't take long for him to discover that she had milk, too, and he latched right on and started sucking ferociously.

Ellie watched in wonder and smiled. "I guess he was hungry!"

"Rosie's such a sweet cow," Libby mused.

Ellie nodded and reached into her pocket for the little bag of apple slices her mom had cut for her that morning and walked over to Rosie. She scratched the big cow's nose and held out two slices, and Rosie's long black tongue slipped out and curled around them, pulled them in, and crunched noisily. Ellie looked into her chocolate-brown eyes. "You're a good mama," she whispered, and Rosie leaned forward, sniffed her ear and then her pocket. "You want more?" Ellie said, giggling. She pulled out two more slices and Rosie's tongue curled out again. "That's it," Ellie said, holding up her hands. "All gone."

She walked around to the calf and scratched his belly, but he was so busy pulling on Rosie's teats, he barely noticed. Finally, she walked over to Buttercup, who was standing by the fence, watching warily. "It's okay, Buttercup," she said, pulling the last apple slice out of her bag and giving it to her. "You'll get used to him."

Libby watched her granddaughter's gentle ways with all three cows, and it reminded her of Jack. Her husband had always spoken softly to their animals and had conversations with them, as if they were people, coaxing, encouraging, praising, and gently scolding. He'd been more patient with their animals than he'd been with people, *and* he would've readily admitted it. He tolerated all their odd eccentricities and quirks better than he did the personalities of the people with whom he came in contact. It was one of the traits that had made her laugh *and* fall in love with him. To watch a six-foot-four seventeen-year-old boy tenderly holding a baby chick or a new kitten in his strong, gentle hands . . . or be reduced to tears when he was digging a grave for one of his beloved hunting dogs had melted her heart.

She smiled wistfully now, knowing from whom her sons, and now, granddaughter, had inherited their gentle ways. Oh, how she missed Jack, Dutch . . . *and* Cale. Why had God visited her life with so much tragedy and sorrow? What was he trying to teach her? Why couldn't they all be alive today? Weren't there lessons they could've learned together, working side by side? It made her heart ache, but it would be wrong to *not* remember, to not think about them. She would never push away all the wonderful memories she had just because their absence was so painful. She recalled one of her favorite pictures—taken in this very spot. Dutch and Jack were sitting on their John Deere tractors in the summer sunshine, and Cale—who was probably around two years old at the time, was sitting proudly on his pedal tractor in front of them. Her three beloved men.

Matt walked over to where she was standing. "Guess we can always count on Rosie," he said, taking off his tattered John Deere cap and running his hand through his hair.

"She always was one of your dad's favorites."

Matt nodded and smiled. "Well, that little guy's gonna need a name."

Ellie climbed up on the fence between them. "How 'bout Never Late for Dinner?" she suggested.

"That's a bit long," Matt said.

"We haven't had a male calf in a while," Libby mused.

"I know!" Ellie said. "How about Tucker?!"

"Tucker's cute," Libby said.

Matt nodded. "Maybe you should show him at the fair this summer."

"Oooh! Can I?" Ellie asked excitedly.

"I don't see why not," Libby said. "We haven't taken a calf to the fair in years, but when you boys were younger, you each took one every year—the cattle trailer would be full, and we'd have to take two pickup trucks full of hay bales, grain, and supplies." She smiled at the memory. "The Tennyson boys and their big bovines used to take up half the livestock barn. It would be fun to show again."

Matt watched his mom's eyes light up almost as much as his daughter's and realized how much she would enjoy watching Ellie show the little calf. "You'll have to get him ready, El."

"I will!" Ellie said, grinning, and then she eyed her grandmother. "Gran, want to teach me how to make strawberry jam today? Maybe we could enter it at the fair, too."

Libby looked over. "We could do that," she said, "but you're going to have to go pick an awful lot of strawberries."

"Woo-hoo!" Ellie shouted, hopping off the fence and running to get a pail, and Libby smiled at the prospect of having several occasions to look forward to. It filled her heart with hope.

34

AMES PULLED INTO HER DRIVEWAY AND WALKED QUIETLY OVER TO PEEK IN HER bedroom window. Ned was sprawled across the sheets, snoring like a freight train, but when she made a *psst* sound, he sat bolt upright, looked around, and started to thump his tail. "You're *so* silly," she said softly, and he hopped off the bed and hurried to the kitchen to greet her.

"Hullo, ole pal," she said, pushing open the door and setting her cup from the Coffee Bean on the counter. She lifted the top off the treat jar, gave him one, scratched his soft ears, reached for her reading glasses, and tapped the screen of her phone to see if anyone—namely, Payton—had texted. She'd stopped to see her the previous afternoon after she'd been moved to a room, but she'd been sound asleep, and although she'd been awake when she and Cash went back in the evening, her throat had been sore, and she'd only nodded or shaken her head to answer their questions. Now, Ames wondered when—and *if*—she would be discharged. She knew getting released from a hospital was often a time-consuming process that included paperwork and a lot of waiting, but she wanted to be ready at a moment's notice.

She took a sip of coffee, which was, surprisingly, still hot. She'd gotten up early that morning to drive Cash into town to open the shop, and then she'd stayed long enough to make sure he was set for the day. By the time she left, Rylee and Jessie were there, too, and the coffee machines had finished brewing, so she'd filled a cup with the flavor of the day—Jamaican Me Crazy—and teasingly told him to put it on her tab. She made him promise to call her if he needed anything, and then she'd headed home to take Ned for their morning constitutional.

"You ready?" she asked, and he hurried off to get his leash. "Good boy," she said when he returned, "but we don't need that today." She tied it around her waist, took another sip of coffee, and headed out through the garage and back into the early morning sunlight. "Looks like it's gonna be a nice day!"

They walked along the road, Ned running ahead, sniffing happily, and as they neared Finley Farm, she saw several cars—including Sarah Whitman's old Subaru—and decided to stop and see how her garden was coming. Ned ran ahead, making a beeline for Sarah, who had her little boy with her, and who—when he saw Ned barreling toward him, stood up and put his hands out. "Whoa, Neddy!" he said, laughing and trying to fend off Ned's exuberant greeting, which included a complete face wash.

"Hi, Daniel! How are you?" Ames asked.

"I'm good," the little boy said. "I'm helping Mom weed."

"I see that," Ames said. "She's lucky to have such a good helper."

"Mm-hmm," Daniel said, turning his attention back to the weeds as Ned wiggled over to Sarah.

"I *am* lucky to have such a good helper," Sarah said, smiling. "How are you, Mrs. Finley? How was your trip?"

"Oh, you heard about that!" Ames said, chuckling.

"Yes, we saw Cash walking Ned every morning, and he told us you had gone to visit Quinn."

"I did, and we had a really nice time."

"Well, Cash took good care of Ned—he was walking him all the time. In fact, we were so impressed, we are thinking of asking him to take care of Samson—our old Corgi—when we go away for a few days this summer. The only problem is Samson is blind—he's fourteen—and he needs eye drops twice a day."

"I'm sure Cash would be able to take care of him and give him his drops—he's really good with animals," Ames said. "He's actually thinking of starting his own pet-sitting service."

"Oh, wow! That would be great! So many people in town are looking for someone to take care of their pets when they're away, or even when they are at work."

"I'll have to tell him you said that." Ames looked at the neatly planted rows and mounds of vegetables. "How's your garden?"

"Good!" Sarah said, pointing. "We have lots of lettuce . . . and we have zucchini, summer squash, cucumbers, carrots, beets . . ."

"And punkins!" Daniel piped.

"Nice!" Ames said. "Quinn used to love punkins!"

Sarah nodded. "How is she doing? I miss seeing her."

"She's fine—she owns her own restaurant now."

"I heard that. Good for her! All those years we worked together at the diner gave her plenty of experience and now, she's off doing amazing things, while I'm just a stay-at-home mom who never left my hometown."

"There's nothing wrong with that," Ames said, surprised that Sarah thought Quinn's life was more exciting than her own . . . when all Ames wished for Quinn was to have what Sarah had—a husband who loved her with all his heart *and* a family. "I never left home, either."

Sarah laughed. "Oh, don't get me wrong—I'm very thankful for my blessings. It's just, sometimes I wish I'd taken a little time to see the world before I settled down."

Ames nodded. "I know what you mean. My trip to visit Quinn was the first time I've ever flown, and my first time seeing the ocean!"

"Wow!" Sarah said. "Well, good for you for going."

"You're young, Sarah, and Jim is such a good guy. I'm sure you two and little Daniel will have a lot of fun adventures together. My Frank was kind of a stick-in-the-mud," she added, giving Sarah a rueful look. "He never wanted to go anywhere. I was lucky to get him to go to the diner once a month!"

Sarah said kindly, "Well, now you can go wherever you want!"

"That's what Quinn says."

Sarah smiled. "I can't remember the last time I saw her."

"Probably at Frank's funeral."

Sarah frowned, trying to remember. "How long ago was that?"

"Almost three years already."

"That's hard to believe," Sarah said. "I think I was pregnant with Daniel back then, but it seems like it was yesterday."

"It does seem like yesterday," Ames said, nodding. "Quinn and I talked about how long it's been, and she said she's going to try to come home this summer."

"Oh, well make sure she calls me—I'd love to see her."

"I definitely will," Ames said. "Well, I guess we better get goin' before it gets too hot to walk. C'mon, Ned."

Sarah nodded. "Good to see you, Mrs. Finley. I'll put some lettuce on your porch."

"That would be great—thank you! Take good care of those punkins, Daniel."

"I will," he said, waving a muddy hand. "Bye, Neddy!"

Ames followed Ned back out to the road and as they continued past the fields, she saw John's cows plodding toward the barn, and the scene reminded her of Frank. Could it really be almost three years since he died?! Back then, she'd been so shocked she didn't know how she was going to manage . . . but she *had* managed. In fact, she'd *more* than managed. She had persevered *and* thrived . . . *and* she was going to live the rest of her life the way she was meant to!

❧

35

"I'm perfectly capable of walking," Payton grumbled as her nurse helped her into the wheelchair for which she, Ames, and Libby had just waited nearly an hour.

"I know you can," the nurse said, smiling, "but it's hospital protocol—we just want to make sure you get safely to your car."

Payton looked at her. "I bet hospitals would save a lot of time if they let people walk out—I've proven I can walk—you've been making me walk up and down the hall all morning."

"I don't make the rules," the nurse said patiently as she wheeled her toward the door. "Have you got everything?"

"I guess so," Payton said, looking over at Ames and Libby, who glanced around the room.

"Do you want the socks with the grippy bottoms?" Libby asked, holding them up.

"No, no," Payton said, waving. "Those socks have absolutely no shape and they're too thick to fit into a shoe. I wonder how many of those dumb socks get thrown away every year. The hospital should at least come up with socks people want to keep!"

"They should," the nurse agreed as she wheeled her down the hall.

"I think a lot of waste goes on in hospitals—it's no wonder medical care is so expensive."

"You're right," the nurse agreed as she pushed the chair toward the exit. She turned to Ames and Libby. "Want to pull your car around?"

"Sure!" Ames said, and then hurried off to get her car.

"I really could walk," Payton repeated impatiently.

"Well, this is the last chance I get to take care of you so stay right here," the nurse said, still smiling patiently.

Payton looked up at her. "I'm sorry to be so grouchy. You will probably be glad to see me go."

"No, no," the nurse said, laughing. "I assure you, I've had much bigger grouches than you."

"Well, thank you for taking good care of me," Payton said, squeezing her hand and eyeing her name tag. "You're a good nurse, Morgan."

"Thank you," Morgan replied, and then she and Libby helped her get into Ames's car. Payton smiled and waved as Morgan pulled the wheelchair away, and Morgan waved back.

"Want to stop for a milkshake?" Libby asked. "My treat."

Payton nodded. "A milkshake would feel good going down," she said, her voice still sounding a little hoarse.

"You sound like Lauren Bacall," Ames teased.

"Ha!" Payton said, lightly touching her bandage.

"How do you feel?" Libby asked.

"I don't think the pain meds have worn off. We'll see how I feel tonight."

They were all quiet as they drove because Libby and Ames didn't want Payton to talk, but twenty minutes later, when they were sitting at a picnic table at Tennyson's Dairy Bar, slurping milkshakes, Payton said, "It's nice to be out in the sunshine and to be *alive*. I'm so thankful it's over . . . and I survived."

"You did survive," Ames said. "I told you that you would."

"I know you did, but I still worried."

"I know you did," Ames said.

"How did the doctor say it went?" Libby asked.

"Well, he took out my whole thyroid and said it was so shriveled up he was surprised it worked at all, but they're gonna biopsy it, along with some lymph nodes, and I still have all my parathyroids—which is a good thing because they control your calcium absorption . . . and he obviously didn't damage my vocal cords because I can still talk. I just have to go back in a week and then maybe do some other follow-up tests."

Libby took a sip of her shake and nodded, feeling very relieved. "I'm glad it went well."

"Me, too," Payton said, smiling. "How are Cash and Ned?"

"They're fine," Ames said, chuckling. "I think Ned might love Cash more than me."

"That could never happen! You're Ned's mom—he loves you more than anyone."

"I don't know," Ames said, "but he wiggles all over the place when he sees Cash."

"That's too funny," Payton said, taking a sip of her shake and swallowing gingerly. "I think the pain med might be wearing off."

"When can you take more?" Libby asked.

"The nurse said to stay ahead of it, so . . ." She looked at her phone. "So maybe twenty minutes." She looked at Ames. "How'd the softball game go on Friday?"

Ames shook her head. "We lost 5–3."

"What the heck?" Payton asked. "We *always* beat Jimmy's Nuts and Bolts."

"Jen pitched because you weren't there, and they just kept hitting off her."

"Dang!" Payton said. "I thought we were gonna be undefeated again this year."

"Well, if our star pitcher didn't have to go have surgery, we probably would be."

"How's the shop? Are the kids managing?"

"They are. Cash is doing a wonderful job. You're gonna miss him when he opens his pet-sitting business."

"Do you think he's serious about that?"

"I do," Ames said. "He talks about it nonstop."

Payton shook her head and took another sip of her shake. "I thought he'd always work at the shop. That way I can keep tabs on him."

"God's plans must be different from yours."

"They usually are," Payton replied, chuckling. "What will be, will be, I guess. At least his plan includes letting me survive surgery so I can enjoy this beautiful day . . . and a chocolate shake. It's such a relief to have it all behind me."

"Having a health scare certainly has a way of putting things in perspective, doesn't it?" Libby mused.

"It does," Ames agreed. "I'll never forget the time my appendix burst—it was right after I had Quinn and I thought I was going to die and not get to see her grow up."

"I forgot about that," Libby said, nodding. "That was scary."

"It was, but it makes you appreciate life," Ames said, "so in a way, it was a blessing."

Payton nodded and touched her bandage again. "I think we better go fill that prescription, but I want to get Cash a shake."

"I'll go get it," Libby said, standing up. "What flavor?"

"Vanilla."

Libby walked over to the window, and while Payton and Ames waited, Payton recalled the two women who'd come into the shop on a bus tour and the obvious affection they'd had for each other. She pictured them sitting at this very table—enjoying their ice cream, and she wondered if they were back at home on Nantucket now. It must've been fun to travel together, have an itinerary all planned—where to stay and dine, and have a glass of wine every evening on the porch or patio of some new inn, and she suddenly wondered if Ames and Libby—or any of the women in their group— might be interested in taking a trip like that.

Libby returned with a shake for Cash and smiled. "Ready?"

The women nodded and stood up to walk to the car. "Thank you for the treat, Libby," Payton said. "That really hit the spot."

"It did," Ames said, smiling.

"You're welcome!" Libby said. "I haven't come down to the shop in such a long time—it's good to check on the kids once in a while."

"It is," Payton agreed.

"Well, now, we need to get you home so you can rest," Ames said, "*and* I have dinner planned."

"You don't need to make dinner. I don't think I'll be able to swallow anything that isn't in liquid form."

"That's why I brought my smoothie maker," Ames said, motioning to the back seat, "*and* I have a bag of fresh fruits and veggies—apple, banana, spinach, orange, celery, carrot, green superfood powder, and raw vegan organic protein."

Payton shook her head. "You are too funny."

Ames looked over and smiled. "Why? We girls have to take care of each other, you know."

"You're right. We do."

Despite the pain creeping into her throat, Payton sank into her seat and relaxed, luxuriating in the simple relief of having her surgery and all the anxiety behind her. They stopped to pick up the pain medicine and then headed over to the shop to pick up Cash, and when he saw her, he leaned in and wrapped his arms around her as if she were made of glass. "I'm so glad you're okay, Mom," he said, blinking back tears. "I was worried."

"*You* worried?" she teased. "I thought you didn't worry about anything."

"I worry," he said, sounding wounded.

Payton searched his eyes. "I'm sorry, Cash. I know you do, and I can't thank you enough for taking such good care of the shop."

He nodded. "You're welcome. It's not as hard as you think."

"We brought you a milkshake," Libby said, holding it out.

"Oh, wow! Thanks!" he said, his face brightening as he climbed into the back seat next to her.

36

⁓

CHASE PARKED THE WHITE MINI COOPER THEY'D RENTED IN FRONT OF LIAM'S parents' house and looked over. "Ready?"

Liam raised his eyebrows and sighed. "Ready as I'll ever be."

SIX HOURS EARLIER, CHASE HAD BEEN ADJUSTING HIS EARBUDS AND CHECKING the aisle for the flight attendant with the beverage cart, and while he waited, he'd opened his Spotify app and tapped the Mumford and Sons song "I Will Wait." Immediately, he started bobbing his head, which caused Liam to look up, and then Chase grinned imp- ishly, and knowing Liam could probably hear the song, started tapping his tray, too, but Liam just rolled his eyes, and turned back to his book. Chase looked up the aisle to see if any progress was being made, and when the cart finally reached them, he pulled out his earbuds and looked over at Liam. "Whatcha gettin'?"

"Coffee," Liam said, yawning.

"Okay, be that way," Chase teased.

"Why? What are you getting?" Liam asked.

"Tonic," Chase said, discreetly producing a shooter of Tito's from his pocket.

Liam shook his head. "It's eight o'clock in the morning!"

"Yeah, so? I'm on vacation."

"I wouldn't exactly call this a vacation."

"Anytime you're on a plane—and you're not going to a funeral, it's a vacation. And if you *are* going to a funeral, that's even more reason to bring your own beverage . . . *but*, if it'll make you happy, I'll get tomato juice and call it a Bloody Mary."

"Do what you want. I can't start drinking this early—I'll be useless later."

"That's because you're a lightweight," Chase teased as the flight attendant took their orders and handed them each a bag of pretzels.

Chase waited for her to push her cart by before adding the vodka to his tomato juice. He took a sip and looked over at the book Liam was reading. "You haven't finished that yet?"

"I'm *almost* finished," Liam said, holding up the tattered copy of *Journey of Souls* Chase had lent him, and showing him that he only had a couple of chapters left.

"Do you like it?"

"I do—it makes you think."

Chase nodded. "I know, right? Like what if we aren't humans having a spiritual experience, but we're actually spirits having a human experience?"

Liam pushed his hand through his dark hair. "It certainly would explain a lot of things."

Chase took another sip and licked his lips. "It certainly would."

Liam blew on the surface of his coffee and found the page he was on, and Chase put his earbuds back in, scrolled to his favorite country playlist, clicked on the bluesy Chris Stapleton song "Tennessee Whiskey," and promptly fell asleep. Airplane travel—even in heavy turbulence—never worried him.

Now, Chase reached behind the seat of the MINI for the bottle of wine they'd brought for Liam's mom and the six-pack they'd picked up for his dad. "I can't believe your dad still drinks Budweiser when there are so many cool craft beers to choose from."

"Yep," Liam said. "Some things never change."

They walked to the front door and Chase looked around at the meticulously manicured lawn and gardens. "Looks pretty perfect around here."

"Oh, everything about my parents is perfect," Liam said, "except me."

Chase nodded. "Well, you're pretty perfect to me." He squeezed Liam's shoulder.

Liam gave him a warning look and said half jokingly, "Remember, no public displays of affection!"

"Got it," Chase said.

Liam's mom opened the door. "You don't have to ring the doorbell, Liam. This is your house."

Liam nodded and gave her a kiss on the cheek. "I wasn't sure."

"Hello, Chase," she said, nodding.

"Hello, Mrs. Evans," Chase said, smiling.

"Oh, pull-ease! Call me Kay! *Mrs. Evans* makes me feel so old."

Chase nodded and held out her favorite chardonnay. "We brought this for you."

Kay looked at the label. "Thank you. I guess it's been so long since Liam was home, he doesn't know I switched to pinot grigio, but that's okay, we can take it to the Johnsons when we go to their picnic tomorrow."

"Oh! Sorry 'bout that," Chase said. "I'll make a mental note for next time."

She nodded. "Well, c'mon in. Mike's out on the deck."

They followed her down the hall and Liam glanced at Chase and shook his head, and Chase smiled knowingly. He'd been preparing himself mentally and emotionally for this, so whatever came, he'd get through it. He just hoped Liam would come through it unscathed, too.

Kay ushered them out onto the deck and Mike looked up from the grill. "I can't get this damn thing to light."

"Did you turn on the propane?" she asked.

"Of course I turned on the propane," he said, sounding annoyed.

Liam cleared his throat. "Uh, hi, Dad."

"Hi, Liam," he said, bending down again to check the connection.

"Want me to try?" Liam ventured.

"Be my guest," Mike said, "but if I can't start it, I doubt you—" But before he could even finish his sentence, Liam had clicked the starter and made the flames roar up. Mike shook his head and didn't say anything.

"What can I get you to drink?" Kay said, standing by the door.

"Whatever you have the most of," Liam said, holding the six-pack out to his dad.

Mike waved him off. "You can give that to your mom to put in the fridge."

Kay eyed Chase. "What would you like?"

Chase pressed his lips together uncertainly and finally decided to just go for it. "Do you have any Tito's?"

Kay frowned. "What's Tito's?"

"It's a brand of vodka."

"Oh, no," she said, shaking her head, "but we might have some Smirnoff."

Chase hesitated—he wasn't a big fan of cheap vodka but he would definitely need a drink—maybe even two—to get through the evening. "Okay—with tonic and lime if you have it."

Kay shook her head. "Sorry don't have those, either."

Chase smiled. "I'll just have a beer then."

Kay held up the six-pack. "I hope Bud's okay."

Chase bit his lip so he wouldn't grimace and nodded. "Yep, perfect."

She broke a can out of the six-pack and handed it to him, and then eyed Liam. "Want one?"

"Sure," he said.

Mike shook his head. "You bring *me* beer and then *you* drink it."

Liam frowned. "You know what?" he said, shaking his head. "I'll just have water."

"I'm kidding," Mike said.

"No, you're not," Liam replied. "And honestly, I don't like Budweiser—it tastes like pi . . . well, I won't even say what it tastes like, but water tastes better. So, Mom, if you can spare it, I'll have a glass of water."

"Ice or no ice?" Kay asked.

"No ice," Liam answered, biting his tongue before he could add: *I don't want you to go to much trouble.* He handed the can back to her, and she offered it to her husband, but he waved her off again.

Chase stood silently, watching the entire exchange. "Guess it's just me then," he said, popping open the can and holding it up. "Cheers!" And then he took a good long swig. There was only so much BS he could tolerate.

Kay sighed, went inside, and returned a moment later with a glass of water and a plate of Ritz crackers topped with cubes of cheddar.

Liam took a sip of his water. "Is Lisa coming?" he asked hopefully.

"No," Mike said, sitting at the table and crossing his legs. "Your mom forgot to ask her, and when she mentioned it last night, she said she couldn't come—she just got a big promotion at work so she's very busy."

"We also think Jim is going to pop the question soon," Kay said sounding giddy. "He took Dad and me out for drinks a couple of weeks ago and asked us for her hand."

"Wow!" Liam said, leaning against the railing. "I didn't know they were that serious."

"Well, they've been going together for almost a year . . . so you know how it is—when you know, you know," Kay said cheerily. "Jim's such a nice guy, and he owns his own business. I can't wait until he finally asks her so we can start planning. I'm sure we'll end up having it at the club, but it'll be fun to look at other venues . . . and then there are gowns to shop for . . . and flowers—it's so exciting. Your father and I already started to make a guest list and I bet we have a hundred names on it."

Liam nodded and looked over at Chase—who raised his eyebrows, and then Liam cleared his throat. "That's exciting . . . and it's kind of funny because that's actually the reas—"

But before he could finish, his dad held up his hand. "Hold that thought," he said, eyeing his wife. "The grill's ready if you want to get the steaks."

Kay nodded and went back inside, and when she came out, she looked at Liam. "What were you going to say?" she asked, handing the plate to her husband.

Liam took a sip of water, feeling his heart pound, and watched his dad open the lid of the grill and start scraping off the rack. "As a matter of fact, I was going to say . . . well, you see, Chase and I have some news, too, and we came out here so we could tell you in person." He hesitated, waiting for his dad to finish putting the steaks on.

Mike finally closed the lid, and then looked at his wife. "You know, I think I will have that beer after all." He smiled at Chase. "You can't have sirloin without beer."

Chase nodded and smiled. "I think I'll have another, too, please, Kay," he said, crushing the now-empty can in his hand.

"Hey, that was my five cents!" Mike teased jovially.

"Oh, well," Chase said, chuckling. "I'll give you a nickel."

Kay came back out and handed the beers to her husband and Chase, and Mike turned to Liam. "So! Big news, huh? Shoot!"

Liam took a deep breath and let it out. "Yeah," he said, nodding. "Chase and I came out to tell you that we . . . well, we are actually engaged, too, and we're planning to get married at Chase's family's farm, and I know it's last minute because we really just decided, but we're hoping that you might co—"

Mike raised his eyebrows and put up his hand, motioning for Liam to stop, and then he shook his head. "I'm sorry," he said, "but where I come from, men don't marry men so there's no way in hell we will attend that *kind* of a wedding, if that's *even* what you're thinking of calling it."

Liam swallowed and looked at his mom, but she shook her head. "Liam, you know we don't condone that kind of behavior . . . the lifestyle you've chosen. We thought you understood that."

"It's not a lifestyle, Mom," Liam said, tears stinging his eyes, "and it's not something we've *chosen*. Chase and I love each other and we want to spend the rest of our lives together."

"Love each other?!" Mike stood up, laughing and shaking his head. "You know what? I don't even want to have this conversation. You *know* how we feel, and if you're going to insist on carrying on, then I really don't know what to tell you." He paused. "To be honest, I don't even know how you can be my son."

Liam looked stunned. "Is that really how you feel?"

"It is *really* how I feel," Mike said. "We don't understand how you can do the things you do—it's not normal, and if this is how you plan to live your life, then . . ." He shook his head.

"How do *you* know what normal is?" Liam said. "What makes you the authority? Because I certainly don't feel abnormal."

"Mammals are on this earth to reproduce and populate the world."

Liam frowned. "Who says everyone has to reproduce? There are plenty of people who—for one reason or another—choose to not have children, and there's no reason Chase and I couldn't adopt kids, or find a surrogate mom. It's about loving someone with all your heart and we'd love to have a family."

"A family?" Mike laughed and shook his head. "What you're doing is wrong. Period."

"It's not wrong, and who are you to judge us?"

"You know what?" Mike said, eyeing Liam. "Since we *are* having this conversation, I'm telling you right now, don't you even think of coming to Lisa's wedding with a male date or a husband"—he made air quotes—"because there is no way in hell that I'm going to let you make a spectacle of yourself in front of our friends."

"I wouldn't think of it, Dad," Liam said, his tears spilling down his cheeks. "I wouldn't want to ruin your precious perfect manly image."

Chase pushed back his chair. "I think we should go," he said, looking at Liam, "before your dad ends up on the other side of the railing."

Mike laughed derisively. "Oh, are you some kind of tough guy now, gay boy?"

Chase clenched his fists but held them at his sides as he stepped closer to Mike, and Mike suddenly realized Chase was a good two inches taller than him. "You know something, Mr. Evans, Liam told me you wouldn't welcome this news, but I had no idea what an asshole you are. If you don't want Liam in your life because you're ashamed he's gay, it's your loss. Liam is one of the most sincere and caring people I've ever met, and I really can't believe you're his father. He is more of a man than you will ever be."

Mike swallowed and took a step back. "You should leave."

"I *am* leaving," Chase said. He looked at Liam. "You comin'?"

Liam nodded and then turned to his parents. "I'm sorry I turned out to be such a disappointment . . . and you needn't worry, I won't show up at Lisa's wedding and embarrass you." He turned to give his mom a hug, but she took a step back. "Wow, Mom," he said, "I'm your son."

But Kay just shook her head.

37

BALANCING AN ARMFUL OF GOODIES, LIBBY AND ELLIE KNOCKED ON PAYTON'S door, and a moment later, Cash peered through the screen. "Hi, Mrs. Tennyson. Hi, Ellie," he said shyly.

"Hi, Cash!" Ellie said, grinning.

"How are you, young man?" Libby asked.

"I'm fine."

"We brought dinner over for you and your mom."

"Mrs. Finley told me you were coming," he said, pushing open the door.

As they came in, Ellie held out a bouquet of blue hydrangeas she'd cut from the garden and a jar of jam.

"Is this strawberry?" he asked hopefully.

"It is," Ellie confirmed.

"Awesome! Thank you!"

"You're welcome," she said, as they followed him to the kitchen.

"How's your mom?" Libby asked.

"She's better," he said. "The doctor gave her some pain medicine, but it makes her sleepy . . . *and* constipated."

Libby suppressed a smile—one of the things she'd always loved about Cash was his honesty. "She's out on the back porch if you want to go see her."

Libby set the still-warm quiche, salad, and brownies on the counter. "Could you two put the flowers in some water?"

"Sure," Cash said, nodding, and then immediately began to unravel the aluminum foil and damp paper towel Ellie had wrapped around the stems.

Ellie stayed in the kitchen to help, but Libby went out to the porch, and Payton opened her eyes. "Hi, there! Is tonight your night to make dinner?"

"It is," Libby said, smiling.

"You girls are too much! You didn't have to go to so much trouble."

"It's no trouble. We're happy to help—it makes us feel useful."

"Mm-hmm."

"So how are you feeling?" she asked, sitting in the chair next to her.

"Better'n I did yesterday, but still tender," she said, reaching up to touch her bandage.

Libby nodded. "I didn't know if you'd be able to swallow so I made a crustless quiche."

"Ooh, that sounds good," Payton said, smiling. "I wasn't very hungry yesterday, but my appetite seems to be returning. Heaven forbid it *not* come back so I could lose a few pounds," she added, laughing.

"I know what you mean," Libby agreed, "but having an appetite is a good thing—it means you're gonna survive," she added, smiling. "I can remember a time when I didn't feel well for several months, and although Dr. Hamlin couldn't find anything wrong with me, I had absolutely no appetite. I lost fifteen pounds, but it was so odd—and disconcerting—to look at food and feel repelled by it. I almost forgot what hunger felt like."

"I think a lot of people wish that would happen to them, at least for a little while."

Libby smiled. "Probably."

"Did he ever figure out what was wrong?"

"No, but he thought it might've been due to stress because it was soon after Cale died, and we had a lot going on, especially with Gage—who'd decided he wanted no part of farming. At the same time, he and Jack both seemed determined to blame themselves for Cale's accident, even though neither was at fault. The chain broke and Cale was standing in the wrong spot. End of story. It was no one's fault, but it didn't help Gage and Jack's already stressed relationship."

"I remember that day like it was yesterday," Payton said sadly.

"Me, too. For a long time, I dreamt about it every night."

Payton nodded. "Cale was following in Jack's footsteps, and then he was just . . . *gone*. It was so tragic and everyone in town was shocked."

Libby nodded and then searched her friend's face. "I came over to talk about *you*, not me!"

Payton laughed. "That's okay. I need to take my mind off myself! I spend way too much time dwelling on my problems. I worry too much."

"Don't we all?" Libby said. "It's our mother hearts!"

"So true!" Payton said. "God tells us to give our worries to him, and put everything in his hands . . . and I try to do that, but the very next moment, I take them all back."

Libby nodded. "I know exactly what you mean."

"Soo," Payton asked. "Are you ready for the big day? It's coming up soon."

"I'm getting there. I went dress shopping with Ellie and Jodi the other day, and I actually found a dress."

"What color is it?"

"It's a pretty coral with white trim around the neck and I'm going to wear Gram's pearls."

"Very nice! She would definitely approve!" Payton said, remembering Libby's grandmother from their childhood.

"You and Cash are coming, aren't you? I gave Gage and Maeve your address a while ago . . . and Amesy's address."

"We are. In fact, we just got our invitation today—it's beautiful!"

"Good," Libby said, smiling.

Payton rifled through the mail on the table next to her chair and pulled the invitation out of the pile. "Ames and I would love to make the centerpieces for the tables. She said she has a plethora of sunflowers—more than any other year."

"That would be wonderful!" Libby said, and then she ran her finger lightly over the illustration. "Gage painted it."

"I wondered! He's such a talented artist. I'll never forget all the blue ribbons he used to win at the fair. No one else's drawings even came close."

"I'll always regret not helping him pay for art school. That's why he never finished, but at the time, Jack held the purse strings, and he told Gage that being an artist was not a way to make a living, so Gage was on his own." She looked up. "I regret not helping him make his dream come true. Everyone has their own dreams, and who are we to say what's worthwhile and what isn't?"

Payton nodded, her friend's words speaking to her own heart.

As Libby started to open the invitation, Payton said, "I think it's wonderful that both your boys are getting married on the same day. That is going to be a fun party! The Tennyson boys' parties were always the talk of the town—I used to hear about them, but I was too old to be invited," Payton said, laughing. "Now I *am* invited!"

"You definitely *are*!" Libby said.

Just then, Ellie and Cash came out on the porch with the bouquet. "Hi, Mrs. Childs!"

"Hi, Ellie, my dear, how are you?"

"I'm fine. How are you?"

"I'm doin' better, thank you. And look at those flowers—they're beautiful—I've always loved hydrangeas."

"Me, too," Ellie said, looking across the yard at her birdfeeder. "Wow! You have a Baltimore oriole at your feeder," she whispered in awe.

"I *do*?" Payton said, sitting up to look.

"Right there," Ellie said, pointing. "I've never seen one before."

"I haven't, either," Payton said as they all watched. "It's our lucky day."

"It is!" Ellie said.

"Well, my dear," Libby said, "I'm sure you're going to have to reheat the quiche now. It was warm when we brought it over, but I'm afraid we've lingered too long. Maybe Cash can heat it up for you . . . or we can stay and fix the plates for you. There's salad and brownies, too . . ."

"No, no," Payton said. "Cash can heat them up. You've already done too much anyway."

"If you're sure," Libby said.

"Positive," Payton assured her. "Cash is a professional in the kitchen . . . and my legs aren't broken."

"Okay, but if you need anything, please don't hesitate to call. I'm just up the road and I can be here in a heartbeat."

Payton nodded. "I'm so thankful to have such good, caring friends. Between you and Ames, I couldn't ask for more. And thank you again for bringing dinner over."

"You're welcome," Libby said, leaning down and giving her a hug. "I brought you some strawberry jam, too. Ellie and I made it today."

"Ooh!" Payton said, "We'll have to have some with our quiche!"

❧

38

"ARE YOU OKAY?" CHASE ASKED AS THEY WALKED ALONG HISTORIC BAKER Beach, carrying their sandals.

"Yeah," Liam replied, even though his eyes were still rimmed with tears. "I don't know why I'm so shocked by their reaction. I knew how they reacted the first time I tried to explain—like if they ignored what I was saying, it wouldn't be true . . . so why'd I think it would be any different now? Why'd I think they would suddenly become accepting?" He shook his head. "It was foolish on my part."

Chase nodded. "You were hoping they would. They're your parents and they're supposed to love you unconditionally, no matter what, but honestly, I can't believe they're even related to you because they couldn't have been more unkind or less compassionate."

Liam ran his hand through his dark hair. "I know, and look at how excited they are about my sister getting married. If they really knew her fiancé, they wouldn't be so happy. They're just brainwashed because he's such a freakin' charmer and because he owns his own sporting goods store, like he's some kind of genius."

"Do they know *we* own our own business?"

"They do—I've told them, but I guess they don't consider a travel agency to be a real business."

Chase didn't say anything. He wanted to tell Liam the way his parents had treated him was an outrage—he was their son! And he wanted to assure him he was better off without them, but he felt like it wasn't his place. He would've never been able to walk away from his own parents—it would destroy him, and he'd be crushed if they'd ever spoken to him the way Liam's parents had or said they couldn't believe he was their son just because of who he loved.

"It'll be okay," he said softly, intertwining his hand with Liam's. "We'll get through it."

Liam mustered a smile. "I know we will." He wiped his eyes with his shoulder. "You hungry?"

Chase laughed. "I *am* hungry. Those steaks were smelling pretty good when we left."

"They were," Liam said, laughing, too.

"It's a good sign that you're laughing . . . *and* hungry—it means you're gonna survive."

Liam gestured to the Golden Gate Bridge looming in the distance. "Why don't we see if we can find a restaurant with a view of the bay."

"Works for me," Chase agreed, and they turned to walk back to the car. "You wanna drive and I'll look for a place? You're more familiar with the area."

"Sure," Liam said, brushing the sand off his feet and slipping into his sandals. They climbed into the little MINI Cooper and Chase pulled out his phone.

"Am I looking for a place that serves steak?"

"Doesn't matter. Pub fare would be good."

Chase tapped his phone and began searching for restaurants overlooking the bay. "Looks like there are quite a few," he said, scrolling down the page, searching for reviews, and then he paused to read the reviews of the highest-rated restaurant. "I found a place," he said. "It's reasonably priced, has outdoor dining, a spectacular view, and everything from steak to wild Pacific salmon."

"Perfect," Liam said, putting on his sunglasses. "Which way?"

"Left," Chase said.

TEN MINUTES LATER, CHASE POPPED A MINT IN HIS MOUTH, PUT ON HIS SUN-glasses, and climbed out, but when he paused to look at his reflection in the car window, muss his short blond hair, and adjust his shirt, Liam frowned. "You have a date or something?"

"Me? Ha! Nooo. Only you!"

Liam eyed him suspiciously, anyway, and then turned to look at the restaurant sign. "Wait a minute," he said. "Quince Café . . . is this your friend's restaurant?"

"Maybe," Chase said, grinning impishly as they walked across the parking lot.

Liam rolled his eyes and laughed. "I forgot her restaurant was out here."

"I forgot, too. I thought of it when the name popped up."

"I wonder if she's here tonight."

"Well, it's Saturday, so I hope so."

They stepped up to the hostess stand and requested a table on the deck, and the young woman seated them at a table with an amazing view of the bridge. "Your waitress will be right with you," she said, setting the menus in front of them.

Chase nodded, and then eyed her. "Is Quinn here tonight?"

The hostess's face lit up. "Quinn? She's *always* here! Is she a friend?"

"She is," Chase said.

"I'll send her right over."

"Thanks," Chase said, feeling his heart pound. He looked at Liam and raised his eyebrows. "Whatcha drinkin'?"

Liam shook his head. "After the day I've had, whiskey, leave the bottle!"

Chase nodded. "That's the truth!"

They perused the list of cocktails and beers. "I don't know," Chase mused. "It all sounds good. We'll have to ask Quinn what she recommends." He looked around to see if she was coming, but there was no sign of her. A moment later, though, he saw a slender young woman with wispy shoulder-length blond hair wearing slacks and a light blue V-neck sweater stop to talk to the hostess. He watched them and when the hostess gestured toward their table, the young woman turned. She raised her eyebrows and then a slow smile crossed her face, and as she walked over, Chase smiled, too. "Damn, woman!" he said, standing up, "you can even make a gay boy cry!"

"Ha!" she said, laughing and wrapping her arms around him. "And *you* can definitely make a straight girl cry!" She pulled back, eyeing him. "Look how you turned out—so tan and buff and hip and handsome! What are *you* doing here?"

Chase smiled. "We're here for the weekend." He gestured to Liam. "This is my partner, Liam Evans."

Liam stood and politely extended his hand, but Quinn laughed and said, "Heck no!" and gave him a warm hug instead. "It's so nice to meet you!" She smiled, studying Liam's handsome face, sun-bleached chestnut-brown hair, and playful, friendly eyes. "Yep, you definitely look like you could be the partner of my old best friend," she said.

"Can you sit for a minute?" Chase said, gesturing to a chair.

"I can in a little bit," she said, looking at her watch and realizing it was almost nine o'clock. "The crowd's starting to thin out. Let me just do a few things and I'll come back."

Chase nodded. "Oh, before you go, what drinks would you recommend?"

"Hmm, for you . . ." Quinn said, eyeing him. "I know you liked JD when we were in high school. Is that still your poison?"

Chase laughed. "It can be . . . that or Tito's."

Quinn nodded and then turned to Liam. "Are you into the hard stuff, too?"

Liam smiled. "Well, since I hang around with him, I drink just about anything."

"Those Tennyson boys, right?"

"Yeah, they're a rowdy bunch!"

"Okay, I'll have James bring over a couple of my favorites from the outdoor bar. Oh! And everything's on the house, so order whatever you'd like!"

"You don't have to do that," Chase said, frowning. "We're here to support *you*."

"I insist," she said firmly, "but you can leave a generous tip for my amazing waitstaff."

"We can do that," Chase agreed.

Quinn smiled. "Dang, Chase, I can't believe you're here!"

He nodded. "It's been too long."

"It has . . . and when I come back, we're gonna talk about why that is."

"Sounds good," Chase said as he and Liam sat back down.

Five minutes later, a young bartender brought over two glasses. "These are special order from the boss," he said, setting them on coasters. "I have a Cool Hand Cuke for the gentleman on the right, and an Old Glory for the gentleman on the left."

"Thanks," Chase said, eyeing the drinks. "What's in them?"

"Sooo, the Cool Hand Cuke is Tito's, Aperol, honey simple syrup, lime juice, and cucumbers, and Old Glory is Tito's, fresh lemon juice, simple syrup, Oregon Pinot Noir, and blueberries."

Chase nodded approvingly. "Sounds good. Thank you!"

"You're welcome," James replied. "Let me know if you need anything."

And after he walked away, Liam smiled. "So gay."

"Oh, yeah," Chase agreed, and then held up his glass. "Here's to us!"

"To us!" Liam said, clinking his glass and taking a sip. He licked his lips. "Damn, this *is* good. How's yours?"

"Really good. Want to try?" he asked, offering his glass.

They exchanged drinks, took sips, and although they both approved of each other's, they were happier with their own—Quinn had chosen well.

Chase looked over the menu. "I think I'm gonna have steak. This one," he said, pointing, "with cabernet sauce and melted blue cheese sounds good."

"It does," Liam agreed. "Can't go wrong with cabernet sauce."

They placed their orders, and even though they hadn't even looked at the appetizers, a waitress showed up with a plate of oysters. "Compliments of the owner!"

"All right!" Liam said.

The two men chatted, drank, marveled at the view, devoured the oysters—and their steaks when they came—and were almost finished when Quinn finally returned. "Sorry!" she said. "Things got a little hectic in the dining room. You never know what's gonna happen on a Saturday night."

"No problem," Chase said. "We're not going anywhere."

"Good," Quinn said. "Anyway, I think my staff has everything under control now. Mind if I sit down?"

"Not at all!" Chase said, pulling over a chair, into which Quinn collapsed with a sigh. "Dinner was excellent, by the way."

"Yes," Liam said. "Maybe we can get the recipe for that cabernet sauce."

"Oh, absolutely," she said. "It's easy."

Chase eyed her. "You look like *you* could use a drink."

"I could," she said, laughing. She caught James's eye and he nodded.

"You boys want an after-dinner drink, or have you had enough?"

Chase grinned. "You're supposed to say, 'Do you want a cocktail or the whole rooster?'"

"Oh, right," Quinn said. "I forgot!"

Chase eyed Liam. "You up for another?"

"Sure, so long as you're driving."

Quinn eyed them. "Have you had Buffalo Trace? It's my new favorite."

"No," Liam said, shaking his head. "What is it?"

"Bourbon."

"I have," Chase said, leaning back in his chair.

"Of course you have," Quinn teased.

Chase smiled and eyed Liam. "Up for some bourbon?"

"What the heck. I've just been disowned by my parents, so keep 'em coming!"

Quinn raised her eyebrows at his comment, and then looked at James. "Three Buffalos, please, sir," she said. "On second thought, just bring three glasses and the bottle."

Chase laughed. "You know me too well."

James brought over the bottle, three glasses, and two more votive candles for their table.

"Seems like he's done this before," Chase teased.

"Maybe," Quinn said, laughing, as she poured two fingers in each glass and held hers up. "To old friends," she said with a smile.

"To old *best* friends," Chase corrected.

"Indeed!" Quinn said, and then she turned to Liam. "You don't have to answer, but you mentioned being disowned . . . and sorry, I can't really let that pass . . ."

Liam took a sip of his bourbon and licked his lips, and then he explained what had happened. The only time Quinn interrupted him was when Liam said they'd come out to tell his parents they were getting married.

"Wait!" she said, holding up her hand and looking at Chase. "You're getting married and you didn't tell me?!"

Chase laughed. "I know . . . well, we kind of lost touch, you know?"

She nodded. "Yes, well, we're gonna talk about that, too!"

Liam smiled. "Anyway, that's how we ended up here."

"That is unbelievable," Quinn said, shaking her head. "I don't know your parents, Liam, but I'd say you're better off!"

Liam gave her a grateful look and took another sip.

"I didn't get along with my dad, either. From the time I was little, I hated the way he treated my mom." She looked to Chase for confirmation. "Right?"

He nodded and took a sip of his bourbon, thankful that Quinn—who had always spoken her mind—was saying all the things he wanted to say to Liam.

"My dad treated my mom like a doormat . . . like she was a maid who had to answer to his every beck and call. He made her give up everything she loved and ignored *her* needs."

Quinn shook her head. "I honestly think people shouldn't feel bound to their families just because they share the same blood. We can choose our family—*our tribe*—just as readily as we can choose our friends. Only we know the right fit, so . . . I know it's hard to let them go, Liam, but you have Chase . . . and along with him, *you* get the entire Tennyson tribe so I hope you know what you're getting into!"

Liam laughed, his heart feeling suddenly lighter. She was right.

"He *does* have the whole Tennyson tribe," Chase said, acknowledging the name because it was perfect—they *were* a tribe. "My brothers—even my mom—have welcomed him with open arms, and Gage and his fiancée, Maeve, are even insisting we get married on the same day."

"Are you going to?" Quinn asked.

Chase looked at Liam and he half smiled and nodded. "Gage already included us on the invitation, so we really don't have a choice."

Quinn eyed him again. "Um . . . I don't remember getting an invitation," she teased.

"I'm not sure if they've gone out yet. Liam and I haven't really invited anyone . . . besides his parents, and we all know how that turned out."

"Well, I better be invited!" Quinn insisted.

"You're gonna come home?" Chase asked. "Don't you have a restaurant to run?"

"I'll figure something out," she replied. "Do you think I'd miss what will probably be the most legendary Tennyson boys' party *ever*?! Besides," she added with a knowing smile, "we literally grew up together." Quinn turned to Liam. "Did Chase tell you we went to our senior prom?"

"He did—he showed me a picture, and said if he could've ever fallen for a girl, it would've been you."

Quinn smiled wistfully. "And then he broke my heart."

"You mean you broke mine . . ."

Quinn frowned. "How so?"

Chase took a sip of his drink, wondering if it was the right time to have this conversation . . . or if there would ever be a right time, especially since it had happened so long ago, but all the alcohol he'd consumed was getting the better of his ability to reason, and he pressed his lips together. "You were the only person I told, Quinn-Fin," he said softly, "and somehow, right afterward, my dad knew."

Quinn raised her eyebrows, his quiet indictment confirming her theory about why they'd lost touch. "You think I told someone," she said, "even though I promised I wouldn't. Even though I crossed my heart."

He searched her eyes. "I never told anyone but you."

Quinn sipped her drink and nodded. "You know, Chase, my mom was visiting a couple of weeks ago." She looked around. "It was a night just like tonight, and we were talking about you, and she told me something I never knew before. She said the night you and I talked about this on our front porch, my dad—who, as you well know, was a busybody and a gossip—was eavesdropping, and she said when he came to bed that night, he told her what he heard . . . and she said she knows she wasn't the only one he told."

Chase raised his eyebrows and slowly shook his head—which suddenly felt like it was spinning. For years, he'd stubbornly harbored a silent resentment toward his best friend, blaming her for his parents finding out before he was ready to tell them. He never once considered the possibility that they'd found out some other way. He'd never once asked Quinn about it or given her the chance to explain. Without a word, he'd judged her, and without any explanation from him, he'd kicked their lifelong friendship to the curb, sentencing her to years of silence. "Wow," he whispered, realizing the depth of his betrayal. "I don't know why you're even talking to me," he said, "when I just assumed it was you."

"I'm talking to you because I love you, Chase. You were my best friend . . . *and* I also know you must've decided to forgive me . . . because you're *here*."

"I did forgive you . . . mostly," he admitted. "It happened so long ago, and it doesn't matter now. I'm not one to hold grudges—I saw what it did to my dad and my brother."

Quinn nodded. "Well, I'm glad we got that settled," she said, pouring more bourbon into their glasses. "How 'bout we talk about something fun . . . like when the heck is this wedding so I can plan my trip," she said, laughing. "*And* are there gonna be any kiddos in the Chase and Liam Tennyson household . . . because I always thought you'd make a great dad."

Chase hooted. "You haven't changed a bit, Quinn," he teased.

"What?" she said playfully. "Because I say what's on my mind?"

"Yep! It's one of the things I love most about you. You're not one of those women who makes a guy figure out what they're thinking."

"Maybe that's why I haven't met anyone," she said. "I scare men off with my brutal honesty. I'm too blunt."

"Nah—you're authentic, and any guy would be lucky to have you!" Chase said. "As far as kids go"—he looked at Liam—"we *do* want to have a family—I love big families and lots of chaos—but we're not sure if we'll adopt or try to find a surrogate."

"It would be neat to have a biological child, but we have to do a little more research," Liam added.

Quinn nodded thoughtfully. "One of my customers works for a dot-com called Surrogate. I can ask him for information."

"That would be great," Liam said.

"It could be a challenge to find a willing womb," Chase mused, "and we don't want to wait too long because we don't want to be old parents."

"Heaven forbid!" Quinn teased. "At least you have the hard part accomplished—finding someone who's willing to raise a family with you."

Chase said confidently, "You will find someone."

She laughed and took a sip of her drink. "Mm-hmm. You sound like my mom."

THEY CONTINUED TO TALK LATE INTO THE NIGHT, LONG AFTER THE WAITSTAFF had said good night. They remembered all the good times they'd shared—their failures and triumphs, their families and hopes for the future until, one by one, the candles flickered out, and the only lights came from the stars above them, and in the distance, the magnificent old bridge and sparkling skyline, too. Finally, they said good night, and when Chase assured her an invitation would be in the mail "forthwith," Quinn laughed and said, "Now I have to figure out what to get you. Are you registered anywhere?"

Chase eyed her quizzically. "Registered?"

Quinn rolled her eyes. "That is where a girl would definitely come in handy!" she said, hugging them both.

39

AMES STOOD IN FRONT OF HER MAILBOX, SIFTING THROUGH THE BILLS AND CAT-alogs, but when she came to a crisp white envelope with elegant handwriting, she tucked everything else under her arm to open it. "Oh, my," she whispered, sliding the wedding invitation—which was really just a formality because everyone who was invited already knew they were invited—out and admiring the hand-painted sunflowers on the front. "We're gonna have to come up with a gift . . . actually, we're gonna have to come up with *two* gifts . . . and we have to make the centerpieces for the tables!" she mused out loud, looking around for Ned, her ever-faithful confidant.

"Where'd you go, silly?" she said, looking around and expecting to see him lying in a sunny spot on the grass. She walked to the backyard, but her big black Lab was nowhere in sight. She frowned and went back out to the road and called him, but all she heard were startled songbirds fluttering from the edge of the road up to the fence. "Shoot!" she said. "Why are you making me worry, Ned?" She scanned up and down the road, praying she'd see his jet-black form trotting toward her, wagging his tail, but there was no sign of him, so she returned to the mailbox, stuffed the mail back in, and walked in the opposite direction, hoping he'd spied

Sarah and Daniel in the garden and gone over to say hello, but when she turned into the parking lot, it was empty.

"Okay, now I'm *really* getting worried," she grumbled. "Ned!" she shouted. She hurried up the road to see if John had seen him. Maybe Ned was there—after all, the farm *was* his old stomping ground, but when she got to the fields, all she saw were peacefully grazing cows.

"Ned!" she shouted again, feeling her heart pound. He never wandered off. *Never!* So where the heck was he? She headed back to the house, hoping he'd returned, but when she got there, there was still no sign of him. She pulled her phone out of her pocket and tried to call Payton—she knew her friend would be home because she was still recovering from her surgery, but when she listened for it to ring, her phone went right to voice mail.

"Okay, this is a little ridiculous!" Ames said, suddenly feeling very alone. "Where *is* everyone tod—?!" But before she even finished her question, her phone rang, startling her. She looked at the screen, hoping it was Payton, but it was Quinn! She tapped the screen and put the phone on speaker. "Hi, hon . . ." she said, her voice edged with panic.

"Hi, Mom! What's the matter?" Quinn always recognized trouble in her mom's voice.

"I can't find Ned," Ames cried. "I've been up and down the road. I've checked the barn and the fields, the garden, and there's no sign of him anywhere! I've called and called, and I just don't know where he can be. He never takes off!"

"Okay," Quinn said, trying to maintain calm from the other side of the country. "He has to be somewhere."

"I know he has to be *somewhere*," Ames said, sounding exasperated and truly panicked now. "I just want to know *where* that somewhere is!" she said, pacing back and forth on the road, still looking. "Is everything okay with you? Can I call you back?"

"Yes, everything's fine . . . and yes, you can call me back. Call me as soon as you find him . . . and don't worry, Mom, you're *going* to find him."

"Okay, I'll call you back," Ames said, hanging up without even saying goodbye. She hurried around the house to the back-yard again, shouting his name, and as she came around the front corner, she felt tears welling up in her eyes. "Oh, Ned!" she cried. "Where are you?" And then she heard a little bark and she looked over at the house and saw his wet black nose pressed against the screen of her bedroom window. "Oh, Ned! What are you doing in-side?" she cried, laughing in relief and walking over to the win-dow. "I was so worried. Did you let yourself in again? I didn't even think of that! I'll be right there," she said, hurrying around to go in through the garage, and when she pushed open the door, he was standing there, wagging his tail as if to say *I'm right here, Mom*. She wrapped her arms around him and he wiggled around her, lick-ing the tears off her cheeks. "What would I do without you?" she whispered into his fur and then she suddenly remembered to call Quinn back.

"Did you find him?!" her daughter asked worriedly without even saying hello.

"Yes, I found him," Ames said, laughing, "and you aren't going to believe where!"

"Where?" Quinn asked.

"*In* the house!"

"How'd he get in the house?"

"The door between the garage and the kitchen doesn't latch, so if he wants to go in, he just nudges it with his nose and it opens. I was coming around the house, calling him and I heard him bark and his nose was pressed against the screen, trying to tell me he was right there all along."

"Oh, Mom!"

"I know. Your mom is losing it," Ames said, laughing.

"Well, I'm glad you found him. I was so worried."

"I was worried, too. I always imagine the worst."

"I know you do."

"So, anyway, did you just call to say hello, or was there something else?"

"I called to tell you I'm coming for a visit!"

"You are?! When?"

"In two weeks. I'm coming home for Chase's wedding."

"Oh, wow! That's awesome! I just got my invitation today," she said, suddenly remembering that her mail was still in the mailbox. "Now I have to figure out what to get them."

"I know! I have to figure that out, too."

"Well, this is such good news! You made my day!"

Quinn laughed. "I bet finding Ned made your day even more."

Ames stroked the sweet head of her big Lab—who was now lying sound asleep on the bed next to her. "You both did," she said, smiling.

⸎

40

"MORE STRAWBERRIES, GRANDMA!" ELLIE ANNOUNCED, TROMPING INTO THE kitchen with a parade of her younger cousins—all sporting rose-stained lips and cheeks—trailing behind her. "And there are a lot more out there!"

"I don't think I've ever cut up so many strawberries," Libby said, eyeing the overflowing buckets they were carrying in. Even little Jack had filled his blue sand pail.

Ellie nodded. "God must've known we needed them for the wedding this year."

"He must've," Libby said, chuckling at the thought that God had planned so far in advance that he'd prepared a bumper crop of strawberries for their wedding dessert.

"Gran, did you know strawberries aren't really berries?"

"What are they then?" five-year-old Elijah asked, biting into one so plump its juice ran down his chin.

"They're fruit . . . just like tomatoes and avocados are fruits, but rhubarb is a vegetable."

"No way!" said Elijah.

"Way," Ellie said, nodding.

"What are these little things that look like splinters?" he

asked, pointing to the strawberry in his hand while all his younger cousins gathered around to look.

"Those are the seeds," Ellie said matter-of-factly.

"Seeds?! And we eat them?!"

Joseph laughed. "You're gonna have strawberries growin' in your tummy!"

"So are you," Elijah said, pushing him.

"Okay, everybody," Ellie said. "Bring your pails, bowls, and buckets over and dump 'em into these colanders for Gran to wash."

The parade of young workers obeyed their revered oldest cousin and then traipsed back out to pick more "straw-fruits" as they were now being called. Meanwhile, Libby rinsed, sliced, scooped sugar, and stacked bags of the juicy fruit on the counter. Later, after they'd had time to swim in the sugar for a bit, she'd stack them in the freezer, and in two weeks, they'd come out, defrost, and be ready for the wedding dessert, newly named *straw-fruit shortcake*.

Libby looked out the window at the activity around their big white barn. It hadn't been used for milking in over twenty years. The summer before Cale died, they'd built a new barn and invested in all new machinery—technology that Cale had learned about at the University of Tennessee's Institute of Agriculture. Ever since then, the big barn—as they always called it—had been used for storage, but when Gage and Maeve announced their engagement the previous summer, Libby had suggested they have their wedding on the farm and the boys had used the upcoming event as an excuse to restore it to its original glory.

For months, they'd been replacing boards, reinforcing framing, and painting. On Mother's Day weekend, when Gage had visited, he'd helped Matt replace some of the more challenging boards, but he'd also repainted the Tennyson Dairy Farm sign on the far end, and in the month since, the entire barn had received a fresh coat of paint . . . and it looked glorious!

Now Matt, Eli, and Grayson were pulling out all the old tractors and parts that had, over the years, found their way into the barn, but never found their way out, and they'd come across all kinds of treasures, including the two John Deere pedal tractors they'd all ridden when they were younger, and which Elijah and Joseph immediately commandeered. They also swept out years of dust and hay, replaced glass, cleaned windows, and jokingly complained that they were doing *all* the work while the three men getting married were not lifting a finger.

"They'd be here if they could be," Libby said, when she brought out a plate of freshly baked lemon sugar cookies.

"I know they would," Matt said, taking a bite of one. "We're just bustin' 'em. Grayson's been sending them pictures of the three of us covered in dust and told them it counts as our wedding presents."

Libby chuckled and walked over to look inside. "Well, there's plenty of room for all the tables and a dance floor now, don't you think?" she said, surveying the space.

"Plenty of room," Matt agreed. "We're getting tables and chairs from the firehouse, and Jodi and the girls are going to hang white Christmas lights from the rafters, but Gage said the caterer is taking care of everything else . . ."

"Everything but dessert," Libby said, smiling. "I'm making strawberry shortcake."

"Well, I'm sure the girls will help you with that."

Libby nodded. "It really looks nice, Matt. Even if there wasn't going to be a wedding, it definitely needed a face-lift."

"It did," he agreed, taking another cookie. "Oh! And look what we did with all the old boards," he said, leading her to the field where they'd piled them.

"That looks like a pile your dad would make for a bonfire," she said.

"That's why we made it—so Dad and Dutch and Cale can see it from heaven!"

Libby sighed. "I wish they could be here."

"I wish they could, too," Matt said, putting his arm around her. "But they'll be here in spirit."

"I know," she said, smiling wistfully and handing him the plate of cookies. "I better get back to my strawberries. Your daughter has a small army of pickers out there!"

"Leave it to Ellie!" he said, smiling.

41

"No swimming, Gus!" Gage called as he and Chase walked along the river behind his cabin.

"This is such a great spot," Chase said, looking up at the old willow trees. "It's so peaceful and quiet—it's like a slice of heaven. You really lucked out."

"We *did* luck out," Gage said, throwing a stick as far as he could for Gus—who looked like a dolphin loping through the tall grass as he searched for it. "You should've seen it before, though. The driveway and gardens were all overgrown and the cabin was . . . well, let's just say it was a little rustic."

"Well, you did a great job restoring it—you'd never expect to find such a nice kitchen in an old hunting cabin."

"That kitchen came from a job we were working on. The owner—who had more money than he knew what to do with—wanted a brand-new kitchen, so Ben offered to take the old cabinets and appliances off his hands, and the guy was happy to unload everything—even though it was all like new. The following weekend we installed it here. We had to move one wall to fit the cabinets, but it wasn't weight bearing so we just took it down and that really opened it up."

"I love the layout."

"Well, you and Liam lucked out, too—you have a cottage right on the ocean!"

"Yeah, we love it. The view is amazing, and we love the beach—whenever we go on vacation, a gorgeous beach is always a must . . . and, by the way, on that topic, did you and Maeve get your passports?"

"Yes, they came the other day."

"Good, because your honeymoon trip to Mykonos is all booked. You're gonna love it!"

"Mm-hmm," Gage said skeptically. "Next time we're going to a national park."

Chase laughed. "Well, if you *do* go to a national park, I would definitely recommend Yosemite. Liam and I drove there last weekend when we were out in Cali, and words just don't do it justice. The mountains and the sequoias—I wish we'd had more time. I'd love to do some serious hiking there."

Gage nodded. "It's definitely on my bucket list." He reached for the stick Gus had dropped in front of him and threw it again. "Mom said Liam's parents aren't coming to the wedding."

"Nope," Chase said, shaking his head. "Our visit didn't go very well."

"That stinks," Gage said, shaking his head. "I really don't get it."

"I don't, either," Chase said, "and Liam was crushed."

Gage nodded. "Mom also said you saw Quinn."

"We *did*," Chase confirmed. "It was so good to see her. She looks great and her restaurant is amazing . . . *and* she's coming to the wedding!"

"Wow!" Gage said.

"So we officially have one guest!"

"Are you sure there's no one else you want to invite?"

Chase nodded. "We're sure. It's just going to be our family and Maeve's, and a couple of Mom's friends, right?"

"Yeah, and even that is quite a few people if you think about it."

"Is Maeve's son coming?"

"He *is*," Gage said. "Mason's coming, and he's bringing his girlfriend, Ali."

"Perfect," Chase said, leaning down to pick up the stick Gus had just dropped again, but as he did, the big yellow Lab shook from head to tail, sending water everywhere and soaking them both.

"Hey!" Gage scolded. "I thought I said *no swimming*!" but Gus just hopped up and down, waiting for Chase to throw the stick, and then he raced off again.

"Dang, I'd love to get a dog," he said.

"What's stopping you?"

"Liam thinks he's allergic—that's why he stayed back at the cabin with Maeve. As soon as Gus came over, his eyes started itching and watering. It happened at the farm a few weeks ago, too."

"You know, they make allergy medicine for that."

"I know. I think he was gonna take some—we'll have to see if it helped."

They passed the chicken coop and Gage stopped to usher his hens and rooster back inside for the night. They protested indignantly but finally hurried inside, and Gage closed and latched the gate.

"Have you seen any more foxes?" Chase asked, recalling the trouble Gage had had the previous spring with a persistent fox getting into his coop.

"No, thank goodness," Gage replied as they rounded the corner of the cabin.

"Well, well, well," Chase said as they climbed the porch steps, "look what we have here!"

Liam and Maeve—who were sitting in the Adirondack chairs on the porch with glasses of wine—both laughed. "You didn't think we were gonna wait, did you?" Maeve teased.

"Someone has to start the party," Liam added. "It may as well be us."

Chase studied Liam's eyes. "Did the allergy tablet help?"

"Calmed it down a little," he replied. "It's just odd because I've never had allergies before."

"You can develop an allergy anytime in life," Maeve said matter-of-factly, "but it definitely stinks to be allergic to dogs." Just then, Gus bounded up onto the porch and dropped his stick at Liam's feet, and a second later, he sneezed.

"Dang!" Gage said, shaking his head. "C'mere, Gus. Leave Liam alone."

Gus nosed over to Maeve. "Don't take it personally, silly," she consoled, "Liam still loves you." He thumped his tail, and Maeve looked at Gage. "He'll have to stay outside while we have dinner."

Gage eyed their dog. "Which is where you'd be anyway since you went swimming!"

Gus seemed to understand this scolding because he plodded out into the yard and lay down in the late-day sun to dry, and Gage looked over at Chase. "Wine, beer, or something stronger?"

"Beer sounds good," Chase said, smiling. "Perfect for a summer evening."

Gage went inside and returned a moment later with two beers and they sat on the steps. "So are you guys ready for the big day?"

Chase looked at Liam, and he raised his eyebrows and smiled. "We are. Are you?"

Gage looked at Maeve and reached up to pat her knee. "You ready for this, hon?"

She laughed. "I'm *ready*!"

"Got your dress?"

"Yup!"

"I think Harper and Ellie are gonna really hit it off," Chase said, smiling as he thought about everyone who would be there.

Gage nodded, and then remembered the pictures Grayson had sent that afternoon. He pulled out his phone to show Maeve and Liam. "They were cleaning out the barn and said it should count as their wedding gift."

"That's fine," Chase said. "I'm sure it's been a huge job."

"In fairness, it needed to be cleaned out *and* painted."

Chase nodded and took a sip of his beer. "We're paying for half, by the way," he said, "so we're gonna need a total for everything, including the caterer."

Gage took a sip of his beer. "You don't have to pay half—you only invited one person!"

"But we share the same family," he said, "so we either split the cost or we're not gonna get married," and then looked at Liam for confirmation, but when his partner raised his eyebrows uncertainly, Chase added, "*that day.*"

"If you insist," Gage said. "Bonni Manning is catering."

"Oh, wow!" Chase said, nodding approvingly. "She makes the best food—she did such a good job at Dutch's funeral."

"She did, *and* we got a *really* good deal on a DJ."

"Yeah?" Chase said, taking a sip. "Who'd you get?"

"Cash Childs."

"Oh, perfect!" Chase said, laughing. "I love Cash, and he loves old music!"

"I know," Gage said, and then his stomach rumbled, and he looked at Maeve. "Do you think dinner's ready? I'm hungry!"

"I do," she said, looking at Chase and Liam. "Are you guys hungry?"

"Starving," Chase said, standing. "I'll come help."

42

"You got this, Jen!" Payton called from the bleachers. She was sitting next to Cash, watching the Bomberettes play a team which—like theirs—was made up of mostly older players. Unlike the Bomberettes, though, the Lunachicks, sponsored by Lenny's Feed Barn, were routinely at the bottom of the standings, so losing to them would be an embarrassment, but, at that moment, they were leading, 4–2, and it was the bottom of the fifth, two outs. "Fire it in there, Jen!" Payton called, and as her teammate wound up, she chanted, "No batter! No batter!"

Cash looked up from his phone in time to see Louise Frederickson, Lenny's wife, swing for the fences, connect, and smack the ball deep into right center—where Mary Lewis was waiting, her glove high in the air, but just as she was about to make the easy catch, Joanne Jacobs—their center fielder—collided with her and the ball dropped between them. Meanwhile, Louise Frederickson huffed and puffed to second.

"Dang it!" Payton muttered. "You guys hafta talk to each other!" she yelled. "Call the ball!"

"Mrs. Lewis never calls it," Cash said quietly, looking back at his phone. "She's like me—she doesn't talk."

Payton looked over and frowned. "What do you mean she's like you?"

"She's an autist, but she doesn't know it. She was never diagnosed—she's too old."

"Really?" Payton said. "How do you know that?"

Cash shrugged. "I just know."

Payton shook her head, thinking of all the times she'd thought Mary was a bit odd. People of her generation, when they were in school, didn't get diagnosed like kids did today. They were called many things back then, but "on the spectrum" wasn't one of them.

"Okay, Jen. Shake it off! You got this!" Payton called, and Jen did just that, sending a fireball straight into Ames's glove; Ames was playing catcher because, thanks to Payton still recovering, everyone had changed positions.

"Strrr-iike!" called the ump.

"Nice one!" Payton called. "Now, two more, just like it!"

Jen watched Ames signal, nodded, and fired in another one, causing Lois Jones to swing, miss, and stagger back.

"Strrr-iike!"

"One more!" Payton called, her heart filling with hope.

Again, Ames signaled, and again Jen nodded and wound up, but when the pitch came in high and Lois swung, she connected with the top of the bat and it sent the ball straight up in the air. Ames pulled off her catcher's mask, and backed up, trying to see where it was, but the sun was in her eyes, and when the ball finally came down, it smacked her right on the cheek, knocking her off her feet, and when she didn't get up, all the players came running in to see if she was okay.

Payton was by her side in a heartbeat, cradling her head. "Someone call 911!"

Jen pulled her phone out of her pocket and dialed, and within minutes, they heard the scream of a siren. By the time the ambulance pulled in, Ames was coming to, and although she tried to protest the idea of going to the hospital, Payton insisted. "You are going!"

Ames touched her tender cheek, which was already turning a lovely shade of violet, and relented. And Dave Peters—one of the local EMTs who doubled as the minister at the Congregational Church, *and* as if that wasn't enough, spent his free time as the conductor on a scenic rail train—took her vitals, strapped her onto a stretcher, and eyed Payton. "Do you want to ride with her?" he asked.

Payton nodded, but when she started to climb in, she suddenly remembered Cash, and looked over to see her son, standing in the crowd, anxiously watching the scene unfold. "Cash!" she called, and he hurried over, towing Ned. "Think you can drive to the hospital?"

His eyes grew wide. "Yes!"

"Okay," she said, giving him her keys. "You and Ned follow the ambulance, but be careful!"

He nodded. "C'mon, Ned," he said, pulling the Lab toward the parking lot.

"This is so unnecessary," Ames said.

"Um, Amesy," Dave countered, "it *is* necessary. Your blood pressure is through the roof, your eye is so swollen you can hardly open it, and you may very well have a concussion." He checked her vitals again and when he turned to call the hospital, Payton reached for her hand.

"I don't have a concussion," Ames whispered, but then her good eye suddenly glazed over and she looked like she might pass out. "Okay, maybe I do," she said, feeling queasy. "Just so you know, I might throw up."

Dave handed her a bag, just in case, and then the ambulance pulled out of the parking lot, with its lights flashing and siren screaming.

Payton looked out the rear window to check on Cash and saw their old red pickup following along. "Where're Cash and Ned?" Ames asked, suddenly remembering them.

"They're right behind us," Payton whispered.

Ames raised her eyebrows—which was actually a comical sight. "You let Cash drive?!"

"Shhh," Payton said, giving her friend a warning look, and glancing over to see if Dave had heard, but he was still on the phone.

Ten minutes later, they turned into the parking lot of the emergency room, and Payton hopped out and waited while Dave pulled out the stretcher. "I'll be right in," Payton called as he wheeled Ames toward the door. Payton hurried over to where Cash was parking. "How'd it go?"

"No problem," he said. "How's Mrs. Finley?"

"She's awake, but she might have a concussion. Do you want to leave Ned in the truck and come in?"

Cash shook his head. "No, I don't think I should do that. Even though the sun's going down, it's still hot . . . *and* he hasn't had his supper. I think I should take him home."

Payton frowned. "You want me to take you?"

"Mom, I'm perfectly capable of driving. Dad let me drive all the time."

"But you don't have a license."

"That's not my fault! And besides, nothing's gonna happen."

Payton shook her head. "I have to go inside. You be very careful and text me when you get there."

"Okay," he said, nodding. "Let me know when you want me to pick you up."

Payton sighed, suddenly realizing that he wouldn't just be driving to Ames's house, but he'd be driving back to get her. "Be careful!" she said, eyeing him.

"I will," he assured her and then he climbed back in, and Payton turned and hurried toward the entrance.

As she went through the automatic doors, Dave was coming out. "They just took her up for an MRI," he said.

"Okay," Payton replied, realizing there was nothing for her to do but wait.

She went inside, let the nurses know she was there, and walked into the empty waiting room. At least Ames was being seen right away—*if you have to go to the ER*, she thought, *Sunday evening is probably the best time to go.* She sat down, pulled her phone out of her pocket, and realized she had a group text from their teammates. She texted back what she knew and asked how the game went, and Jen texted they'd lost. They'd been down a player after Ames had been hit by the ball, and Lois had recovered from the 2–0 count, hit one more foul, and then smacked one deep into center.

Payton sent back a frowning emoji, put her phone back in her pocket, and looked around. The last time she'd been to the hospital was for her own surgery, but the last time she'd been in the ER was when Lonny had his heart attack. He'd been standing outside the diner, talking to Jack when it happened, and although Jack had done everything he could to save her husband—and his best friend—calling 911 and giving him CPR until the ambulance arrived, the attack was too much for Lonny's weak heart, and she later learned that one of his arteries was a classic widow-maker. Jack had met Payton at the ER and held her as she cried, even though he was crying, too. She was sure that the tragic event reminded him of Cale and the helplessness he'd felt as he'd held his oldest son in his arms.

Now Jack was gone, too, though, and his passing was just more proof that life was too short and much too unpredictable. You never knew, when you woke up in the morning, if you'd be back in your own bed that night . . . or if you'd be heading for that proverbial bed, six feet under. Payton closed her eyes and whispered a prayer for Ames. She couldn't bear losing her, too. A moment later, her phone hummed and she pulled it out—it was Cash, letting her know Ned was eating supper and then he was going to take him for a walk.

Okay. Thanks! ☺ she wrote back.

43

"GRANDMA, DID YOU KNOW GOD MADE TUMBLEWEEDS TUMBLE SO THEY WOULD spread seeds?" Ellie asked as she carefully lifted mason jars out of an old cardboard box and lined them up on the kitchen table.

Libby looked up from stirring wax. "I guess I never gave it much thought."

Ellie nodded and continued to read the article she'd just found in the old *Knoxville Sun* Libby had spread on the table to protect it from dripping wax. "This article says tumbleweeds are actually an invasive weed, and although they grow in every state, the trouble began in South Dakota when Russian immigrants brought flaxseeds over that were contaminated with thistle bush seeds." She continued to read the article in the faded yellow newspaper. "Russian thistle bushes have tender leaves and delicate flowers that animals—like prairie dogs, mule deer, and pronghorns—eat, along with birds. Thistle bushes even saved cows from starvation during the Dust Bowl because they were the only thing available to eat."

Libby smiled. "Did you ever hear the song about tumbleweeds?"

Ellie looked up from dropping wicks into the jars. "There's a song about tumbleweeds?!"

Libby nodded and started to sing, "See them tumbling down, pledging their love to the ground. Lonely, but free I'll be found, drifting along with the tumbling tumbleweeds. Cares of the past are behind. Nowhere to go but I'll find just where the trail will wind, drifting along with the tumbling tumbleweed . . ." and then, forgetting the words, she continued to cheerfully hum the song from the old Gene Autry movie with the same name.

"You're such a good singer, Gran," Ellie said wistfully. "I wish I could sing."

"You're a good singer," Libby said. "What's wrong with your singing?"

Ellie shrugged. "I don't think so."

"Well, everyone has their own gift, hon, and you happen to be very knowledgeable about so many things. You're always teaching me something new."

Ellie nodded. "I just find the world interesting. I mean, think about all the different kinds of animals and plants and bugs and butterflies and birds there are. It seems like there's no end to the varieties and traits and colors and habits."

Libby continued to stir the wax—which was finally reaching a smooth pourable consistency. "There's no end to God's creativity, but I've never taken the time—or I guess *had* the time—to read and explore and learn, like you do. You have an insatiable curiosity, and that's what makes *you* special—your innate quest for knowledge."

Ellie nodded thoughtfully. "You know, I was reading about the ways animals communicate with each other in frequencies that are either too low or too high for humans to hear, and then I read that humans can listen to different frequencies and be healed from disease. I think I'd like to study something like that someday. I'd like to find cures for dementia and cancer."

"The diseases Dutch and Grandpa had," Libby said, looking over.

Ellie smiled sadly and nodded.

"Well, if anyone can find cures for those two dreadful diseases, you can . . . and they would be so proud of you. Of course, they will be proud of you no matter what you do."

Ellie felt a wave of confidence wash over her. "Are we adding a fragrance to the candles?"

"No, I think it might be overpowering to have twenty-four candles all smelling like pine or lilac or begonia," she said, "so we're just doing plain soy."

"We could do cow manure or sweet hay," Ellie suggested, giggling.

Libby laughed. "I think there's enough of those scents around here, don't you?"

"I guess."

"Are those ready?" she asked, looking over her shoulder.

"Yup." Ellie pressed her lips together as she prepared to systematically move the jars into position for her grandmother to fill.

"Be careful," Libby warned, making sure her granddaughter's hands were not near the jars when she poured the hot wax.

"Are we putting the ribbons on the jars tonight?" Ellie asked.

"We can if you'd like."

"There's no time like the present!" she said, using the phrase she often heard her grandmother use. "Did you already cut the ribbon?"

"Not yet."

"Good!" Ellie said, looking forward to the next step in the process. "So we're gonna have bouquets of flowers with blue gingham ribbons and two candles with red gingham ribbons on each table?"

Libby nodded. "Yes, Mrs. Finley and Mrs. Childs are making centerpieces with the sunflowers in Mrs. Finley's garden."

Ellie moved more jars into position. "Gran, do you know how sunflowers got their name?"

"Because they look like the sun?" Libby ventured.

"That's one reason," Ellie confirmed, "but their faces also follow the sun . . . *and* if the sun isn't shining, they look down and it almost seems like they're sad—it's called heliotropism."

"I guess they're like us then—we need the sunlight on our faces, too, to keep us cheerful."

"We do," Ellie agreed as her grandmother filled the last jar. "The tables are gonna look really nice!" she said, her growing excitement for the wedding was palpable. "I can't wait till next weekend!"

"I can't wait, either," Libby said, and she meant it. They hadn't had a big family gathering since the funerals of Jack and Dutch, and those had both been sad occasions, but a double wedding on the farm! That was cause for celebration!

44

"I VOLUNTEERED TO HELP AT THE SOUP KITCHEN THURSDAY NIGHT," CHASE SAID, "so we'll have to take both cars to work that day."

Liam looked up from his phone. "Aren't we heading to the farm Friday morning?"

"We are, but it's only for a couple of hours and I won't be late. They need volunteers, and I thought I might see Matthias. I haven't seen him in a couple of weeks and I'm a little worried."

"You have such a good heart," Liam teased.

"Thanks," Chase said. "Even though you sound sarcastic."

"I'm not being sarcastic. I mean it."

"Mm-hmm." Chase took a sip of his drink. "You could volunteer, too."

"I might, but I'll let you see how it is first."

Chase watched the beachgoers walking along South Beach. "I think we should wait till September to go to Cancun. It'll be less crowded and not so hot. Besides, I told Gage I'd feed the chickens while they're away. He said we could stay at the cabin if we want."

Liam looked up from his phone. "I don't know if I could stay there with my allergy. I barely made it through dinner last weekend."

"Gus won't be there," Chase said. "Maeve's sister and brother-in-law are taking him."

"I don't think that matters—there will still be dog hair floating around. But I'm fine with going on our honeymoon in September. It's a little late to book something right now anyway."

"I'm sure we could find something if we really wanted to."

"Nah, I don't want to rush it. I want to have fun planning it." Liam took a sip of his wine. "Besides, September isn't too far off and it'll give us something to look forward to."

Chase nodded. "Did you hear from your sister?"

"I did," Liam replied. "She's not coming. She said if she had a little more time to plan, she might've been able to pull it off, but she and Jim already have something going on that weekend."

"I wonder if your parents had anything to do with her decision."

"Probably," Liam said, "but she's my twin—you'd think our bond would be stronger than that."

"You'd think."

"Is Quinn coming?"

"She is . . . *and* she asked me if she could bring someone."

"Wow! I thought she wasn't seeing anyone."

"She wasn't, but she said something unexpectedly happy happened—her words, not mine—and she wants to bring him so she has someone to dance with . . . and so her mom can meet him."

"Okay," Liam said thoughtfully. "She's such a great person—she really lifted my spirits that night when she talked about her relationship with her dad. She was spot-on about choosing your own tribe."

"She was always such a good friend. I can't believe I ever doubted her, but I had no idea her dad was eavesdropping that night—it had to be well after midnight when we were talking." He finished his drink and stood up. "Need a refill?" he asked, nodding to Liam's empty wineglass.

"No, thanks. I'm good."

"Suit yourself," he teased, and a few minutes later, he came back with a fresh drink. "Next time we go to the store, we need to pick up limes and vodka."

Liam nodded, and while he added them to the growing shopping list on his phone, he said, "Seems like we're going through a lot of vodka lately . . ."

"Does it?" Chase said, grinning impishly and feigning innocence, but then his smile faded. "Do you think I drink too much?"

Liam shrugged. "Sometimes, maybe . . ."

Chase nodded thoughtfully and pressed his lips together. "I think it's probably a habit I picked up from my brothers . . . *and* from years of life experiences . . . dealing with everything, you know? Wondering, when I was a kid, why I was different from my brothers—how I was the one to draw the lucky card, and then thinking my best friend betrayed me . . . and having to find the courage to tell my parents. To be honest, I've sometimes wondered if it would just be easier to fake it . . . you know, pretend to be straight, marry a girl, and have a family the conventional way."

Liam looked up. "I think a lot of people *do* do that, especially before it wasn't as widely accepted, and in some ways, it probably is easier—especially if you live in a country where they'll throw you off a building if you're gay, but then, again, you aren't being authentic . . . so how can you be truly happy?"

Chase smiled. "That's why I'm *not* faking it. If I had, I would've never met *you* . . . and that would've been the biggest loss of my life."

"It would've been a huge loss for me, too."

"You have more reason to drink than me," Chase said, "the way your parents treated you . . ."

"Yeah, well, I *could* drink more," Liam said, smiling, "but I'm not gonna let my parents ruin my life and my health. I also think drinking can get out of hand—alcohol is a slippery slope."

Chase nodded and sighed. "It *is* a slippery slope," he agreed, and as he said it, he thought of Matthias. "Maybe I'll cut back."

"Don't do it for me."

"I'd do anything for *you*, though," he declared. "Besides, you're right. My devil-may-care attitude might end me in a heap o' trouble someday."

Liam looked back at his phone. "We need bread and milk, but I don't want to get too much food since we won't be here next weekend."

"That reminds me—did the marriage license come?"

"It did. Yesterday."

"Good," Chase said, sipping his drink, but when Liam eyed him, he laughed. "What? I can't throw away a perfectly good drink. Besides, I'm getting married this weekend and we'll be celebrating . . . sooo there's no point in starting now!"

◈

45

"WE'RE JUST GONNA SIT OUT ON THE PATIO FOR A FEW MINUTES," AMES CALLED as Rylee wiped down a table.

"Okay," he called back, looking up to see who she meant by *we*. "Hi, Mrs. Tennyson," he said. "It's nice to see you."

"It's nice to see you, too, Rylee," Libby replied.

"Are you helping Mrs. Finley because she has a concussion?"

"I'm trying to," Libby said, laughing, "but she's a bit stubborn and says she doesn't need any."

Rylee laughed. "My mom says I'm stubborn, too."

"You should let Mrs. Tennyson help you, Mrs. Finley," Jessie said, overhearing their conversation. She was draining the last coffee machine into a pitcher for the next day's iced coffee. "You have a 'cussion and Rylee and I can handle the shop."

"Thanks, Jessie," Ames said. "I know you can." She looked over at Libby. "I know you're a tea drinker, my dear, but would you like some iced coffee?"

"I would love some iced coffee," Libby replied, "but don't go to any trouble."

"It's no trouble at all," Ames assured her. She filled two clear plastic cups with ice and held them out to Jessie. "Hon, would you be so kind as to pour some into these cups?"

"Absolutely," Jessie said. "Need room for cream?"

"A little," Ames replied, and then she eyed Libby. "Cream?"

"Yes, please," Libby replied.

"How's that?" Jessie asked.

"Perfect. Thank you."

"You're welcome," Jessie said, looking up. "Your eye looks better."

Ames chuckled. "You think so?"

"Mm-hmm."

"It's less dark purple and more puke green now," Ames said.

"Kind of like a rainbow," Jessie said, smiling.

"Exactly," Ames said, laughing.

"I'm glad you're okay," Jessie said, reaching out to hug her. "I was worried."

"Thank you," Ames said. "I'm glad, too."

Finally, the young woman released her. "Need tops and straws?"

"Please," Ames said.

Jessie poured half-and-half into the cups, snapped on tops, unwrapped two straws, and slid them in.

"What service," Ames said, smiling.

"Thank you, Jessie," Libby said.

"You're welcome," she replied and then continued draining the coffee into pitchers.

Libby followed Ames out into the late-afternoon sunshine and looked around in surprise. There were big clusters of all of her favorite old-fashioned perennials—from daisies to cheerful black-eyed Susans, and from lilies of every color to lavender echinacea and allium, not to mention fiery-red bee balm—which had the honeybees buzzing all around them . . . *and* it looked like the sedum would be blooming soon, too. "Wow! It's so pretty out here," she said. "I didn't even know Payton had a patio!"

Ames looked around at the raised beds framing the cozy space. "I know!" she exclaimed. "I should get Cash to come over and work in my garden. He does such nice work!"

"Cash did all this?" Libby asked.

"He did," Ames said, taking a sip of her coffee. "Mmm, this hits the spot," she murmured. "Maybe it'll help my headache."

Libby frowned. "Your head still hurts?"

"A little. Not as much as it did, thank goodness."

"It takes time," Libby said, sipping hers. "Matt got hit in the head with a baseball when he was in high school, and he had to take it easy for several weeks. He missed the whole second half of the season . . . and I think that hurt more than his head did."

They heard a vehicle pull in and looked up to see Cash parking the truck behind the shop. "Well?! How'd it go?" Ames called as he and Payton came up the walk.

Payton looked over at her son and he proudly held up his new license. "I got it!" he said, beaming.

"Congratulations!" Libby said.

"Thank you."

"You didn't have to get a learner's permit?" Ames asked, frowning.

"No, I told Mom, if you're over eighteen you can just get a license," he said. "Besides, I already knew how to drive—Dad taught me. Now, I just have to get his old Bronco running."

"God help me!" Payton said, shaking her head. "*Now*, the fun begins," she added, laughing.

"I'm gonna go show Jessie and Rylee," Cash said, pulling open the door.

"Okay," Payton said, sitting down across from her friends. "Thank you for covering for us."

"You're welcome," Ames said. "It was no trouble—these kids run this place like a top." She looked over at Libby and smiled. "And I had Libby as backup."

Payton smiled at both of them. "It's nice to have old friends you can count on."

"It is," Ames agreed.

Payton eyed her. "How're you feeling?"

"Just tired."

"Does your head still hurt?"

"A little, but Jessie made us some iced coffee and it's helping."

"It looks like the swelling is going down," Payton said, leaning closer.

"Jessie says it looks like a rainbow."

Payton laughed. "Well, that'll go away."

"Not in time for Saturday."

Payton frowned. "What's Satur . . . oh, the wedding!"

"Yes, the wedding. I haven't been to a wedding in years, and I finally get to go to one and now I look like Quasimodo!"

"You don't look like Quasimodo," Libby consoled. "He had a hunched back."

"He also had a funny face," Ames countered glumly. "And Quinn's coming home with her new friend . . . and this is how I'm going to look when I meet him."

Payton chuckled. "I didn't realize you were so vain!"

"I'm not vain—I just don't want to look like Quasimodo." She half smiled and took a sip of her coffee. "Oh, by the way, did you get your test results back?"

"I did," Payton said, smiling. "And all my margins are clear!"

"Oh, wow!" Ames said, her face brightening. "Praise God!"

"That's wonderful news," Libby said. "I've been praying, too. You must be so relieved."

"I *am* relieved," Payton said.

"Do you have to go back?"

"I have to have some scan in the fall that involves taking a radioactive iodine pill and staying away from people for three days, so I'll probably need someone to keep an eye on the shop again . . . *if* I still own it . . ."

Libby raised her eyebrows. "What do you mean, *if you still own it*? You love the Coffee Bean!"

"I *do* love it," Payton acknowledged, "but I'm sixty-five, and all this"—she motioned to her neck—"has me wondering how much time I have left on this earth, so I've actually been thinking about Cash's suggestion to retire."

"I didn't know you were thinking of retiring," Libby said in surprise.

Payton nodded. "I only started considering it recently and he is right—why am I working so hard when I don't need to? Why am I getting up at the crack of dawn every day? By the time I get home, I can barely stay awake. There are so many things I'd like to do with my time before I'm too old."

"What kinds of things?" Ames asked curiously.

Payton smiled. "Well, a few weeks ago we had this tour bus full of people come into the shop, and two ladies from Nantucket said they'd been to DC and Williamsburg; and that night, they were going to Pigeon Forge, and on the way home, they were going to Gettysburg. It sounded like so much fun to me—I'd *love* to go on a bus tour. Everything is planned for you . . . *and* paid for, and I'd love to see the country, especially the national parks. I looked at the cost of some trips, and they're really quite reasonable.

"So," she continued with a chuckle, "from bus tours I ended up looking at cruises, too, and I found cruises for all around the world—Alaska, the Panama Canal, the Mississippi River, even Europe—the options are endless!" She smiled and eyed them both. "But I don't want to go alone. You guys are welcome to come—we could even do a group trip with the Guild ladies . . ."

"Ooh! That would be fun!" Ames said. She looked over at Libby. "Would you go, Libby?"

"Oh, I don't know," Libby replied, the question catching her off guard. "It took me almost nine months just to come to the coffee shop!" Ames and Payton laughed, knowing it was true. Libby continued to think out loud. "But I might go. It *does* sound fun. I always wanted to travel, but Jack never felt comfortable leaving the farm. Now the boys have taken over and they really don't need my help, so I *could* go . . . and I know a really good travel agent!"

"Ooh, that's right!" Payton said. "I bet he could get us a good deal for a group. We just have to ask the other ladies."

"I bet there would be a lot of interest," Ames said, and then she frowned. "What about Cash? Are you going to leave him?"

"I am," Payton said. "He's gonna stay home and take care of Ned . . . and any other animals that need a pet sitter. He has his driver's license now, he's determined to get Lonny's old Bronco running, and he's already designed a business card—it's called *Cash's Doggone Awesome Pet Service*—which is actually a pretty cute name."

"That *is* cute," Ames said. "And that reminds me! I keep forgetting to tell him that I saw Sarah Whitman and she said she's looking for someone to take care of their dog while they're away, but she said it's a little more complicated because he's fourteen, blind, and needs eye drops twice a day. Do you think Cash would be interested?"

"I would definitely be interested," Cash said, peering through the screen door. "I can do it. Mrs. Finley, did you tell her I can do it?"

Ames looked up and laughed. "I *did*, and she said there are a lot of people in town who are looking for someone to take care of their pets."

"See, Mom?" Cash said. "I'll have plenty of business."

"I guess you will," Payton said, and then she looked over at them. "Anyway, that's what I've been thinking—selling the shop, retiring, and traveling."

"It sounds wonderful!" Libby said, surprising herself.

Ames nodded in agreement. "We can stay in lovely inns, drink wine on beautiful verandas . . ."

"Or tea," Libby chimed.

"Or tea," Ames agreed.

"Yes!" Payton said, smiling. "Oh, I'm so glad I have old dear friends for this stage of life!"

Ames and Libby smiled, too. "And we are so glad we have *you*!"

46

ELLIE PUSHED OPEN THE MUDROOM DOOR. "GRAN, COME QUICK! THERE'S SOMEthing wrong with Mercy!"

Libby left her mending on the table, hurried outside, and found Ellie kneeling in front of a cushioned porch chair on which their old gray tiger was curled into a tight ball with his pink nose tucked under his paws.

"I was watching Tucker and Rosie," Ellie said, motioning to the fence, "and I kept hearing this sad howl, and I turned around and saw Goodness pacing up and down on the porch."

Libby knelt down next to Ellie, and the orange tiger cat put her paw gently on Libby's knee, crying. "It's okay, Goodness," she said softly, stroking her soft fur, but the little orange tiger cat was inconsolable, and Libby turned her attention to the gray cat curled up in the chair. With two fingers, she gently stroked his solemn forehead but he didn't stir.

"Is he sleeping?" Ellie whispered.

Libby laid her hand on his side, feeling for warmth or a heartbeat, and then gently lifted his chin. "Oh, hon," Libby said softly, "I think our sweet Mercy has crossed over the rainbow bridge."

"He's dead?!" Ellie asked, her eyes brimming with tears.

Libby nodded and put her arms around her. "He looks so peaceful, though," she consoled. "I don't think he was in any pain. He just went to sleep and didn't wake up."

Ellie nodded as tears streamed down her cheeks. "He was just chasing Goodness around yesterday—he didn't seem sick," she sobbed.

"He's pretty old, though—Chase brought these two home when he was younger than you, so he had a good long life with lots of time to lie in the sun—which was his favorite thing to do."

Ellie nodded tearfully and looked down at the little orange tiger cat still pacing and crying mournfully. "What about Goodness?" she asked. "Her heart's broken."

"That's because she knows he's gone. Animals understand death . . . and they mourn, just like we do. Sometimes I wonder if they understand it even better than we do."

Libby sat down in the chair next to Mercy, and Goodness immediately hopped up on her lap, meowing and circling and stretching her neck so her nose touched Libby's chin. "It's okay, little girl. We know you're sad," she said softly. "We know you loved him." She stroked her soft orange head. "We know just how you feel." And finally, the little cat sat, but she continued to meow, telling the whole world about her grief.

Hearing the commotion, Matt walked over from the barn. "Who's making all that racket?" he said, and then he saw the tears on his daughter's cheeks. "Uh-oh, what happened?" he asked, looking over the railing.

"Mercy is dead," Ellie said tearfully.

Matt came up on the porch and put his arm around her. "Well, death is a part of life, El," he said softly, "especially on a farm." He looked at his mom. "I remember when Chase brought those two home. He was towing a wagon with his bike and he had them all nestled into a bed of hay."

Libby smiled. "I remember that, too, because we already had

too many barn cats, but he told Dad they were not barn cats, and even though Dad told him not to, he kept sneaking them up to his room."

"Uncle Chase will be sad," Ellie mused.

"He will be," Libby agreed. "They're supposed to get here tomorrow afternoon."

Matt sighed, knowing this was true—Chase had always had such a tender heart when it came to animals. He looked at his mom. "Want me to take him?"

"I guess you better," Libby said.

Ellie looked up. "Are you gonna bury him, Dad?"

Matt nodded. "Yeah, I'm sure there's a box in the barn . . ." He looked back at his mom. "Do you have an old towel or something to lay him on?"

"I do," Libby answered, setting Goodness on the porch and watching her go right over to the chair on which her brother lay, put one foot on the edge, and sniff him again. Then she hopped up and curled up next to him.

Libby felt tears sting her own eyes, too, but she brushed them away. "I'll get a towel."

"I'll be right back, too," Matt said, eyeing Ellie.

The little girl knelt next to the chair again and tried to console the sibling that had been left behind. "It's okay, Goodness," she whispered, gently stroking her fur.

Matt returned with a small wooden box and a shovel, and Libby came out with an old blue towel. "Where do you think would be a good spot?" he asked.

"I was thinking out under the pines. He loved to stroll through there and roll in the soft needles." She tucked the towel neatly into the box.

Matt lifted the gray cat off the cushion and gently laid him in the box, and Goodness hopped down, and hurried over, meowing loudly. "You're gonna talk about this the whole time, aren't you, girl?" he said, kneeling to pet her. Then he looked up at Ellie. "You comin'?"

Ellie nodded and he handed the shovel to her and picked up the box.

Ellie looked back at her grandmother. "I'll come get you when we're ready."

Libby nodded and watched the sad procession make its way slowly toward the pine grove with Goodness following them, still meowing mournfully.

An hour later, Ellie slipped her hand into Libby's as they walked back to the house. She turned to see if Goodness was following them, but she was still lying on the mound of fresh dirt under which her lifelong companion, playmate, and brother—after being prayed for and blessed—was buried.

"I don't know about you, my dear child, but I could use a cup of tea," Libby said, trying to lift her granddaughter's spirits.

"I could, too," Ellie replied.

"I have a lovely Yorkshire tea that is wonderful with condensed milk and a spoonful of honey," Libby suggested.

"Okay. Do you have any more of those cranberry scones we made the other day?"

"I *do*," Libby replied. "I even have some clotted cream."

"Mmm," Ellie said, smiling, "I didn't think I'd be hungry, but I guess I am."

"Being hungry is a good sign—it means you're going to survive."

"It's funny how you can be really sad, and still feel hungry."

"Well, your body knows it needs food, even if your heart doesn't think so."

"I hope Goodness gets hungry and doesn't stay out there all night."

"She will," Libby assured her as they climbed the porch steps. "She just needs time."

Ellie pulled open the screen door and held it for her grandmother. "Gran, do you think animals have souls?"

"I do," Libby answered without hesitation. "We've had so many animals live and die on this farm, and they've all had unique personalities, eccentricities, and soulful story-filled eyes—especially the cows, but even the chickens . . . so I absolutely believe they have souls, and they mourn, *and* go to heaven." She filled her kettle with fresh water. "Do you remember how the cows—after Grandpa died—used to stand under that big oak tree in the field where he and Cale are buried?"

Ellie nodded. "They missed him, too."

Libby smiled wistfully as she set the kettle on the burner. "They wore a path in the grass."

Ellie watched her grandmother drop two bags into her teapot and drape the strings over the side. "Two bags?" she asked, raising her eyebrows.

Libby smiled. "Two. I think we can both use a little extra comfort today."

"I think so, too." Ellie sat at the kitchen table and lightly traced her finger over the grooves and scratches. "Gran, did you know elephants mourn when a member of the herd dies?"

"I've heard that," Libby said, setting the scones and clotted cream on the table. "I also heard they have good memories."

Ellie nodded. "One time, Dad took me to the Elephant Sanctuary in Hohenwald and there were these two elephants there, Shirley and Jenny, who had performed together over twenty-four years earlier, and when they were reunited, they remembered each other and gently stroked each other's scars with their trunks."

"That's amazing," Libby said. "Seems to me I saw a story on the news about an elephant from that same sanctuary who was friends with a dog, and they were inseparable, and when the dog died, the elephant was devastated."

Ellie looked up in surprise. "That was Tarra and Bella! I have a book about them." She smoothed some clotted cream onto one of the scones. "I heard Shirley died recently—she was seventy-two!

And the other elephants at the sanctuary stood by her grave—just like Goodness with Mercy . . . and the cows with Grandpa."

Libby brought over the tea and sat across from her. "Which is all proof that animals *do* have souls and they *do* grieve."

"Mm-hmm," Ellie agreed, taking a bite of her scone.

❦

47

"I'LL BE HOME LATER," CHASE SAID AS HE OPENED THE OFFICE DOOR.

"Any idea what time?" Liam asked. "We're having burgers and I need to light the grill."

"Mmm, burgers," Chase hummed, and then pondered his answer. "Well, we serve from five to six and then we have to clean up, so I guess I'll be home around seven thirty."

Liam nodded. "Just text me when you're on your way."

"I will."

"I hope Matthias shows . . ."

"Me, too." Chase stepped out into the steamy late-day heat, and as he walked through the streets of downtown Savannah, and through historic Forsyth Park, he kept his eye out for the tall man with the little white dog, but he didn't see him.

He kept going until he came to an old white church, and when he pulled open the door, he was greeted by the heavenly aroma of beef and onions. "Dang, that smells good," he murmured. He went inside, asked for Big Bob, and was directed to the kitchen, where he found a mountain of a man stirring a huge pot of gravy. "Are you Big Bob?"

The man nodded and held out his hand. "You Chase?"

Chase nodded.

"Thanks for volunteering," he boomed and then pointed to a pile of aprons. "You're gonna serve mashed potatoes and gravy. That's Daisy—she'll show you."

Daisy smiled. "Hello, young man," she said. "Follow me."

Chase followed Daisy out into a big room where tables and chairs were set up. "There's already a line waiting," Daisy said, leading him over to the buffet table, "and they'll be coming in in about five minutes, so you stand right here next to these two characters," she teased, nudging her friends. "This is Dell," she said. "She's serving salad and rolls, and this is Fran—she's serving the pot roast and carrots." They both smiled as he tied his apron.

"Nice to meet you," he said, smiling back.

Daisy handed him a ladle and a serving spoon. "So you're last in the line, and they all love their mashed potatoes and Big Bob's gravy so be prepared!" She eyed her friends. "Y'all ready?"

They nodded and Daisy walked over and pushed open the heavy metal door, and a parade of people of all shapes, sizes, and colors started to filter in. They chatted quietly, picked up heavy-duty paper plates, and gratefully held them out to be filled, and then helped themselves to lemonade or iced tea from Coleman jugs, or hot coffee from a big percolator, and sat down across from their friends. For an hour straight, Chase piled mashed potatoes, made little pools for gravy, filled them to overflowing, and drizzled extra gravy over the tender beef; and after everyone had been served, people started coming back for seconds or going to the dessert table and taking a couple of cookies or a piece of cake.

Before Chase knew it, an hour had gone by and everyone began clearing their plates and leaving, but on their way out, Daisy and Bob handed them each a paper bag with a sandwich and a piece of fruit—a banana, apple, or peach in it. It was such an organized system that it went off without a hitch, and the time flew by. In fact, Chase was so caught up in serving and chatting, he forgot all about Matthias . . . until it was over, and he realized he hadn't come.

He helped carry the empty food trays back to the kitchen and set them on the counter, and then Daisy asked him if he could stay to help wipe down the tables. He nodded and she handed him a bucket of hot sudsy water and a cloth. He went back out, cleared the remaining plates, and thoroughly wiped down the tables, and when he carried the bucket back, they all beamed at him.

"Dang, you're a good worker!" Big Bob said. "You comin' back tomorrow?"

Chase laughed. "I can't come tomorrow, but I can come back next week."

"Please," Daisy begged, smiling and squeezing his arm.

"You come anytime you want," Dell said and Fran nodded.

Chase untied his apron and handed it to Daisy. "You don't happen to know an older gentleman named Matthias, do you? I thought I might see him here tonight."

"You mean tall handsome Matthias?" she asked, her eyes sparkling in recognition. "And little Marmalade?"

"Yes!" Chase said. "He's a friend of mine."

Daisy laughed. "Matthias is everyone's friend."

"How come he doesn't come to dinner?"

"Oh, he comes sometimes, but we can't let Marmalade in—some dumb state law about dogs, and he doesn't want to leave her outside. We tol' him he could come to the door and we'd give him a plate, but he's only done that a couple times, when he's absolutely desperate, or worried that she doesn't have enough to eat."

"It's too bad she can't come in," Chase said, shaking his head. "She's such a sweet dog."

Daisy nodded. "She is, but our hands are tied. Matthias is welcome to come to the door, though."

"Well, if you see him, would you please tell him I was asking for him."

"I will," Daisy replied, "and if you see him, tell him to come by and get a hot meal."

"I will," Chase promised.

"Thank you for helping tonight, Chase. We'll see you next week."

"You're welcome," Chase said. "I'll definitely be here."

He stepped out into the cool evening air and as he walked back to his car, he listened to the usual evening hum of downtown Savannah, but as he cut through Forsyth Park again, still checking park benches for any sign of his friend, the peaceful night was suddenly pierced by the scream of sirens, and he realized they were coming his way. He turned to look and saw them stop at the far end of the park, their lights flashing through the trees and against the old brick buildings, and he felt an odd wave of worry wash over him. Drawn to the lights and commotion, he hurried across the park to see what had happened.

A crowd was forming as yellow tape was stretched from a flickering streetlamp to the edge of a building and across an alley. "What's going on?" Chase asked a man standing nearby.

"They found some old homeless guy in the alley," the man answered.

Chase tried to swallow the lump in his throat and watched in dismay as two EMTs steered a stretcher out of the alley toward a waiting ambulance.

"Oh, no," he whispered, his heart pounding. He ducked under the tape and hurried over. "Who is that?" he asked, trying to see, but the body was covered with a white sheet. "Can you tell me who that is?" he asked one of the EMTs.

The EMT turned to him. "It's some old homeless guy. You think you know him?"

Chase swallowed. "I . . . I might," he stammered. "Can you show me?"

The EMT lifted the sheet and Chase saw Matthias's weathered face. "Damn," he whispered, tears springing to his eyes.

"You know him?" the EMT asked.

Chase nodded, his shoulders sagging. "He's my friend," he said, wiping his eyes.

"Well, maybe you can go talk to the officer because we couldn't find an ID on him."

Chase looked over to where a policeman was talking to a woman trying to tug a reluctant scrawny white dog to a van that said CANINE CONTROL. "Marmalade," he cried, and hearing her name, the little dog looked over, and even though her ears were back and her eyes were full of fear, when she saw Chase, she started to wag her whole hind end. "Thanks," he said to the EMT, and approached the woman, and without a second thought, said, "I'll take her." He knelt in front of Marmalade and she climbed into his lap.

The animal warden looked stunned. "Are you serious?"

"Absolutely," Chase said. "She's my friend's dog and I'll take care of her."

"Works for me," she said, slipping off the choke chain.

"Do you have her leash?"

"You mean this ratty old thing?" the woman replied, holding up the tattered rope Matthias had always used.

Chase nodded, took it from her, and hooked it to Marmalade's old blue collar, but he needn't have used it—the little dog was sitting on his foot. Chase stroked her side, and when he realized she was shaking, he scooped her up into his arms and held her against him.

The policeman pulled out his pen. "Did I hear you say the deceased is a friend?"

Chase nodded. "His name is Matthias Abraham. He's a Vietnam vet and his family lives in Atlanta."

The policeman jotted down this information, thanked him, and then held out his pen and pad. "Can I just have your info, too, in case I have any questions."

Chase set Marmalade on the ground and wrote his name and number down, and while he did, he felt her trembling between his legs. "If you can't find his family, please let me know and I will make the arrangements and cover any funeral expenses," he said, handing the pad and pen back to him, before scooping Marmalade up again.

The officer eyed him. "That's very generous of you. How did you know him?"

"I would see him around town and we chatted—that's all."

The officer reached up and gently stroked Marmalade's soft ears. "I'm glad you're taking her. She had her head on his chest when we got here and she wouldn't leave him. I didn't like seeing the warden tugging her like that with a choke collar."

"She's a sweet dog," Chase said as Marmalade licked his chin.

"Thanks for your help," the officer said. "I'm sorry about your friend."

"Thanks," Chase replied, extending his free hand. "Have a good night."

"You as well," the officer replied.

Chase turned to walk away. "You want to walk, Marmy-girl?" he asked softly, but when he tried to set her down, she resisted and he ended up carrying her all the way back to his car. He set her on the passenger seat and went around to the driver's side but when he opened the door, she was on his seat. "Um, are you driving, missy?" he teased and then he gently nudged her, but once he got in, she moved closer and rested her head on his lap. "It's okay," he said softly. "Everything's gonna be okay." And then he pulled out his phone to call Liam.

〜

48

"Did Cash come with you?" Ames asked, holding the door open for Payton—who was carrying a big cardboard box. "I told Ned he was coming."

Payton shook her head. "He's been working on the music for the wedding every night this week and said he still has more to do. Gage and Chase sent him playlists and he wants to be ultraorganized. You know how he gets."

"I *do* know," she said, chuckling. "But I also know he'll do a good job—he would do anything for Chase—and Libby said he was thrilled when Gage asked him, so I'm not surprised by his enthusiasm."

"Enthusiasm bordering on obsession!" Payton said, setting the box on the counter.

"How much more do you have?"

"Two more boxes."

Ames propped open the door and followed her through the garage, and Ned took advantage of the opportunity to scoot out and lie in the sunny driveway—his favorite spot. "Are you staying out here?" Ames asked as she walked back by with a box, and he responded by lazily thumping his tail.

"You're so silly, Ned," Payton said, chuckling as she walked past him, too. They set the boxes on the counter. "You leaving this door open?" she asked.

"Just don't let it latch, so he can come in if he wants to."

Payton chuckled. "Doesn't he know how to bark and let you know?"

"He knows," Ames said, chuckling, too. "If he hears something outside at night, he tears down the hall barking like a maniac, and it scares the bejesus out of me, but it doesn't happen very often. He finds other ways to communicate, like flopping his ears or groaning. He really is a character."

"That reminds me—Sarah Whitman called Cash and asked him if he'd be available to house-sit and take care of Samson for a week in July."

"Is he gonna do it?"

"He is," Payton said, nodding. "He also had business cards printed and put them in a little holder on the counter at the shop . . . and he's had to refill it twice already!"

"Wow! He's gonna have more business than he can handle!"

"And now, both Rylee and Jessie have said they want to work for him!"

"That's too funny," Ames said, "but if you decide to sell the shop, it'll make it easier if they have different jobs lined up."

"Well, Rylee said he wants to do both. I'm not sure about Jessie . . . *and* at the last softball game, I mentioned I was thinking about selling and retiring, and Jen said she and her husband might be interested."

"Wow. That would be too easy!"

Payton nodded. "Guess we better get going on these or we'll be up all night." She gestured to the vases. "So they're all washed and I cut the ribbons and picked up some baby's breath. I also brought some sustenance," she said, smiling and pulling a bottle of chilled chardonnay out of one of the boxes.

"You think of everything, don't you?" Ames said, laughing and reaching into her cabinet for two wineglasses.

"I try," she said, and then her smile faded. "Are you allowed to drink with a concussion?"

"It's mild. I'm fine," Ames assured her. "Besides, we're going to a wedding this weekend so I'm not gonna miss out on all the fun!"

Just then, Payton noticed that the sink was full of sunflowers. "Oh, my goodness! Look at all those—they're gorgeous!"

"Thanks! I told you I had a bumper crop!"

"You weren't kidding. They're gonna look so pretty on the tables."

Ames nodded and then eyed the bottle. "Do we need a corkscrew?"

"No, it's twist-off," Payton said, opening it and pouring two glasses. "Cheers!" she said, holding up her glass. "Here's to a fun weekend!"

Ames clinked her glass. "Cheers!" she said, taking a sip.

"So what did you end up getting them?"

"Oh, I got my usual—Woodstock wind chimes."

"Those are always nice," Payton said, nodding approvingly.

"What did you get?"

Payton smiled. "You're gonna laugh."

"Why?" she asked, already laughing.

"I got them both smoothie makers like the one I gave you."

"Oh, that's a great idea! I love mine."

"Now that you finally use it!" Payton teased.

"Have you decided what you're wearing?"

"Noo . . ." Payton said, raising her eyebrows. "I can't remember the last time I wore a dress, so I think I'm just gonna wear a pantsuit—maybe that beige one."

"I was thinking the same thing!" Ames said. "Libby said it's not really formal, although she bought a new dress."

"Well, she's the mother of the grooms, plural! And you look cute no matter what you wear."

"You think so?" Ames asked, feeling her cheeks flame.

"I do," Payton said, briefly searching her friend's eyes. "Even cuter with that shiner!" She started to lift the vases out of the boxes and set them in rows on the table. "I think we should tie the ribbons on first," she said, pulling out a pile of blue gingham ribbons.

"Okay," Ames said, clearing her throat and sitting across from her with her wine. They began tying the ribbons around the vases. "So Quinn is getting in around ten thirty."

"Are you pickin' them up?"

"I am."

"Do you want me to drop these off?"

"I thought we could do it tonight when they're done—it's not supposed to be hot so they'll stay fresh. Besides, I already asked Libby and she said they have the tables all set up and we can just put them on them."

Payton nodded and took a sip of her wine. "Sooo . . . what do we know about this new fella?"

Ames sipped her wine. "I peppered Quinn with questions and tried to find out as much as I could! So, in a nutshell, she said his name is Ezra Hamilton, he's twenty-nine, and he has a golden retriever named Esther. He's originally from Tennessee—which is so crazy . . . or serendipitous, but he's lived in San Francisco since college—not sure where he went. She said he comes into the restaurant pretty often, sometimes with friends, but sometimes by himself, and one night recently, when he was there by himself, she wanted to ask him something about his business, and they ended up talking about hiking, and the next thing she knew, he'd asked her if she wanted to go hiking with him, and she said yes, and he brought Esther—who she said is beautiful, and they had such a good time, she decided to ask him if he wanted to go to a wedding in Tennessee, and he said yes!"

"Wow! You got a lot of information!" Payton said, laughing. "She must really like him if she wants you to meet him."

"She must," Ames agreed, setting a vase on the table and taking a sip of her wine. "I hope he's a good guy. I've been praying for her to meet someone who likes the outdoors and dogs and kids—like she does. I've been pretty specific in my prayers," she said, "and I don't know if he likes kids, but he likes dogs and hiking, so we're two out of three so far!"

"You're funny," Payton said, smiling, "but I believe prayer works . . . and you can't be too specific. God loves details."

Ames nodded. "I also want her to find someone who's gonna love her with all his heart, you know? Someone who puts her first and wants her to be happy." She smiled sadly. "I never had that with Frank. The only good thing that came from our marriage was Quinn—and although I wouldn't trade her for anything, I sometimes wonder if I settled because I was worried no one else would come along."

Payton smiled and searched her friend's eyes. "I know just what you mean."

❦

49

IT WAS DUSK WHEN PAYTON AND AMES TURNED ONTO TENNYSON ROAD WITH the centerpieces. They'd snugly tucked them between towels in the back of the truck—which they'd doubly lined with a moving blanket. Payton drove slowly down the quiet dirt road, avoiding potholes and ruts, the beams of her headlights bumping up and down.

"Someone's walking," Ames said, pointing, "with a dog."

"I see them," Payton replied.

"Oh, I think it's Chase!" Ames said. They pulled up next to him. "How are you, young man?"

Chase turned to see who was talking and a slow smile crossed his face. "Mrs. Finley!" he said, and then he looked over to see who was driving. "And Mrs. Childs! I'm fine. How are you?"

"Able to sit up and take nourishment," Payton said.

Chase laughed. "That's good." And then he eyed Ames. "Oh, no! What did you do?"

Ames reached up and touched her still-tender cheek. "You should see the other guy!"

Payton shook her head. "She tried to catch a softball with her face and it didn't go well."

"Ouch!" Chase said, cringing sympathetically.

Ames nodded. "I have a concussion, too."

"Well, remember to use your glove next time," he kidded her.

Ames laughed. "I'll try."

"Are you guys coming tomorrow?"

"Absolutely!" Ames said. "We wouldn't miss it."

"We brought over the centerpieces," Payton said, gesturing to the back of the truck.

Chase looked. "Wow! Those look great. Do you need help?"

"We never turn down help," Ames said.

"Well, sometimes we do," Payton interjected.

Chase laughed and then eyed Ames. "Is Quinn coming?"

She nodded. "I'm picking them up tomorrow morning."

"Good! I'm so glad she's bringing someone—I can't wait to meet him."

"You and me both!" Ames said.

He looked over at Payton. "Is Cash stressed about being the DJ?"

Payton chuckled. "He's thrilled, but he's probably a little stressed, too."

"Well, he shouldn't be—we're all family and I'm sure he's gonna do great."

Payton nodded. "I'll tell him you said that."

Ames looked down at the little white dog sitting on Chase's foot. "Who's that cutie?"

Chase scooped Marmalade up and held her so Ames could pet her. "This is Marmalade."

"Oh, my, she's so sweet," Ames said as Marmalade licked her hand. "Is she yours?"

Chase shook his head. "I wish she could be, but Liam seems to be allergic to dogs. She even had to ride over from Savannah with Gage and Maeve because Liam's eyes were itching and watering so much."

"Where'd you get her?" Payton asked.

"She belonged to a friend of mine. He passed away unexpectedly, and the dog warden was going to take her to the pound."

"Oh, no, I'm so sorry to hear that," Ames said as Payton nodded in agreement.

"Thanks," he said. "Anyway, there was no way I was letting her go to the pound, so here she is. I wish we could keep her. She's been through a lot, and she was very attached to my friend—they were homeless together, and I'm sure she can't figure out what has happened to him. I don't even know if she had ever even ridden in a car before last night, so everything is new and she's a little shy and traumatized." He nuzzled her head against his cheek. "You guys know of anyone who wants a dog?" he asked.

Ames shook her head. "I have Ned and he's really enough for me." She looked over at Payton, who shook her head, too . . . even though she could see the lightbulb popping on in her friend's brain, but Payton gave her a warning look: *Don't even!*

"Well, let me know if you think of anyone."

"We will," Ames replied.

"I'll be right up to help you unload."

"Okay," Ames said, and as Payton turned and pulled up the driveway, Ames looked over. "Why not?"

"Because."

"Didn't your mother ever tell you that *because* is not a reason?"

"Let's not ruin what has been a fun evening."

Ames sighed and didn't say anything more, but a few moments later, when Chase came in with Marmalade, she nosed right over to Payton—who was setting a centerpiece on a table.

"Hello, there, missy," she said, smiling and reaching down to pet her. She looked up and saw Ames watching. "What?" she asked. "My heart isn't made of stone, you know."

"I know it's not," Ames said. She turned to Chase—who had just come in with two more centerpieces. "Did you have your rehearsal tonight?"

"We did," Chase said, nodding. "Mom made a wonderful dinner and I think there are still a few people inside." He looked toward the house and saw Reverend Dave Peters—the minister who would be officiating the ceremony the next day, and his wife, Susan, coming down the porch steps. A moment later they appeared in the doorway and surveyed the scene. "Wow!" Susan said, admiring the centerpieces. "Did you two make these?"

"We did," Ames said, stopping to give them both hugs.

"Are they from your garden?"

Ames nodded.

"They are beautiful!"

Dave nodded in agreement and then eyed Ames's cheek. "Your eye is looking better."

"Thanks," Ames said, "and thank you for taking such good care of me on the way to the hospital."

"Just doing my job—my other job . . ." he added, smiling. "Did you end up having a concussion?"

"A mild one. Not enough to slow me down."

"Well, you should take it easy."

"I am," she assured him.

Payton walked over. "You are, except when you're *not*," she said, hugging the minister and his wife, too. "I told you Cash would walk Ned, but you insist on doing it yourself."

"I'm fine," Ames insisted. "Walking is good for you."

Chase put the last two centerpieces on tables and walked over to join them with Marmalade still glued to his leg.

"Your mom makes the best lasagna, Chase," Susan said. "I just want to take a tray home."

Chase laughed. "She'd probably give you one. It's the least she can do after you made all those yummy lemon meringue pies, which are our favorite!"

Susan waved her hand. "That was nothing. I make them all the time."

"Not to mention all the cookie favors," Liam said, coming up behind them.

Susan nodded. "You're most welcome. I had fun making them." She knelt down to pet Marmalade again. "I wish we could take you home, honey, but we already have two pups." Marmalade wiggled her whole hind end and licked Susan's hand. "Oh, my goodness, you're so sweet!"

Dave watched his wife becoming more enamored by the little white dog and chuckled. "All right, we better get going before we *do* take her home."

Chase laughed. "I'm sure she'll still be here tomorrow."

Dave shook his head and began gently steering his wife toward their car. "Don't tempt her."

Chase laughed and turned to Ames and Payton. "You've met Liam before, haven't you?"

"Oh, yes," Ames said, looking over at Payton for confirmation. She nodded. "We met him at your dad's funeral."

"I thought so," Chase replied, and Ames and Payton both gave Liam a hug. "Mrs. Finley is Quinn's mom, and Mrs. Childs is Cash's mom," Chase explained, and Liam nodded.

Ames suddenly felt self-conscious about her cheek. "Don't mind me," she said.

Liam smiled. "It looks like it hurt."

"It did," she admitted, "but it's a lot better."

Payton nudged her and grinned. "Thank goodness you're still cute!"

"Oh, you!" Ames said, her cheeks becoming rosier than they already were.

"Well, we better get going," Payton said. "We both have to be up early—you to pick up Quinn, and me for my half day at the shop."

"You're only opening for half a day?" Ames asked, raising her eyebrows.

Payton nodded. "What did you think I was doing?"

"I guess I hadn't thought about it."

Payton turned to Chase and Liam. "We will see you tomorrow!"

"Okay!" Chase said as Liam smiled. "Thank you very much for the beautiful centerpieces."

"You're very welcome," Ames said as Payton nodded.

"G'night," Payton said.

"Night," Chase replied. "Be careful driving home."

"We will."

Chase and Liam watched the two older women walk toward their truck, and then noticed a quick intimate moment when their hands brushed together and they briefly intertwined pinkies. The two women separated, climbed in, and waved, and Chase and Liam waved back, and then they looked at each other with raised eyebrows. "No way!" Chase said.

Liam nodded. "Way . . ."

50

THE SUN HADN'T EVEN PEEKED OVER THE HORIZON WHEN LIBBY QUIETLY PUSHED open the screen door. She heard a soft meow and looked over to see Goodness curled up in her favorite chair. "Well, good morning to you, too, missy," she said softly, stroking the cat's soft chin and ears. The little cat responded by pushing her head up into Libby's palm and purring loudly, but a moment later, two hummingbirds zipped past Libby's head, and the cat sat up attentively and watched as they sipped from the feeder. "No hunting," Libby admonished as she headed down the steps.

She walked down the driveway and looked out across the misty field at the milking barn where the cows were mooing impatiently. She glanced at her watch, wondering where her boys were, but she didn't have to wonder long because, by the time she reached the road, Matt was turning in. "You're up early," he said, stopping beside her.

"I couldn't sleep," she said.

"Wedding day jitters?"

"I don't know about that," she said. "I just keep thinking about the details—I want it to be perfect."

"I'm sure it will be."

"I'm sure it will be, too."

"Where's Ellie? She's not walking with you?"

"She's sound asleep. She and Harper were chattering late into the night. They're both so excited, I'm surprised they ever fell asleep."

Matt chuckled. "I knew they'd hit it off." He sighed. "Well, I'm sure the ladies are waiting."

"They are—I heard them mooing."

He smiled. "Have a good walk."

"Thanks," she said, leaning down to pull out a dandelion.

He turned into the driveway, and just as he rounded the bend, Eli and Grayson arrived too. They chatted with Libby for a minute, and then headed up to help their brother with the morning chores—it was going to be a busy day for all of them.

Libby watched Eli's truck disappear and smiled—she was thankful to have all her boys home—it didn't happen very often anymore and it made her heart full. She continued to walk, the sun filtering through the trees, dappling the road and the old stone wall with blotches of light. She listened to the morning symphony of songbirds and then heard the unmistakable singing and chirring deep in the woods of a wood thrush. The bell-like song of the elusive bird always reminded her of Dutch, and she decided it was appropriate for her dad to make his presence known on this special day . . . or, as he would call it, this *day of days*! Her hand brushed the daylilies as she tried to spy the little speckled-breast, but per usual, the bird—whose song was so magical and clear—eluded her. In all of her sixty-five years, she'd never seen a wood thrush, but Dutch had. One time, when she was little, they'd sat together in the woods all afternoon, waiting because he wanted her to see one, but they never did.

Libby smiled wistfully, remembering that day, and then her mind, of its own accord, drifted back further to a story—a fable of sorts—that he'd told her that day—a story she'd all but forgotten . . . until now.

They'd sat side by side, listening and watching, and then

Dutch—with an impish smile—had whispered, "Did you know birds didn't always have wings?"

At nine years old, she'd frowned skeptically. "Yes, they have."

He'd shaken his head. "Nope. God made them without wings at first. It wasn't until later that he made their wings, and he didn't call them *wings*. He called them *burdens* and he laid them in front of them and told them to pick them up and carry them. The birds were beautiful—they had lovely feathers and pretty voices, and they didn't want to carry burdens, but eventually they obeyed and picked them up and put them on their shoulders to carry. At first, these burdens were cumbersome and heavy, but they didn't give up and continued to carry them, even folding them over their hearts, and then, as time went by, don't you know those burdens they'd been carrying attached to their bodies—they became a part of them!"

"No!" Libby said, wide-eyed.

Dutch nodded. "Indeed, and it didn't take long for the birds to figure out how to use them, either. Before they knew it, they were being lifted high up into the air by them. Their burdens had become wings!"

"Wow!" Libby had whispered.

Dutch nodded. "Same thing goes for us hapless humans. God gives us problems and heavy loads to carry, but if we're willing to carry them in our hearts and soldier on, those burdens will lift us up, just like wings, and bring us closer to God. Our burdens will become our blessings."

"Our burdens will become our blessings," Libby murmured now. "I can't believe I forgot that story, and never even told Ellie, my bird lover!"

She smiled, and then a flash of feathers caught her eye. She followed the little bird's flight to a branch above her head, and then caught her breath in astonishment—it had a snow-white breast sprinkled with cinnamon speckles, and then it fearlessly sang its cheery song, punctuated with chirring, and she knew exactly what it was. The little wood thrush cocked its head, studied her, sang once more, and flew off, deep into the woods.

Libby stood still, stunned by the serendipitous encounter, and wondered if her dad was nearby, watching over her. It was so odd that she would remember a story he'd told her so long ago on a day that meant so much, and she felt a comforting peace wash over her—it was almost as if the burden of her loss was becoming her wings. She looked up through the whispering trees and smiled.

❧

51

"DID YOU KNOW BLACK SWANS CAN LIVE TO BE FORTY YEARS OLD?" ELLIE ASKED as she scooped a spoonful of cereal. She was sitting at the kitchen table across from Harper—who, she'd just discovered, also loved Lucky Charms.

"I believe it," Harper said, brushing her copper bangs out of her eyes and scooping a spoonful, too.

Ellie took a sip of orange juice. "A male swan is called a cob, a female is a pen, and babies are cygnets."

Just then, Chase came into the kitchen to get a cup of coffee and saw them sitting there. "Uh-oh," he said, "double trouble!"

They looked up and laughed. "*You* are double trouble all by yourself," Harper teased back.

"How can I be double trouble all by myself?" Chase asked, mussing her hair and sitting next to her.

"You just are," Harper said, grinning at Ellie—who nodded in agreement.

"So are you two solving all the world's problems this morning?" he asked.

"We're working on it," Ellie said, grinning at Harper.

The day before, when Harper had first climbed out of her parents' car, the two girls had eyed each other like cats in an alley. They'd both heard so much—Harper from her uncle Gage and aunt Maeve as well as from her parents, Ben and Macey Samuelson, Maeve's older sister and maid of honor, and Ellie from her dad and grandmother—about how well they were going to get along that they'd both grown increasingly skeptical, but after a half hour in each other's company, swinging on the old tire swing in the backyard, they'd happily discovered that the adults' prediction had been 100 percent correct. And ever since they'd been chatting nonstop, covering every topic they could think of—from sea turtles to ostriches, and now they were on swans.

"We were just talking about black swans," Ellie reported matter-of-factly. "Did you know they can live to be forty years old?"

Chase raised his eyebrows. "Forty years?!"

"Mm-hmm," Ellie said, nodding. "Another fun fact is they mate for life . . . *and* sometimes, two *males* will even pair up for life."

Chase laughed. "Wow! I guess black swans are pretty hip."

Ellie nodded. "They are. You know how the two males have babies?"

"I do not," he said, sipping his coffee.

"They either take over another pair's nest, or they have a three-some with a female, and after she lays eggs, they kick her out."

"A threesome?!" Chase said, practically snorting coffee out his nose and causing the two girls to almost fall off their chairs with giggles.

Just then Maeve came in, in search of coffee. "Uh-oh," she said. "What's goin' on in here?" she asked, eyeing them suspiciously as she filled a mug.

"Your nieces just told me that black swans have threesomes." And Maeve, who'd just taken a sip, almost choked on it.

"How do you know what a threesome is?" she asked, looking alarmed.

"Everyone knows what a threesome is, Aunt Maeve," Harper said, still giggling.

"Not when they're ten years old!" Maeve said.

"I'm eleven," Harper corrected.

"Ten, eleven, doesn't matter!"

The two girls looked at each other, grinning, and started scooping their cereal.

Chase raised his eyebrows and looked at Maeve and she shook her head in dismay.

"What is that funny sound?" she asked, looking around the kitchen, and when Chase pointed, she realized the sound was coming from Marmalade—who was curled up on the dog bed next to the woodstove, snoring. "I guess she finally relaxed a little."

"Yeah, she needed to," Chase said. "I think she must be exhausted. Between riding all the way over here and meeting so many new people, it's been more than a little overwhelming. I'm also sure having a full belly has helped."

Maeve nodded. "She's such a good dog—I wish we could take her, but we have our hands full with Gus." The mention of her dog reminded her of the potential escapades going on back home, where one of her brother-in-law Ben's employees was taking care of Gus as well as Harper's three-legged golden retriever, Keeper, and their cat, Big Mac, at her sister's house. She looked at Harper. "I hope Gus and Keeper are behaving for John this weekend."

Harper nodded. "I know Keep is behavin', but you never know about Gus!"

Maeve laughed and refilled her cup, knowing all too well how true that statement was. "Well, I'm going up to shower while no one else is in there."

Ellie stood up to clear their cereal bowls. "I'll show you where Mercy is buried," Ellie said solemnly, eyeing her uncle. "Grandma said he died peacefully—he was all curled up." She shook her head. "But poor Goodness was so sad she wouldn't stop meowing."

Chase nodded. "Those two cats followed me everywhere when I was little." He sipped his coffee. "She'll be okay."

As he said this, the little orange tiger sauntered in, eyed Marmalade suspiciously, and hopped up on Chase's lap. "Hey, there, little girl," he said softly, scratching her chin and she curled up on his lap and started to purr like a motorboat.

"Boy, Uncle Chase, she really does love you!"

52

CHASE STOOD IN FRONT OF THE MIRROR IN HIS CHILDHOOD BEDROOM—THE mirror into which he'd gazed when he was a boy trying to understand life—and deftly tied his new dark blue paisley tie.

"How'd you do that so quick?" Liam asked, looking over his shoulder.

"I'm an expert at tie tying," he replied.

Liam looked back down at the folded piece of paper he'd printed with directions on it and tried to tie his tie again. He held out the narrow red paisley fabric that matched Chase's and kept consulting the paper as he folded first one way and then the other and pulled it through.

Chase looked in the mirror at the end result. "Hmm," he murmured, which resulted in Liam pulling it off in frustration.

"Easy there," Chase teased, and then he reached up, held the tie at the perfect length, folded it over, one way and then another, pulled it through, tightened and straightened it, and turned him to look in the mirror. "The handsomest groom out there," he said, squeezing his shoulders.

"Except for you," Liam said, smiling and laying his hands over Chase's.

"All right, you two—you're not married yet . . . *and* I need help with this damn tie." Gage's hair was still damp from showering after helping his brothers milk the cows. "I have to check on Cash and make sure he has everything he needs."

"Cash is here?" Chase asked, his face brightening.

"Mom said he's unloading his equipment from the back of his dad's old Bronco."

"Wait! Mrs. Childs let him get his license . . . and he's driving his dad's old Bronco?! That thing is a classic!"

"That's what I heard, but I can't say for sure because I'm up here waiting for help with my tie!"

"Well, why didn't you say so." Chase reached up to tie his brother's tie. He cinched it tight, straightened it, and adjusted his collar. "There you go. Another handsome groom!"

"Thanks," Gage said, and then he eyed his brother's and Liam's slim perfectly creased dress slacks and pressed fitted white shirts. "How come you two always look sharper than the rest of us?"

"Why do you think?" Chase teased.

Gage laughed and then frowned. "Dang! I almost forgot! I'll be right back." He disappeared down the hall to his old bedroom and returned with three boutonnieres, an unopened pint of Jack Daniels, and three shot glasses. "A pre-wedding toast!" he said, smiling.

Chase laughed. "I'm surprised I didn't think of this. You're a man after my own heart!"

Gage filled three glasses and handed one to each of them. "I know we'll be doing official toasts later, but this is just for the three of us because, by some miracle, we all found someone to love, and I hope you guys have a lifetime of happiness," he said, holding his glass up solemnly.

"Same to you!" Chase said, clinking their glasses.

"Welcome to the fam, Liam!"

"Thanks!" Liam said as they all swung them back.

"Shall we have another?" Gage asked as they pinned on their

boutonnieres. "I don't want to be a bad influence on my little brothers."

"Heck, yeah!" Chase said. They had another round and then Gage set the bottle on the bureau. "I'll leave it here, but you should probably tuck it away so Mom doesn't find it." He grinned. "She might think we were drinking *before* the wedding."

"Thanks for the boutonnieres," they said.

"You're welcome," Gage said. "Maeve actually thought of them. She got boutonnieres for her dad and Mason, too, and really pretty corsages for Mom, and *her* mom."

"Nice!" Chase said, nodding approvingly.

Gage shook their hands and then headed down the stairs, and Chase tucked the bottle in the top drawer of his bureau and turned to Liam. "Ready?"

"I am."

Chase leaned forward and softly kissed him. "Let's do this then," he said, taking Liam's hand.

They went downstairs, and except for Marmalade—who was still asleep on the bed, the kitchen was empty. "Hey, sleepyhead," Chase said softly, kneeling next to her. "You comin' out?" She sat up, yawned, licked his hand, and started wiggling around him. "Well, c'mon then. Just don't get too close to Liam—we don't need him sneezing through the ceremony!"

As they stepped out into the beautiful June evening, they saw rows of white chairs set up under two oak trees in the backyard and they saw family and friends—including Mrs. Finley and Mrs. Childs, standing with Quinn and a slender outdoorsy-looking fellow—milling about, drinking, and chatting. Marmalade stayed close to Chase as they headed toward the barn. A small white catering tent had been set up on the far side of the barn and Bonni Manning's catering crew was bustling back and forth to the barn, getting ready for the reception. As they drew near, one of Bonni's girls, dressed in black slacks and a white blouse approached them with a tray of festive-looking drinks. "Peach Bellini?" she asked.

"Sure! Thank you," Chase said as they both took one.

They stepped into the barn and surveyed the scene—it looked amazing with white lights sparkling everywhere. Two girls were lighting the candles Libby and Ellie had made, and the sunflower centerpieces looked gorgeous. The catering crew was setting up a festive-looking buffet in one corner, and Cash was busy organizing a stack of CDs on another long table. "Hey, brutha!" Chase said, and Cash looked up.

"Oh, man, hey, bro!" Cash said, a shy smile crossing his face.

"How are you?" Chase asked, reaching out to bump fists.

"I'm fine. How are you?" Cash said, beaming at his old friend.

"I'm well, thanks!" He gestured to Liam. "Cash, you remember Liam?"

Cash nodded and extended his hand. Then he turned back to Chase. "Quinn's here, too!"

"I saw her," Chase said. "Have you talked to her?"

"Only to say hi. I've been busy."

"I heard you've been busy. I hope you're not stressing about all this."

"I'm not. My mom told me what you said so I'm not worried." Cash looked down and, for the first time, noticed the little white dog sitting on Chase's foot. "Oh!" he said softly, and then he came around the table. "Is this your dog?" he asked, holding out his hand. Marmalade immediately gave his hand a lick and then left Chase's side and started to wiggle all around Cash. "What a cutie," Cash said as she put one paw on his knee and stretched up to lick his cheek. "What's her name?" he asked, laughing at her enthusiastic greeting.

"Her name is Marmalade, and she's not mine. She belonged to a friend, but he passed away, so I'm looking for a home for her."

"You *are*?" Cash asked. "She doesn't have a home?"

"No, we would keep her, but we just found out Liam is allergic to dogs. Plus, we travel a lot."

Cash nodded. "She's such a sweetie."

"She is. My friend used to call her Marmy-girl."

"Is that your name?" Cash asked softly. "Marmy-girl." And hearing her old nickname, she tried to climb onto his lap.

Chase laughed. "I think she likes you."

Cash looked up. "Maybe I could give her a home. After all, I'm starting my own pet-sitting service."

"You are?" Chase said. "That's awesome!" He smiled. "I don't know how you can own a pet-sitting service, and not own your own pet. That's like owning a coffee shop and not drinking coffee."

Cash laughed. "I work at a coffee shop, but I don't drink coffee."

"Well, that's okay," Chase said.

Cash nodded thoughtfully, and Chase could tell his mind was spinning. "I know you're gonna be busy during the reception, but maybe you could keep an eye on her during the ceremony."

"I can do that!" Cash said, smiling.

"Perfect!" Chase said, and then he glanced up and saw Dave Peters standing with Gage, and when Dave saw him, he motioned for them to come over. "All right, bro, I guess Liam and I better go get ready." He bumped fists with him again. "Thank you so much for all you're doing."

"You're welcome," Cash said shyly. "I'd do anything for you, bro."

Chase pulled him into a hug. "I know you would, and I'd do the same for you." He smiled and handed him his untouched Bellini. "Finish this for me, would ya?" And then he smiled at Liam. "I already had a drink upstairs and I want to be completely present for the big day."

Cash's face lit up. "Sure!" he said and then, as they walked away, he knelt down to give Marmalade another hug, and the little dog seemed perfectly content to stay with him.

"You boys ready?" Dave asked.

"We are," they confirmed. And then Chase eyed his brother. "Where's Maeve?"

"She's still getting ready," Gage said, shaking his head, "but I hear she'll be right out."

"Okay," Chase replied, sweeping his hand through his short blond hair. They all turned to walk out and Ellie and Harper, who were running across the yard, just about mowed them over.

"Whoa! Who the heck are you two?" Gage teased, eyeing their dresses. "And what did you do with our nieces?"

They both giggled. "We *are* your nieces!"

"No, you're not. Our nieces wear jeans and T-shirts and know all kinds of trivial facts about wildlife."

"That's us!" Ellie said.

"And we have two messages to deliver," Harper added.

"What are they?"

"We have to tell *you* that Maeve is ready and to head over," Ellie said.

"And we have to tell Bonni 'a half hour,'" Harper added.

Chase smiled and looked at Liam and Gage. "Guess that means we're *done in thirty*!"

"Okay," Reverend Peters said, "I'm going to ask everyone to find their seats." He eyed them. "Don't linger too long."

They all nodded, and Chase called over to Cash, "You comin' for the ceremony?"

Cash looked up. "Yep, be right there!"

The girls headed off on their mission to warn Bonni, each happily taking a fat shrimp off the tray she offered, dipping it in cocktail sauce, and racing back across the yard.

Libby—who looked elegant in her new coral dress with the beautiful rose corsage pinned to it—was standing on the porch, waiting for Matt to escort her to her seat, but when her sons stopped to give her hugs, her eyes teared up. She gently touched their cheeks and told them she loved them, and then Liam and

Chase, who had decided to not steal Maeve's big moment, stepped aside and waited with everyone else for her to appear.

A moment later, a young trumpeter began to play, and while the cows peered curiously over the fence, and everyone stood, Maeve, looking stunning in a simple white gown, and escorted by her dad on one arm and her handsome nineteen-year-old son, Mason, on the other, followed her sister, Macey, across the sun-dappled lawn.

Ever composed and not showing any sign of being nervous, she smiled as she reached Gage, kissed her dad and son, and turned to stand next to him. Finally, Chase and Liam smiled at each other, clasped hands, and solemnly crossed the lawn to join them.

Reverend Peters welcomed everyone, gave a short homily—because he "knew the Tennyson boys were eager to get the party started," and stood in front of each couple to guide them through their vows and bless them. Chase felt his heart race as he and Liam faced each other and slid on the handsome wedding bands they'd chosen. "You may kiss the groom," Reverend Peters said, smiling. "And so may you!" he said, winking at Maeve.

"Done in thirty!" Chase whispered, grinning. "I love you so much!"

"I love you, too," Liam said, kissing him.

"Hot damn!" Chase said, turning and smiling. "Let's get this party started!"

53

"DO WE HAVE TO TAKE PICTURES?!" CHASE ASKED, FEIGNING DISMAY.

"Just a few quick ones," Maeve said. "You'll be all right."

"But Cash is playing Sinatra . . . I can hear it."

"Don't be such a little kid," Maeve teased.

Chase sighed, and while they waited for the photographer to set up, he and Liam chatted with Quinn and Ezra, and afterward, Chase was glad they'd taken the time for pictures because the images the photographer captured as the sun set on the farm were stunning—the sky was every color, from mango to cobalt to deep purple—it was as if God had painted the palette just for them; Chase even pulled Quinn into a picture with Rosie, and her adopted calf, Tucker—it looked just like the one they'd taken when they were kids.

Finally, they made their way to the barn, and Reverend Peters—because Cash was reluctant to speak into the mic—introduced the new couples and invited them to dance to the first song, "At Last" by Etta James.

Afterward, an elegant buffet dinner was served, Bonni and crew pulling out all the stops and serving several of her signature dishes—from field greens with beets and goat cheese, sprinkled with candied pecans, to homemade rolls and a variety of bread; from filet mignon with chimichurri sauce to cedar-planked salmon with dill sauce; and from roasted red potatoes with rosemary to quinoa and scallion salad as well as grilled tender asparagus. Bonni had also assured Libby that, later in the evening, they would be happy to assemble and serve the strawberry shortcake and luscious whipped cream Libby had made from fresh cream that morning so she didn't have to worry about a thing. They also set out the lovely basket of Susan Peters's beautiful wedding cookie favors.

As the rush of dinner slowed, Cash—who'd been sitting with his mom and Mrs. Finley—both of whose cheeks were rosy from wine, and Reverend and Mrs. Peters (and with Marmalade sitting on his feet, happily eating filet mignon tidbits he slipped her)—returned to his post and invited Maeve and her dad to come out to the dance floor. Ames smiled and squeezed Payton's hand under the table and, as Nat King Cole's "Unforgettable" drifted from the speakers, she whispered, "He's doing such a good job!"

Payton nodded, smiling proudly, and as they sipped their wine, they watched Maeve dance with her dad and realized there wasn't a dry eye in the place. Next, Cash invited Gage and his mom to the floor to dance to the song he'd chosen—Louis Armstrong's "It's a Wonderful World." Finally, just as the song ended, Cash looked around for Chase, spotted him, nodded knowingly to acknowledge their prediscussed plan, and reminded Mrs. Tennyson to remain on the dance floor. Gage stayed with her until her youngest son approached with the sweet smile she loved so much, and then Cash began to play Ben E. King's "Stand by Me," and Chase solemnly searched his mom's eyes. "Thank you for everything, Mom," he said, his voice choked with emotion. "Today has been so special. I can't thank you enough for always being there for me, no matter what."

"Oh, Chase," she said, searching his eyes. "You have no idea how much I love you and I couldn't be more proud. You are an amazing man and I'm so thankful you've found such a good person to love . . . and to love you back. That's all I've ever wanted."

"I love you, too," he whispered, his eyes glistening.

Just then, Cash lowered the volume and invited Liam—who was leaning against the wall—to come to the dance floor. At first, Liam shook his head, but then, at the crowd's insistence, he set his beer on a table and made his way over. Chase grinned as he gave his mom's hand to him, and when Libby danced with her new son-in-law, she saw tears in his eyes and gently touched his cheek. "I'm so happy you're joining our family, Liam," she said. "Now I have six sons again!"

Liam nodded and tried to stop the tears from spilling down his cheeks, but it was no use, and when the song ended, she held him for a long time.

"Okay!" Cash—who was suddenly emboldened by the two beers and two peach Bellinis he'd had—said deeply into the mic. "Let's get this party started!" He switched the CD and turned up the volume, and the familiar rhythmic drumbeat of Leon Redbone's "Come and Get Your Love" began to rock the rafters of the old barn, and everyone, including Ellie and Harper, hit the dance floor. Chase grabbed Liam, making him smile, and Cash watched wistfully, feeling a little left out, but then Quinn came up behind him and pulled him onto the dance floor, too. They joined right in, and Cash looked over and saw his mom and Mrs. Finley dancing as if no one was watching, and when they suddenly kissed, he raised his eyebrows and pointed and Quinn looked over, her eyes growing wide. "Wow!" she shouted. "Maybe we're gonna be related, too!"

"Maybe!" Cash said, laughing.

The song neared its end, and Cash left Quinn in the capable hands of her new boyfriend and went back to his post, but when he picked a slow song from their childhood, Elvis's "I Can't Help Falling in Love with You," Chase appeared at Quinn's side and eyed Ezra. "Sorry, pal, but this one is mine!" Ezra nodded, and

power of prayer, and I know she's been praying for me to meet someone, but you're right, when you give of yourself, good things come back to you in unexpected and amazing ways."

Chase put his arm around her and kissed her forehead, and as they walked into the barn, Cash was just bringing Marmalade back from getting busy. "Chase," he called excitedly. "My mom said if you're still looking for a home for Marmalade, I can keep her!"

"Wow! That's awesome, Cash—I think you're the perfect person to give her a good home."

Cash grinned and looked down at the little white dog sitting on his foot. "I think she'll be happy."

"I think she will, too," Chase said. Then he looked over at Liam and Quinn and smiled. "See? Serendipity."

Cash returned to his post with Marmalade and reached for the next CD. A moment later, unmistakable slow guitar strumming filled the barn, and all the Tennyson boys grabbed their drinks and headed to the dance floor to sing along to the famous Garth Brooks song, "Friends in Low Places." Libby stood by the door with Ames and Payton and watched as their kids started dancing. "What a wonderful wedding," Payton said.

"It is," Ames agreed. "We are all so very blessed."

Libby nodded. "Gram used to say, 'The music of life lies not in your circumstances or in external things, but in your soul' and she was right."

"She was," Ames agreed, "and this old soul wants to keep on dancing." She laughed and pulled them both back out to the dance floor. The three old friends joined in, dancing and singing along, and remembering all they'd been through together. Through thick and thin, loss and heartache, triumph and tragedy, they'd always been there for one another, and they always would be. Finally, Libby slipped away to watch—she wanted to etch this beautiful summer night of celebrating life with her two dearest friends and her beloved family into her mind forever. "No matter what comes,

Lord," she whispered, "I will always choose joy." As she said this, she felt a small hand slip into hers and she looked down to see Ellie standing beside her.

"Gran, come listen," the little girl whispered.

Libby followed her outside, and a moment later, they heard a faint *who-who-who cooks for you* . . . and then, a much closer reply. "It's a pair of barred owls—they're talking to each other," Ellie said. "Did you know they mate for life?"

"I *didn't* know," Libby said, squeezing her hand. "I haven't heard a pair of owls since I was a little girl." Then she remembered the encounter she'd had that morning. "Guess what I saw today."

"What?" Ellie asked eagerly.

"A wood thrush."

The little girl's eyes grew wide. "You did?!"

"Mm-hmm . . . *and* I have a story to tell you."

Ellie grinned. "Okay! Well, Bonni just put out a basket of all different kinds of tea . . . *and* they're serving your strawberry shortcake so you can tell me while we have some."

Libby laughed. "There's nothing like a cup of tea and a good story, is there?"

"There isn't!" Ellie said, pulling her inside.

Epilogue

の

One year later . . .

"HERE WE ARE!" MATT SAID, PULLING THE PASSENGER VAN HE'D BORROWED from a friend into an empty spot in front of the airport terminal.

Ellie—who was serving as copilot—looked back at the eight chatting ladies. "Ding! Ding! Ding! Welcome to Nashville International Airport! Next stop, Jackson, Wyoming! Be sure to check under your seat for all personal belongings—phones, purses, boarding passes, and any other items that might have fallen between the seats."

Ames looked up from searching under her seat for her phone and laughed. "I really think we should bring Ellie! She would keep us all in line and help us not get lost . . . or lose anything!"

"It's not too late," Ellie cried hopefully. "You can fit me in one of your suitcases!"

Matt feigned dismay. "What about me? I need your help on the farm."

His daughter rolled her eyes. "You could manage without me for ten days." And even though she would've loved going on the trip with all the ladies, she knew it would be good for her grandmother to go with her friends. Initially, when Libby had first mentioned "going on a bus tour with the ladies," her family had barely paid attention, but when she called Chase and asked him to start looking at travel packages, they'd just about fallen over, especially Ellie, who couldn't believe her grandmother was actually going on a trip!

One week later, Chase had called back with an amazing package and said he'd even managed to finagle both senior *and* group discounts. The women would fly from Nashville to Jackson Hole, and from there, over the course of ten days, they'd visit five national parks: Grand Teton, Yellowstone, Bryce Canyon, Zion, and the Grand Canyon, and their last night would be spent at the luxurious Venetian Resort in Las Vegas, from where they would fly home the following morning; and when Libby told all the Guild ladies about it, everyone wanted to go.

Now here they were, clambering out of the van, wearing new outfits and sunglasses, and as Matt commandeered a cart and loaded their luggage onto it, Ellie reached for her grandmother's hand. "Gran, make sure you take lots of pictures of any birds and wildlife you see, especially the raptors—you know, eagles, falcons, hawks, osprey . . . but I'd also love to see pictures of bison and elk. And don't forget, juvenile bald eagles look a lot like golden eagles so try not to mix them up."

"I'll do my best," Libby said, pulling her into a hug. "Meanwhile, you keep me posted on baby watch."

"Oh, I will!" Ellie said, beaming. "You *and* Mrs. Finley, because I'm sure she'll want to know, too!"

"What's that?" Ames said, hearing her name as she searched her bag for her boarding pass.

"Grandma wants to know when Quinn has Chase and Liam's baby."

"Oh, yes! I want to know, too! That was one thing we didn't plan on when we planned this trip because we didn't realize how soon Quinn would be pregnant . . . and now she's due in less than two weeks!"

"I know," Libby said, shaking her head. "I'm really glad they decided to have just one. I think twins would've been overwhelming."

"I agree," Ames said, triumphantly producing her boarding pass.

"You know, you could have that right on your phone," Ellie said.

"And knowing how to do that is another reason why we should be bringing you," Ames said, laughing.

Ellie grinned, and Libby—who was still thinking about the baby, continued. "God certainly works in mysterious ways, doesn't he?"

Ames nodded. "He certainly does."

"You always say God's timing is perfect, Gran," Ellie piped, "so there must be a reason it's all happening at the same time. We just have to keep the faith."

"You're right, as usual!" Libby said, putting her arm around her granddaughter.

Payton walked over, smiling as she slid her phone into her pocket. "Cash just texted and said he and Ned and Marmalade drove past the coffee shop and it's as busy as ever."

"That's good," Ames said. "I knew Jen and her husband would do a good job."

"Do you miss it?" Libby asked.

"Not for a second," Payton replied. "Not when I can go on a trip like this with my dearest friends." As she said this, she put her arm around Ames, and Libby smiled. She was very happy her two oldest friends had finally found the courage to be together—it was long past time.

Just then, her phone rang and she looked at the name on the screen. "It's Chase," she said, frowning. "I wonder why he's calling so early."

"Maybe he wants to make sure we made it to the airport," Ames offered.

"Maybe," Libby said, putting her phone to her ear, and as she listened to her son's excited voice, tears filled her eyes. Ames, Payton, Ellie, and Matt all gathered around, and the five other women, sensing something was going on, grew quiet and watched. Finally, Libby smiled, her tears spilling over as she looked at all their faces. "It's a girl!!!" she whispered, and then she eyed Ames and smiled. "Baby and mom are fine, and Chase and Liam are flying out this afternoon!"

"Woo-hoo!" Ellie shouted, jumping up and down. "We have another girl on our side!"

P.S.

Insights,
Interviews
& More...

Meet Nan Rossiter

About the author

NEW YORK TIMES and *USA Today* bestselling author Nan Rossiter loves to weave together stories about the complicated relationships to which all readers can relate—motherhood, sisterhood, friendship, marriage, and romance. She draws from her own life experiences to create authentic situations that mirror the trials and triumphs we all face. Compassionate, real, and funny, her books take readers on emotional journeys that often include heartbreak and joy but also include threads of faith, a furry friend or two, and an uplifting ending. Nan's books have been highly acclaimed by reviewers from *Publishers Weekly* to *Booklist*. Her novel *Summer Dance* was the 2018 winner of the Nancy Pearl Award.

Nan is a graduate of the Rhode Island School of Design and began her writing career in the world of children's books. Along with her many contemporary fiction novels, Nan is also the author/illustrator of several books for children, including *Rugby & Rosie*, winner of Nebraska's Golden Sower Award, and *The Fo'c'sle: Henry Beston's "Outermost House."*

Nan lives on a quiet country road in Connecticut with her husband and a solemn black Lab named Finn, who diligently watches her every move and can be roused from slumber in a distant room by the sound of a banana being peeled or a cookie crumb hitting the floor. Nan and her husband are the parents of two handsome sons who have struck out on life journeys of their own.

For more information, please visit nanrossiter.com, where you can sign up for her newsletter, or follow her on Goodreads, Facebook, Twitter, and Instagram @NanRossiter. ∾

Recipes from the Ladies of the Guild

Libby's Deviled Eggs

INGREDIENTS

1 dozen eggs

1 cup chopped celery

½ cup chopped green pepper

½ cup mayo (or less)

1 teaspoon yellow mustard

2 teaspoons minced onion

½ teaspoon curry powder

¼ teaspoon salt (or to taste)

Freshly ground black pepper, to taste

Paprika

Parsley, for garnish

DIRECTIONS

1. Place eggs in a saucepan and cover with water. Bring water to a boil, cover, and remove the pan from the heat. Let the eggs sit in the hot water for 15 minutes.

2. Drain out the water, refill the saucepan with cold water, and let the eggs cool in the water.

3. Peel the cooled eggs, halve them, scoop out the yolks, and place yolks in a large bowl.

4. Mash the yolks and then add in the celery, green peppers, mayo, mustard, minced onions, curry powder, salt, and black pepper.

5. Blend everything with a beater until creamy and smooth.

6. Spoon the yolk mixture into the hollowed eggs halves.

7. Finish with a sprinkle of paprika or garnish with parsley.

The secret ingredient in this recipe is the curry!

Ames's Famous Banana Bread

INGREDIENTS

½ cup melted butter

1 cup sugar

2 eggs

1 teaspoon vanilla

1 ½ cups all-purpose flour

1 teaspoon baking soda

½ teaspoon salt

2 very ripe, medium bananas, mashed

½ cup sour cream

½ cup chopped walnuts

½ cup semi-sweet chocolate chips (optional) ▶

Recipes from the Ladies of the Guild
(continued)

DIRECTIONS

1. Preheat the oven to 350 degrees and grease a 9 x 5-inch loaf pan.

2. In a large bowl, stir together butter and sugar. Add in eggs and vanilla and mix well. In a separate bowl, combine flour, baking soda, and salt. Add this dry mixture to the butter mixture and stir together until smooth. Fold in the mashed bananas, sour cream, and walnuts (and chocolate chips, if desired). Spread the mixture into the greased pan.

3. Bake at 350 degrees for 1 hour or until a toothpick inserted into the center of the loaf comes out clean. Let the loaf cool in the pan for ten minutes before unmolding and transferring to a wire rack to continue to cool. ∾

Have You Read?
More by Nan Rossiter

THE GIN & CHOWDER CLUB

SET AGAINST THE beautiful backdrop of Cape Cod, *The Gin & Chowder Club* is an eloquent, tender story of friendship, longing, and the enduring power of love.

The friendship between the Coleman and Shepherd families is as old and comfortable as the neighboring houses they occupy each summer on Cape Cod. Samuel and Sarah Coleman love those warm months by the water, the evenings spent on their porch enjoying gin and tonics, good conversation, and homemade clam chowder. Here they've watched their sons, Isaac and Asa, grow into fine young men, and watched, too, as Nate Shepherd, aching with grief at the loss of his first wife, finally finds love again with the much younger Noelle.

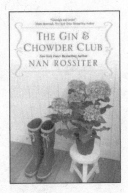

But beyond the surface of these idyllic gatherings, the growing attraction between Noelle and handsome, college-bound Asa threatens to upend everything. In spite of her guilt and misgivings, Noelle is drawn into a reckless secret affair with far-reaching consequences. And over the course of one bittersweet, unforgettable summer, Asa will learn more than he ever expected about love—the joys and heartache it awakens in us, the lengths ▶

to which we'll go to keep it, and the countless ways it can change our lives forever.

"Eloquent and surprising. . . . I loved this story of faith, love, and the lasting bonds of family."
—Ann Leary, author of
The Good House

"Nostalgic and tender . . . summons the passion of first love, the pain of first loss, and the unbreakable bonds of family that help us survive both."
—Marie Bostwick, *New York Times*
bestselling author

WORDS GET IN THE WAY

FROM THE AUTHOR of *The Gin & Chowder Club* comes an exquisitely heartfelt and uplifting novel that explores the infinite reach of a mother's love—and the gift of second chances.

The modest ranch house where Callie Wyeth grew up looks just as she remembers it—right down to the well-worn sheets in the linen closet. But in the years since Callie lived here, almost everything else has changed. Her father, once indomitable, is in poor health. And Callie is a single mother with a beautiful little boy, Henry, who has just been diagnosed with autism.

Returning to her family's quiet New

Hampshire community seems the best thing to do, for the sake of both her father and her son. Even if it means facing Linden Finch, the one she loved and left, for reasons she's sure he'll never forgive. Linden is stunned that Callie is back—and that she has a son. Yet in the warm, funny relationship that develops around Henry and Linden's menagerie of rescued farm animals, Callie begins to find hope. Not just that her son might break through the wall of silence separating him from the world, but that she too can make a new start amid the places and people that have never left her heart.

"Rossiter's second novel is an intimate portrayal of a family in crisis, with good character development and a bucolic setting." —*Publishers Weekly*

MORE THAN YOU KNOW

BESTSELLING AUTHOR NAN ROSSITER weaves a poignant, empowering novel in which three sisters gather to celebrate their mother's life—and find new inspiration for living their own.

Losing their father on the night Beryl Graham was born could have torn her family apart. Instead, it knitted them together. Under their mother's steady guidance, Beryl and her older sisters, Isak and Rumer, shared a childhood ▶

filled with happiness. But now Mia
Graham has passed away after battling
Alzheimer's, and her three daughters
return to their New Hampshire home to
say good-bye.

Swept up in memories and funeral
preparations, the sisters catch up on each
others' lives. Rumer and Isak have both
known recent heartache, while Beryl has
given up hope of marriage. But
surprising revelations abound, especially
when they uncover Mia's handwritten
memoir. In it are secrets they never
guessed at: clandestine romance,
passionate dreams, joy, and guilt. And,
as Beryl, Rumer, and Isak face a future
without her, they realize it's never too
late to heed a mother's lessons—about
taking chances, keeping faith, and loving
in spite of the risks.

"A gripping story of three sisters, of love
lost and found, and of a family's
journey from grief to triumph. A sure
winner."
—Debbie Macomber, #1 *New York Times*
bestselling author

"Rossiter's patient, deliberate pacing
makes this one a perfect bedtime read."
—*Publishers Weekly*

"Rossiter's writing style is compelling. The setup of the novel provides a number of passages that tug at the reader's heartstrings, and the situations evoke realistic compassion."
—*Houston Chronicle*

UNDER A SUMMER SKY

BESTSELLING AUTHOR NAN ROSSITER transports readers to Cape Cod with a warm, compelling story of family, new beginnings, and finding the courage to love honestly and well.

The old Cape Cod house that Laney Coleman shares with her minister husband, Noah, and their five boys is usually brimming with cheerful chaos. There's nothing fancy about the ancient kitchen or the wooden floors scuffed by the constant parade of activity and the clicking claws of their two Labrador retrievers. It's a place to savor the sea breeze wafting through the windows, or sip coffee on the porch before another hectic day begins. This summer, life promises to be even busier than usual, because Noah's younger brother, Micah, wants to hold his upcoming wedding on their property.

Although thrilled that Micah has found happiness after past heartache, Laney is apprehensive about having her home turned upside down. She has other concerns, too—her youngest son ▶

Have You Read? More by Nan Rossiter
(continued)

is being bullied at school, and Noah's father is not the robust patriarch he once was, in mind or body. As the bride and groom's large, close-knit families gather, there will be joyful celebration but also unexpected sorrows and revelations, and a chance to store up a lifetime of memories during the fleeting, precious days of summer.

"The setting, with its sea breeze and quaint charm, is immediately inviting, adding to the overall sense of familiarity that the author so beautifully evokes. . . . [T]o read this book is to feel like you've come home."
—John Valeri, *Hartford Books Examiner*

NANTUCKET

FROM BESTSELLING AUTHOR Nan Rossiter comes a tender, moving story of rekindled passion, set amidst the timeless beauty of Nantucket.

More than twenty-five years ago, Liam Tate and Acadia McCormick Knox fell in love. It was summer on Nantucket, and seventeen-year-old Liam knew that wealthy, college-bound Cadie was way out of league for a local boy who restored boats with his uncle. Yet the two became inseparable, seizing every chance to slip away in Liam's runabout to secluded spots, far from the world that was trying to keep them apart.

After Cadie returned home to New York and discovered she was pregnant, her parents crushed any hope of communicating with the boy she'd left behind. The silence that greeted Liam's calls and letters couldn't change his heart, but over the years he's settled into a simple, solitary life in his rambling beachfront house. Now he's learned that Cadie is returning to Nantucket for the opening of her son's art show. Over a weekend of revelations and poignant memories, Cadie and Liam have an opportunity to confront the difference time can make, the truths that never alter, and the bittersweet second chances that arrive just in time to steer a heart back home.

"There are moments of pure gold in the story that will undoubtedly touch readers' hearts. With wonderful characters and a charming idyllic setting, *Nantucket* does pack an emotional wallop along the lines of a good Kristan Higgins book."
—RT Book Reviews

FIREFLY SUMMER

BESTSELLING AUTHOR NAN ROSSITER's touching new novel reunites four sisters at their childhood vacation spot on ▶

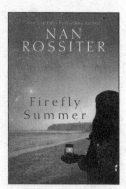

Cape Cod—where they uncover the truth about a past tragedy to find their future as a family.

The close-knit Quinn siblings enjoyed the kind of idyllic childhood that seems made for greeting cards, spending each summer at Whit's End, the family's home on Cape Cod. Then comes the summer of 1964, warm and lush after a rainy spring—perfect firefly weather. Sisters Birdie, Remy, Sailor, Piper, and their brother, Easton, delight in catching the insects in mason jars to make blinking lanterns. Until, one terrible night, tragedy strikes.

Decades later, the sisters have carved out separate lives on the Cape. Through love and heartbreak, health issues, raising children, and caring for their aging parents, they have supported each other, rarely mentioning their deep childhood loss. But one evening, as they congregate at Whit's End to watch the sun set, the gathering fireflies elicit memories of that long-ago night, and a tumult of regrets, guilt, and secrets tumble out.

Poignant yet hopeful, *Firefly Summer* is an uplifting story of the resilience of sisterhood and the bright glimpses of joy and solace that, like fireflies after rain, can follow even the deepest heartaches.

**WINNER OF THE 2018 NANCY PEARL
BOOK AWARD**

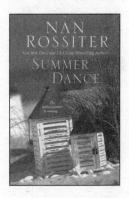

Bestselling author Nan Rossiter brings together characters from her acclaimed novel *Nantucket* in a powerful, heartwarming love story that bridges past and present.

When Liam Tate was seven years old, his Uncle Cooper opened his heart and his Nantucket home to the boy. In the intervening decades, Liam has found both love and loss on the island and, since learning that he has a son, Levi, a new kind of happiness. Yet one piece of his family history remains elusive—the long-ago romance between his uncle and Sally Adams. Now Sally makes a revelation that sets the whole town abuzz: she's publishing a book about what happened during the summer when she and Cooper first met, painting a picture so vivid it feels like yesterday.

In 1969, recently discharged veteran Winston Ellis Cooper III landed on Nantucket with only a duffel bag and a bottle of Jack Daniels. He found a sparsely furnished beach cottage, about as far from Vietnam as he could get. But even here, Cooper couldn't withdraw from the world entirely. Especially once ▶

his eyes met Sally's in the flickering lights of a summer dance. The effects of that fiery affair can still be felt decades later. As the story unfolds, there are new lessons for all to learn about life's triumphs and heartaches, and about loving enough to let go.

PROMISES OF THE HEART

Can the course that they've set for the future handle a slight detour . . . ?

MACEY AND BEN Samuelson have much to be thankful for: great friends, a beautiful—if high-maintenance— Victorian house on idyllic Tybee Island, and a rock-solid marriage. The only thing missing is what they want the most. After her fifth miscarriage in six years, Macey worries that the family they've always dreamed of might be out of reach. Her sister suggests adoption, but Macey and Ben aren't interested in pursuing that path . . . until a three-legged golden retriever named Keeper wags his way into their home and their hearts.

Harper Wheaton just got kicked out of another foster home and it won't be the last if she keeps losing her temper. She's not sure why she gets mad; maybe because no family seems to want a nine-year-old girl with a heart condition.

She loves her social worker, Cora, but knows that staying with her forever isn't an option. Will she ever find a family to call her own?

As a physician's assistant, Macey meets lots of kids. Harper Wheaton's a tough one, but Macey knows the little girl has already struggled more than most. It gets Macey and Ben to thinking about all the children who need homes. Then Harper goes missing, and one thing is suddenly crystal clear: life is complicated—but love doesn't have to be.

"A multileveled, beautifully written story that will glow in readers' hearts long after the last page is turned."
—Kristan Higgins, *New York Times* bestselling author

PROMISES TO KEEP

In this heartwarming sequel to Promises of the Heart in the Savannah Skies series, USA Today *bestselling author Nan Rossiter returns to Tybee Island off the Georgia coast to focus on beloved characters Maeve and Gage as their relationship is tested by secrets they are keeping from each other.*

THIRTY-FOUR-YEAR-OLD MAEVE LINDSTROM loves her job at Willow ▶

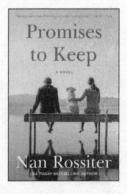

Pond Senior Care. Her older sister Macey thinks Maeve is the only human being on earth who can make working in a nursing home sound like fun. Maeve enjoys being around the sundowners, as she calls them, helping them navigate their senior years—brightening a time that can be, all too often, a lonely, sad stage of life.

Thirty-three-year-old Gage Tennyson—who brings his mischievous yellow Lab, Gus, to whatever restoration job he is working on with Macey's husband, Ben—loves Maeve with all his heart. He's a handsome country boy and a true southern gentleman. But as he and Maeve grow closer, they both sense that they haven't been completely forthcoming about their pasts.

When Maeve realizes Gage might be planning to propose, she knows she must finally be honest with everyone she holds dear. She can no longer live with the secret she's been dragging around like an anchor, and she knows the only way she will be free to build a lifetime relationship with Gage is to risk everything—including his (and her family's) love and respect. Before she finds the courage, however, her past comes careening into her life in a shocking and unexpected way. ∾